## Praise for W. DALE CRAMER and *Bad Ground*

"Cramer has a delicious way with a pen, whether he's crafting a lush Southern backdrop or offering glimpses of [his characters'] interior lives. . . . With its notes of hope, humor and redemption, this delightful book exemplifies what good Christian fiction should aspire to."

—*Publishers Weekly* (starred)

**Selected by *Publishers Weekly* as one of the "Best Books of 2004."**

"Cramer's second novel offers a refreshingly inventive perspective with its portrait of the dangerous world of hard-rock mining and the men who do it for a living. The spiritual message is clearly about the healing power of forgiveness, but the well-developed characters never fall into the cookie-cutter stereotype of being 'too perfect' as so often happens in Christian fiction. Both male and female readers will identify with Aiden Prine's physical and spiritual struggles. Highly recommended for its excellent storytelling and believable characters."

—*Library Journal* (starred)

***Library Journal* listed *Bad Ground* in the Top 5 of "Best Genre Fiction 2004," Christian Fiction category.**

"Skillful storytelling, beautifully described settings, and original, fully realized characters set this novel of faith by W. Dale Cramer apart from typical coming-of-age stories. . . . This novel confirms Cramer as one of the brightest new voices in faith fiction."

—*Christianity Today*

"*Bad Ground* proves that *Sutter's Cross* [Cramer's debut novel] wasn't just beginner's luck. Cramer has an uncanny command of dialogue that can put a smile on your lips as easily as a tear in your eye. With a truckload of danger, a few traces of romance, and a heart that reflects God's own, *Bad Ground* should appeal to fiction lovers. Highly recommended."

—*CBA Marketplace*

"The lush landscape of south Georgia jars against the harsh beauty of the subterranean world of the hard-rock miners with satisfying clarity, and Cramer makes masterful use of both dialogue and description to get across his message of love, forgiveness and brotherhood in this intriguing coming-of-age novel."

—*Bookpage*

"Cramer's detailed, enthusiastic portrait of rough men following the dangerous trade of hard-rock mining is original, and in the end, the novel is almost a hymn to working men."

—*Booklist* (starred)

**Chosen by *Booklist* as one of the "Top 10 Christian Novels 2004."**

"*Bad Ground* breaks new ground in Christian fiction! Edged in reality and bold in characterizations, this book digs deep into the complex makings of genuine Christianity in today's world. . . . Not only was [Cramer] able to describe the world of mining in an understandable and interesting way, but he has a masterful use of dialogue and a skill in applying spiritual truths. . . ."

—*Love Romances*

"Sparkling character studies grace this powerful tale of hope regained and the miracle of inner healing. A page-turning blend of humor, knuckle-biting action and deep introspection. Cramer is a new author to watch."

—*Romantic Times*

"This is a richly written book, filled with evocative language. . . . Poignant and thought-provoking, *Bad Ground* will stay with you for a long time."

—*BookLoons*

"Cramer's simple, muscular prose and spare poetical images reflect an artist in full control of his medium. . . ."

—*Southern Scribe*

"I liked the first one better."

—Mrs. Cramer
(W. Dale's mother, and a fan of *Sutter's Cross*)

# W. DALE CRAMER

*A Novel*

# *Levi's* Will

BETHANYHOUSE

MINNEAPOLIS, MINNESOTA

*Levi's Will*
Copyright © 2005
W. Dale Cramer

Cover design by Lookout Design, Inc.
Author photograph by Larry McDonald

Published by Bethany House Publishers
11400 Hampshire Avenue South
Bloomington, Minnesota 55438

Bethany House Publishers is a division of
Baker Publishing Group, Grand Rapids, Michigan.

Printed in the United States of America

ISBN-13:   978-0-7642-2995-4
ISBN-10:   0-7642-2995-8

**Library of Congress Cataloging-in-Publication Data**

Cramer, W. Dale.
   Levi's will / by W. Dale Cramer.
      p.  cm.
   Summary: "A family saga of pain and reconciliation set behind the closed doors of an Amish community. Spanning three generations, the story follows the life of Will McGruder, who having fled as a young man, seeks to heal the past by bringing his new family to meet his Amish relatives"—Provided by publisher.
   ISBN 0-7642-2995-8 (pbk.)
   1. Amish—Fiction.  2. Conflict of generations—Fiction.  3. Inheritance and succession—Fiction.  I. Title.

   PS3603.R37L48    2005
   813'.6—dc22

                                          2005004602

*For Larry McDonald, the real Jubal.*

# Books by W. Dale Cramer

*Sutter's Cross*

*Bad Ground*

*Levi's Will*

*Summer of Light*

# *Levi's* Will

What power has love but forgiveness?
    In other words
             by its intervention
what has been done
    can be undone.
                What good is it otherwise?

—William Carlos Williams,
    from *Asphodel, That Greeny Flower*, Book III

CHAPTER | I

*January 1985*

He reaches out, not quite awake yet, and his forearm comes to rest on the other pillow, cool and vacant, before he remembers where he is. It's a strange bed, not because it's a thousand miles from home, but because Helen isn't in it. Sitting up, rubbing his face, he thinks of calling her, but it's too early. After forty years he knows he will find no kindness in Helen at five o'clock in the morning. She's been known to cuss at that hour. There is no clock. He knows the time without turning on the light to look at his watch. All his life, as far back as he can remember, with or without an alarm clock, he has always awakened at five.

There's a snap and a rumble when the gas furnace ignites and pumps warm air through the little mobile home as it has done often during the night, fending off the brunt of an Ohio winter. Still, the air is cold on his legs when he flings the covers back. He steps into the pants he left on the chair last night and pulls yesterday's sweater over his head. The floor is cold too. His feet slip into his shoes.

Drawing back the curtain he sees the snow has stopped falling sometime in the night, and now the stars burn fiercely, as if the newly departed clouds had polished them in passing. The valley rests under an endless white comforter, a shroud of tangible silence quickened and sharpened in the glow of a crisp full moon hanging above the hilltops. The road in front of the trailer has disappeared during the night, and no grinding, clanking snowplow has yet come to break the landscape with a belt of salt and slush. Here in the country there are no streetlights to cast a pall of darkness beyond their own garish glow. The cold luminescence of a sea of moonlit snow is challenged only by the distant glint of yellow lamplight in the kitchen window of a farmhouse tucked in against the eastern hillside, where a thin ribbon of smoke stretches from stovepipe to stars. The barn is quiet, the cows out of sight. The trees are heavy with snow. Nothing moves. A deep sleep lies over the valley.

He has come to bury his father. The event is a milestone for any man—the falling of the last barrier before his own yawning mortality—but for Will McGruder it is more, having lost great chunks of his father in the tempest of his life, a tempest that with every passing year seems more preordained. *Men are grass,* he thinks. He stands very still at the window and lets his mind wander over the hills until, in a little while, he begins to merge with the night and the land. The aches and sorrows of his sixty-year-old body fall away and he ceases to be aware of himself as he is. The earth—this particular earth, beneath the snow—holds the memory of him as he was. The eyes of his mind see another night, another season, another valley.

## CHAPTER 2

*June 1943*

The two-story white frame house shone pale blue in the moonlight. There were no lights on, not because of any wartime blackout or other of Roosevelt's conservation plans, but because it was an Amish house and it had never coveted electric lights. It was a big, square, solid farmhouse, *gutgemacht,* a stark fortress between the road and the farm, between the World and the earth. Upstairs, the six boys slept in a large corner bedroom—Mose, the eldest, in his own single bed, Will and Tobe stacked in bunks, and the three youngest together in a double bed. Across the hall, three girls shared roughly the same arrangement. Clara, Will's older sister, had married and left home back in the spring. The other nine children remained. Opposite the stairwell, on the other end of the house, slept the parents—Levi, the patriarch, and Elizabeth, his second wife.

Will, the next to the eldest son, lay staring at the ceiling, listening to the sounds of the night. Since midnight the rhythmic buzzing of insects had quieted as the window-shaped rectangle of moonlight had inched its way along the heart-pine floor to the middle of the room. Mose breathed evenly and deeply, immersed in the sleep of the just, exhausted from a long day of cutting hay. The low rumble of their father's snore swelled and ebbed all the way from the other end of the house, a snore that had held steady for the last hour.

It was time.

Will slithered out of the top bunk and down to the floor carefully so as not to make the faintest whisper of sound, but it did no good. Tobe had been waiting. He flung back the covers, swung his legs over from the bottom bunk, fully dressed, and wiggled his feet into his boots. Always the hasty one, Tobe finished tying his laces first and rose, starting for the door. Will snagged his suspenders to stop him, then shook his head, pointing at the window.

Tobe went first, out the window and across the tin roof of the summer kitchen, dropping his hat to the ground, grabbing onto the limb of the walnut tree and swinging out. The limb bowed under Tobe's weight, but it would hold. It had held before. His legs flailed for a second, then clamped on the limb, and he monkeyed down. Will followed, and moments later the two boys picked up their wide-brimmed hats from where they had dropped them among the gladiolas. Will paused there, reaching down to run his fingertips up the length of a thick leaf.

Elizabeth Mullet took pride in her flowers. Her beds of tulips and roses and lilies were the envy of even the Amish women. Her kitchen garden, in the flat just below the house, was ringed about with a thick bank of marigolds, which she claimed kept insects away, and sprinkled with mothballs she claimed kept out the rabbits, though rabbits had been scarce for the last two years thanks to Tobe and his four-ten. It was the one thing he did well. The moonlight was bright enough so that Will could make out the shapes of the potato plants, overlarge this year, and he wondered briefly how the potatoes would fare after the wet spring, whether it would be a bumper crop or if the growth had all gone to the plants and the potatoes themselves would be full of rot. The green beans were almost ready, even if Will would not be around to eat them. He snugged his hat on his head and moved on.

Limping slightly, favoring a sore knee as they neared the woodshed, Tobe said softly, "I don't know why we wouldn't just come down the stairs."

"Well, little brother, do you know which step creaks? Is it the third or the fourth?"

"It's the third one, I'm sure."

"It's the fifth," Will said, glancing back at the house. "And his bed is just on the other side of the wall. You would awaken the bear, and then what would become of me?" He flinched involuntarily as the thought flashed across his mind and left its thumbprint, as a bright light seen for a moment leaves a print upon the eye: What was a man, that one loose tread could alter the course of his life?

Tobe sighed and said nothing, his customary response to the constant criticism he endured from his brothers and his father. He was flighty, and Will would not have let him come if he'd had any choice. On this night choice itself seemed a thing of the past, a childhood memory. Tobe had caught him hiding his bundle in the woodpile yesterday and instantly guessed his plans, so now Tobe would come with him. Burrowing into the pile, Will's sure hands tossed aside sticks of firewood until he reached the burlap bag. Drawing it out, he flipped the bundle over his shoulder and set off at a trot, making for the wooded ridge silhouetted in the distance.

Near the barn the air still held the cloying scent of butchered chickens, for his sisters had cleaned out the chicken house early in the week. One of the big Belgian draft horses—Will's favorite, the one who liked ruta-bagas—snuffled in his stall, saying goodbye as the boys glided past the barn door.

He paid little attention to where he stepped as he crossed the straw-berry patch—the strawberries were nearly finished now anyway—though he avoided the raspberries entirely, since they were just getting ripe.

Running on the even ground between the windrows he heard Tobe's steps falling behind, felt the crunch of stubble underfoot and smelled fresh-cut hay on the night breeze. He flexed his broad shoulders against the slight soreness left by the hay fork—a good soreness, the residue of strength and youth. Will knew he would be badly missed in the fields this coming week, the last week of June. After three days of sunshine the anxious farmers would be rushing to get hay in before the next rains came. These would be the longest days of the year. Levi Mullet and his sons would fill every minute with work from well before daylight until pitch dark. Will's hands and back and legs were strong, this he knew. If he could have chosen, he would have left in the wintertime. Leaving now, with so much work to do, drove yet another nail through his heart.

Skirting the upper cornfield, nearing the woods, he dodged around the depression left by the stump he and Mose dug up last winter where lightning had killed the old oak tree. Will's feet knew where it was, even in the dark, but he heard the "Oof!" behind him as Tobe plowed straight into it and went down face first in the damp grass. Will stopped at the edge of the woods where the land began to slope upward, and waited.

Limping even worse after tripping over the stump hole, Tobe finally caught up to him, laughing that peculiar little snorting, derisive laugh of his—the impish laugh of a sixteen-year-old boy.

"Brother, we'd better be a long ways gone before morning," he said, doffing his wide straw hat and dragging a sleeve over his brow in a single practiced motion. "I wish I could see the old man's face when he finds out."

Tobe saw the whole thing as an adventure, a lark. For all his faults he was a sweet boy, full of light and laughter. He kept no record of grievances, and he had not lived long enough nor fallen hard enough to understand that other people do. He thought no more of running off to the World with Will than he would think of hitching a horse to the hack and driving to the store for a bag of salt. Even now, the punishment Levi would heap upon him at his returning would last only a little while, and then life would be good again. Tobe didn't allow people to expect too much from him, and so they were never deeply disappointed.

Will, however, stood at the edge of an abyss. Looking back across the moonlit fields at the only home he had ever known, it was a watershed moment in his life and he knew it. If he left now, he could never return. If he stayed, he could never leave.

Beyond this ridge lay the World, with all its wonder and terror and mystery, though for Will the mystery was not so deep as it might have been for some. Except for the last three weeks, Will had been farmed out for more than two years to Abel Elliot, an Englisher farmer a few miles up the road, and he had used the time well. Abel had been kind to him, partly because the war had made good help scarce—the average Amish teenager would outwork two Englishers, and Will was above average— but also because he just plain liked the boy. After the first two months Abel had loaned him a horse and buggy for his own personal use, arguing that it just made sense, for the hour and a half Will spent working instead of walking would more than pay for the rig in a year's time. Abel had also loaned him old copies of *The Saturday Evening Post* to read, and Will had devoured them, hiding them here and there, reading whenever he could do so without being seen. When Abel gave him a pocket dictionary he took the name literally and carried it in the deep front pocket of his home-made trousers for the better part of two years. He would read a magazine while driving to the Elliot farm and back every day, and whenever he encountered a new word the dictionary would flash from his pocket. Like all Amish, his first language was Dutch; he had learned English in school. Attending the local public school until he finished the eighth grade, he had always admired the English boys—their facility with language, their fancy clothes, their modern haircuts. Some of them wore shoes, even in warm weather, and sometimes they had a nickel for a candy bar. One of them, Earl McGruder, had been Will's friend in spite of their cultural differences, and shared store-bought Hershey's bars with him. It was a kindness Will would long remember. He hadn't seen Earl in several years. He was probably away at the war.

Whenever Will ate lunch in Abel Elliot's kitchen he would drop hints about the radio until Abel, smiling patiently, turned it on. Music, stories, war news, baseball, Will didn't care—it was radio. It was the World, and it called to him.

It called to him now, hesitating on the threshold as the realization settled in that he was saying a last goodbye to every warm thing he had ever known. Goodbye to the farm six miles outside of Apple Creek, Ohio, whose every rock and shrub he knew blindfolded; goodbye to home and family and friends; goodbye to field and forest, plow handle and ax—all the solid, familiar things that had anchored his hands and feet and heart to the earth. His mouth formed silent words in his native Dutch, and though he would not have called it a prayer—for it was a certainty now that in the morning he would be excommunicated and even God would have no more to do with him—they were words from the bottom of his heart. Mattie would be there, and then she would know.

Mattie.

In his mind he could see her standing before them in the cold morning light with no one to stand beside her and no place to hide her shame. He could see, as plainly as if he were there, her ankle-length black caped dress, the starched white covering, the flush of her cheeks, her tender downcast eyes. As always, a fierce grief welled up within him, filled him to bursting, and might yet have turned him back had not his father's wrath planted its iron feet, *as always,* in the short breech between remorse and repentance. Levi Mullet's thundering demands for immediate and unconditional surrender, delivered in the innate fury of his coal-fired contempt, might well have been the only force on earth capable of preventing the very repentance he demanded.

Things might have gone differently. Remorse might have won out and life might have been somehow redeemable if only Will's father hadn't been so *right,* if only Levi Mullet hadn't been the very model of righteousness. Yet there it was—that heaping measure of condemnation could only be meted out by a truly righteous man. No soul could long thrive in the glare of such withering and justifiable wrath. Will chose exile because it seemed a lesser kind of death.

Even now, his heart pounded with anger over the path he was being forced to take, but take it he would. He would wrest control of his life away from his father, away from the constricting coils of a church that said to him: *You will live in this house and do this kind of work. You will marry this girl, wear these clothes and cut your hair this way. You will have as many children as your wife can bear, and teach them to live the same.*

He would not. He would turn instead to the World, with its infinite choices, where he would control his own life and choose his own destiny. Mattie was the price. Though he thought sometimes it would worry a hole in his heart, he knew he must abandon her or stay.

And he simply could not stay.

A train whistle sounded in the distance. Tobe shifted his feet and glanced up the ridge. "Shouldn't we be going?" he asked.

Will nodded absently, his eyes on the fields. "There's still a lot of sweet corn to plant," he said quietly, a final apology, then turned his back and trotted up into the woods.

The engine puffed and grunted and hissed, leaning into its work, dragging an infinite string of coal and cattle cars across the trestle and up out of the valley. At the first sight of a black rectangle denoting an open door on the side of a cattle car the two boys broke from the trees and ran up alongside the train, stumbling in the cinders, straining to get up to speed before the open door caught up with them.

The floor of the car was higher than Will had expected. His feet arced underneath the belly of the train and he came close to falling, but then he managed in the next second to swing a leg up and roll himself inside. Tobe, who was shorter of leg than his older brother, panted through gritted teeth, struggling, neither gaining nor losing ground. Even at full speed he was visibly limping from the pain in his knee, and Will could see he wasn't going to make it. Cinching the end of the burlap bag tightly around his hand Will leaned out the door as far as he could and swung the bag toward his brother's face. Tobe caught hold in the same instant that his eyes went wide with surprise, for his toe had snagged a crosstie. Any other boy falling beside the wheels of a moving train would have let go, but Tobe trusted the resolve of his brother. He clung to the burlap, and before his knees could hit the ground Will hoisted him up, swung him bodily through the door, and sent him tumbling all the way across the rough oak floor of the cattle car. He sat up against the far wall rubbing his knee.

Will went over and sat down beside him, opening the bag and reaching inside to see if any damage had been done to the food he had brought along.

"What do we have to eat?" Tobe said, still grinding his palms against his knee.

"Yeah. What do we have to eat?" said another, deeper voice from the shadows at the end of the car.

Tobe sprang to his feet, peering into the darkness, his body taut and ready to bolt. Will drew his feet under himself and closed his fist about the bag, but he didn't get up. His eyes were growing accustomed to the darkness inside the cattle car and he could make out movement. The blackness shifted. Moonlight flashed through the slats like a strobe, and he caught a glimpse of a man rising, first to a sitting position and then standing at the front of the car. Tobe's eyes switched nervously from the man to Will.

"We didn't know you were in here," Will said.

"You do now," the voice answered, and the man moved closer. Will rose to face him and saw, as the stranger moved into the half-light of the open door, that he was slight of build and the hair showing below his sweat-stained felt hat was gray. His clothes hung on him like a scarecrow's, and the left sleeve of his moth-eaten coat lay oddly flat and empty against his side. Will was no fighter, but even he could see that this one-armed old man posed no threat. The rhythmic clacking of steel wheels quickened as the train picked up speed on level ground, and yet despite the rocking of the car Will noticed the old man's upper body didn't sway, his legs automatically compensating for the motion.

"We got some trail bologna and some cheese," Will said, reaching his arm down into the bag.

The man's eyes watched suspiciously. His hand slipped into a trouser pocket and came back out hiding something. Very slowly, Will extracted a foot of dark burgundy bologna and held it up for him to see. The man took it, gripped the knot in his teeth, snapped open the pocketknife he had palmed, sliced off the top quarter of the bologna, handed the rest back to Will, and then folded the knife against his thigh and slipped it back into his pocket. All of this was done quickly and without taking his eyes off of Will. He bit off a chunk of bologna, dragged a sleeve across his lips, and giving a slight nod toward Will's wide, flat-brimmed straw hat, said, "Pennsylvania Dutch."

"Amish," Will answered.

"Same thing. You running away?"

Will hesitated, unsure of his ground. "Why do you say that?"

The man coughed—or laughed, it was hard to tell. "I been ridin' these rails better'n ten years, and I know this part of the country up and down. You ain't the first Amish boys I seen." The bologna in his hand waved roughly at Will's chin. "You got no beard. Means you ain't married, right?"

Will nodded.

"Just a kid." Chuckling, he bit another plug from the bologna and abruptly sat himself down against the slats where the boys had been sitting. He patted the floor next to him.

"Sit down, kid. You need old Peavey's help, I can see it in your eyes. I ain't got a dime to my name, but I'm a veritable fount of wisdom," he said, tapping his temple. "Peavey always pays his way. Boloney for bologna—seems fair enough, don't it?" His own joke got the better of him, and his gravelly laugh evolved into an uncontrollable fit of coughing.

Will sat down next to him, cautiously, keeping his knees raised and holding the bag between his feet. Tobe crossed his arms and remained standing despite the constant and slightly embarrassing struggle to keep his balance.

"I gotta tell ya, first of all, yer nuts," Peavey said. "I *seen* them farms like where you come from. It's heaven, I tell ya. I don't know what your problem is—whaddaya, bored?—but if I was you I'd turn right around and march back home and square things with my old man before it's too late."

"It's too late already," Will said.

Peavey snorted a little laugh, but there was no mirth in it. Staring out the door at the sparse lights of Fredericksburg, something hard and cold surfaced on his face. "No," he said. "You're too young for it to be too late. Go back home, son."

Twisting the neck of the bag in his rough hands, Will said nothing, shook his head.

"All right, then. All right." Peavey nodded, staring cross-eyed at the bologna, picking out his next bite. "Then you gotta get rid of the hat and the clothes. And the hair too—makes you look like a rube. Things ain't like it was ten years ago when *everybody* was hungry and guys looked out for each other. Nowadays it's dog-eat-dog. Rule number one—don't trust nobody. You're on the lam, right?"

Will's fingers played absently with the hair hanging down over his ears in a thoroughly Amish bowl cut. "I'm on what?"

"On the lam—running, hiding. Kid hops a freight in the middle of the night, he's runnin' from somebody. It's your old man, right? He'll come after you, won't he?"

"Yes. He'll be looking for us, sure." *He'll move heaven and earth. You don't know him.*

"Then rule number two is never use your real name. What *is* your real name, anyway?"

"William Mullet."

Quick as a snake, without even dropping the bologna, Peavey whipped his hat off and swatted Will over the head with it. "Wha'd I tell ya? I give you two simple rules and you break both of 'em in ten seconds flat! You ain't got a prayer, kid."

Peavey, who had spent a fair portion of his life as an unwelcome guest in freight cars, knew how to make friends quickly. Will was beginning to like the little man but wondered how Peavey, even though he did seem to know a great many things, could possibly know that he could not pray. He would have to learn to hide himself better.

"So, William Mullet, where ya headed?" The old man stuffed the last of the trail bologna in his mouth and wiped greasy fingers on a dirty pant leg.

"South," Will said.

"How far?"

"Till morning."

Peavey choked on a chuckle, then knifed his hand out in front of him and said, "Now that's what I call a flexible plan. You might just make a hobo after all, William Mullet."

"We thought we might be able to find work on a farm."

"You might. Lots of people short of help these days. Even thought about takin' a job myself, now and again." This, Peavey found terribly funny. He slapped his leg and laughed, choked on the bologna and laughed some more.

They talked through most of the night, or rather they listened to Peavey talk. Blessed with a captive audience, he spun story after story about life on the rails, people he had known and things he had seen. Past Millersburg and Glenmont he discussed the relative comforts of the Pennsylvania line versus the B & O. When the train stopped in Columbus he made them get up and sit near the door because, he said, "If you hear the bulls coming you want to hit the ground runnin'. Can't let 'em corner you in the car." Trundling past Wilmington he talked misty-eyed about a plump young lady he once knew there. Nearing Cincinnati he stood up and stretched, belched, spat, and said it was about time for him to go. Urgent business in the city.

"Pay attention now. When you get ready to get off the train, don't wait till it stops. You'll know you're comin' into town when you see lots of houses near the tracks, so when she slows down enough, go ahead and skedaddle. Most of the young bulls are gone now, and the old ones won't come after you if it means having to hike a ways to catch up to the train. I seen 'em catch a pal of mine asleep outside of Akron, once. They laid his heels up on the track and stomped his knees backwards."

Tobe winced, and a look of horror passed over his face.

"Thank you for the advice," Will said.

Looking out the door as the train began to slow, Peavey pushed his hat back on his head, took his empty sleeve in his hand and wiped his forehead with it.

"One other thing," he said, spurred on by the fact that somebody, anybody, would value his advice. "Rule number three—keep your own counsel. Fancy words for 'don't listen to nobody.' I learnt that from books. Philosophers. Them guys are all standing in line waitin' for a chance to tell you what you ought to think, but once they get their shot all they ever say is, 'don't never let nobody tell you what you ought to think.'"

Then he doffed his hat, bowed his head sedately, said, "See ya in the funny papers," and leaped out into the World.

"What time do you think it is?" Tobe whispered, crouching next to the door.

"Nighttime," Will said.

The whole time the train was stopped on a siding in Cincinnati they sat perfectly silent and still, except for Tobe's head, which snapped wide-eyed toward the slightest sound. But no one ever came to check the car. They never had to run for their lives, or to keep their legs from being broken, and soon enough the train grunted and rattled and heaved itself ponderously southward once again. Tobe remained quiet for a long time, even after the train was under way. Will thought he had fallen asleep, sitting with his back to the wall and his arms propped across his knees, until he raised his head.

"Why do you think they got so mad?" he asked.

"Who?" Will knew then that Tobe hadn't been sleeping. He'd been thinking. His mind had circled like a beagle until it came across a day-old trail and bayed a question.

"Dad and the other elders."

Will sighed. "Because Mattie is going to have a baby."

"I know *that*. And I know you and Mattie . . . sinned. It's just, well, other people sin sometimes too, and the church corrects them and then everything is all right. Like when Uncle Enos put the stuffed fish on his wall. They made him take it down, but nobody shouted at him. I've never seen the elders get angry like that. They scared me last meeting, they got so mad."

"They had a moral dilemma," Will said.

Tobe stared blankly, waiting for a definition.

"When a boy and a girl get caught in sin like that, they get put in the ban," Will began, choosing his words carefully.

"Everybody knows that. The elders have to do that to protect the church. I heard them say it—*'What has righteousness to do with unrighteousness?'* But they still wouldn't have to yell, would they?"

"Well, Tobe, this problem is different. It's not like a stuffed fish, that you can just take it down and throw it in the burn pile and it's gone. *This* problem won't so easily go away. The girl is going to have a baby yet, and she has no husband. Both families are shamed, and the only way they can begin to cover their shame is for the boy and girl to be married."

Tobe shrugged. "All right. Well then, let them be married. That's only a little more trouble than the burn pile."

"But they can't get married," Will explained. "They aren't in good standing."

Tobe's eyes widened. He finally saw it. "So they must be banned, and they must be married, yet they can't be married because they are banned. That's a moral dimenna?"

"Dilemma. Yes. It makes the elders very angry when there isn't any right way. So they put you in the ban, and then at the next meeting, two weeks later, if you have repented, they take you out again so you can be married. The elders don't like being made to bargain with sin. It makes them angry, but they don't have any other choice." Will bit his lip. "Anyway, if you think they were angry two weeks ago, just wait till I don't show up in the morning."

Tobe pondered this for a bit, and his expression slowly darkened as he became aware of the gravest implication.

"If you're not there in the morning you'll stay in the ban."

Will nodded. He had thought these things were common knowledge by now, but as usual Tobe's short attention span had left some holes.

"Forever?"

"Oh yes. I'm a lost soul, little brother. There's no hope for me now." Will said the words easily, with even a little smile, but Tobe still took it hard. He said nothing and yet he could not hide the sorrow in his face. He was a sweet boy.

Tobe asked no more questions, and Will offered no more answers. Yet plummeting into the darkness, Will's thoughts traveled again the worn pathways that had led him to this forsaken place, and a splinter of suspicion festered. He would say no more to Tobe about it, indeed might not ever mention it to anyone, but in his heart he knew somehow that there was more blame to be had than one boy should bear alone. It was only a suspicion, disembodied, flitting through the shadows of his mind, and he could not put words to it—his wounds were too fresh, his heart still too close to home. But it was real. However vague, his suspicion would not go away. Suspicion fanned the embers of a bitter and unaccustomed self-pity which, as self-pity often does, fed on itself until it burst into full flame and a mindless rage overwhelmed him.

Leaping to his feet as if something had bitten him, he snatched off his Schwartzentruber hat and sailed it out the door, then turned and kicked the slats of the cattle car. He smashed the walls again and again with his heels, venting a fury whose source he could not name, grunting and cursing and shouting his frustration. When his legs grew weary and his breath short he drew back to drive his fist into the wall, but he stopped himself; underneath his rage was self-preservation, and he would need his hands to live. Tobe shrank from him in fear as he snatched up the burlap bag by its bottom and shook it out, scattering two new pairs of English bib overalls, two clean shirts, some socks, an old blanket, and a quarter hoop of newspaper-wrapped cheese. What was left of the trail bologna rolled blithely across the dung-littered floor of the cattle car.

"Put these on," he said, throwing a pair of overalls at Tobe, then jerked the hat off the boy's head and sailed it out the door as he had done with his own. "They'll be big on you, but you can cinch up the galluses and roll up the legs."

He dressed himself quickly, without a word, then gathered up his Amish clothes and hurled them into the night. The wind took them, and he stood for a long time staring out the door into the blackness, his fists buried in his hair.

CHAPTER | 3

*June 1943*

He guessed it to be about an hour before first light when the train stopped to take on water somewhere south of Cincinnati. Sitting by the door they heard the ticking of hot metal cooling—somewhere in the undercarriage of the cattle car a bearing had gone bad. A rooster crowed in the distance. A moment later they heard voices, broken and indistinct but definitely voices, and they were drawing nearer. Peering between the slats Will caught glimpses of a lantern swinging, slowly approaching, though it was still a ways down the track.

Tobe saw it too, and his fear overpowered him. Without warning, he sprang to his feet and leaped out the door. Shouts came from the direction of the lantern. Tobe managed only a step or two before the darkness fooled his feet and he tumbled down a long grassy slope. Will snatched up the burlap bag and took off after his brother, stumbling himself but managing to keep his footing. Near the bottom of the hill he caught up with Tobe, who had fallen a second time. He grabbed Tobe's arm and jerked him to his feet in passing. They sprinted, tripping and reeling, looking over shoulders, splashing across the stream at the bottom of the slope, slipping on wet rocks, faces lashed by limbs as they clambered up through the woods on the other side. Only when they neared the top of the little rise did they dare to stop. Panting heavily, hands splayed against ribs, they saw no lantern coming after them, heard no voices. Through an open place in the trees they could still see the lantern swinging alongside the train, now directly across from them, and they knew they had not been pursued.

"Well," Will said, then turned and started walking, angling up toward the ridgetop where he would keep moving south, parallel to the tracks.

By sunrise they had broken out of the woods and stood on a high grassy knoll overlooking the lights of a large town. Nothing moved in the streets, and the chimneys of the factories stood grim and silent in the pearly light.

"What town is this?" Tobe asked.

Will shrugged. "I don't know."

"I've seen bigger." Having passed through the lights of Columbus and Cincinnati in the night, Tobe was now a jaded, World-weary traveler.

Will turned and started walking into the lightening east.

Tobe called after him, "Aren't we going into town?"

"Not today," he said, without looking back. "It's Sunday."

He kept walking, avoiding civilization, staying to the farm fields, rarely speaking. Tobe limped along behind, complaining only rarely of hunger, veering occasionally into the edge of a wheat field where he would rake the stalks with his fingers, rub the heads between his palms, blow off the chaff, and munch the raw wheat.

Will knew when it was nine o'clock. The angle of the sun told him, almost to the minute. They would be gathering for Sunday service at the Nisley house now, filing in and sitting on the rows of wooden benches that had been set up the night before, women on one side, men on the other. This same bright sun would light grim faces in the big stark front room of the Nisley home, for they would already know. The news would have spread like a grass fire through the stables and around hitching rails as families tied their horses, brief whispered headlines altering the mood as swiftly and profoundly as the news of Pearl Harbor had done. *Did you hear? He's gone. Will Mullet ran away last night!*

The men would say nothing. Beards would twitch and eyes would harden under hat brims as they looked to the horizon while hands and shoulders continued their business with horse and buggy, but they would say nothing. The women would hide their faces, though for once they would have words when the men did not.

"Poor Mattie," they would say.

When they stopped to rest in the shade of a sycamore alongside a fair-sized creek Tobe revealed what for him was an uncharacteristic bit of foresight: He pulled from his pocket a tangle of fishing line and hooks, and began sorting it out. Will cut a couple of green willow limbs, trimmed them with his pocketknife, and set about digging under patches of damp leaves for worms and grubs. Within an hour they had spitted several small fish and were roasting them over an open fire. A line of little wood ducks paddled past in the edge of the creek, and a brown thrush called from the opposite bank. A light breeze stirred the upper limbs of the sycamore.

"This is good," Tobe said, leaning back against the tree, holding a fish like an ear of corn and picking it clean with his teeth. More than once he had commented with a proud grin that their father would surely have killed them had he caught them fishing on Sunday.

For Tobe it was a sun-spangled afternoon of rare, sweet freedom, but for Will it was nothing of the kind. Squatting by the fire, stirring the embers, his mind replayed a litany of harsh, condemning voices. He said nothing. After a while he stood up and wandered over to the edge of the creek where there lay a little curved beach littered with good smooth stones. For a long time he just threw rocks, sometimes skipping them across the water, sometimes hurling them into the woods on the other side. Sometimes he threw them very hard.

Country boys would never go hungry in the summertime. Besides the fish and cheese and what was left of the trail bologna, they foraged nuts and berries from the countryside but stopped short of raiding a vegetable garden when they came across it. That would have been stealing. The weather held fine, and they spent a pleasant evening beside the creek. Tobe wrapped himself in the blanket and fell asleep long after dark. Will lay on his back next to the fire, staring at the stars, longing for a forgetfulness that would not come. His heart was torn and bleeding, and his thoughts would not go away.

The next morning at daylight they smothered the remains of the fire, packed up their meager possessions, and followed the nearest road straight into town. On the outskirts they passed an occasional farmhouse surrounded by its outbuildings and separated from neighbors by tilled and tended fields. But as they neared the town, the houses closed in on each other and crowded up against the gates of massive, stark, ugly buildings with rows of narrow windows mounted far too high for anyone to see out of. Fences had been built around the factories, which gave them the look of prisons. Tobe gaped in astonishment at the houses all in rows between the factories and mills. He had not envisioned a place where people lived in such close quarters, and he said so.

"Yes," Will said. "It's a little claustrophobic, isn't it?"

Tobe didn't answer, and after they'd gone a few steps in silence, Will tugged a battered dictionary from the hip pocket of his overalls and handed it to his brother. He liked having lots of pockets. Pockets were the best part of English overalls. Amish pants had big, roomy pockets in the front, but that was all. There were none in the back.

Men with lunch pails hurried past without speaking, barely nodding, most of them older men dressed like Will and Tobe, in overalls. A few wore khakis. All wore hats, and it was probably because of the hats that it took a while for Will to notice that some of the men passing them were not men at all, but women dressed as men, going to work like men. The World, in this latest upheaval, had done strange things to itself.

Just across the railroad tracks in town they passed through a solid block of red brick buildings. The right side of the block was taken up by two long warehouses. On the left stood Swint's Feed and Seed, Dindy's Hardware, Parson's Dry Goods, and down on the corner past the row of stores Will saw what he had been looking for: the candy-striped pole of a barbershop.

A gangly old man sat carving a tiny horse with his pocketknife on a bench in front of the window, long legs crossed in the manner of a man with no worries and no gainful employment on a Monday morning, his dangling foot keeping time to music no one could hear. His hat was pushed back to reveal a shiny, bulbous, liver-spotted forehead, and his bottom lip bulged with snuff. He glanced up, squinting, as the boys approached out of the rising sun and their shadows fell in front of him on the sidewalk. It was only a brief glance, but his countenance changed. Something the old man saw, some little thing—the bowl-shaped haircuts or the burlap bag dangling from Tobe's hand, Will figured—brought him back from wherever his mind had taken him and planted a knowing smile in the wrinkled corners of his eyes. As they walked past him he folded his knife, dropped the half-finished horse into his shirt pocket and brushed shavings from his knee. When they turned in at the recessed doorway of the little barbershop he rose to follow them.

A small cowbell made a racket when Will pushed the door open and stepped into the shop. Tobe followed closely, peering over his brother's shoulder at the two strange pedestal chairs bolted to the hardwood floor, the mirrors on the wall, the vast collection of ointments and lotions on little shelves and nooks under the mirror, the razor strop hung on its peg. The air smelled of cigarettes and shaving lotion. To the left, a little pregnant wood stove sat cold and empty with a clutch of cane-bottomed chairs scattered around it, but the chairs were vacant. A ceiling fan turned lazily overhead.

" 'Scuse me," the old man said, touching the boys on their shoulders as he brushed past them and shuffled, stoop-shouldered, to a door at the back corner of the shop. He opened the door, stuck his head in and, looking up, said in a loud rasp, "Arliss! Gi'down here, boy! You got work to do!"

Turning from the door, leaving it open, he aimed himself at one of the chairs by the wood stove and shuffled toward it muttering, "He'll be down d'rectly."

Will fidgeted, not sure what to do with his hands while he waited in a strange place without a hat to hold on to. He mumbled a thank-you, then hooked his thumbs in the bib of his overalls to quiet his hands.

Footsteps on the stairs, then a little man in a white coat like a doctor burst through the door.

"Arliss Compton!" he boomed, introducing himself in a voice larger than his body, and shook out an apron as he hurried across the room to one of the pedestal chairs, then draped the apron over his arm and spun the leather chair to face them. "What can I do for you gentlemen today?"

He was a dapper-looking little man, polished and groomed, with a pencil-thin mustache and neatly parted slicked-down hair. He smiled a broad, toothy smile that somehow made Will distrust him deeply.

"We need haircuts," Will said, rather sheepishly, "if it's not too much trouble." He had never been in a barbershop before and wasn't sure what he should say. His stepmother had always cut their hair.

"No trouble atall, son. Just have a seat right here!" The barber's voice was too large for the confined space. He patted the leather seat, and Will stumbled toward it, nudged gently from behind.

As soon as Will scooted himself up into the seat, the barber flung the apron into the air and brought it billowing down around his neck.

"So, what'll it be today, sir? A little off the top?" There was more than a glint of satire in the barber's eye. Will and Tobe had belonged to the Old Order Amish, who were always careful to keep their bowl haircuts completely covering their ears, and Will felt sure he owned more hair than Arliss Compton had ever seen on a man.

He pointed at one of a line of pictures above the mirror. "Can you make me look like that?"

The barber glanced up at the picture, winced, then raised a hank of hair over Will's right ear and looked underneath.

"Clark Gable? Oh, I don't know, son. I don't think your ears are big enough, but we can air 'em out and see." He backed away, frowning. "You *sure* you want that much cut off? It'll take a lot longer for you to grow it back than it will for me to cut it."

Will nodded resolutely, glancing at Tobe in the mirror and holding his tongue, wondering who Clark Gable was. Tobe took a seat against the wall behind him and watched with openmouthed fascination while his brother's hair fell away in clumps.

"What's your name, son?" Arliss boomed. "And don't jerk your head like that unless you want to lose an ear."

"William," he said, "William Mu—" He stopped after catching the widening of Tobe's eyes in the mirror and instantly remembering Mr. Peavey's advice. In the space of a second he pictured himself shriveling in the buggy next to his father on the long ride home, saw the set of his father's chin. In the same instant he spotted a Hershey's bar in one of the cubbyholes in front of him, and the freckled face of Earl McGruder pressed itself upon his mind so that he spat out, with no conscious thought and only the briefest pause, the name that was to become his own.

"William McGruder," he said, watching his brother's reaction in the mirror.

The barber stopped clipping and stepped back from him in mock surprise, scissors raised in one hand and comb in the other. "You hear that, Mister Roy?" he said, his eyes big. "We got *Wicked Willy McGruder* right here in chair number one! The infamous Willy McGruder! What do you say to *that*, Mister Roy?"

The old man slapped his hands down on his knees and leaned forward from the edge of his seat, grinning at Will. "Why, I b'lieve you're right, Arliss! At's him, all right. Reckon they still got a re-ward for him down to the post office?"

Near panic, Will was watching Arliss closely, so he saw the pretense in the barber's face, the laughter in his eyes, and figured out that Arliss was pulling his leg. He had brought his hands up to grip the leather arms of the barber's chair, preparing to bolt, but now he decided against it.

"Hold still now—you'll want to look good for the hanging," Arliss said, returning to his work. "You know, Mister Roy, now that I think about it, old Willy here might not be a wanted man anymore. The statute of limitations has surely run out by now."

"Is there a statue of limitations on train robbery?"

"Why, sure there is!" Arliss trimmed studiously around an ear. "Seven years, just like everything else. After seven years they can't hang you for anything, except murder. Say, Willy, you didn't kill anybody when you robbed that train back in thirty-five, did you?"

Tobe was on his feet, inching toward the door.

"Oh, I don't think so," Will said. "But I wouldn't remember everything. I was only eleven years old."

Mister Roy cackled, slapping his knees and pointing. "He's got ya there, Arliss! By gum, that's a good'un!" He laughed until he wheezed.

The cowbell clattered and a portly man in a brown three-piece suit ambled into the shop with a newspaper under his arm.

"Mornin', Jack!" Arliss shouted. "Say, Willy, you know who this is? It's the infamous Jack Pelham, that's who! Do you two gangsters know each other?"

Will shook his head. The new face in the mirror tipped his hat, smiling patiently at Arliss's nonsense, and sat down next to Tobe.

"Say, Jack, did you hear about the blooper pitch?" Arliss made a little arcing motion with his scissors. "Some guy on the Pirates throws it. Calls it a 'dewdrop.'" Will was beginning to understand that Arliss was one part barber, one part entertainer.

Jack crossed his legs, snapped his paper open.

"Psh, dewdrop. Sewell's a chump. The only reason he's getting away with that stuff is he's only throwing it to little kids and fat old has-beens. Let some real ballplayers come back from the war and see what happens."

Mister Roy's eyes lit up and he pointed a bony finger.

"You mighty right, Jack! First time he serves that lollipop to the likes of DiMaggio he's gonna git shellacked!"

"Whole country's gone nuts," Jack muttered. "*Night* baseball at Crosley, for pete's sake. Who wants baseball without sunshine?"

"I heard they even got a one-arm guy playin' in the majors. Next thing you know they'll be wantin' to let niggers in," Mister Roy said.

Jack lowered his paper, looked at him. "You ever seen 'em play?"

The old man's back straightened, his eyes narrowed.

"Who?"

"The Negro Leaguers. Some of those nigras are pretty good ballplayers."

Mister Roy pulled a deep breath and stared for a minute. Arliss shot a hard look at Jack, but said nothing. This was not a new argument.

"No, and I ain't a-goin' to, neither." The old man pushed himself to his feet and shuffled to the door, jerked it open and went out to take up his post on the outside bench, clearly betrayed but not ready to air it out in front of strangers.

Jack shrugged, went back to his paper.

"It's good they have the Reds on the radio now," Will said, uncomfortable with the tension. It was his considered opinion, having come from a place where nothing ever changed, that change was good. Arliss was putting the finishing touches on his new haircut, rubbing in a healthy dose of tonic and combing it into place with a flourish. Facing the mirror, the barber spread his arms.

"Well now, how do you like the *new* Willy McGruder?"

Will turned his head side to side, smiling at himself in the mirror. There was still a little wave in his hair, and he looked good. He'd traveled a hundred years in the space of ten minutes. Change was definitely good.

While the infamous Tobe McGruder was getting sheared, Will took a seat next to Jack, who was still buried in his morning paper. But after a few minutes he folded the paper, laid it aside and pulled out a pack of Pall Malls, thumping it against his palm before he shook one out. As an afterthought he offered one to Will, who took it, then lit them both with his Zippo.

Seizing the opportunity, Will blew a cloud, spit out a shred of tobacco and said, "If a fellow was looking for work around here, where would he go?"

"Well." Jack pointed a chubby thumb in the direction the boys had come from. "The mills are always hiring."

Will could see Tobe's face in the mirror, and he almost laughed out loud at the intense, purposeful frown.

"I don't think we would do very well in a mill," he said. "Is there anything else?"

Jack pointed with the two fingers that held his cigarette. "About three blocks down that way, there's a bus stop. Right past that is an old soup kitchen—closed now, but the street corner in front of it is where guys stand around in the morning, waiting for day work. What *can* you do?"

"Oh . . ." Will shook his head, took a drag, coughed. "Just work. You know. We make pretty good farmhands."

Will bought both of them a decent felt hat at the dry goods store, mostly to cover their conspicuously bare heads, but partly because Tobe insisted Will owed him one for having flung his old one out of the train. Tobe wanted a cap instead, but Will held his ground.

"We want to look like working men," he said, "not boys, and not bums."

It was pretty much for the same reason that he also bought his own pack of Pall Malls. Looking at his reflection in a shopwindow with his new haircut and city hat, a cigarette clinched in his teeth, he didn't look at all like some hayseed Amish kid. "Clark Gable," he said to his reflection.

Walking down the sidewalk toward the soup kitchen, Tobe asked, "Where did all that money come from?"

It was a legitimate question. Working for the last two years, Will had followed the Amish custom of bringing all his pay home to his father, who then doled out a little pocket money as he saw fit. *Very* little. When he paid for the hats Will had pulled out a wad of five-dollar bills—more money than Tobe had ever seen outside of a horse auction.

"Abel gave it to me."

Several paces later Tobe said, "You kept your pay? That's Dad's money."

"No. Abel gave Dad the last of my pay two weeks ago when Dad went over to take back the horse and buggy—and to tell him what happened. I saw Abel in town, day before yesterday, and he gave me fifty dollars. He said it was a loan."

"So you're going to pay him back, then."

Will nodded. Somehow. Someday. They both knew he wasn't supposed to accept money from an Englisher, even if he was a friend.

A minute later Tobe spoke up again. "You told Abel you were going to leave?"

"No."

"Then why did he loan you money?"

"He just knew. He never said, but I believe he was thinking I could either use the money for getting married or for not getting married. Either way."

"He didn't tell you what to do with it?"

"No."

Tobe pondered this for nearly a block, then said, "Abel Elliot is a good friend."

They hadn't been standing in front of the soup kitchen very long when a black car pulled up to the curb and stopped. Will didn't know what kind of car it was, but he could tell it was almost new—it shined, and there were no scuffs on the running board. Jack Pelham's round face peered out of the driver's window.

"I forgot to tell you. If you want to go out on day labor you have to get here early. Most of 'em get picked up around first light." He hung his hand over the steering wheel, wiggled his fingers on the other side. "Tell you what, just hop in and I'll take you out to my cousin's place. I think he could use a hand bringing in his wheat."

CHAPTER | 4

*January 1985*

Will's forehead is leaning against the cold glass of the trailer window when the distant grumble of a snowplow brings him back to himself. Headlights crest the hill to his left and tilt down, spilling artificial light across the snow. Cruising down the hill, a yellow strobe light heralding its steady march across the valley, the snowplow passes in front of the trailer and up the opposite slope, rooting aside new snow and scattering salt in its wake. Two cars trail behind, far enough back to avoid the spray of salt but close enough to let him know they're in a hurry and they wish he would move a little faster.

Will runs a hand over what remains of his receding gray hair.

"Clark Gable," he whispers. "Pfff."

Still dark, the valley lies quiet again after the snowplow is gone, but it's not the same. Now that the road has been cleared, even when a car doesn't come to spoil the view, there is still the expectation of it, and the snow is broken anyway. He turns away and goes into the kitchen to put on a pot of coffee.

He doesn't know where things are. It's Sylvia's home, but she's in

Sarasota for the winter and he's borrowing the trailer for the weekend. He finds the coffee maker on the counter beside a can of Maxwell House but doesn't spot the filters right away. They're on top of the refrigerator, behind a framed photograph of Tobe, all grown up, grinning, sitting in the middle of a sofa with his wife and two daughters under his arms. Will turns on the overhead light, and with his thumb wipes dust from the glass over Tobe's face.

In the picture Tobe is happy. Really happy. He is lit with a bone-deep contentment in himself, the world, and his place in it. The light—his light—spills out through Sylvia's face, and the faces of his two daughters. Sylvia is young and thin. It's an old picture, and Will knows things now that they did not know then. Part of the reason Sylvia's face shined in the picture was that she was already pregnant with Tobe's only son; she just didn't know it yet. She wouldn't find out until after Tobe was dead.

*June 1943*

Will and Tobe hired on with Jack Pelham's cousin, who took an immediate liking to the "McGruder" brothers and treated them well enough, even if he didn't pay handsomely. It didn't matter to Will. Work was work and a roof was a roof, even if it was just a harness room with cots. There was nothing he could not, or would not, do. He had never been taught to divide work into categories of good work or bad, easy or hard, dignified or undignified; he had only been raised to recognize work done well, work done poorly, and work not done at all. If manure needed shoveling, in Will's mind the only true indignity was leaving it unshoveled.

There were many things he did not know about the World, but he knew himself. In the earthbound economy of the Amish there had always been certain standards, clear goals a boy could strive for, measure himself against and know for a quantifiable certainty when he had passed a milestone in his life. Like field corn. To help feed the livestock over the winter everybody raised field corn. On the cusp of autumn, after the grain was fully developed and before the frost had driven out the sap, the men would cut the stalks and gather them into shocks. Once the ears were dry enough to store without mildew or spoilage the church would come for a husking bee, and afterward the stalks would be chopped up for fodder.

Because everyone did it the same way, it was easy for a boy to measure himself against other boys his age. There were lots of little competitions. Even the fathers did it sometimes. While an Amishman could not indulge in prideful boasting, he *could* strike up a conversation about bushels per acre and let the numbers speak for themselves. Farmers took pride in their yield, courting couples took pride in their husking prowess, and growing boys took pride in how much field corn they could cut. It was widely understood that the standard for a full-grown Amishman was one hundred shocks a day.

Will remembered the first time he did a man's share. He remembered the hot, sore pride in his hands and his back, the blister raised on the outside of his right ankle by the foot-mounted corn knife. He remembered the lay of the field and what sort of day it was. He remembered exactly how the pink fingers of cloud stretched across the setting sun, and how his legs felt walking back to the house, damp with sweat, with daylight left and a hundred shocks behind him. He had walked differently on his way to the house that evening, emulating, not quite unconsciously, the swaying man-walk of his bowlegged father, and fairly bursting with the compressed anticipation of the moment when his father would ask him how he had done. He was fifteen years old at the time.

Jack Pelham's cousin was heartbroken when he ran out of things for Will and Tobe to do and they had to move on. They migrated south, picking corn, then tobacco, then cotton, taking whatever they were paid and living however they could. When they reached Florida they discovered that the economics of war had created a sugar shortage and raised up a whole new industry overnight. It was a labor-intensive business, cutting sugar cane, because it was a new enterprise and the owners had not yet learned how to mechanize it. Desperate for help in the fields, plantation owners imported boatloads of Cubans and Bahamians to help. Armies of old men, children, and islanders took up machetes and hacked and slashed against a wall of green in the tropical heat and humidity of central Florida, sticky with sweat and sap and hounded by swarms of gnats and mosquitoes.

At night, Will and Tobe bunked with the single men in a long, low, dirt-floored building that had obviously been a chicken house before the war. The smell of chicken droppings clung to the walls, and bits of white feathers remained caught here and there in the chinks of the exposed rafters. The damp, oppressive heat and militant mosquitoes might have been unbearable had it not been for the freshwater spring down at the edge of the cypress swamp, where crystal clear water welled up out of the ground to form a broad ice-blue pond big enough for everybody to swim in the evenings.

Most of the women stayed away from the big spring, preferring the smaller one farther down in the woods, where the men did not go, where they could bathe in relative privacy after a hard day in the fields. The men put on trunks or short pants or whatever they had and plowed straight into the bracing cold water of the big spring within sight of the camp. Some would carry a bar of soap and wash themselves in the shallows where the spring funneled itself into a stream, and the current would carry away the cloud of their bathing. Some of the girls in their bathing suits came to the big spring in the evenings too, if they were young and unattached and thought themselves pretty. It was a kind of advertisement. Will understood. He was polite, but quiet. He never spoke unless he was spoken to, and never stayed long in the company of women. They brought a kind of sorrow upon him and drove him further into his self-imposed exile. After a bath and a swim he would retreat to the bunkhouse and read, or play poker for cigarettes on a makeshift table under a bare light bulb.

But not Tobe. While Will had been shrinking into himself, Tobe—who bore none of Will's secret guilt and brooding anger, who would soon turn seventeen a thousand miles from home, who had discovered he could earn his keep, and more, alongside grown men, and whose teenage heart was beginning to chafe under the constant disapproval of his older brother—was expanding.

It started in the cane fields, when a man named Kouros came to work there with his daughter, Carmela, who was sixteen years old. She had dark sultry eyes, full lips, shining black hair and a body that even in dungarees was a danger to men who worked all day with razor-sharp machetes.

The first day that Kouros and his daughter worked in the same crew with the McGruder brothers, Will could see that it was going to be a problem. Sooner or later Tobe was going to cut off his own left hand if he didn't keep his eyes in his head. For a long time the girl didn't seem to notice Tobe, but then someone kicked up a snake that panicked and darted in the wrong direction. Instead of slipping into the dense forest of uncut sugar cane it coiled itself and then shot straight out into the stubble toward Carmela, who was just returning from putting an armload of cane on the mule cart. She backpedaled when she saw it and let out a little shriek. Tobe's machete descended in the same second, leaving the headless reptile tying itself into a knot. Carmela gave Tobe a demure smile, then tiptoed around the dying snake and went back to work, but Will saw the look in Tobe's eye and knew that he was smitten.

"It was a black snake," he whispered to Tobe. "Harmless."

"Yes, but *she* didn't know that."

"You don't know *what* she knows. She probably keeps one for a pet."

The girl's father also saw the looks between them, but Kouros did not know much English. He spoke animatedly to his daughter in his native Greek, while speaking to Tobe only with his eyes. The next day Kouros got himself and his daughter assigned to the cane press, but in the evening Carmela put on her bathing suit and went down to the spring where the boys were. When Tobe smiled at her, she smiled back.

If they had been at home, if none of this had ever happened, Will wouldn't have had to deal with his younger brother when he started to spend all his evenings with the dark-eyed girl. At home their lives had all been strictly controlled by the laws of the farm and Levi Mullet's will. Tobe would have answered to his father. But things had changed. Adrift in the World, cut loose from the binding ties of land and family and name, Will McGruder felt the weight of only two responsibilities. One was the need to work, to carry his share of the load and earn his keep. The other was Tobe.

Late one evening, after most of the others had turned in, Will propped himself against a tree below the bunkhouse, smoking a cigarette while he waited for Tobe.

Kouros and his daughter had come to the plantation with a group of families who traveled together in an old broken-down two-ton stake bed truck, and they had made a little tent village down between the bunkhouse and the spring. A dying cooking fire between the tents still gave a little light, and Will could see Tobe and Carmela silhouetted against it, facing each other, their hands touching. He could not hear what they said to each other, but he could guess. He could remember.

Kouros came out of the tent and said something to Tobe, loud enough for Will to hear. Though he didn't understand the language, there was no mistaking the meaning of the backhanded wave, the raised voice. Tobe stuck his hands in his pockets and, with a casualness bordering on insolence, turned toward the bunkhouse. Carmela ducked into the tent. Her father stayed outside for a long moment staring at Tobe's back.

Will dropped his cigarette butt and ground it with his toe as Tobe approached. Tobe stopped short, his face in the dark. He pushed his hat back on his head, crossed his arms and waited.

"You should leave the girl alone," Will said.

"I should?"

"Yes." He wanted to slap some sense into the boy, but he controlled himself. "She's too young."

"She's sixteen. Same as me."

"*You're* too young."

Silence. Tobe's head tilted belligerently.

"You're going to get yourself in trouble," Will said. "Or her." He heard the note of pleading in his own voice. Tobe just shook his head and brushed past him on his way to the bunkhouse.

"You're one to talk," he said.

Will grabbed his shoulder and spun him so that they faced each other, inches apart.

"Yes!" he hissed, and his eyes flared. "I am!"

Tobe stared for a moment. There was no fear in him any longer, just the arrogance of the untested.

"That's right!" Tobe said, in an almost cheerful voice, "You had *your* fun, didn't you?"

It might have been a true thing, but it was still uncalled for. Will stewed in it for a second before he managed to nod and say, "Yes, and it wrecked my life."

"Well then," Tobe said, his eyes locked on Will's, "leave me alone and let me wreck my own life."

He reached up and calmly removed Will's hand from his shoulder, then turned and went into the bunkhouse without looking back.


A party broke out in the tent village that Saturday night. The ground between the circled tents had been cleared, the trees hung with lanterns. Two old men cranked up fiddle and squeeze-box with surprising energy as the wine flowed and dancing commenced. Caught up in the spirit of celebration it was some time before Kouros looked around, noticed that his daughter was missing, and went looking for her.

Will, himself caught up in the spirit of celebration and enjoying the wine being passed around, did not know any of this had happened until he heard, above the uproar of the music and dancing, what sounded like a girl's scream coming from the direction of the swamp. He dodged between the tents to the outer edge of the light cast by campfire and lantern, cupped his hands around his eyes and peered down toward the dark cypress woods. The first thing he saw was a white, shirtless chest bounding toward him from the mouth of the trail, then white arms and legs pumping as Tobe came tearing up the hill, still soaking wet from the spring. Kouros was hot after him. The Greek was maybe thirty yards behind Tobe, brandishing a machete and shouting unintelligible curses.

Carmela, in her black bathing suit, brought up the rear, screaming for her father to stop.

A handful of people had followed Will to see what was going on. When Tobe shot past them barely touching the ground, Will broke from the crowd and tackled Kouros. The old Greek was surprisingly strong for a forty-year-old man. Even so, he was no match for Will. He stopped struggling as soon as Will took away the machete. He kept up a steady diatribe, venting his rage and frustration in words Will didn't understand, but as soon as he stopped fighting Will got off of him. Kouros lay propped on an elbow, breathing hard, gesturing toward the bunkhouse and spewing venom. Will picked up his hat, which had fallen off and gotten crumpled in the melee, dusted it off, put it on his head, and backed away, holding the machete loosely at his side.

The music had died and the whole cast of the party spilled out into the edge of the darkness to see what all the excitement was about. They gaped at Will, with the machete in his hand, and the old Greek sitting on the ground flinging curses. Now that Tobe was out of sight, Kouros turned his attention to Will. Will felt the crowd watching him, watching the machete, and he sensed their fear. He stabbed the machete into the ground and raised his hands, palm out, to Kouros.

Kouros snatched a fistful of grass and flung it at him. Sitting on the ground defeated in front of his friends, righteous indignation fueled his anger. His face twisted into a mixture of rage and frustration that made him look like a kid about to cry. The only word Will thought he could pick out from among the wild diatribe was the name "Andre." Kouros said it several times as he rose to his feet. Ignoring the clump of grass stuck in his hair and the swelling bruise on his jaw, he slowly closed in on Will.

Will could see that Kouros wasn't attacking—it was in his eyes. The fight was over. Kouros just wanted to say his piece. He didn't stop railing at Will or pointing his finger at him, but his voice dropped to a much quieter snarl. At the last he stood toe-to-toe with the larger, younger man. Slowly, he reached up toward Will's hat.

Will recoiled at first, but Kouros showed him his palms and somehow made it clear with his eyes that his intent was at least peaceful. Will let him remove the felt hat from his head.

Kouros turned to the machete still quivering in the ground at Will's side and carefully hung the hat on top of it. He straightened up and a quietness came over him. The anger drained out of him, leaving only pain. He said some more things, softly, looking Will in the eyes but pointing at the hat, then leaned close and asked a question. Will understood none of it and could not answer.

Kouros spat in the direction of the bunkhouse, spat again at Will's feet, then turned and shoved his way through the crowd toward his tent.

Will started after him when the fiddle player stopped him, holding fiddle and bow in his right hand and planting his left against Will's chest. Seeing the look on the man's face, Will allowed himself to be stopped.

"You wish to know what Kouros say?" the fiddle player asked.

Kouros went into his tent as the crowd dispersed. Will nodded.

"He say, 'If Andre Kouros is here, he kill you. *And* your brother.'"

Will didn't know who Andre was, but he said nothing because he felt sure the fiddler would explain, which he did.

"Andre is son. Big brother to Carmela. Very big. Kouros have no words, but he try to say to you Andre is *man*."

The fiddler paused, took a deep breath, then continued. "Was man," he said, pointing to the hat on the machete. "Now Andre is helmet on stick in mountain. New Geenee."

He pointed two fingers at his eyes. "Kouros see you are man like Andre. He know. He ask why *you* are here, and not his Andre."

Will said nothing. He lifted the hat from the machete and pinched the crown of it, trying not to look the fiddler in the eye.

The fiddler tilted his head, searching for Will's attention.

"Why?" he repeated.

Will ducked his head and walked away. He had been a fool. He had overlooked what to everyone else was a perfectly obvious and primary question: Why was he not in the Army? Thinking back on all the places he had worked in the last few months, he could not now remember any other men near his own age in any of those places, except for the one he had met in a Georgia cotton field, who was almost blind. The truth was that shreds of Will Mullet still lived under his skin, habits and attitudes and thought processes so ingrained as to be invisible to him. Will Mullet had been a conscientious objector, whereas Will McGruder enjoyed no such status. Nearing the age of twenty, he had no legitimate excuse. Legally, though Will McGruder had only existed for a few months, he had been a draft dodger for almost two years.

And there was a war on.

He drifted away into the dark and spent the remainder of the night wandering the sandy trails between the sugar plantation and the swamp, thinking.

When he threw his Amishness out the door of a train in Ohio, when he left his hair and his name on the floor of a barbershop in Kentucky, when he ceased to be Will Mullet and became Will McGruder, it had not occurred to him that a man cannot align himself with nothing. He had always accepted the Amish belief that it was wrong to kill a man, even in war, because he had grown up with it and never had a reason to challenge the issue. He'd heard the stories all his life, about how Amish resistance to military service had been a source of conflict and persecution even from the time of Switzerland. In the Great War, before Will Mullet was born, conscientious objectors had their beards forcibly shaved; they were cursed, beaten, and tossed naked into cold jail cells for refusing to wear the uniform or support the war.

His father loved the stories of men who had stood firm in their convictions despite the personal cost. It took a superior brand of heroism, he said, to refuse to fight. Levi Mullet loved to tell the story of a favorite cousin who had been drafted and sent to a training camp where Army officers gave him a tour of his own grave and matter-of-factly described his execution if he didn't put on the uniform. He refused. He was not executed, *"But,"* Levi always proudly pointed out, *"that was not his fault."* Levi refused even to use rationing stamps because they bore pictures of weapons of war, a position that cost his family no end of added inconvenience but which paid for itself in the pride of self-sufficiency.

By the time World War II started, Roosevelt's Civil Public Service programs were putting conscientious objectors to work in noncombatant jobs where they didn't have to wear a uniform, and yet this only complicated things for Will. He had choices. He could keep moving, never tell people how old he was, and maybe never get caught, but given what had just happened he figured he would inevitably end up in jail. He could walk into a recruiter's office and tell the truth—that his name was Will Mullet, that he was born and raised Amish, and so was a conscientious objector.

At first he figured the worst that could happen was that they would ignore his CO status and ship him off to basic training, but then he realized that if he gave his real name and lineage they might stick him in a CPS program someplace near home and then contact his father, which would lead to a fate far worse than any the Japanese or Germans could devise. His last option was to forget the name Will Mullet, join the Army as Will McGruder, and take his chances in the war.

Then there was the question of ethics. Should he—*could* he—take up arms and fight? It surprised him to learn how tightly his Amish upbringing held him, even now.

In the pale light of dawn, when the birds were awakening and distant roosters crowed, Tobe came down and found him sitting on the end of the rickety little pier that jutted out over the blue hole where the big spring boiled up out of a limestone cave.

Tobe sat down next to him and ticked his toes on the surface of the water.

Leaning over with his elbows on his knees, Will watched a catfish nuzzle the grit at the bottom of the spring.

"Look at that," he said. "Thirty feet down, and you can see his whiskers. I've never seen water so clear."

"You been out here all night?" Tobe asked. His eyes were sleepy and his hair had been stiffened by the pillow.

Will nodded.

"I heard what happened," Tobe said, waving vaguely toward the tent village. "After you took the machete away from him. Thank you, by the way."

"Don't mention it."

Tobe watched the catfish with him as it wriggled into a patch of weeds, stirring up silt.

"It was my fault," Tobe said.

Will looked at him.

"What he said to you," Tobe explained, "about being draft age and all. It was my fault. I lied. I told Carmela I was seventeen and that you were three years older than me." He picked a gray splinter of wood from the edge of the pier and tossed it onto the water.

Will sighed, watched a bream creep up under the splinter, suck it in, and then spit it back out. He said nothing. He was tired.

"What will you do?" Tobe asked.

"I'm going to join the Army." There. The decision was made.

Tobe's face was grim. He didn't say anything for a while, then he looked Will in the eye and asked, "Could you really shoot somebody?"

Will nodded slowly. "If I had to."

"Why?"

"Because I was born in Mexico." This was where he had arrived after thinking all night. Tobe waited for the explanation he knew would come in Will's own good time.

"Paradise Valley," Will said, and snorted at the irony in the name. "You've heard Dad talk about it. They bought a big parcel in Mexico and a bunch of families went down there to work it. Packed up everything they owned on a train and moved to Mexico."

"I remember the stories. You and Clara were both born while they were there."

"Yes. It was a big adventure for Dad and Mama. They were young and strong, and he likes to tell about how they went down there and cleared the land, cut the trees, put up houses and barns, and broke the ground."

"They did real good for a while."

"Until Pancho Villa's men found them."

Tobe laughed. "I think Dad likes telling that part, even though it hurts him a little—how the bandits came and took everything. And the next year they came again."

Will nodded. "They would always come at harvest time and take everything before the men could go to market."

"But they never fought the bandits." There was confusion in Tobe's eyes. He couldn't untangle Will's reasoning. "They stayed true."

"No, they didn't fight—none of them did. They starved. They went and pleaded with the Mexican authorities to protect them from the bandits. The Federales told them, *'We will look into the matter and let you know what we find,'* but they were afraid of Pancho Villa so they did nothing. When the men saw they couldn't make it through another winter they packed up the women and children and came back to Ohio."

"I still don't understand. You're going to join the Army because bandits took Dad's crops twenty years ago?"

"No, it's not as simple as that." Patience was important when explaining anything to Tobe. "It's hypocritical, that's all. Sure, Dad believed it was wrong to fight, but he also believed it was wrong to take something he didn't earn."

"That's true."

"Well, when his family starved because men with guns came and took his food, his answer was to come back to this country so he could live in peace."

"Yes. He said America is a more civilized country."

"That's what he said, and they are very pretty words, but sometimes pretty words can make you look away from the truth. They came back to this country because *here* bandits don't steal your crops. Because *here* there are men with guns who will protect you and your crops."

"All right. But I still don't see your point."

Will sighed, leaned on his palms and watched a leggy blue heron stalk through the reeds in the shallow water at the far edge of the spring, his thin beak poised to spear breakfast.

"I was born in Mexico, and I was just a baby when they came back. If they had not come back to this country they probably all would have died where they were, including me, and you never would have been born. So, how is it right to seek out the protection of men with guns and yet refuse to take part in that protection? Is there not a debt? Is it not hypocrisy?"

Tobe sat watching his bare toes tick the surface of the water for a long time.

"You think too much," he said, then planted his hands on the edge of the pier and plunged into the spring.

At sunrise the tent people broke camp. They loaded tents, cots, clothes, cooking pots, blankets, lanterns, fiddle, squeeze-box, an antique dressing table, five adults, six children, and two bleating, bellicose goats into the back of the old stake bed truck and trundled out of Tobe's life. Carmela was not allowed to see him or speak to him at all. She waved to him once from the truck as they were leaving.

Tobe said he thought he knew where they might have been heading and intended to follow them. In the cold light of day Will could see that his talk was mostly bravado—the boy wanted no more of Kouros and his machete. Will kept ten dollars for traveling, gave his brother the rest, and told him to go home. Tobe, naturally, refused. Will was pretty sure he'd go home anyway, once on his own, though he could never be sure of anything with Tobe.

Will caught a ride into St. Pete and showed up at the recruiter's office with not much more than the clothes on his back. He didn't want to go to jail, so after he lied about his name, he shaved two years off his age and then, for good measure, lied about where he was from. For *Place of Birth* he wrote down Canada. People sometimes told him he talked like a Canadian, so he incorporated it into his identity. The only true thing to come out of his mouth that day was when they asked him for a social security number and he said he didn't have one. The recruiter never challenged him, never questioned any of it. Will figured it didn't really matter what he told them as long as he signed up to fight.

CHAPTER | 6

*January 1985*

The chuckling of the coffee maker brings him back. He is leaning against the counter, still holding the picture of Tobe, and he knows he has been here for a while because the kitchen window has gone from black to gray.

Carefully, he sets the framed photograph back on top of the refrigerator and then, since no one is watching, touches it once more, lightly, with his fingertips.

Everything in the trailer is scaled down, including the bathroom. The tub, the sink, the room itself—everything is small. It suits Sylvia, whose life and needs have shrunk since her children left home to go raise families of their own, but when Will crowds in over the sink to brush his teeth his elbow keeps turning off the light.

The shower has steamed the mirror. He takes the hand towel and wipes a hole in the steam so he can see to shave. It surprises him, as it often does when he first sees his face covered in the morning's silver whiskers, to see how old he has become. He doesn't feel old in his heart, though his heart has been overhauled with parts from his leg.

He wants to go back across the years, the way sometimes on a cold morning he wants to get back under the covers. He feels the need for it like an ache—a longing to travel again the pages of a book already read and closed and put away. He wonders briefly why he is drawn so, until he recalls why he has come here and what the day will bring. It's his father. It has always been his father, and he knows it is not just wistful remembrance of things past. Remembering salvages nothing. It can't bring back what has been lost any more than looking at Tobe's picture can bring back Tobe.

But he begins to understand. As if someone had come in the night and tucked it around him like a blanket, he has awakened on this day with the profound awareness that he has come full circle, and his own life will tell him the truth now if he will only turn the pages.

Jubal Barefoot's face comes to him, a photograph laid on the desk of his mind by an unseen hand. The picture is clear, and it is not the weathered face of the Barefoot he knows now, but the young man he once was.

## CHAPTER 7

*November 1943*

On the train to Maryland Will watched from a corner while the other raw recruits put their fear on display. Some of them acted rowdy and bullish, others more subdued. Some sang to themselves. It all came from the same place, he was sure of it. Sometimes he felt like a spy infiltrating a foreign culture, picking up subtle mannerisms and speech patterns and incorporating them into his own persona.

The talk on the train led him to believe basic training would be so brutally hard that some guys wouldn't survive it. Will doubted it, mainly because he doubted the judgment of eighteen-year-old boys. As it turned out, he was pleasantly surprised. Yes, there was the running through drab winter woods in combat boots at dawn, the digging, filling in, and redigging of useless holes, the peeling of potatoes and cleaning of latrines, but it was all just work to Will, and work had never been a problem. Getting up at five o'clock, marching on the parade ground, swinging on ropes, and crawling under live machine-gun fire was like play. The drill sergeant, whose sadistic furies and insane perfectionism drove other boys almost to tears, actually made Will a trifle homesick.

He had not expected to like the military, but he did. The rigid discipline of the Army was only marginally different from the rigid discipline of the farm. Like his father, the Army made sure he did not have to worry about what to do with his days, or where his meals would come from.

When he finished basic training they didn't stick a rifle in his hands and send him to Europe as he had figured they would. Instead, they sent him to a vehicle maintenance school in Georgia. Through whatever mystical means of divination the Army used, they had decided that Will McGruder, who was infinitely more familiar with the outside of a horse than the inside of a tank, would make an excellent tank and half-track mechanic. This was fine with him. He was in no great hurry to die, and working on tanks turned out to be, after all, just work.

He had never seen anything like the Atlanta Army Depot, never *dreamed* of anything like it. A sea of olive drab jeeps and tanks and half-tracks and canvas-covered deuce-and-a-half trucks stretched to the limits of the post—acres, *oceans,* of machines stockpiled and ready, waiting, quivering in anticipation of some massive onslaught. He had known about the war, had heard about it constantly, even before he joined the Army, but he had not for one moment imagined the scale of it.

Will spent long days taking tanks apart and putting them back together under the tutelage of a stumpy little cigar-chewing tech sergeant, while his nights, and sometimes his weekends, were now free. Mostly he kept to himself. Always conscious of his secrets, he learned not to talk at all, especially now that he didn't have Tobe to talk to. Sometimes in the evenings, however, he would join the other guys hunched over a table, chain-smoking cigarettes and playing hearts. He learned quickly not to get into the poker games—there were sharks in the Army—but the hearts games helped pass the time. That was how he met Jubal Barefoot.

Barefoot was six-three and might have weighed a hundred and forty pounds with his boots on. He had sandy hair and piercing blue eyes set too close together, a condition amplified by a splendid hawk nose that testified to a scant Cherokee heritage and made his slightly twisted smile even more comical. Born and raised in Georgia, Barefoot talked with a slow drawl, and he was a natural complement to Will McGruder because he liked to talk. While Will quietly tossed off tricks, squashed out cigarette butts, and deftly avoided the queen of spades, Barefoot rambled on about everything from abacus to Zoroaster. Most of the time he even seemed to know what he was talking about.

Will, who had lived all his life in the company of simple and taciturn men, and who had recently become, out of necessity, taciturn himself, enjoyed Barefoot immensely. And Barefoot, who found Will to be not only an astute cardplayer but a pretty good straight man as well, referred to him as "my Irish Canuck buddy."

Barefoot also had a strange habit of slipping a little King James into the conversation whenever he could, which was often. He seemed to have a limitless supply. When an irascible redheaded private from Brooklyn tried to "shoot the moon" and run the hearts, Barefoot busted him and then drawled, "Seems to me you're gatherin' stones together when you ought to be casting 'em away, Red. Gotta learn to play the hand you got."

It was Barefoot who introduced Will to the big city, taught him how to get around on the trolleys, and where to meet girls. It was Barefoot who took him to his first USO dance. "I would not have you ignorant, brother," Barefoot said. Will's Amish feet would not do the jitterbug, and the sheer foolishness of it kept him from trying it more than once, but he loved the excitement.

Now that he was no longer chained to Tobe, Will tested the limits of his new freedoms with the eagerness of a man freshly paroled from prison. Driving a car, he simply couldn't allow another car to remain in front of him—it must be passed. With the war in Europe looming he developed a deep fondness for beer, and his meager military pay ran through his pockets like water, though he remained awkward around girls because of Mattie. Somewhere out there was a girl who had been almost a wife to him, and she would soon bear his child. Alone. Not a day went by when he didn't think of her.

One night during mail call, Barefoot came and sat down on the bunk opposite Will. He stuck his finger under the flap of an envelope and tore it open. As he started to pull out the letter his eyes turned to Will, who was reading a book.

"It's not good that a man should be alone," Barefoot said. "How come you never show up for mail call?"

Lying with his back propped against a pillow, Will looked up from his book and shrugged. "I don't have any mail," he said.

"Well, all right. But you don't even *go* to mail call." He looked around the barracks. Guys with letters invariably retreated to the privacy of their bunks to open them. Those who received no mail either left the room or gathered at the card tables lighting cigarettes.

"The other guys all crowd around at mail call because they think they might get a perfumed letter from Mary Lou or a package from Mama. Sometimes they do and sometimes they don't, but nobody skips mail call. Except you. How is it a fella *knows* he's not gonna get any mail? Who are you, Will?"

Peavey spoke to Will then—the old hobo he'd met the first night in the cattle car—a gravel voice saying, *"Rule number one, don't trust nobody."*

"I'm Canadian, eh? The stamps don't work." He tried hard to look nonchalant.

Barefoot's eyebrow went up. He smirked, shook his head, and retreated into his own letter from home. When he had finished reading he tucked the letter back into the envelope, sighed, stood up, slapped Will's raised knee, and drawled, "Well . . . if you ever want to crawl out of your foxhole and talk, let me know."

As the weather warmed, the grass greened, the sap rose, and the azaleas and dogwoods exploded in blooms, Barefoot and Will found themselves hanging around Piedmont Park in the heart of the city on Sunday afternoons.

The boardinghouses around the park were ripe with young single women who had come to the city to take up jobs left open by men, so there were lots of girls in the park on Sunday—*fancy* girls. Will saw Helen for the first time when he was playing third base in a pickup softball game. A gaggle of girls wandered over and stood around the sidelines watching for a while. They were young, but not teenagers—no bobby socks or saddle oxfords in this crowd. These women wore close-fitting dresses up to the knee, and some of them even wore slacks.

One of them stood watching him from the near sideline. She was wearing slacks and flat-bottom shoes, unlike the really fancy girl with the short dress and poufed hair who giggled too loud and carried her high heels in her hand because she couldn't walk on the turf in them. Will tried not to look at her, the girl with the honey-colored hair that swept softly to her shoulders and the sweater that she filled out so nicely, but he knew she was watching him. He was sure she had been watching when he snagged a hard grounder over the bag, planted and fired a strike to first to beat the runner by two steps. He flexed his shoulders and held his stomach a little tighter going back to his position, all the while keeping himself from looking over there. She was watching.

It was beyond his powers to speak to her. He would have waited for her to approach him, and most likely never would have met her, if Barefoot hadn't been paying attention. Barefoot was playing first base, so when the inning ended he had the ball in his glove. As Will ran off the field Barefoot called to him, then threw him the ball. The throw sailed high and headed straight for the gaggle of girls standing on the sidelines. Will put on a burst and made a leaping catch, but his momentum carried him crashing into the girls and he knocked two of them down.

The girl with the poufed hair and short dress picked up her high heels and primped her hair before she bothered to rearrange her dress. Will could see she was enjoying the attention as four guys rushed to help her up. So he held out a hand to the other girl, the one who had been watching him. She didn't say anything as he pulled her to her feet, but then her brown eyes met his, and he was shaken.

She regarded him narrowly for a second and then looked away, swiping grass from the back of her pants, yet in that moment he glimpsed a kind of strength and self-assurance that he had never seen in a woman before, and certainly never expected to find in a woman of the World. When she looked up again she had gone back to being a demure Southern girl embarrassed at having been knocked off-balance, and Will wondered if what he had seen was real or if perhaps he had been mistaken. He had been knocked a little off-balance himself.

He stammered an apology and, blushing, started to make his escape. If Barefoot hadn't arrived and made a great show of trying to dust off her backside for her and then launched into a long and colorful list of the failings of his "clubfooted Canuck buddy," she might never have smiled at

Will, and he might never have learned that her name was Helen Shelby, or that she liked black-walnut milk shakes from the Miss Georgia on Peachtree Street.

Helen worked evenings for the phone company and couldn't see Will again until the next Sunday, but she promised to come back to the park. He talked her into coming dressed for the game. Something about her, a sweet Southern mystique, made him want to draw her closer into his world and show her who he was. He wanted her in the game so she would have to stay with him until it was over, so they could stand together on the sidelines and people would know she was with him, and so he could put his arms around that soft white sweater and show her how to hold a bat.

She showed up the next Sunday wearing Bermuda shorts and tennis shoes. She had what the guys called "Betty Grable legs." On the sidelines before the game he took time to make sure she knew how to stand at the plate. She paid attention, nodded politely, and didn't object when he put his arms around her to correct her grip. Barefoot was over by first base, playing catch with Novak, and a crooked grin came over his face when he saw Will with his arms around Helen. Barefoot gave him that little thumb-across-the-nose move that when they were playing hearts meant *Way to go.*

But when they chose up sides for the game Helen and Will ended up on opposing teams. Will was pitching, and when she came up to bat he took it easy on her. He spoke to her from the mound, reminded her to keep her eyes on the ball and not to feel too bad if she missed. She smiled sweetly, pulled her hair back and said okay. He lobbed her a nice easy pitch—not too fast but not with too much arc on it either. Right down the middle.

She did manage to keep her eyes on the ball and her head down. She leaned in, wiggled the bat, and when the ball was about halfway to the plate she bent her knees and shifted her weight to her back foot. As the ball dropped in over the plate she lunged forward, pivoting at the waist, her arms lashing out and her thin wrists snapping the bat with astonishing authority. There was a resounding *THWACK*, and a white bullet whizzed back through the space where Will's head would have been if he hadn't bailed out. He actually heard it *whiff* past his ear as he was going down. By the time he got back to his feet, Helen was standing at first base with that same sweet expression on her face, and when he glanced over there she looked him in the eye and very deliberately raked a thumb across her nose.

He grinned stupidly, and his concentration left him for a long time after that.

After the game was over, Barefoot made the acquaintance of Helen's roommate, a tall brunette from the same part of south Georgia as Helen. They all went to Miss Georgia for ice cream, and the four of them arranged to go to a movie together the following weekend.

Will saw Helen at every opportunity, spent every penny he earned on her, and pestered the sergeant for weekend passes so he could see more of her. Weeknights he lay awake worrying that some sophisticated English boy would cut in on him while Helen was at work and steal her away.

She introduced him to the South. He went with her to a showing of *Gone With The Wind* at Loew's Grand, where the film had debuted a few years earlier and the foyer was still plastered with blowups of the stars arriving on the red carpet—Atlanta's one great shining moment immortalized in posters. Finally, he figured out who Clark Gable was. She took him to see the Crackers play, climbed Stone Mountain with him, and taught him how to talk. He learned that much of his English was flawed, that he had been badly mispronouncing words without knowing it. Helen seemed to think this was a severe and deeply ingrained problem, yet with great patience she set about correcting the gaps in his education. The name Houston, for example, he learned was supposed to be pronounced House-ton. Cairo was pronounced Kay-ro, and Vienna was pronounced Vye-anna. It mattered not one whit that the rest of the World pronounced these words differently. This was the South, and the rest of the World was uniformly and matter-of-factly wrong about a great many things. The honey-haired girl with the mischief in her eyes could have told him anything that magical spring, and he would have believed it. He woke up every morning to a new astonishment that such a woman could find him worth her time.

But early summer brought news of D day, and the endless rumors that had been circulating on post for months culminated in a sobering reality. The storming of Europe had begun. There would now be all-out war on yet another front.

He promised to write, and he made Helen promise too. Lying in his bunk on the crowded transport, staring at her picture for hours as the ship plowed across the Atlantic, he knew that his life had changed. Everything had changed. He would be afraid of the war now, because now he had a reason to live. Now he would show up for mail call.

## CHAPTER 8

*January 1985*

Hello?" Helen's voice is low and rusty, almost a whisper, and he knows she is still asleep.

"It's me. Did I wake you?"

A long pause, the sound of slow breathing. "No. I had to get up to answer the phone anyway. Are you okay?"

"Yeah. It was late when we got in, so I figured it'd be better to wait and call you in the morning."

Another long, sleepy breath. "Miss you," she murmurs. "There's a hole in the bed."

"I know," he answers quietly, remembering how warm she is in the morning. Forty years is a long time to be married.

"Did Riley do okay?" she asks.

"Yeah, he's fine. He's not up yet. He has a hard time getting to sleep— I think that's the worst of it."

"Well. Remember what the counselor said—go easy on him, but watch him."

A long silence follows, and Will's ears echo with the babbling, unintelligible voices of the past, the hauntings of family history and the struggles of men, one generation grating against another.

"We talked yesterday. A little, anyway," Will mutters. "It was a start. I think maybe he's finally turning a corner."

Now Helen is quiet. It's delicate ground, and she's afraid to step on it. "Good," she says at last. "That's good. Maybe the trip will be good for him."

Will looks at his watch. "I guess I better go roust him out. It's gonna be a long day."

## CHAPTER 9

*January 1985*

The call had come right after supper, while Will was watching the weatherman wave his arms around over a map, trying to predict what the convergence of three fronts would bring. The silver-haired weatherman clearly didn't know how bad it would be; only that it would be bad. The worst of the ice buildup, he guessed, would be in a wide band across Tennessee, Kentucky, North Carolina, West Virginia, and Virginia. North of that would be snow—to the south, rain.

The route from Georgia to Ohio would cut right through the middle of the winter storm. Will could imagine what it would be like driving fourteen hours on treacherous roads with Helen. The seats in the new car aggravated her back, and that wasn't the worst of it. Helen had always been an outspoken critic of his driving, and slick roads raised her criticism to another level, well beyond the tolerance of a normal human being.

Watching the forecast, Will uttered one of those brief silent prayers he'd become accustomed to since his bypass surgery. "Please don't let the call come now. I'd have to kill her," he explained.

That was when the phone rang.

It was no surprise. The doctors had said anytime. Could be five minutes or a month, but soon, they said. Will had just been up to Ohio two weeks ago—the first time Mose called and said their father had taken a turn for the worse, the first time he'd said the end was near.

"In my mind it chust doesn't seem right for him to linger so," Mose said disdainfully when, sitting with Will day after day in the hospital room, the old man's leather heart refused to quit. "It's that machine, I'm thinking."

Will gently disagreed. "Mose, that's only a monitor—it doesn't really do anything except tell us what's going on inside him. He's just *strong*."

Will had returned home after four days, saying he'd come back whenever Mose called. Levi Mullet was already gone. Only his heart kept working. So when the phone call came, Will had already dealt with the loss of his father—the stopping of his heartbeat was a mere formality.

Helen stroked his back. She didn't have to say anything. He hung up the phone and his fingers rested on top of it for a long moment.

"I have to go," he said quietly.

"We could fly," she offered, glancing fretfully at the weatherman and the colorful splotches spread across the tube.

"No. Dad's place is hours from the airport. It would still be a bad drive. Besides, it looks like the airports may close down."

"I'll go," Riley's voice said. He was standing in the kitchen in his standard rumpled T-shirt and jeans, barefoot, unshaven, hair a mess. He had apparently sensed the nature of the phone call and come out of his room to hear. "I can help drive. You know . . . Mom's back and all. She should probably stay home."

"I don't know," Will sighed, trying not to look at his son for the same reason he would try not to look at a car wreck. "I'll think about it."

Hands in his pockets, Riley shuffled back to his room. If his feelings were hurt, Will thought, it didn't show on his face. Nothing did.

"I think it's a good idea," Helen said.

"What?"

"To let Riley go with you."

Will answered with silence. His lip twitched.

"Why not?" she asked.

Another non-answer, more silent than the first.

"Will McGruder, you've told me a million times yourself—'There's something in a man that needs to be needed.' You and me both know you'd never make it all the way there with me in the car. You'd kill me before we got halfway."

Clairvoyant, she was. "But I'd feel terrible about it afterwards," he said, biting back a smile.

"You know I'm right."

He didn't know any such thing, though he knew when he was beaten.

Once it was settled that he would make the trip with Riley it became a job, a task to be accomplished with as little aggravation as possible.

They left early in the morning. For the first few hours, plunging through a gray freezing rain up out of Georgia and into middle Tennessee, he and Riley were very polite to each other and even managed a little small talk about what they expected from the weather to the north. Mostly, they left each other alone. Will was indebted to Riley for coming along and helping with the drive because he knew he couldn't have made the trip otherwise, but they had never had any common ground. They had never really talked to each other.

When the sky began to spit sleet near Nashville and the cars left tracks in the slush on the expressway, Will slowed down and gripped the wheel tightly with both hands. In Kentucky they began to see ice collecting on tree limbs.

And when Will's sixty-year-old bladder forced a stop at a rest area, Riley stood out in the sleet the whole time just to smoke another cigarette, and Will, though he regarded smoking with the self-righteous contempt of an ex-smoker, said nothing. Riley took the wheel and Will's muscles tightened, sitting in the passenger seat. It would be hours before he could relax with Riley driving, if ever.

Before long he found himself doing Helen's job, applying imaginary brakes on the passenger side when Riley crowded too close to the back of a truck, latching on to the grab bar every time he saw brake lights a quarter mile ahead, squirming whenever Riley changed lanes across the little band of accumulated slush on the centerline.

An eighteen-wheeler alongside put his blinkers on. Will, thinking their car was in the trucker's blind spot, shouted a warning and braced himself.

Riley calmly put his own turn signal on, checked his mirrors, and slowly drifted left to allow the trucker room.

"You know, Dad," he said, with just a touch too much sincerity, "I'm clean right now. My vision is documentably unimpaired."

"I just didn't know if you—"

"I see the truck. I see *all* the trucks, Dad. And I'm thirty-five years old. I know how to drive."

There was twenty years of baggage in the tone of his voice. It was Riley's way of yanking his father's chain. His consummate chain-yanking skill was the prime reason Will had thought it a bad idea to bring him along.

"Yeah. I always forget how intelligent and perceptive you are." Will wasn't above yanking a chain himself if the occasion called for it.

Riley held his tongue for a minute. Will could almost hear his gears grinding.

"It's a curse, being smarter than everybody else," Riley said.

"Obviously," Will said, thinking even as he said it that sarcasm seemed to be hereditary. "It's ruined your life, hasn't it? The fact that you think you're smarter than everybody else is ninety percent of your problem, Riley."

He had said this to the window. As soon as it was out he wished he hadn't said it, but a man could only take so much. He stared out the window and waited for the flare-up, the cold-eyed fury, the shouting. When it didn't come, he turned, slowly, and looked at his son.

Riley chewed on a corner of his lip, and there was a devilish half grin in his eyes. He took a deep breath, and his head tilted curiously as he spoke.

"Given the dizzying vagaries of the human psyche," he said thoughtfully, "the spectrum of inherently esoteric disciplines requisite to any demonstrable psychoanalytical acumen, and absent the sheer mental acuity and exhaustive empirical evidence exigent to a cogent or even tenable analysis, such an extemporaneous diagnosis, particularly from someone of your plebeian sensibilities, would have to be dismissed as either vacuous or pedantic. Don't you think?"

Will chuckled. He laughed a quiet, wheezy laugh that intensified until he found himself wiping his eyes. Somehow this unexpected jolt of self-deprecating humor, after decades of war, had succeeded in doing something that nothing else had been able to do. It changed his perspective and tore down a little piece of the wall they had built between them. He stepped back from the mask of expectations through which he had always viewed his son. For once he just saw another human being, and one who, for all his obnoxious ways, wasn't so bad.

"I'm sorry," he heard himself say. "We were raised in different worlds, you and me. Sometimes I forget."

CHAPTER | 10

*January 1985*

Will pours a cup of coffee, dumps cream and sugar into it and carries it to the far end of the trailer, where he knocks lightly on the door of the little spare bedroom. After a second he eases the door open. Riley's feet stick out the bottom of the too-short single bed, and his head is buried under the pillow at the other end.

"You awake?" Will says.

The rumpled pile of quilts stirs. The feet retract and Riley sits up, rubbing his face. Bleary-eyed, he sees the coffee and reaches for it. As he takes the cup he glances up, just for a second, smiles a little and mutters thanks.

After a two-handed sip he closes his eyes and says, "At least I still have caffeine, thank God."

*Even his thank-you comes with a barb,* Will thinks, but he doesn't say it. He has learned to pick his battles. The mere fact that Riley thanked him means that the bridge they began building yesterday, no matter how frail, is still intact.

Will goes back to the kitchen and pours himself another cup of coffee.

He's still there when Riley comes out of his room wearing his down coat over yesterday's clothes, bare feet stuffed into unlaced shoes. Will returns to his room to get dressed while Riley goes out to stand on the porch in the bitter cold for the first cigarette of the day.

*The kid is lost,* Will thinks, for the ten-thousandth time. *He's hit bottom, but at least he's finally starting to look for the light.*

It has taken Riley's selfishness thirty-five years to shatter his illusions, to rob him first of his wife and kids, then his precious career, and leave him wallowing in self-destructive habits he could no longer afford to support. Thirty-five years from cradle to drug rehab. Will himself had hit bottom a lot younger.

Saving his good blue suit for the funeral tomorrow, Will hangs the gray suit on the back of the door to steam the suitcase wrinkles out of it, and his mind drifts back again.

The war. He remembers it in bits and pieces, ghosts bobbing to the surface of his mind at random.

Faces, voices.

## CHAPTER II

*August 1944*

The war made sane men monsters and made seasoned monsters cry like breathless children, crushed under the weight of terror. It was a brutal time, tinged with the smell of cordite and the sight of scorched and contorted bodies frozen into the foreground of a picturesque winter landscape, beauty and horror mingled in surreal, unforgettable ways. There were whole months that winter when Will forgot what it was like to be warm, when his new definition of life included the assumption that even if he survived, his feet would never be warm again.

The repple depple—the reception depot where they took him after he got off the ship in LeHavre—was a place of crowded isolation, and it filled him with a sense of nothingness, of nobodyness.

His own nobodyness was sealed and stamped that first day in the repple depple when they took away his alias and replaced it with a number. He and Barefoot waited—milling around among the other nervous recruits, trading rumors, shifting their loads and waiting, waiting. Barefoot, whenever he was under stress, turned quiet and philosophical. He sat on his helmet, propped against a brick wall while watching recruits pass and stop and talk in the cobblestone street, observing the fidgeting of eyes and hands, the too-frequent lighting of Lucky Strikes and the too-loud retelling of old jokes. After an hour of unaccustomed silence Barefoot leaned over to Will and, with his eyes still fixed on the troops in front of him, muttered his assessment.

"And they were sore afraid," he said. There was fear in Barefoot's voice too. It was in the air. It was everywhere.

They sent Barefoot out the second day, assigned to Third Army. An old staff sergeant told him to shave and button his shirt before he got there, and he was serious. Patton was all spit and polish, the sergeant said. Barefoot gave Will an exaggerated salute as he climbed into the back of a truck, still grousing about the monumental absurdity of having to wear cologne to a fight. Will wanted to go with him but there was no mechanism he was aware of by which he could even suggest such a thing. The repple depple sent men out individually, not as battalions, companies, or even platoons. One digit at a time. The number system and the warehoused rows of identical bunks gave Will the distinct feeling that the repple depple was nothing more than a large sheep pen where nameless livestock waited to be sorted and shipped to different slaughterhouses.

Then there were the horror stories from the veterans filtering back the other way, some of them wounded, some of them headed to Paris for R and R. They were changed men, all of them, grim and detached. Will could see it in the emptiness of their hard, veiled eyes. Pressed by the newcomers, they told their stories—some of them. He wouldn't have admitted it to anyone, but Will was profoundly grateful not to have been at Omaha Beach to see the surf and barbed wire and steel obstacles choked with ruined bodies, nor in the grueling, yard by yard, murderous entanglement of the French hedgerows. He was glad not to have been there, and he granted a kind of sainthood to the iron-eyed men who were.

He missed Barefoot. The nervous chatter of a thousand voices merged into a dull drone that in time disappeared from his conscious hearing so that, even in a crowd, silence reigned. For a man with no name, no home, no family and no friends, silence was a ghastly thing. In fear and loneliness his thoughts bent once or twice toward God, but the God of Will's youth had long ago crossed His arms and turned His back, so Will looked to Helen instead. A hundred times a day he took off his helmet to look at the picture he carried there—the face of hope and salvation. Mattie's face intruded once in a while, though it had gotten easier to push her aside. She belonged to another world, another life. The odds were growing daily that Will would soon pay the ultimate price for his sins, and he would have thought it fair enough if it hadn't been for Helen.

For more than a week he waited at the repple depple in his helmet and field jacket, carrying the requisite three days' rations, rifle, ammunition, canteen, trenching tool, and with a carton of cigarettes tucked into the bloused legs of his fatigue pants. When orders finally came he shipped out with twenty other guys in an open coal car heading north into Belgium, assigned to a maintenance battalion in support of an armored division approaching the Siegfried Line. That was all he knew, except that GIs coming back the other way shuddered whenever they said "the Siegfried Line."

In the fields and villages of Belgium that fall the talk was optimistic, all about how the war would be over by Christmas. Then the rains came.

"The leaves aren't turning colors," the soldiers said, "they're just rusting." Rivers swelled and hurried, roads became swamps where even tanks and half-tracks sometimes got stuck, supply lines bogged down, foxholes turned into sump pits, and everybody's feet started to rot.

The war stayed just beyond Will's reach. His maintenance battalion remained clear of the front lines most of the time, usually working in or around a supply depot far enough back from the front to keep from being overrun by German counterattack. Will's days were filled with tanks and half-tracks, patching and piecing them together from scraps and spares and sending them back to the front. It was good, heavy, hard work, and it lasted as many hours as he could stand. When he finally gave out he would crawl into a hole to sleep for a few hours, then drag himself back to work. He still didn't know if he could fight, didn't know if he could face killing or being killed, but he did know how to work.

Pushing across Belgium he could always hear the rumbling of guns in the distance, and at night he could see the flashes. A steady stream of fresh men and new equipment was heading for the front, with a steady stream of broken men and broken equipment coming back. It was not unlike walking behind a plow, he thought, treading among the fresh destruction. Still, the road home ran through Berlin, and everybody knew it. In the end it was all just work. The sooner the work was done the sooner they could all go home.

Will made a good friend that fall—a pudgy, freckled boy named Ralph Sedgewick, from Maine. And then one bright, clear day on the edge of a choppy sea of blue-green cabbage somewhere near St. Vith, Ralph went to jump on a moving tank and his foot slipped. He had only wanted to trade some K rations. His combat boot snagged in the steel gears driving the treads and he was drawn in. He died screaming shortly after they got the tank stopped. Will would make no more good friends after that.

Not long after Ralph was killed, the sarge sent Will down to the big depot near Bastogne to trade some parts for a Sherman. On the way he was flagged down by a staff officer, a captain with ropes on the shoulders of his tight fitting waist-length battle jacket. The captain wore a tie and carried a briefcase. A hundred yards down a side road his jeep had hit a mine and flipped, tossing him into the mud twenty feet from the road, shaken but unharmed. The jeep had landed on top of his driver.

Will winched the jeep off of the driver, then wrapped the dead corporal's body in a piece of canvas and loaded him into the back of the truck. He found some rags and helped the captain get cleaned up and then, once he managed to get his own truck out of the mud, gave the captain a ride down to regimental HQ in Bastogne. The captain had lost his cigarettes in the wreck. Will offered him one, then lit it for him, the *clang* and *swish* of his Zippo photographing another face for him to remember.

"If you don't mind me asking, sir," Will said, "what's a staff officer doing this far from home? We don't see a lot of pink and greens out here."

"Dangedest thing," the captain said. He was a young guy from Lubbock, Texas, and his drawl reminded Will of Barefoot. "The Old Man sent me out into the field to find this Sergeant Marecki, to drag him back so we can decide whether to give him a medal or court-martial him. 'Hang a star on him or hang him,' the general said."

"What did he do?"

"Well, he was with the Ninth a couple months ago outside Mortain—buck private, rifleman. He's made sergeant since then, mostly through attrition. Anyway, he gets separated from his outfit, and all by himself he takes out a little Kraut bunker on a hillside where he finds a stockpile of *panzerfausts*—German bazookas. He hadn't slept in a couple days, the sun's shining and it's warm, so he crawls up into the woods and lays down, you know, just to close his eyes and rest for a couple minutes while he waits for his unit to catch up. When he wakes up it's dark, and he hears tanks. His little hill overlooks the main road, and a column of Panthers is toolin' along, right in front of him. All he's got with him is his carbine, so he goes back in the bunker, figures out how to fire a panzerfaust, and takes out three tanks before they chase him out of there."

"All by himself?"

"Yeah, you believe that? There was a platoon dug in on the other side of the road, but they laid low—didn't want to tangle with the tanks. They saw the whole thing."

"Well, sir," Will said, tentatively, "maybe it's none of my business, but would you have to court-martial a soldier for falling asleep after he did something—"

"Oh, it wasn't *that*!" the captain said. "They don't care about the little nap. Ol' boy was dogged out, you know? Nah, the real trouble started when his CO put him in for a medal. When word got around back home in Chicago they put Private Marecki's picture on the front page of the *Trib*—WAR HERO!" The captain grinned, and painted the headline splash with spread hands.

"But as soon as his picture hits the stands, we find out his name's not Marecki. It's Parnelli, and he's got a rap sheet long as your leg. The only reason he joined up in the first place was to let things cool down around home."

At the moment it wasn't raining, although the sky threatened, and Will had the window down. He hung his elbow out of the bouncing deuce-and-a-half and drove one-handed, trying to look casual.

"You mean the general is mad because this guy lied to the Army about his name?"

The captain chuckled. "That and a bunch of other stuff. Fraudulent enlistment is a serious offense, and let me tell you, son, the Army don't like a liar. Worse than that, they don't like being embarrassed."

"So . . . what are they going to do with him?"

"Well, fortunately, Sergeant Marecki went and got himself killed day before yesterday in the Hurtgen Forest. So now I expect we'll just make it all look like a paper-work snafu and go ask Mrs. Parnelli what name she'd like on the posthumous medal."

"But if he was still around, would you really put him in the stockade? Just for lying about his name?"

The captain thought about this for a minute while he peeled his leg up from the passenger seat and flaked more of the drying mud off of his pants.

"I don't know, Corporal McGruder. It's a federal offense, but he's got two things going for him—he's dead, and he's a hero. Under other circumstances, who knows? If he was alive and they decided to make an example out of him, yeah, he could end up makin' gravel at Leavenworth."

Will flipped his cigarette butt out the window. "Just out of curiosity," he said, as coolly as he could, "would there be a statute of limitations?"

The captain looked at him for a bit too long without saying anything. "Now that's an odd question," he said. "Where'd you come up with something like that?"

"Read it in a book, I guess." Somebody's Guernsey milk cow had gotten loose and plodded, ignorant as a cow, into the soupy road in front of the truck, giving him an excuse to slow down and keep his eyes forward. "I just wondered if they have something like that in the Army, like on the outside. Statute of limitations, I mean."

"Well, yeah," the captain said, shrugging. "But I can't see how it would ever be used. Shoot, with Army scuttlebutt traveling the way it does, if a guy could keep his yap shut that tight for seven years they ought to pin a medal on him and put him in Intelligence."

Will changed the subject then, steering the captain away from the truth. He had gathered a bit of intelligence of his own—one that would cause him to guard his secrets much more closely.

Through that bitter winter the divisions in front of Will plowed doggedly through the forest, beyond the Siegfried Line, over the Rhine and across the German countryside, wrecking towns and villages, scarring the beautiful black-earth bottomland and paying a price in blood for every foot of it. The Allied armies cut a swath all the way to Berlin in the spring, and Will McGruder trudged along behind in the furrow. He never got near the fighting.

It was inevitable that Will's fluency in German would be discovered in the crossing of Belgium and Germany. His native Pennsylvania Dutch was a kind of melding of languages but it was essentially a German dialect, so it didn't take him long to adapt to High German. When his superiors learned he could speak the language they moved him up to Headquarters Company. His facility with German, his stoicism, and his workmanlike determination to plow through the mounds of paper work made him indispensable to the officers at headquarters, who rewarded him by making sure he didn't get relieved when the war ended. He had become the perfect soldier; he never said anything much beyond "Yes, sir" and "No, sir."

The end of the war found Will sitting on a bunk on the third floor of a bombed-out factory by a canal in Berlin, rereading Helen's letters. Through that fall and winter her letters had followed him across Europe, reaching him in clusters of three and four. He tore them open and devoured them in the order of their postmarks, trying to remember what he had written to her in between and piecing her answers together with his questions.

It had become increasingly difficult to remember what he had told her because he'd made up most of it. He told her that his parents were dead. He lied about his past and his family because no one could know—not even Helen—and he lied about the war because he didn't want her to worry. Mostly, he learned to be vague.

Both of them fumbled for words when they wrote letters and tried to name the goodness they saw in each other. She saw in him a steadfastness he did not know he possessed, and he saw in her a strength and grace she did not know she possessed. They tried to name these things, and failed, but they tried anyway because they knew they were right. Against the backdrop of death and devastation, in total isolation on the far side of the World, the wonder of her belief in him shined like a beacon.

His young heart burned, for youth and wonder were kindling for the brightest kind of love, but in the beginning he simply didn't believe he would survive the war, or that he might actually live to see her again. Once he reached Berlin and found himself still alive he was faced with a terrible choice, and in the end he knew he could not continue with Helen. He could write to her—he could pour his heart out in writing—but the knowledge settled upon him like a blanket of snow that he could not go home and look her in the eye and offer himself to her as he was. If his love for her was real he could not go home and offer her, as if it were the truth, the grand lie that had become his life.

Tormented by Helen, he found it hard to sleep at night. And half the time when he did finally doze off he'd be awakened by bullets zinging through the factory windows high over his bunk. Russian soldiers in the early days after the war mingled with Americans in the streets of Berlin, which led to problems.

The Russians, for the most part, were big, rough peasants. Will ran into them in the streets from time to time, usually traveling in packs. They were boisterous and friendly—like everyone else, glad to be alive after all—and some of the GIs made friends with them. It was at best a brittle friendship, forged between distrustful allies bristling at each other over the spoils of war. The Russians wanted Berlin. The Americans were there to see that they didn't get it.

It was bound to happen. Eventually, one of the Americans took a Russian into the Post Exchange in the basement of the factory and let him buy a few things. Word spread quickly about the wealth of American cigarettes and food to be had there, and deprived Russian soldiers came by the hundreds to load up on these treasures. It was inevitable that the hordes of Soviet troops would be denied entry to the PX, and equally inevitable that they would answer by standing a block away and shooting out the windows of the headquarters building.

Will met Mikhail in a local *gasthaus* one night. The Russian was sitting at a table by himself looking a little red-faced, having already had a few pints. When he heard Will order a beer in German, Mikhail waved him over to his table because he spoke some German himself and wanted to show off.

He treated Will like a long-lost cousin. Mikhail wore a standard Russian greatcoat with a thick black belt around his waist. The bulge of the coat above the belt served as the Russian equivalent of a backpack, where he carried his ammunition and rations. As a gesture of friendship the Russian pulled out a slab of raw bacon wrapped in greasy paper, whipped out a knife the size of a machete, sliced off a hunk and offered it to Will.

He wanted no part of the Russian or his rancid meat, but he looked at the bacon in the one hand and the knife in the other and accepted the gift as if it were a prize beyond reckoning. Mikhail took a pack of Pall Malls in return.

Two nights later Will came down the street toward the same gasthaus and heard shouting in the dark between streetlights. Mikhail stood across the street, over by the canal, with his back to Will. In the darkness, Will could just make out the khaki uniform of an American officer facing him. Apparently drunk, Mikhail was bellowing at the officer. The few words Will could pick out from his slurred English led him to believe the officer had told him to get out of the American sector and go home. Mikhail had obviously refused. Crouching bearlike, the Russian moved a step closer to the officer, and Will thought he saw the flash of a knife.

For two days he'd been thinking about that rancid bacon, and how it seemed to be the story of his life. He had left home in search of freedom so he could make his own choices and not be forced to live by someone else's rules, and then he had been forced to join the Army. The Army had forced him to come to Europe and work on tanks, forced him to remain here while others were going home, and forced him to lie to Helen just to stay out of prison. It seemed a small thing at first, to be forced to trade a pack of cigarettes for a slab of rancid bacon, but it ate at him. He'd had enough of being forced. There was nothing he could do about the Army, but Mikhail the Russian was going to *pay*.

He glanced left and right. It was late, and the street lay empty. He didn't know how to fight, yet something had cracked inside him and the strength of rage swelled through the opening. He approached quietly and took the Russian from the rear, pinning his arms to his sides. With surprise and momentum and pent-up fury on his side, Will levered most of the Russian's weight from the ground so that he could only resist with his toes. In one great straining burst he swept the larger man bodily to the edge of the canal and, roaring, heaved him over the rail.

There was a lot of splashing and cursing as Will turned back to the officer, who turned out to be Colonel Phillips, the battalion commander. Will picked up the Russian rifle lying against the curb and hurled it into the canal.

"Thank you, soldier," the colonel said, then took Corporal McGruder into the gasthaus for a beer. Looking over his shoulder, Will asked the colonel if the Russian had pulled a knife.

"I don't think so," the colonel said. "If he did, I didn't see it. Big as he was, why would he need a knife?"

Two days later Colonel Phillips called Corporal McGruder into his office, closed the door and stood him at ease.

Will tried very hard to keep the shock from showing on his face as he eyed the open folder on the colonel's desk. In that moment he was sure that he'd been found out, all because he'd drawn the attention of the battalion commander. There was a saying in the trenches: No good deed goes unpunished.

"How good are you at keeping a secret, soldier?" The colonel's voice was grave.

"Pretty good, sir," he rasped, now certain that the jig was up. The incident with the Russian had focused someone's attention on him and they had pulled his file, tried to check his background. Will's throat was very dry.

Phillips leaned back in his chair and studied Will. "This morning they fished a Russian soldier out of the canal, drowned. Been AWOL for a day or two." He watched Will's face. Will knew now what this was about, and it wasn't what he had expected. It was worse.

"I'm pretty sure you and I know how the soldier got *in* the canal, but nobody else does. Do they?"

"No, sir."

He thumbed the thin sheaf of papers in the center of his desk. "The Russians are upset because the body was found in the American sector. They want an investigation. They want blood."

Will squirmed, but remained at parade rest, hands clasped behind his back. He could think of nothing to say. He waited.

"The thing is," the colonel continued, "if anybody finds out how the Russian got in the canal we're going to have an international incident on our hands, and nobody wants that, do we?"

"No, sir."

"They've already cordoned off their sector and started stringing barbed wire around it. The American sector is now officially off-limits to Soviet troops. Things are . . . *ticklish* right now. We don't want any reprisals, and we don't want any shooting to start between us and Ivan, do you understand?"

"Yes, sir."

"It would seem best to me, for all concerned, if this Russian simply got drunk and fell into the canal all by himself." He tapped his West Point ring on the sheaf of papers and looked Will in the eye. "Have you told *anybody* about what happened the other night?"

Will shook his head firmly. "No, sir."

"Good." And for the first time, the colonel smiled. It was a fatherly smile. "So I ask you again, soldier, can you keep a secret?"

Will bit his lip. "I think so, sir. Yes. Yes, I can keep a secret, sir."

The keeping of secrets had become a way of life for Will McGruder. That wasn't the problem. The problem was that, although on the surface he appeared no different than a thousand other soldiers whose eyes had been hardened by what they had seen, underneath the surface he was still Will Mullet. He was still an Amish kid, raised in simplicity and utterly unprepared for the crushing guilt brought on by what his father would have called murder, plain and simple. He had killed a man.

In the end, he escaped the pressure in the only way he could. He got drunk. In his off-duty hours he went straight to the gasthaus and got gloriously drunk. It was on one of those desperate nights, and in that condition, that he made up his mind and sat down on his bunk and wrote his last letter to Helen. In his clumsy way he told her that he would not be coming back, that she should find someone else. It was a short letter.

Amid a sea of battle-hardened veterans he was certainly not alone in his drunkenness, but it didn't go unnoticed at headquarters. After a few days the hangovers, the rumpled uniforms, and the less than stellar performance landed him on the colonel's carpet, again. This time he was told to remain at attention.

Colonel Phillips tore into him, circling Will for what seemed like ten minutes, dismantling him verbally while Will's eyes remained straight ahead, chest out, knees locked.

And then the commander did a curious thing.

He picked up a piece of paper from his desk, stood reading it for a minute, and then said, "It has come to my attention that our honored dead, who have heretofore been buried in foreign soil, are being disinterred and shipped home to their families. We have received a request to supply a clerk to accompany the bodies to the States, maintain accurate records, and see that the bodies are turned over to their respective families, or the representatives thereof."

He laid the paper down and crossed his arms, staring at Will.

"You've been in the European Theater of Operations over a year now, haven't you?"

"Yes, sir."

"This is a cream-puff assignment," he said quietly, "and we've decided to award it to the Battalion Soldier of the Month. Now, I may have some small say in who gets to be that lucky soldier, and it looks to me like you could use the three weeks' Stateside leave that comes with it."

He closed on Will. His arms were still crossed, and he leaned over them a little so he could get nose to nose.

"The first ship leaves in nine days. In the meantime, do not," the colonel said, then his eyebrows and his voice went up, "I repeat, DO NOT cause me any further embarrassment, *sad sack*! For the next week I expect you to make General Patton look like a slacker! Do we understand one another?"

"Yes, sir."

## CHAPTER 12

*September 1945*

Will shared a cabin with a little gray-haired priest aboard the ship crossing the Atlantic—a thin, silent, punctilious man who lined up his scant possessions on the single shelf over his bunk with obsessive care. He had brought dozens of cans of sardines with him, as if he were afraid there would be no food on the ship. Will avoided him, spending most of his time on deck or in the crew's mess listening to the stories of the merchant marine. The last thing he needed was an officer of God underlining his sins.

The merchant marine were proud of their Liberty Ship, and they were convinced they had won the war single-handedly. To Will, it was a ship of dead. There were twenty-four hundred wooden boxes in the holds, and a dead man to watch over them. It was clunky and ugly and small compared to the huge converted cruise ship on which he'd made his first crossing, and yet there was something in the no-nonsense, workmanlike nature of the thing that appealed to him. The ship seemed to be made entirely of dull gray paint trimmed with rust, and it plowed through waves rather than riding gracefully over them, making a whopping twelve knots, rain or shine. Not much faster than a horse and buggy. But it never stopped, and it got the job done. Will admired that.

On the third day out, the swells grew impossibly large and the stodgy little ship rose and fell with them, shuddering when the prow dove into the trough and the props lifted clear of the sea, churning and beating. At least he didn't get seasick. He had enough troubles without that. Gripping the rail while the ship pitched and groaned under an endless overcast, he reached the burnt-out end of solitude. His soul ached. The sky was as gray and impassive as the ship, and land was beyond the reach of all but memory. The sea surged up to meet him, dropped away and surged again, black and unforgiving, whispering of relentless judgment. One of the sailors had told him the water here was twelve thousand feet deep.

Twelve thousand feet. He had traveled the World and found it broad and deep and magical—everything that home was not—but it seemed always that for every gift the World gave it took something back. In Europe, every sunset wrought with unnamed colors from God's own palette had brought another freezing night of thunder and terror. Every purple dawn brought a new day of brutality and slaughter. He had watched the madness from a distance, like a newsreel, and wondered where God was. His father had always said that God did not move. *"He is where He always was. Watching."* His father's God was a vengeful God whose eyes missed nothing, and He would be waiting with judgment, swift and sure.

Will was standing at the rail staring into the depths when the little priest came, unannounced, and stood beside him. Will ignored him for a while but the man didn't take the hint. Finally, he pulled his Pall Malls from his shirt pocket, lit one for himself and offered one to the priest, who took it.

Feeling he had been polite enough, Will leaned his forearms on the rail and waited for the priest to go away. A swell rose up and he watched coins of foam hurry past.

"Gaze long into the abyss," the priest said quietly, "und the abyss gazes also into you." He spoke with a German accent, pronouncing *also* as if it had a *z* in it.

"Nietzsche?" Will said. He had heard of Nietzsche in the bunkers and foxholes, in the endless discussions about what made Nazis tick. He had heard this particular quote from a lieutenant who had been an English teacher in his former life. Shortly after that conversation the lieutenant had moved on to yet another life.

*"Ja,"* the priest said, smiling, holding his cigarette backward between thumb and forefinger.

*"Sind sie Deutsch?"* Will asked.

*"Ja. Und sie?"*

"American," Will said, glancing at the shoulder patch on his jacket to accent the obvious. The priest was only making polite conversation, but Will was in no mood for company. He turned away again, and waited.

The priest still didn't take the hint.

"I was wondering, why is an American soldier on this ship alone? These ships usually are full of young men going home. Why only you?"

"This ship *is* full of men going home. In the holds, in boxes."

"Ahh." The priest's head tilted back. "So."

"What's a German priest doing here?" Will asked. If he couldn't make the old man go away, he could at least steer the conversation away from himself.

"I could not stay," the priest said, gazing to the east. He turned the collar of his black wool coat up around his neck—he didn't have enough meat on his bones to keep himself warm. "I could not bear it. Perhaps someday I will return."

Will probed further, speaking German because he could tell that the priest was uncomfortable with English. He learned that the priest had been interred in a work camp for the last year and a half for speaking against the Nazis. He also learned that the man was only forty years old. He looked sixty.

"You do not speak German like an American," the priest said after they had talked at some length. "What puzzles me is that neither do you speak German like a German. Yours is not the Hoch Deutsch, but neither is it Bavarian, and your words have an antiquity about them. Some words you do not have—you use the English *airplane* instead of *Flugzeug*."

Will held tight to the rail and didn't answer. The airplane didn't exist when the Amish moved to America. Isolated, they learned only the English names of new things, and words like *airplane* became part of the language. It was clear the German priest listened closely and heard things that had not been said. Will wanted only to be left alone, but the old man would not grant it.

"Forgive me, I do not mean to pry. Things appear strange to me and my mind asks questions. It is the cloth, I suppose," and he ticked at the clerical collar with a finger.

Maybe it was because Will had reached the bottom, and self-preservation had come to mean a whole new thing, or maybe it was just that the little priest seemed so straightforward and trustworthy, or maybe it was only that they were alone in the middle of an ocean and did not know each other's names. Whatever it was, Will decided in that moment to tell the truth.

"I was Amish," he said.

"Amish! Of course! There are few Anabaptists left in Europe, but I have heard of them. Pacifist, are they not?"

"Yes. My father would not approve of my uniform."

The priest let out a sharp, surprised laugh and said, "We have much in common, you and I. My father also would not approve of my uniform. You are a warrior from a line of pacifists, and I, a pacifist from a line of warriors!"

"I'm not a warrior," Will said, "but I have killed." He pulled his eyes away and tried to draw the veil down, yet the priest saw.

"There is a time for war," he said gently. "A time to kill."

"The war was over. And he was not my enemy." Will told the priest the whole story—how he had thrown Mikhail into the canal and caused him to drown.

The priest was silent. His hands gripped the rail and his steel eyes reflected the endless sea. A fine mist drifted on the wind to Will's cheek and he thought for a moment it was rain. He hoped it would thicken and drive the meddlesome priest away, but the mist came and went, came again—salt spray dashed up and scattered on the wind by the prow of the ship.

"You blame yourself for this man's death?" the priest said without turning.

"Don't you?"

"Blame is the province of the innocent and the omniscient. Forgiveness is what I aspire to these days."

"Strange words from a man who quotes Nietzsche," Will said.

Little continents of rust marred the rail where layers of paint had chipped away. The priest lifted a hand from the rail, looked at the rust stains on his palm with a kind of detached curiosity, and then put it back down.

"Nietzsche is dead," he said. "God has taught me much these last two years, about forgiveness. There are times when the murderer is as much to be pitied as the murdered. Tell me, have you ever witnessed men—*old* men, like myself, who have known the horrors of war before—forced to choose between madness and death? Have you seen a grandfather kill a child—not because he chooses to, but because he *must*?"

Will had heard of the camps. Rumors had swept through the Army, stories of death camp guards who, once captured, tried desperately to defend actions that could only be seen, in daylight, as atrocities.

"I was not ordered to kill the Russian," Will said.

"Nor did you *mean* to kill him. His death was an accident, and yet you cannot forgive yourself. You meant only to stop him. You are a soldier—it is your job. And now you are angry, but you do not know why."

"Angry?" The accusation surprised him. And it made him angry.

"Yes, there is great remorse in you, and underneath is anger."

Will's eye twitched and his breathing deepened. "If I'm angry—and I'm not saying I am—I don't believe it is your concern," he hissed.

"I am a priest. That is *my* job." And then, smiling, he turned away and left Will alone.

Will managed to avoid the man for two days, but he was tormented by his words. On the last night before they were to arrive in New York, Will spent the evening playing poker in the crew's mess, losing badly because he could never manage the brand of bluffing and lying that was required. He found it easier to live a lie than to tell one. They were playing for dimes and quarters. Will started with five dollars, and when his last fifty cents lay on the table and a one-eyed seaman raised him, he folded on a full house rather than go into his wallet again. His heart was not in it.

He went to his cabin and found the priest still awake, sitting there in his T-shirt, reading from a *Heilige Schrift* with gold edges. Will sat on the edge of his bunk and lowered his face into his hands. He still did not know the name of this priest, nor did he want to. It was only anonymity and isolation that allowed him to speak at all.

"There is more, if you want to hear it," Will said, in German. "I did something wrong. Before. And it has caused great harm to people I love."

The priest closed his Bible and laid it aside. He unhooked his glasses, folded them and placed them on top of the book.

Palms pressing his eyes, fingers entwined in his hair, Will slowly unveiled the story of how he had left home, and why. He told the priest about leaving Mattie behind, pregnant, and because he felt sure that a Catholic priest would not understand, he went on to explain the Amish practice of "bundling": when a boy and girl were courting they would spend Saturday night at her house. Following ancient tradition, the boy would sleep in the girl's bed—under her father's roof, and with his unspoken sanction.

"I have heard of such a thing. But they sew the boy into the sheets, do they not?"

"No." Will chuckled. "A myth. And there is no board. I've heard that one too."

"It is a strange custom," the priest said, eyebrows raised. His hands lay clasped calmly in his lap.

"Perhaps," Will agreed, "but it has always been so. I remember my father talking about it, saying how it was when he was young."

The priest was silent for a minute, and then he said quietly, "So this is why you are angry."

Will looked up at him, puzzled.

"In the camps, I learned that some men have little sense of justice and others drown themselves in it. You tell your story as if you believe that your father, your church, perhaps God himself, have complicity in your wrongdoing."

"Well, if you put a nineteen-year-old boy and a seventeen-year-old girl in bed together and leave them all night, what do you *think* will happen?"

"And you believe this was their intention." Pity mixed with disbelief to form a sad kind of smile.

Will's eyes roamed. "It *must* have been. My father, when he talked about it at all, treated it lightly, like a joke. I remember him laughing about how, in his younger days, they did not have any fancy flashlights. They would light their way to the girl's bed with a match, and then dive in." He put his hands together in a comical mime of a dive. "He never, not once, ever talked to me about what to do—or *not* do—when I was with her. Not once."

"But this makes no sense. Why would a father condone, *encourage* such a practice?"

Will clasped his hands in front of him and stared down at them, avoiding the eyes of the priest. "Because the sons leave," he said softly. "The Amish are farmers. They have many children—ten or fifteen, sometimes—because they need sons to work the farm. There is always work to do."

"Work will make you free," the priest whispered. His eyes fell, and Will could see a deep bitterness behind his words.

"But the simple life is a hard life," Will went on, "and the World is full of temptation. I know, I was tempted always. The plain folk's rejection of the ease and pleasure of modern life is hard for the young. Many of the sons, when they are old enough, leave the Amish and never return. The fathers worry about this, and they use what they can to keep the sons from leaving—mostly the promise of a fine piece of land—but even that is not enough. They must find other ways."

The priest's brow furrowed. He still did not see it.

"The girls are much more deeply bound to their mothers, and to their traditions," Will explained.

The priest's mouth opened, his eyes widened, his hands came up. "Ach, I see! So when the boy is forced to marry the girl, he is obliged to honor his father's wishes and remain! And you believe this is by *design?*"

Will nodded weakly. "I think it is understood," he said. "It would never be spoken aloud."

The priest sighed, turned his palms up and examined them as if he hoped to find some answer written there. When he looked up, a great compassionate sorrow deepened the lines in his face.

"My eyes have seen too much of man," he said quietly. "I am not as wise as I once was, or perhaps wiser, and answers do not come easily anymore. Given all that you have endured, no penance I could assign would be very meaningful to you, but somehow you must come to understand that God is love, that love is the proof of God, and that forgiveness is the proof of love. This is the seed I can plant. Only God can make it thrive."

The priest made the sign of the cross, from his forehead to his chest, the left to the right shoulder, very quickly, two fingers projecting from a fist. "I absolve you of your sins in the name of the Father, the Son, and the Holy Spirit," he said.

Something deep within Will shuddered, as if the sea itself trembled. There was an authority about this man, yet his words flew in the face of the God of Will's youth. Until that moment Will had not suspected that God could be looked at in that way. He had been excommunicated, condemned by his own people. It had never occurred to him that God might not be Amish.

*"Danke,"* Will said, nodding dumbly, avoiding the priest's eyes. He said nothing else because he didn't know what else to say. Rising from his bunk with a great sigh, he picked up his coat and went back out on deck.

The sea had calmed. Standing at the rail in the light of a fingernail moon, Will smoked and thought and gazed into the abyss for most of the night while the Liberty Ship groaned and waddled toward home. The priest's words held hope, although it was simply too far outside Will's experience, then, to entirely trust a Catholic priest.

But the words.

*"I absolve you,"* the priest had said, and the words shook something deep within him. He still didn't think God could forgive him, and Levi certainly wouldn't, but at least someone had. He had been granted at least some measure of forgiveness, and *that*, as small as it was, was enough to keep him going. He could go on. And if this little priest could forgive him, perhaps Helen could too. Before the morning sun glinted on the Statue of Liberty he had made up his mind. He would go to her and take his chances. He could face whatever the World demanded from him so long as he didn't have to do it alone.

At dawn a whale broached a hundred yards out, his barnacled back silvering in the pearly light as a plume of spray escaped him. Will watched with a sad smile.

"Not yet, great fish," he whispered.

It was necessary to get death out of the way before getting on with life. The Army had notified the next of kin, and they came to the docks in New York, throngs of them, dressed in black, somberly waiting to receive the boxed and catalogued remains of sons and brothers and husbands. Waiting to bury their dreams and get on with lives forever altered.

It took three days for all twenty-four hundred pine boxes to be delivered and signed for. After the last one was gone, Will McGruder grabbed the duffel bag containing everything he owned and *ran* to catch a train bound for Atlanta. In the station he counted the dimes in his pocket and almost called her, then decided against it. He might only get one chance, and he wanted it to be face-to-face. From a window seat he watched the country pass by and willed the train to hurry. He could have run faster, he was sure.

The next evening he got out of a cab, paid the driver, slung his bag over his shoulder, and rushed up onto the porch of the pale yellow two-story boardinghouse on the edge of Piedmont Park. He wore his dress uniform, complete with green coat and tie, and discovered that in Georgia even the autumn could be oppressively hot and humid. His breathing deepened and a trickle of sweat crawled down the side of his face. The door stood wide open, as did all the windows. As far as he could see through the screen door, there was no one home. An antique grandfather clock ticked loudly in the hallway.

He rang the doorbell. After what seemed like an hour he heard footsteps, and Nancy, the girl with the tall hair and short dress, stared blankly at him through the screen.

"Yes?" she said. It had been a year, and they had met only in passing. She didn't recognize him in his dress uniform.

"Is Helen here?" he asked, pulling his cap off. "I'm Will McGruder."

Painted eyebrows went up in surprise. "OH! Sure. I'll get her." She pushed the screen door open in invitation, then turned and flounced up the stairs, pleated skirt swinging.

A moment later she was there. Helen. She came halfway down the stairs and stopped when she saw him. Nancy stood on the landing at the top of the stairs watching with a catlike smile. She clearly had not told Helen who it was that had come to see her. Helen froze on the stairs, her mouth open in shock. One hand went absently to the curlers in her hair and the other gripped the front of her quilted housecoat.

She literally took his breath away. He had come halfway around the world to find her, and in his rush to get here had forgotten the power of her presence—what it felt like just to look at her. She hovered there on the stairs, waiting for him to speak, and he could not find words.

"Will?" she finally said, as if she needed to get his attention.

"Helen," he rasped, surprised to find even a part of his voice. "Have I come at a bad time?"

She came to him quickly, yet she didn't run. Floating down the remainder of the steps and across the hardwood foyer, she stopped in front of him and slapped him as hard as she could.

"Maybe you got me mixed up with some other girl," she said. "Remember me? I'm *Dear Jane*." Her nostrils flared. He could hear her breathing.

He turned the flat-topped dress cap in his hands, stared at the brass insignia on the front. He remembered sending the letter, but not precisely what it said. It didn't matter. Not now. Nothing in the past mattered now. He had come here to talk about the future.

"You want to get married?" He said it just like that, bluntly, with his eyes on his cap.

She slapped him again, harder, with the other hand. She was a switch-hitter. "I have a date."

The slap didn't faze him. Her words made him flinch a little.

"Well. After that, then. Maybe tomorrow or the next day. Or the day after that."

He saw it happening in her shoulders first. Her will weakened, and then her anger collapsed. She threw her arms around him and kissed him, then pressed her cheek against his and whispered into his ear, "Yes. You're the one."

Nancy giggled, clapped her hands together, jumped up and down and ran into an upstairs bedroom to tell somebody.

They were married two days later by a justice of the peace on the grass under a live oak tree in Piedmont Park. Barefoot was there, thinner than ever. The Army had let him go, and he called Helen as soon as he got home to give her his number in case Will showed up. Nancy said Will's best man looked "positively Lincolnesque" in his black suit.

Helen had chosen a simple wedding band, claiming she didn't want anything fancy. She knew he didn't have a lot of money—he was a soldier. There was a nervous moment when they filled out the papers for the marriage license and he put his name down as William L. McGruder.

"What does the *L* stand for?" Helen asked.

"Levi," he said. Caught without an answer, he told her the truth. He did not, however, explain that it was his father's name, or that every Amish boy took the name of his father as his own middle name. All of his brothers had the same middle initial, but he didn't tell her about the brothers either. He told her that he was an only child.

The little wedding ceremony went well as far as Will could tell, though he had no point of reference. He'd never been to an English wedding before.

CHAPTER | 13

*January 1985*

The sun is well up now, and the valley shouts with light. Will cranks the car and scrapes snow from the windows, his hands numbing quickly in the biting cold. The sky is clear. Yesterday's dense ceiling of snow clouds has hurried eastward, leaving only a brittle gusty wind beneath a solid dome of polished turquoise. He's forgotten to bring gloves. Blowing into his red hands and jamming them into his armpits for a minute, he looks down the valley and sees the flat expanse of a frozen pond ringed about with naked trees and he smiles, thinking of Tobe. The day is flush with memory. One of his earliest is the time they went to cut ice, just about this time of year, to stock the icehouse for the summer. Tobe was just a sprout, not more than four. One of the men, Abe Shetler, he thinks, noticed Tobe's hands were red and raw and told him he ought to put them in his coat pockets to warm them up. *"Ich kann nat,"* Tobe said. He hadn't learned English yet. *"There's no room—my gloves are in there."*

Tobe.

He shakes himself and, smiling, goes back to scraping the windshield.

He thinks maybe he should stick his head in and tell Riley to get a move on. There's no predicting what Riley will look like. He hasn't worn a suit since he lost his job, and he never shaves anymore.

But as Will is putting away the scraper Riley comes out the door dressed and ready. His hair is still wet from the shower and he has removed the three-day stubble from his face, though he wears the same jeans he had on yesterday.

"I could eat a horse," Riley says. "Must be the weather."

"I know a place where they serve horse. You want to drive? I don't have my sunglasses."

Riley tiptoes around to the driver's side, stepping in Will's footprints to keep snow out of his athletic shoes.

A horse and buggy clops down the road with two Amish women in it, bundled in buggy robes. This time of the morning Will figures they're on their way to work up at the Dutch Door. The dark standard-bred horse holds his head high and trots vigorously, snorting his pleasure at being able to work some warmth into his muscles this frosty morning. The younger woman, the one not holding the reins, stares at Will and Riley as she rides past.

On the way into Winesburg Riley turns on the radio and fishes for a rock station. Will tunes it out easily. He looks out the window at the soft white hills and opens his memory.

CHAPTER | 14

*April 1946*

When he came home from the war and married Helen, he thought she would save him. And she did, for a while. They were young then, and full of ideas about how married life would be— none of which mattered, of course, because all of their ideas were wrong.

Will finished his tour in Berlin and came back for Helen in the spring. They spent a few days with her family in south Georgia, in a cramped, creaking clapboard cottage in the middle of a flat, dry, red clay expanse planted in cotton. Helen's older sister wasn't there; she had married a banker and moved to Augusta. Her brother was a greaser who actually kept a pack of Luckies rolled up in his T-shirt sleeve. He stayed gone most of the time, tearing in and out in a souped-up '32 Ford, dividing his time between working at a garage and chasing girls. Welch Shelby, Helen's father, was a hard, terse, redneck dirt farmer who every morning ate a mammoth breakfast and left the house before sunup to work his fields. At noon he would come in and clean up at the sink on the back porch, eat a mammoth lunch, wash it down with too-sweet iced tea from a quart jar, then clap his hat on his head and go back to work. Around dusk he would put away the mule, come in and eat a mammoth dinner, then settle down in a ladder-back rocker on the front porch with a quart of iced tea, put his feet up on the rail and watch the dirt road in front of the house. He didn't talk much. When he did he kept it short and to the point. Welch Shelby would have made a good Amishman, Will thought.

Helen's mother, Erma, was a short, plump woman in a frayed cotton-print dress who tended her house and garden and chickens. The garden was just getting started, and they were eating the last of the previous summer's canned vegetables. Erma was always cooking. If it was meat she fried it, and she seasoned vegetables, always, with a hunk of fatback. She kept the radio on the mantel tuned to a gospel station, humming all day long to the crooning of tenors who promised fairer worlds on high, and the twangy wailing of wilted sopranos who dreamed of flying away. She talked, mostly about her ailments and her no-account neighbors, to anybody who got within earshot. After she and Helen finished cleaning up the kitchen in the evening she would sit for a while on the porch, but neither she nor Mr. Shelby lasted long.

"I'm plumb wore out," one of them would say, yawning. Then the other would yawn, and they would grunt up out of their rockers and drag themselves off to bed.

On the porch swing alone with Will in the cool of the evening, Helen would get as contented as a cat and tell him stories about growing up.

"I used to sleep out here on the porch in the hot summertime," she said. Her mother had saved up her loose change once and purchased a jar of peanut butter from a cousin who stopped by in his Model A to deliver it. Erma had never owned any store-bought peanut butter. Coming back through the dirt yard to the house she stumbled and dropped the jar.

Helen pointed. "It broke all to pieces on a rock, right there. Mama got down on her hands and knees and gathered up every bit of it that she could—whatever didn't have dirt in it," she said. "Brought it in the house and set at the kitchen table for an hour and a half picking out every sliver of glass. She saved the biggest part of it."

Helen remembered one year when she was little, the rains fell just right and her father brought in a bumper crop of peas. The pea crop in California was ruined that year and he made a killing.

"Only time I ever seen him get crazy with money," she said. "Went into Cordele that Saturday and came home driving a Hudson Roadster. Convertible. Drove that thing up in the yard with the top down—done lost his hat—and got out grinning ear to ear. Mama came out on the porch with a dishrag in her hand and just stood there for a minute looking at Daddy and his shiny toy. Then she raised her arm and pointed. Never said a word, just pointed her finger toward town and then went back in the house. Daddy went and got his money back. Far as I know, they never mentioned it again, either one of them."

"I didn't know," Will said, shaking his head. "I had no idea you were so poor growing up."

"Poor? Psh. If we were poor we sure didn't know it."

"Then what were you talking about? I mean, with the peanut butter and the Hudson?"

She raised her head from where it had been lying against his chest and stared into his eyes.

"That wasn't about being poor," she said. "It was about being strong."

He was quiet for a while, staring at a line of clouds on the horizon whose copper bottoms reflected a departed sun.

"I'll never understand Southern girls," he finally said.

Erma didn't show much emotion when Will and Helen left. She hugged them both goodbye, then just kept wiping her hands on her apron and looking back at the house like she'd left something on the stove. Helen's father looked like he was going to cry. Welch Shelby didn't talk a lot, but there was something in his hard blue eyes that said to Will, "You better take care of my daughter." They were good people.

He and Helen put everything they owned in a secondhand Chevy and drove to west Texas. He had reenlisted. The Army provided a steady, if meager, income for a married man, and now that the war was over the Army wasn't a bad place to be. Though the pay wasn't much, it was stable employment, food was cheap at the commissary, and Army doctors were free.

The romance of living in a run-down trailer in grassless west Texas wore off quickly, though they both came to understand that there was a lot to be said for hammering out the beginnings of a marriage far away from family. The first big fight came when Helen insisted she was going to get a job.

"No wife of mine is going to work," he told her, and that was final.

"You hide and watch," she said.

"You can't do it. I won't let you."

"I didn't ask you, and you can't stop me."

"Yes, I can."

"Not if you plan on going to work every day. You gonna handcuff me?"

"We've only got one car, and I'm taking it."

"I'll walk. I'm not spending my days sitting in a lawn chair counting rattlesnakes and horned toads. And I don't plan on living in a house trailer the rest of my life. We need money."

"You're not going to work. If we need more money I'll get a part-time job."

"Good. If you're gone all the time I can put in more hours."

"Who's going to cook?" He expected dinner on the table. It was part of the deal.

"I'll still cook. Dinner might just be a little late sometimes, that's all."

"A woman's place is at home with the kids."

"We don't have any kids."

"We will."

"Okay. When we have kids, I'll quit my job."

She took a job stocking groceries in a store a half mile from the trailer park. A year and a half later, she quit. Seven months pregnant, the walk got to be too much for her.

She was a pretty good cook when she wanted to be, but she cooked a lot like her mother. "A Georgia girl would starve to death without a black-iron skillet and a can of Crisco," she said.

Will ate like an Amishman—he was omnivorous. The only complaint an Amishman would make at the table was if there wasn't enough to eat, and then only if he was absolutely certain he had provided the raw materials for a meal. It was not his job to cook, or his right to complain, but Helen stumped him now and then. She had quirks. Her mind made strange connections, and her logic took odd, inexplicable leaps.

Once, in the middle of making an apple pie, she discovered she was out of butter and so substituted peanut butter.

The pie ended up in the neighbors' dog dish. Will watched from the window as the dog, a bizarre mix of collie and chow whose stuffing appeared to be coming out in hunks, circled the bowl, sniffed at it, shook his head and circled some more. Finally he skinned his lips back, gripped the edge of the bowl delicately in his front teeth and shook Helen's pea-nut-apple pie out on the ground. Then, to Will's eternal delight, he turned around and scratched dirt over it with his hind feet.

Once Little Welch was born Will bought a motor scooter, a small Vespa to get him back and forth to the base when the weather was good. He didn't want Helen stranded at the trailer without transportation, in case the baby got sick or something. Not long after Helen took over the car he noticed the gas tank was always full. He thought at first the gauge might be broken, but then, on a trip to White Sands for a picnic, Helen insisted he stop and buy gas even though the tank was still three-quarters full.

"I like to keep it full," she said, and there was a smugness in her tone as if she knew something he didn't. "It saves money."

He rolled this over in his mind for a mile or so but couldn't see the logic. "How does it save money to keep the tank full?"

"The car gets a lot better gas mileage when it's full."

"Huh?"

"Well, after I fill it up the needle doesn't even move for the first fifty miles, but once it starts burning gas it drinks a quarter of a tank right away."

That was why he hadn't seen the logic—there was none. Already he had learned a thing or two about getting along with a Southern girl. He pulled into the next filling station and told the boy to top it off.

Riding his scooter to work that winter Will came down with pneu-monia, and when Helen mounted a campaign to make him quit smoking, he refused. He was a grown man and he would smoke if he wanted to, except he did switch to filtered cigarettes. Nor would he stay home from work, as long as he could get to his feet. It was his job. He had just made sergeant, and he would live up to his responsibilities. A man goes to work, period. His only compromise was that he drove the car to work until his lungs cleared.

Over time, he began to feel trapped again. Helen had liberated him at first and given him a home, but her presence also meant that he had to guard his words even more tightly. Alone with Helen his lies interwove and tightened around him like vines.

Helen was unlike Amish women in a million little ways. It would never occur to an Amish woman to question her husband's authority because it came from the Bible. Since Will couldn't claim his Amish roots, he couldn't say that to Helen. He could tell her what he thought sometimes, but more often than not he couldn't say where his thinking came from. So he compromised the best he could and fell increasingly silent, having long since learned that it was easiest to keep track of what he'd said if he said nothing at all. He swallowed his opinions, and some of them soured in his stomach.

When the Army sent him back to Germany in the fall of 1948, his wife and son went with him, and the gap between them slowly widened. What should have been a great adventure for a young couple was overshadowed by his brooding silence and the turning of her attentions to her child. As far as Will was concerned he was fulfilling his contract with her, bringing home a paycheck and keeping a roof over her head, but she eyed him with an increasing suspicion. No matter how careful he was, the part of him that Helen didn't know was too large and unwieldy. Pieces of it slipped out now and then.

The first time they went shopping on a little cobblestone street in Mainz he took her into a butcher shop where the woman at the counter made a huge fuss over Little Welch. The German shopkeepers loved babies. The butcher's wife snatched Little Welch away from his mother and prattled at him. Baby talk. Then she turned and asked Helen how old he was, in German. Helen didn't understand a word. Will told the woman Welch was ten months old and then fell into friendly conversation with her. It took a minute for him to realize Helen was staring at him. She was frowning, and her mouth hung slightly open.

"When did you learn to speak German?" she asked.

He scratched his nose, thinking. "You've heard me speak German before."

"Not like *that*. Just a word or two at the airport, not *blaba-laba-laba-lab* like you've been talking it all your life." She made a little duck-bill motion with her hand.

"Oh, uh, yeah, I had some German friends when I was a kid. Then I brushed up on it when I was in Berlin. I didn't have anything better to do."

"You're just full of surprises, aren't you?" Her eyes reflected a dark suspicion.

He shrugged. "I thought you knew. Anyway, it's not a hard language. I can teach you if you like."

He tried to teach her, and she learned a little, but her Southern mouth had trouble wrapping around a German accent. For a while it was great fun coming home every day and hearing about her adventures with the locals.

"Germans are rude," she told him one afternoon. She'd gone into a shop to buy a brush and the clerk laughed at her. To top it off, he had called the other clerks over to hear what she said.

"They horselaughed me," she said. She left in a huff. Never did find a brush.

"What did you say to him?" Will asked.

She told him, word for word. Will laughed too. Hard. She went slit-eyed. He laughed harder.

Wiping tears from his eyes, he apologized and then explained. "I guess when you speak German with a Southern accent, 'Can you show me a brush?' isn't really that different from 'Can I show you a breast?'"

Riley was born at the Army hospital in Wiesbaden. They had been married four years by then, and Will was in the middle of a three-year tour at a missile base near Frankfurt. When Riley was born Helen wanted to name him Will. Will refused. He couldn't quite understand it himself, let alone explain it, but he would not force any child to bear his name. Let the boy have his own name.

"Well, then, what about Levi?" she asked. His middle name.

No again, even more adamantly. No explanation.

She eventually named the baby Riley, after her brother—he of the slicked hair and the Lucky Strikes. Will didn't care. A kind of distance had grown up between them.

Helen spent all day in their quarters on the fourth floor of a twenty-four-family apartment building in an Army housing project, changing diapers. That was her job. Will spent all day manning a radar station, watching the Russians, because that was *his* job. During the Cold War the Russians posed an imminent threat on the eastern border, and the Army set up missile bases to counter the threat. Short-range nukes. It was Sergeant McGruder's job to watch, and there was constant pressure in it. In those days the Russians put pressure on everybody. Schoolchildren practiced huddling under desks, and grandparents dug bomb shelters, stocking them with canned goods. Part of the pressure fell on Helen too. In her early twenties, living in the shadow of the Russians, with a toddler and an infant clinging to her, she was required by the Army to keep suitcases packed and ready by the door in case the godless Communists made their move. She had to memorize the procedures, the escape route down through France to the sea, and be prepared to leave at a moment's notice—with or without her husband. It was months before she stopped jumping every time the phone rang.

The pressure reached critical mass when Little Welch was almost four and Riley a toddler, not long before Will's tour was up. Will had taken to working longer hours at the radar installation to keep from coming home. The apartment was noisy, and it seemed he had no say in anything. It was Helen's territory. She let the kids run wild and do as they pleased, and it grated on him. Discipline had ruled in Levi Mullet's house—with ten kids, a hundred and forty acres, and a full complement of livestock to look after, there could be no nonsense. It was the law of the farm. Will had been raised that way, and the Army had done nothing to mitigate his opinions about the value of discipline. Children, in his experience, were to be seen and not heard, but Helen seemed to know nothing of discipline, and Will had no say in the matter. He started going out with the guys in his outfit once or twice a week after work and having a beer at a local gasthaus. Anything to keep from going home.

After one particularly harrowing day when they'd been on alert all day long without knowing why, he went out and downed a few. It might have been more than a few, but what difference did it make—he was a man, wasn't he? He could do as he pleased as long as he provided for his family. Coming home later than usual he ate a cold dinner, then turned on the radio and parked himself in his favorite armchair with a cigarette. Little Welch came ripping and tearing through the room, and before Will knew what had happened he knocked the ashtray to the floor and a lit cigarette bounced across the rug, scattering sparks and ashes. Will snatched up the cigarette, righted the ashtray, and grabbed the kid by the arm on his next pass. He swatted Welch twice on the bottom, and drew back a third time before Helen caught his wrist. In the heat of his anger and frustration he might have hit the boy too hard, but he was drunk, so he was never sure.

Welch screamed. Helen's eyes threatened. Will let go of the child. Later, he would admit to himself that it crossed his mind for an instant. The impulse flashed through him only for a second, but in that second he came within an eyelash of taking a swing at Helen.

"You're drunk," she said. "You can leave now . . . or you can go to bed, and we'll talk in the morning."

Partly because of the look in her eye, and partly because he knew what he had almost done, he complied. He didn't say anything; he just pulled away and went to bed.

The next morning she fixed his normal breakfast of two eggs over easy, bacon, and toast. While he was eating she came and sat beside him, leaning an elbow on the table. The kids were still asleep.

"About last night," she said. Here it came. She was very calm, almost smiling. The calmness frightened him.

"If you ever come home drunk again, I'll wait until you go to sleep and sew you up in the sheets," she said quietly. "And then I'll take the broom handle to you. I'll beat you like a cheap rug, and then I'll take the kids and leave. My daddy'll get me home somehow, and you won't get a second chance."

He picked at an egg with his fork. There was nothing to say.

"And if you ever hurt one of my kids? I'll use a baseball bat."

She said it sweetly, patting his forearm, yet meaning every word. She never bluffed, and he had seen what she could do with a bat. He left quietly that morning, and remained silent for the rest of the day, thinking. Helen was right. In the sober light of day he saw that he had shamed himself. It was a deep and stubborn pride that kept him from apologizing for the incident, but it was the same pride that kept him from going out drinking again.

## CHAPTER 15

October 1951

Even from thirty thousand feet up, the Atlantic stretched from horizon to horizon, glittering like a distant pond in sunlight. Looking down on the endless ocean and the white feathers of cloud, though he was traveling three hundred miles an hour, Will would not have known the plane was moving at all if it hadn't been for the occasional buffeting of wind currents. Little Welch lay curled up asleep in a seat just across the aisle despite the horrendous vibrating drone of the engines. Hard to believe he was nearly four years old. Riley slept on Helen's lap, churning and kicking fitfully. Helen's eyes still showed too much white, fear of flying written all over her. It was the first time for all of them.

The plane lurched and Helen tensed, tightening her grip on the baby.

"I don't trust this thing," she said for the tenth time. "It's noisy and clanky. It's going to fall apart. I don't trust it."

"It's all right. Everything is fine. It's noisy because it was designed to be a bomber, and fly-boys *like* being able to hear the engines." Will had to raise his voice to be heard above the roar. Helen kept peering past him, out the window at the riveted aluminum wings to make sure the propellers were still turning.

"We'll be on the ground in New York by dinnertime," he said.

The words did not impress Helen, but they haunted Will. An idea had festered in him for months now, ever since *the date* passed. Seven years. He had checked the files himself to make sure. The end of his seventh year in the Army had come and gone last fall without incident. The statute of limitations said he could not be sent to Leavenworth now even if they found him out. And yet the lifting of his greatest burden, his deepest fear, bore unforeseen consequences. When the need for his elaborate fiction had passed, it had slowly settled upon Will that what he wanted most in the world was to go back home. To Ohio. He wanted to see his family again—his stepmother and brothers and sisters and aunts and uncles and cousins.

And Levi. He wanted to see the family, but he *had* to see Levi. His father. Levi's judgment lay on him, even now, after eight years, a palpable weight on his shoulders, a tension in his neck. He had tried to convince himself that even Levi Mullet couldn't stay angry forever. A thousand times he had tried to imagine his father welcoming him home with joy and celebration. *Kill the fatted calf, for the prodigal has returned.* But he knew his father; Levi Mullet was not likely to forgive and forget. Still, he dared to hope, and in the end he knew that sooner or later he would have to go home to Ohio. It was inevitable, and the inevitability of it had made up his mind for him months ago. That wasn't the problem.

The problem was the web of lies he had spun for Helen over the last seven years—how to correct them, which ones to correct, and when, exactly, might be the best time to attempt it. It was going to be bad, he knew that much. Living in Germany, an ocean away from Ohio, the matter never seemed pressing enough to inspire the kind of courage he would need to face Helen with the truth. But now New York approached, and time was running out. Sitting beside Helen in an aluminum tube high above the Atlantic Ocean, Will steeled himself.

She was quiet. The kids were asleep. Engines droned.

"Maybe I'll get another Chevrolet," he said. "A new one."

She nodded. They had already talked about this. He would buy a car in New York and they would drive south to see her folks.

"I was thinking. Maybe on the way to Georgia we can stop by and visit my family." There. That ought to get it started.

She blinked and looked straight at him, her attention diverted from the clanky airframe for the first time since leaving the ground.

"Your family? Did you say your *family*?"

He nodded. "My father and stepmother."

"I thought you said they were dead. You did! You told me your parents were dead!"

"Well, my mother . . ." He swallowed hard. His real mother was dead, but that was a technicality far too frail to uphold such a volume of lies.

"The thing is, I may not have been completely truthful," he said. "They're both alive, as far as I know."

"As far as you know. When was the last time you talked to them?"

"When I was nineteen. I left home eight years ago and haven't heard from them since."

She frowned. "You're twenty-five. Nineteen and eight is twenty-seven."

"Oh, that. Well, I kind of neglected to sign up for the draft. I figured the Army would be mad because I was overage when I went to join, so I fudged my birthday a little."

She blinked—a long, purposeful blink. "Okay. That's why you lied to the Army. What I want to know is, why did you lie to me?"

"You mean about my parents being dead or about how old I was?"

"Pick one."

He looked away, shrugged. This was not going well at all.

"I don't know, babe. It's complicated. At the time they didn't seem like very *big* lies." He knew—they both knew—that he never called her "babe" unless he was in trouble.

Although she couldn't move much with a sleeping baby on her lap, she leaned away from Will and glared at him as if he were a complete stranger who had said something unspeakably rude.

"Those are pretty big lies where I come from," she said.

*The truth*, he reminded himself. *Wherever possible.* "Well, I couldn't let anybody know I lied about my age, because the Army would have sent me to prison for it. I never told *anybody*—it wasn't just you."

"They'd send you to jail for putting down the wrong age?" An eyebrow went up, clearly skeptical.

"That, and not signing up for the draft in time."

"That still doesn't explain why you didn't tell me about your parents. And how does a man run off from home and not even write his folks a letter for eight years? Will, if your folks were alive how could you not go see them, or call them, or write a letter? How could you do that?"

"Well, we're . . . uh . . . we're not on speaking terms. My father and I . . ." He jerked his thumbs in opposite directions.

"Uh-huh." There was a note of sarcasm in her voice. "That must have been one humdinger of a fallin' out. What did you do to start it?"

He squirmed in his seat for a few seconds. He and Helen had not been on the best footing lately anyway, and the tone of her voice made it clear that if he told her about Mattie now she'd grab the kids and head for her daddy's house without him. Then he would have to face Welch Shelby if he wanted her back. He had been over all this already in his mind. She would find out most of it anyway, the first time she set foot in Ohio. But this—the reason for all of it—she did not necessarily need to know, and it was the biggest bombshell of all. Mattie would have to wait for a better day.

"He didn't want me to join the Army," he said.

Her mouth skewed to one side. "That doesn't make a bit of sense. Why would they not want you to join the Army? There was a war, for pete's sake—*everybody* signed up."

"The thing is—" he stammered, juggling his hands and trying to find the right approach, deciding finally to just lay it out—"he's Amish. They all are. My family, I mean."

"Amish. What's Amish?"

"You know. Horses and buggies, no electricity, plain clothes, beards . . ."

The furrows between her eyes deepened. "Never heard of it. Anyway, what's that got to do with the Army?"

"Well, the Amish are conscientious objectors. They don't believe in war."

"You mean it's a religion? Like Baptist or Methodist?"

"Right. Growing up, none of us were allowed to even think about joining the Army. That's why I didn't sign up for the draft."

Another blink, more pronounced. "Us? You got *brothers*?"

He had slipped, and she'd gotten ahead of him. The lies really had seemed so small, before. Now it seemed a mushroom cloud went up over every new revelation.

"Five," he said, shrinking into his seat.

Her eyes widened. "Sisters?"

"Four."

She whistled softly and sat back. Her eyes turned toward the front of the plane for a long time, her mouth slightly open.

"Six years," she muttered, looking down as if she was talking to the baby asleep on her lap. Riley stirred, and she bounced him a little. "We've been married six years and you never told me any of this. What else have you lied to me about?"

"Nothing," he said, with all the sincerity he could muster. "That's pretty much it."

He fell silent then, watching Helen. Though she still wouldn't look at him, he could read the slow change in her features as she sorted it all out in her mind. She had no choice, really. This was the situation and, as always, she would adjust. Her strength and adaptability constantly surprised him. It took her a few minutes to work through the shock, but then she arrived at a thin, suspicious kind of sympathy. He saw it in her face when she turned back to him.

"Of course we have to go see them," she said. "Your daddy'll forgive you. He has to. You're his son."

Will nodded. He had his doubts, but there was no point in voicing them now. He seemed to have gained her sympathy.

"Well, it'll be nice," she said, attempting a brave smile. "I've never been to Canada before."

"Oh, uh, well, they're not exactly in Canada. They have a farm in Ohio."

Her mouth made the O first, silently, then she said, "Ohio." The brave smile went away, just like that. Her head thumped back against the seat and she muttered, "I'm married to a *Yankee*."

So much for sympathy. He was back to being a liar, *and* a Yankee.

"It's not that different from being a Canadian," he said defensively.

"Okaaay," she said, very slowly. "We'll stop off in *O-hi-o* and visit your dead parents and umpteen brothers and sisters. I can't wait to meet the rest of the McGruder clan. Are they *all* bald-faced liars? Shoot, I pity anybody that stops and asks for directions in that part of the—"

"Uh, babe? There's just . . . Well, there *is* one other thing you probably ought to know. It's not the McGruder clan. I mean, their name's not McGruder."

Two blinks and a sigh like steam escaping. He thought about fastening his seat belt.

"And . . . what is it, then? Their name."

"Mullet. My father's name is Levi Mullet."

"Well, I swan," she said. By now Will was able to interpret most of her Southernisms. She used *I swan* in place of *I swear* because her mother used it to keep from swearing. It was a little heavier than *Good night a'livin'* and a lot worse than *foot* or *shoot* but, at least in Helen's vernacular, not as bad as *durn*. One of her eyes started to twitch.

"So why'd he name his son Will *McGruder*? Is that a custom of the . . ."

"Amish?"

"Yeah, is that an Amish custom? Do they give all their young'uns a different last name, or just you?"

"No, actually my name is—*was*—Mullet. I changed it to keep him from finding me."

"So, you had your name legally changed when you left home?"

"Not exactly. I just . . . whenever somebody asked me, I told them my name was McGruder, that's all. And I gave it to them when I joined the Army. That's another thing that would've gotten me in trouble."

*Now* she was in shock. Her mouth hung open a little. Her chin quivered. He was glad he'd chosen the airplane as the time and place to tell her. There was no telling what might have happened if she'd had room to maneuver. Most likely somebody would've been injured.

The plane jostled, hard, but she paid no attention. She cleared her throat.

"So, you're telling me you never legally changed your name. It's not even your real name! It's just a . . . what's the word?"

"Alias?"

"Yes, thank you. It's a durn alias?" Riley raised his little round head and squinted at her, sleepy-eyed. The folds of her blouse had left red lines across his face. She looked at her baby, then turned back to Will with a fierce question in her eyes. If her husband's name was in question, then so was hers—*and her children's.*

"Well, no," Will said. "I think it's legal now. Or at least we can see about it. Making it legal, I mean. I guess we can do that."

She didn't say anything else. She pressed Riley's head back down and kissed his crown, then sat stroking his back. She looked dazed. The rules of her world had changed as drastically as if the law of gravity had suddenly been suspended. Will had the distinct impression that the airplane could have disappeared and left her alone, hurtling through the atmosphere with a baby on her lap, and at that moment she would not have been greatly surprised.

"I'm sorry," he said quietly. "Really, I didn't mean for things to—"

"Leave me alone," she said.

And so it was that Will Mullet, after eight long years out in the World, came home to Apple Creek at the wheel of a secondhand '49 Chevy Fleetline he'd bought on a lot in New York. He liked the clean, fenderless lines of the car, the sloped back, even if Helen said it looked like a capsized boat. Helen sat beside him and his two sons played in the back seat, so he was not unaccompanied on the long drive across the low mountains and gray mining towns of Pennsylvania, but he was, nonetheless, alone.

Will had taken no part in the raising of his sons thus far, especially since the night Helen stood between him and little Welch. There had been no defense for him that night—he was just wrong, and he knew it— and their differences over the raising of the boys made him aware that, besides being wrong, he was ignorant. He didn't know the right way to bring up an English child—*couldn't* know. His own father had been hard, even for an Amishman, and over time Will stopped pretending to know how to be a father. He simply abdicated. To tell the truth, he had never been that involved anyway, so there had been no great and noticeable divide, no defining moment before which he was a fully vested father and after which he was not. It happened incrementally. One by one he stifled his opinions about the raising of children until he retained no voice at all. They were Helen's.

It seemed to Will that Helen had come to their marriage complete with an unfair set of expectations about what a husband and father should be like. Over time he came to understand that most of her expectations came from her own father, with whom she had enjoyed a deep friendship, and who had managed, even in relative poverty, to always surprise her. Will had provided her with adventure all right. Before she married Will she had never traveled outside the state of Georgia, and since then she had scarcely done anything else. The World was a wider place than either of them had ever imagined. But she came from a different culture, where husbands and fathers behaved in ways Will simply didn't understand.

Helen had turned to the children and Will had turned to his work, and by the time the statute of limitations ran out and he told her the truth it was almost too late. The bond between them had been reduced to a strand of responsibility as thin and tight as barbed wire.

Crossing Pennsylvania, Will took care of the driving and Helen took care of the kids. There was a silent, tight-lipped tension in her when the boys were sleeping and she found herself alone with Will. He tried to put himself in her position. She'd lost her anchor and the wind was up. She must have been disoriented and disillusioned, and she had to have asked herself a hundred times how she arrived at such a place: a thousand miles from home with two small children, plummeting headlong into who knew what fate at the hands of a newly discovered and monstrously large family. She didn't even know what Amish was. On top of everything else her husband had only recently told her his real name. After six years of marriage. It was all there, all written in her taut face, her straight back, and the knuckles of her hands.

They slept at a dingy motel outside Pittsburgh where neon flashed the curtains red and green all night long, and a coal train woke them up rattling the windows long before daylight. As the day brightened they migrated from the brown haze of Steel Town into northeastern Ohio where autumn had peaked. Driving through postcard scenes of rust and gold and flame-red rolling farmlands, a growing apprehension held them both captive in their separate silences, Helen afraid of what she didn't know, and Will afraid of what he did. The boys, trapped too long in the

car, fidgeted and screeched and fought and cried in the back seat, energy
building under pressure.

Around noon they topped a hill a few miles outside Apple Creek
where Will slowed the car, leaning against the steering wheel, peering at
a large white farmhouse.

Little Welch's head popped up behind the seat. "What is it? Are we
there?"

"That is your grandfather's house," Will said.

Helen's fingernails dug into the fabric of the seat.

"They're not home." Will let the big car ease past the mailbox, not
quite stopping, driving one-handed and bending down to look up the neat
little driveway. He didn't turn in.

"How do you know?" Helen asked.

"The buggies are all gone." Across the drive, the doors of the buggy
shed stood open and he could see to the back. He glanced at his watch.
"They're away at church—won't be home until late afternoon. I was hop-
ing it was an off week." It was a lie, he realized even as he said it; he was
*relieved* not to find Levi at home. Even now, eight years removed, it felt
like a stay of execution.

He read the farm like an open book. He knew the season, knew that
the farmers would all be busy combining soybean and harvesting corn
from bleached, frostbitten cornfields, filling the root cellar with potatoes,
spreading fertilizer for next year. He could see at a glance that Elizabeth
was still alive. Her signature was on the flower beds and the well-kept
kitchen garden, neatly tended even at the tail end of the season. His father
was still there too, his personality printed in the trim of the place—the
crisp edge of grass and gravel, the compost bin already filling with leaves
from the spotlessly raked yard, and especially the freshly dredged and

scraped drainage ditch at the roadside. Will smiled. His stepmother had always complained that she could never grow flowers at the end of the driveway because of Levi's constant cleaning of the drainage ditch. *"Mustn't let it get out of hand,"* Levi would answer—his philosophy of life.

"You should have called first," Helen said. "Let them know you were coming."

"No phones." Will speeded up, turned his attention ahead, and made no sign of coming about.

She puffed, flipped a wrist. "So just drive over to the church." The boys needed to get out and run. They were losing control, and Helen was losing patience.

"They don't have a church building, Helen. They take turns meeting at each other's houses, and I don't know whose turn it is. Since they only meet every other week, I figured there was a fifty-fifty chance they'd be home. I guessed wrong."

"Then we can wait for them. It's almost noon, they'll be out soon."

He chuckled. "They preach for three hours. Then they have dinner together. Then the men sit around and talk crops and livestock while the women clean up. Then the men load up the benches and talk some more. After that, everybody has to hitch up for the long drive home. They'll be all day." He topped the next hill and his father's farm fell from sight in the rearview mirror.

"So where are we going?"

"Abel Elliot's. I need to see him."

She didn't even ask him who Abel Elliot was. She just looked out the window at a herd of Holsteins scattered across the still-green pasture, tugging patiently at the grass.

Abel was out in his barn when they arrived. He came out of the drive-through and stood there, sleeves rolled up on ropy forearms, wiping his hands on a rag, staring at the strange car in his yard. Will got out first and paused near the open door of the car long enough to let Abel get a good look at him. Abel hadn't changed much—maybe a little thinner, the same old khaki cap pushed back on his balding head. He didn't recognize Will. Will closed the car door, leaned down and told Helen and the kids to wait just a minute, then strode unsmiling up to Abel Elliot and held out a fold of cash.

Abel looked at the money.

"It's yours," Will said. "It's the fifty dollars I owe you."

His voice did the trick. Will had gained a little weight and maybe even gotten an inch taller; his hair was cut short and he was wearing a uniform, but as soon as he spoke the light of recognition came into Abel's eyes.

"As I live and breathe, if it ain't Will Mullet." Ignoring the money, he wrapped Will in a hug. Abel was not a man given to displays of affection, but he was misty-eyed and speechless for a moment. "I thought you were dead," he finally stammered.

Abel's wife, May, stepped out from the kitchen door then, intent on finding out why her husband had just hugged some stranger in the front yard. Her name was Mabel but she insisted on being called May because very early in their marriage she had grown tired of the singsong way everybody said "Abel and Mabel." A great bear of a woman—twice the bulk of her husband—she hugged Will half to death once she found out who he was, literally lifting his feet off the ground. She reminded him of a Liberty Ship: a bust like a prow and a foghorn for a voice.

May Elliot insisted they all stay for lunch, and then she put out a big spread—roast beef, new potatoes and gravy, homegrown green beans. Over lunch, Abel told Will what he knew of his family. Levi and Elizabeth were still reasonably healthy considering their age, and Mose had gotten married.

"He married that little auburn-haired Detweiler girl—um . . ."

"Lydia," Will offered.

"Yes! Never could remember names. They got four kids now, I think."

"Oh! And Clara has remarried too!" May said.

"*Re*married!" Will's head jerked upright in alarm. "What happened to Joe?" Clara had married Joe Stutzman a few months before Will left home. He was a good Amish boy, which ruled out divorce, leaving only one other, rather ominous, possibility.

"Oh my!" May said, and the pained look on her face confirmed Will's fear. "You didn't know? Oh my . . ."

For once, May was at a loss for words. Abel came to her rescue.

"I'm afraid Joe's gone, Will. An accident. You knew they moved off up to Geauga County, right?"

Will nodded. They had moved before he left home.

"Well, they'd been there a couple years when Joe got a new horse, a standard-bred," Abel said. "Supposed to have been buggy-broke already, but he was checking it out on the road that afternoon and it balked on him. While he was sideways in the road some fool in a Cadillac came flying over the hill, killed him *and* his horse."

Will sat in stunned silence. Joe had been a good friend.

"They were doing so good too," May said. "Had two of the prettiest little girls you ever laid eyes on. Used to come by and see us whenever they got down this way."

Helen touched his arm. "Who's Clara?" she asked quietly.

"My sister," Will answered. "She used to clean house for May, back when I was working here."

"You worked here? Doing what?"

"Farming. Clara would ride over with me one day a week."

"I hated to see her go, too," May said, refilling the gravy boat from a pot on the stove.

"And now she's married again?" Will said.

"To Simon Schlabach," Abel said grimly.

Will lowered his fork, frowning. He knew Simon Schlabach, and the man was no match for his sister. He was peculiar, everybody knew that. He'd never make much of a farmer, and Will couldn't imagine what he'd be like as a husband.

"I can't imagine Clara with Simon," he said. It didn't add up.

Abel's eyes stayed down. He wasn't really eating; he was just moving food around his plate. "It's a long story. She was in kind of a hard way when she married him. I forget how long you've been gone, Will. Seems like yesterday. Everything feels the same, but so much has changed, really."

Abel pushed his plate back, propped his elbows on the table and linked his fingers under his chin. "It was a real bad time. We heard about the accident, of course, but it was a long time before we heard the rest of the story. Clara was off up there by herself with those two little girls and no way to support them. If I'd known about it, I would have moved them in here."

"What about the church?" Will couldn't believe this. It was practically chiseled in stone—the Amish didn't let widows go hungry.

Abel shrugged. "They didn't do a lot for her. I don't know why, exactly. Heard rumors, you know. Since I'm not Amish, they don't tell me everything. Some of them apparently thought she ought to move back down here and let your dad take care of her, and then there was some trouble over Social Security money—least that's what I heard."

"Social Security money?" This was puzzling. Amish didn't pay, or accept, Social Security.

"Yep. Way I got it, Joe worked out—"

May saw confusion in Helen's face and laid a hand on her forearm. "He had a job," she explained. "In a factory. Most Amish work at home on the farm. Joe didn't."

"Yep," Abel continued, "and he paid Social Security. So when he got killed, the government started sending checks to Clara."

Will winced. "That was probably the trouble, then."

"That's how I figured it. They wouldn't help her because they didn't like her taking government assistance. Must have been a pretty big stink because they still didn't help her even after she quit taking the checks. She cleaned houses, sold eggs, worked nights butchering chickens—anything she could find to do, for a while, and still went hungry." Abel shook his head sadly. "I just wish I had known." Abel and May had always treated Clara like a daughter. They never had any children of their own.

It was starting to make sense. Will saw the shadow of his father's hand in it.

"You're right," he said. "She was in a bad way. If it came down to feeding her kids I can see why she might marry Simon."

Abel nodded. "Simon was a widower himself. Had a couple kids of his own. They got a few more, now. You know—'yours, mine, and ours' kind of a thing. We stopped by to see Clara not long ago, and she seems content. Simon's not a bad sort, I guess. He's just . . . odd."

"Where do they live?"

"You know the old Amos Coblentz place, down toward Winesburg? Just about a mile past the covered bridge."

Will nodded. "I know the place. They bought that?"

"Nah, they're renting. Tenant farming. Simon's still poor as dirt and probably always will be, if you want my opinion."

After lunch they decided to pack the kids in the car and drive down to visit Clara.

Once on the road Helen was silent for a long time—not a good sign. Will could see she was getting worked up about something. Then, out of the blue, she said, "I don't understand why your father wouldn't take your sister in after her husband was killed."

Will had his suspicions. "I can't say for sure, but my guess is Clara didn't ask him to. Dad didn't approve of Joe Stutzman. He even gave me a hard time about hanging around with him. Dad could be pretty gruff."

"Why? What was wrong with Joe Stutzman?"

"Well, nothing, really. It's just that he was New Order—a little too modern for Dad's taste."

"Your father is a hard man," she said.

"Yes. He is."

CHAPTER | 16

*January 1985*

A stop sign stands half buried in a bank of dirty snow where the freshly plowed road empties like a tributary into a larger highway. Riley brings the car to a full stop.

"Which way?" he asks.

"Right." It seems a shame that Riley knows so little about the place, that he has spent so little time here. Will looks out the window. Mittened and capped Amish kids are already making sled tracks on hillsides sculpted smooth and round with new snow.

When they get to town Will directs Riley to Yoder's Kitchen, a little corner restaurant that has been here as long as he can remember. It sits right in the bend of the road in the middle of Winesburg, shouted down by the trinket shops where New Yorkers sell Chinese-made quilts and faceless dolls to gawking tourists; Yoder's is about the only place in town still owned and run by Amish people. Riley parallel parks on the street.

Yoder's smells like an Amish kitchen. Noodles with gravy, mashed potatoes with gravy, fresh baked bread with gravy—a farmer's diet. Knowing what he knows now, Will figures eating like that would surely kill any man who didn't work like a plow horse all day long.

Teenage Amish girls wait the tables, smiling, ruddy-cheeked. In contrast to Riley's gauntness they glisten with health. They wear caped dresses with full skirts, aprons tied around the front. Their uncut hair is tightly bunned on the back of the head, held there by a starched white covering. The laces dangle.

When the waitress comes, Will says good morning in Dutch, just a word or two so she can relax, and then switches to English. He orders oatmeal, yielding to the nagging voice of his cardiologist. Then, out of pure belligerence, he puts butter and brown sugar in it.

Riley glances at the waitresses once or twice while he attacks a pile of pancakes.

"They seem happy," he finally says, frowning, as if the notion puzzles him.

Will nods, his mouth full. He almost tells Riley about the article he read where the writer states, as a minor sidebar, that depression is nonexistent among the Amish. Like disease in sharks, there is none. But the article was about depression and everybody skirts the issue with Riley, instinctively avoiding his prickly defenses.

"They are," Will says. "They're happy people, for the most part."

"Huh. Go figure. But these aren't Old Order Amish, are they?"

"No. Old Order wear black, most of them." These girls wear blue or brown—subdued colors, but solid—no print dresses like Mennonites wear. "And sometimes the coverings are bigger, like bonnets."

Riley shakes his head, sneers. "Man, the places people draw the lines. Like you can go to hell for wearing the wrong color."

He's on the verge of snickering, and it ticks Will off. Breakthrough or no breakthrough, Riley still knows how to get on his nerves.

"There's a little more to it than that." Will manages to hold back, but he knows the rancor still shows on his face. Too bad. "It's about simplicity and humility—things it wouldn't kill you to learn a little more about."

"Yeah, maybe I should have more respect for my forefathers' religious traditions." Riley looks over his shoulder, holds up his cup to signal for more coffee. Will ignores the sarcasm.

The waitress comes with the coffeepot, and Will watches her face while she's filling the cups—anything to keep from joining battle with Riley. Riley says something vaguely flirtatious to the girl. She blushes, crimson rolling up to her neatly parted hairline, and Will notices for the first time that she has an angel's kiss—a pale birthmark on her forehead, tornado-shaped, wider at the top and narrowing as it disappears between her eyebrows. Will has never seen this young girl before and does not know her, but he is very familiar with such a birthmark. It's very faint now, but it would have been more pronounced when she was a child. He falls silent. He knows Riley mistakes his silence for anger and doesn't bother to correct him.

Riley takes a couple of sips from his full cup, shoves it away, and goes outside for a quick cigarette.

The angel's kiss fills Will's mind like wind in a sail and carries him back.

CHAPTER | 17

*October 1951*

C lara's house sat well back off the road in a narrow valley at the end of a long driveway that wove along between a weed-choked brook and a line of trees at the peak of color. There was good bottomland here, but not enough of it. Most of the arable land lay on slopes. Hard plowing. The house was big, though it needed paint. The barn and assorted sheds—smokehouse, sugar shanty, woodshed—had all gone gray, and some of them seemed to lean a little out of plumb with age and disrepair.

When Will saw the crowd he knew Simon's church was holding services at his home that day. There was a long row of black buggies parked between the trees nearing the house. A cluster of teenage boys in the front yard stopped whatever they were doing and turned toward the driveway when they heard the car coming. Small children ceased chasing each other around the side of the house and stared.

"They all look just alike," Helen said weakly. Welch and Riley peered over the seat, quiet for once. As the car pulled past the line of buggies and slowed, bearded men rose from rockers on the expansive front porch and stared at the car from under their black, wide-brimmed Sunday hats. The cluster of boys moved like a school of fish, ringing about the car as it stopped in front of the house. Will could see how they might all look alike to Helen. The men and boys all wore the same dark homemade breeches and vests, wide hats, suspenders, broadcloth shirts, and their hair was all cut to precisely the same bowl. The girls all wore dark, full dresses, and kept their hair bundled under identical starched white coverings. The smaller kids were all barefoot.

Only now, when it was too late, did it occur to Will that he should have bought some civilian clothes for the occasion. He'd always been proud of his uniform, but now he was painfully aware that it might not be the best thing to wear to an Amish church gathering.

Jockeying for a better look, the ring of young boys pressed so close to the car they had to back up a little when Will opened his door. Everybody stared at him, though he was sure he saw no sign of recognition in their eyes. Helen looked petrified. Will stood in the shelter of the open car door to let the line of men standing on the porch get a look at him. He recognized one or two of them, but Simon was nowhere in sight.

"Is this the home of Simon Schlabach?" he asked, in Dutch. They glanced at each other, surprised to hear their language coming from a soldier in uniform.

The oldest of the men, the only one wearing a coat—Will figured him for an elder—finally nodded. His beard was longer than the others, and it wiggled as if he were chewing.

"Ja, and who might you be?"

"I'm Clara's brother, Will."

The elder's eyes widened noticeably amid whispers and rumblings, a few gasps, a general murmur. One of the men on the porch sat down heavily, and the older boys crowding around the car moved back a half step, pulling the children along with them.

The elder had Will's undivided attention. Will was an outsider now, and if he was going to be condemned and turned away from his sister's house this would be the man to do it. But the moment passed. The elder whispered something to the man nearest the front door, dispatching him into the house with a flip of the hand, then turned back to Will and cleared his throat.

"We thought you were dead," he said. He didn't sound particularly overjoyed to learn otherwise.

Will looked around, saw a host of tense faces, and decided to try to lighten the moment. He smiled, a little awkwardly, and said, "No, but I'm not feeling very well."

His sense of humor had always been a bit out of sync with the Amish, and this was no exception. Nobody even chuckled.

The screen door opened and Clara stepped out onto the porch. The Clara in Will's mind was a young girl, slim and bright-eyed with wonder. The woman looking at him now was thirty pounds heavier, with lines in her face that weren't there before and a gravity in her eyes that surprised him. But it was her.

There was something very like fear in her face, and her hand went up, involuntarily, to cover her mouth. She moved. Though she crept down slowly she still almost stumbled on the last step, as if she were uncertain of her feet. Will stood waiting as the throng of young ones parted to let her come up to the car. Her eyes stayed riveted as she came and stood on the other side of the open car door—he had not moved—and reached up to touch his face with a shaky hand.

"Willy?" She had always called him that, before.

He nodded, tried to smile. "Clara."

Her face moved slightly, side to side, a barely perceptible shake. "We thought you were dead," she said, her voice unnaturally high.

The words hung there for a long moment. Fifty people watched, standing very still, gawking at Will and his sister in utter silence. Humor had already failed him, and he could not think what else to say. Clara made no move to step around the car door that stood between them. Riley squawked, and Will suddenly remembered he was married.

Closing the door, he leaned into the open window and asked his wife if she would like to get out of the car and meet his sister. Helen clung to Riley like a life preserver, and Will thought for a moment she would say no, but then she opened the door and struggled out with her baby. Welch, wearing a red cowboy hat and brandishing a chrome-plated six-shooter, scrambled over the seat and followed her. Awkwardly, riding Riley on her hip with one hand and corralling Welch against her pleated skirt with the other, she made her way around the front of the car.

Will introduced them, and Clara shook Helen's hand—once up and down, stiffly, the Amish way.

"This is my little Riley," she said, jostling the baby on her hip and wrinkling her nose at him to make him smile. "And my cowboy's name is Welch." She tugged his hat off and handed it to him.

Welch gave Clara a circular wave, said, "Howdy, ma'am," and retreated behind his mother.

Two little girls peeked out at him from around Clara's full dress, one on either side. Clara put a hand behind each of their heads.

"These are my two oldest—Cassie and Katie," she said. She glanced at Will for a second and again he could swear there was a trace of fear in her unsmiling face. The two girls were exactly the same size. They looked to be seven or eight years old and a ruddy-cheeked picture of health, both of them. Except for being barefooted they were dressed just like the women. They shared the same walnut brown hair, what could be seen of it, neatly parted in the middle where it disappeared under the covering.

"They're darling," Helen said. Cassie beamed, and there was devilish merriment in her bright blue eyes when she leaned out and looked around her mother's waist, peering at her sister. Katie smiled too, rather primly, then lowered her eyes. She had a pale pinkish birthmark running down the middle of her forehead in a vague V shape. It wasn't very noticeable, but it flashed a darker pink when she blushed.

"Look! Katie has an angel's kiss," Helen said. "Are they twins?"

Clara seemed distracted for a second, looking at Katie, but then her head snapped up. "Hmmm? Ohhh, heavens no! They are almost the same age, though. They are chust stepsisters, but they quarrel like real sisters yet." Katie looked pleadingly up at her mother, mouthing a word. Clara nodded and Katie spun away, bounding around the corner of the house with Cassie in hot pursuit.

By this time the rest of the women had begun filing out of the house and the men had come down from the porch so that Will and Helen found themselves working through a sort of impromptu gauntlet, shaking hands. Though Will tried to smile and say a few words to the ones he recognized, it was all rather hushed and formal until Welch broke the ice. Peeking out from behind his mother, he tugged on her skirt. There was childish wonder in his eyes, and when she looked down at him, he announced excitedly, "Mom, they're *pilgrims!*"

A general laughter ensued, and Will began to think things would be all right. His people loved to laugh, although it was a measure of their humility that they were only really comfortable laughing at themselves. One of the young women made a fuss over Riley, prying him away from his mother and hustling him off into a crowd of giggling, fawning girls. Welch, who was never out of place for very long, went running off with two barefoot boys not much older than he was. They spoke little English, but somehow they made him understand that they had ponies out back. He was hooked. They went tearing around the corner of the house and disappeared, the three of them, as if they were old friends.

Simon appeared out of nowhere, standing next to Clara and gawking unabashedly at Will and Helen. Everybody had stared at first, yet there was something different, something uncomfortable, in the way Simon ogled them. He was about Will's age, but he looked forty, gaunt and bug-eyed.

"Simon," Will said with a nod. Simon shook his hand, once up and down, hard. He said nothing, and his wide white eyes bored into Helen until she squirmed.

Clara took Helen by the arm and gently steered her toward the steps. "Let's go inside," she said, glancing at Simon, "and talk. Oh, there's so much to talk about!" Helen looked back over her shoulder from the middle of a formidable gaggle of women, as if she were being dragged against her will.

Simon crowded Will, looking him up and down, examining the uniform.

"So. You were in the war, then?"

"Yes," Will said, but didn't elaborate. Other men eased closer to listen. The elder, he of the long white beard and black coat, stood at Simon's shoulder, his hands clasped behind him. He had hung back during the initial introductions. Now his curiosity got the better of him. Will stuck out a hand and he pumped it, once.

"Eli Schlabach," the elder said, nodding toward Simon. "Simon's dad."

"Will McGruder."

The elder Schlabach's broad hat brim lifted in surprise. "Ahhh! You changed your name, then."

"Well . . . yes, I uh . . . yes." There was no point in explaining further. They would put it together themselves.

Simon leaned even closer, his hat brim almost touching Will's hair. Like all married Amish men, Simon wore a beard around the perimeter of his face but kept the mustache shaved off, and there was a slight bulge to his naked upper lip that reminded Will of a baboon.

"We thought you were dead," Simon said, and his glare made it feel like an accusation.

The elder Schlabach explained. "Your brother told us you went off to the war. After a long time and nobody got a letter, we all thought you got killed over there."

"Tobe came home?" Will's heart leaped.

"Ja, he came home twice!" Simon said, to a ripple of laughter from the others. "About a year after y'unce left he came back, but Levi wouldn't let him in the house now, so he turns around and left again. He was here chust long enough to tell us about you goin' off to the war."

"So, where is he now?"

"Oh, he came back again a couple years ago and married that Sylvia Troyer. Now he built himself a fancy new house down by Millersburg—electric and all."

"They went Mennonite," Simon's father explained, and Will discovered that the elder Schlabach had an accusatory stare of his own. Mennonites, for the most part, were far more liberal than the Amish. Most of them allowed cars and electricity. If his words didn't get it done, the set of his chin made it perfectly clear how he felt about Tobe. And he wasn't too crazy about Will either.

But Tobe was *here*. Will would see him again. That was all he needed to know for now. He didn't care what else the Schlabachs had to say about Tobe, so he changed the subject.

"We drove by Dad's house earlier, but they were out."

The elder nodded, stone-faced. "They would be meeting today. A man should have his family at meeting on the Sabbath if he is able."

As soon as he could break away Will wandered around the homestead, catching up on what had happened since he left and satisfying everybody's curiosity. He stayed out of the house because he knew, what with the elders here and all, there was bound to be a little tension over the ban. Some people wouldn't want to associate with him at all, and it would be easier for everybody if he stayed out in the open where they could avoid him altogether if they wished. Likewise, if he went in the house and somebody wanted to raise the issue of the ban, Simon would be put on the spot because it was his house. Fortunately the weather was nice.

It felt good, his speaking the old language again. Two of the men here had gone to school with Will—Arlen Chupp and Iddo Miller—and when he first arrived he had not recognized them, all grown up, filled out, and bearded. They were happy to see him again, and they spent a long time together leaning on the barn lot fence and talking about old times. They talked about wild teenage Friday nights when they raced buggies on a quiet stretch of Fredericksburg Road, and when nobody was listening they laughed, hard, about the night they moved old man Hostetler's outhouse three feet back.

But nobody mentioned Mattie. There were a few furtive glances and whispered conversations just out of his hearing, and knowing how the Amish liked to gossip, Will was sure everybody knew the story, and yet nobody brought it up. Even Arlen and Iddo, while Mattie was part of the fabric of their teenage memories, carefully avoided her name. So did Will. It was as if she had never existed.

Iddo, his sharp eyes still eager with youth, asked vague questions about the wider World.

"What was it like in Europe?"

Will told them about the farms and fields, the kinds of crops and cows and chickens he had seen. He painted the lay of the land, the look of the mountains and rivers, the dense darkness of the forests, the sameness of the snow. Instinctively, he made no mention of war and death. These were people whose lives moved in quiet unison like trees in a wind. Because they all had roots into the same ground, they were led to each day's labor by the urging of the same earth, patiently, mindfully, humbly living one step ahead of the season. They would have seen no meaning in the grinding up of Ralph Sedgwick by the geared wheels of a tank. They would have felt only confusion and horror. Will understood the need for the war, having been a part of it, but he knew he could not explain the experience to them. More than once he thought of Mikhail, the Russian he'd thrown into the canal, and he prayed they didn't ask him if he'd ever killed anyone.

After a while they fell to talking about wives and kids. Everybody Will's age had at least five or six children. It was the Amish way. They married young and had a baby every year until the wife wore out or died. Arlen Chupp told them about a man he knew in Lancaster County whose first wife bore fourteen kids in the space of seven years—all twins and triplets. When she died he remarried—apparently right after the funeral—and his second wife was as fruitful as the first, spitting out babies like watermelon seeds. After fifteen years of marriage there were thirty-two children in the house.

It was an extreme case, though Will didn't doubt a word of it. Most Amish women had a baby every year, and because of their natural distrust of doctors, it took a heavy toll on them. Will's own mother had died in childbirth. He couldn't even remember her now, and there were no pictures.

Kids were everywhere, flashing past in groups of two and three and twenty while Will leaned on the fence talking to Iddo and Arlen. One of the children, a girl, ran over and climbed up on the fence facing Will, bare toes hanging over the bottom rail and elbows hanging over the top. When he saw the impish grin and bright blue eyes, Will recognized her. It was Cassie, one of Clara's two girls who Helen thought were twins.

He smiled at her. "Where is your sister?" he asked.

Cassie's grin rotated toward the barn. "Oh, she's hiding in the hayloft. She's angry with me."

"What did you do to her?" It was clear from the way Cassie grinned while biting her bottom lip that she was up to something.

Her eyes flashed as she hugged the top rail of the fence. "I told her you're not her uncle. Katie is Dad's girl, and I am my mother's. You're my mother's brother, so you're *my* uncle but not hers. She's very moody. Katie is always pouting."

A tabby cat stalking through the grass at the edge of the barn lot caught Cassie's attention, and suddenly she jumped down, hiked her dress, and took off after it.

"I bet she is," Will chuckled.

"Cassie thinks your uniform is exciting," Iddo said, watching her go. "She's a real fireball, that one. I pity her dad, one of these days."

With the men starting to lead horses out to the buggies, and mothers rounding up children to go home, Will headed for the house to rescue Helen. He found her sitting in a wooden kitchen chair in the big living room, trapped in a large circle of women whose attentions seemed primarily focused on Helen. The walls of the living room were bare, the hardwood floor scratched and scuffed, yet spotless. When Will stepped inside the front door the smell of woodsmoke and kerosene stabbed him with a rare pang of homesickness. Helen was sitting very straight in her chair, knees together, feet flat on the floor, Riley hugging her shoulder. Her eyes said she was near panic, and she kept tugging nervously at the hem of her pleated skirt even though it more than covered her knees. Seeing Will come in, she stood up abruptly. It was almost a leap.

"Where have you *been*?" she huffed, glancing at the back of her wrist as if she were wearing a watch. A dozen white-capped heads turned instantly toward him, and he knew he was being measured. The women watched to see how he would respond to what they saw as impertinence.

"Get your things," he said curtly. "We're going." Keeping his head up and giving not an inch, he turned and went back out the door.

As soon as he collected Welch from the pasture they said their goodbyes and left. They were a mile or two down the road, heading toward his father's house and driving slowly because of all the buggy traffic on the hills and curves, before Will noticed Helen was too quiet. Her mouth had turned into a thin, white line. He lay low, thinking she was mad at him.

A few minutes later she started muttering to herself, spitting angry words under her breath.

"What's the matter, babe?" he asked, bracing himself. It had been in the back of his mind all afternoon, what the women might be telling Helen while he was outside. Maybe, he thought, just maybe the women had been too polite to mention Mattie to her, especially at the first meeting. They didn't know her that well.

Helen's face contorted, clearly mimicking some poor Amish woman who had bought herself an unfortunate and indelible place in her memory. "Ohhhh, you can *cook*?" she crooned. "Do they think I grew up in some antebellum mansion with slaves waitin' on me hand and foot? Shoot, there ain't no silver spoon in *this* girl's mouth, I'm here to tell you! I was raised on a farm same as they were. Cook, my hind leg, you come to my house and I'll *show* you some cookin', missy."

Will knew better than to laugh. When he got firm control of his voice he said, "I guess they have as many misconceptions about fancy English women as you do about them."

"You weren't there," Helen said. "They got me off by myself and grilled me like I was applyin' for a bank loan. Where were you?"

"Oh, I was out back talking to some old friends. I figured you could handle yourself."

"You figured wrong. You threw me under the train is what you did. Don't you *ever* leave me alone with that bunch again!" She wrinkled her nose and looked over the back seat. "What's that smell?"

"I don't smell anything." Will had spent the afternoon out near the barn so his nose was temporarily immune to farm odors, but he could guess. Riley was stretched out on the shelf under the back window serenely doodling on the glass with a chubby finger. When riding in the car he liked to pull himself up onto the shelf. Welch was looking quietly out the side window, cowboy boots bobbing in front of the seat.

"It's probly me," Welch said absently. "We were playing Red Rover out in the pasture."

And then Welch told them what he had stepped in. He dropped the

S-word casually, as if he'd been using it all his life.

Helen turned all the way around and stared at him, her chin hanging. "Robert Welch McGruder, did you say what I *think* you said? Soon as I get near a bar of soap you're getting that trashy mouth washed out, little man!"

The red cowboy hat perked up and Welch, incredulous, said, "What? That's what Mahlon called it!"

"Well then, Mahlon needs to eat some Ivory too! No son of mine is gonna talk like that. It's common!" Then she turned on Will, who was biting his lip trying to keep from laughing. She slapped his shoulder. "What kind of people are they, anyway, talking like that?"

"But he's right," Will said. "Mahlon wasn't doing anything wrong; it's just what they call it."

"Well, it's considered hypocritical where I come from, walkin' around all high and mighty in your pilgrim clothes and cussin' worse than Ferdy Pruitt."

"That's what I'm trying to tell you—it's not a cussword to them. It's a different culture, babe. They do lots of things different from you."

"Really? They got any other bad habits I need to warn the kids about?"

Will scratched his head. "Sometimes they belch after they eat. It's kind of a compliment." So far they hadn't been in an Amish house at mealtime. Will was grateful for that, although it was bound to happen sooner or later.

"And they talked Dutch half the time so I couldn't understand what they were saying," Helen said.

"Well, some of the older ones have never gotten very comfortable with English. It's a courtesy to them, in a way." It was strange: he found himself, in spite of everything, defending his people to his wife. He hadn't expected that.

"And the *names*," Helen continued. "Best I could make out there were at least three Marys, and they put other names in front of them so they could tell which one they were talking about."

"Right. They put the husband's name in front. Let's see, there would have been a Menno Mary, an Eli-Jake Mary"—he pronounced it Aylee-Check Mary, the Dutch way—"and . . . I don't know the other one. Also, there are several *Checks*—Aylee-Check, Henry-Check, Uri-Check, and a couple others. They put the father's name in front to distinguish men. So Aylee-Check Mary would be Mary, the wife of Jake, the son of Eli. If they're talking about a child, they'll do the same thing except they'll use the possessive. My older brother's name is Mose, and when we were kids at church there was always another Mose or two, so my brother was Levi's Mose. Now that he's grown they drop the *s* and hyphenated it—Levi-Mose."

Helen flopped back against the seat and let out an exasperated sigh. "I'm never gonna get this," she said.

CHAPTER | 18

*October 1951*

Twilight. The yellow glow of kerosene lamps shone dimly from the living room windows as Will turned in and the headlights swept his father's house. He could make out the dark shapes of a couple of men out back, near the barn. There would be one or two more in the buggy shed or the stable, putting away the horses. The younger ones would have seen to the cows already. There were evening chores to do, even on Sunday.

Will could feel his own heart thumping as he eased up past the house. One of the men, walking into the half-light just beyond the corner of the barn, turned around and stopped, having spotted the car. It was Mose, the firstborn, Will could tell by the way he stood, his head tilted slightly forward, hands hooked into the back of his pants. Mose was always the serious one, deliberate and thoughtful. He would watch, motionless until he saw a reason to move.

Will switched off the lights, killed the engine. The motor ticked and cooled. Helen's eyes shone white in the near darkness, and he knew she was almost as afraid as he was. The boys had both fallen asleep, Riley in the window ledge and Welch stretched out on the back seat with his hat over his face, a grubby hand holding a chrome six-shooter across his chest.

As his hands kneaded the steering wheel, Will watched Mose for some sign of recognition.

"Maybe you should wait here for a minute or two," he said. "This may be kind of a shock for them, so I'll just see how it goes, and then I'll come get you."

No answer. Helen was staring at the house, wringing her hands in her lap.

"Okay?"

She turned to him and her face was grim, but she held out a hand, palm down. "Yes, all right. Will," she said, and squeezed his hand. "It'll be okay. He's your father. You'll see."

He did not share her confidence, but he smiled and said, "Sure."

When he got out of the car his brother started toward him. He could tell by the cautious gait that Mose didn't recognize him. Nine times out of ten when a car pulled up in the yard it was some lost Englisher in need of directions. For the first time in his life, Will understood how the Englisher felt. He didn't announce himself; he just jammed his hands in his pockets and ambled across the yard past the clothesline up to the barn lot. Mose swung the gate open and met him there.

"Can I help you?" Mose asked, in English. They were face-to-face now, and there was just enough light to see the burnt copper of Mose's thick hair, cut clean and straight below his ears. Will said nothing, waiting to see if Mose would recognize him. He did not.

"Are you lost?" Mose asked, clearly beginning to lose patience with this mute Englisher.

"Depends on who you talk to," Will said. "How have you been, brother?"

Silence. The sound of breathing—Mose had always breathed loudly through his nose. A pronounced swallow, and then Mose shifted his feet.

"Oh my..." he stammered. "Can this be?" Tentative fingers reached out to touch Will's shoulder. Then, once he had established it was no ghost, he took Will's hand in an iron grip, pumped it once and held on as if he didn't know what to do next. It wasn't in him to hug a man, and words had always eluded him, so he held on to Will's forearm and squeezed until his steel arms trembled.

"I thought I would never see you again in this life," Mose finally whispered. He let go suddenly and, turning back toward the barn, shouted, "Ben! Daniel! Come!"

Daniel, who had been watching from the barn lot, came quickly. Ben, the next to the youngest son, stuck his head out the door of the barn to see what the commotion was about, saw the little gathering at the fence and walked slowly toward them, tucking his shirt into the high waist of his pants and straightening his hat. Mose clamped a hand on Will's shoulder as if to hold him there until they assembled, as if he was afraid Will might disappear again.

When they were together facing Will, Mose said, "Do you know who this is?"

They couldn't see him very well in the gathering dark, and the oldest of the two was barely seventeen—half their lives had passed in Will's absence. They both shrugged, shook their heads. They knew no one who wore an Army uniform, and the nametag above the pocket said *McGruder.*

"This is your brother, Will, come home."

Will was moved by the little celebration that took place then. They were genuinely glad to see him, and he sensed no hesitation, not the slightest hint of condemnation or ostracism. He dared to hope that his father would react the same way. But why did his brothers not rush him into the house to share the good news with the rest of the family?

"Oh," Will said, glancing back at the car, "I want you to meet my wife."

"A wife! Did you hear that, brothers? We have a new sister-in-law!" They were ecstatic. They stumbled over each other, trooping across the yard to Will's car.

The evening had cooled. Helen got out clutching a white cardigan around herself and closed the door very softly. "The boys are asleep," she said in a hushed voice. As Will introduced his brothers they shook hands with Helen and then peeked in the windows of the car, grinning broadly at their new nephews. It was like Christmas.

Will heard the groaning of the screen-door spring at the back of the house and he stiffened, realizing suddenly that it was precisely the sound his ears had been waiting for. Feet clumped down the back steps and crunched on the gravel of the walk. The dark shape of Levi Mullet materialized, his jerky, bowlegged walk and splayed elbows unmistakable even in silhouette. He was shorter than Will remembered. The brothers straightened and fell silent. Will stood with his back to the car, waiting.

"What are you boys doing out here?" Levi called, stalking toward them. "Who is there?"

No one answered.

Will waited. Visions flashed across his mind at light speed, visions alternating between a weeping father welcoming his lost son home and an enraged judge striking him across the face. In the end, fatalism took hold. Will had done all he could. He had covered endless miles, not to mention confessed a good many lies, to come and put himself in this very spot. All he could do now was to wait and see.

His father stopped one pace short and stared, letting his eyes adjust to the darkness. For a long moment he made no move, no sound. Will could feel his own pulse hammering. Levi's head turned slowly, taking in the car, Helen, Mose, Daniel, and Ben standing mute. Will realized then—it was in his father's movements, somehow—that his brothers' refusal to answer their father had identified Will more clearly than if they had announced his name.

Levi Mullet moved a step closer. With a shaky hand he produced a kitchen match from his pants pocket and struck it with his thumbnail. The match flared to life and he held it cupped sideways in his hand, at arm's length so that it flickered within inches of Will's face.

The blackened end of the match shriveled and curled. Orange flame crawled up the wood toward Levi Mullet's rough fingertips. Will held his breath. In the close stillness he could hear the faint hiss of the match burning. His eyes fastened on the light. He could see nothing else.

Levi's gruff voice penetrated the darkness.

"I thought you were dead," he said flatly, and the breath of his words made the flame dance a little.

He held the match a beat longer and then, before the flame could reach his fingers, blew it out, flung it away, turned about, and stormed back to the house. Night-blind from staring at the light, Will heard his father go away but could no longer see him. He heard the screen door screech open but it didn't close, so he knew Levi had paused in the doorway.

"Don't bring that in my house," the darkness said, and then the screen door slammed and a black silence fell. It was something of a shock, that silence. Will had always imagined hell would be a bright and clamorous place.

Mose cleared his throat.

"Well," he said, and shuffled his feet in the gravel.

The silence rushed back in for a long moment, and then Mose laid a hand on Will's shoulder and said quietly, "I think you might want to come back tomorrow. I will speak with him in the morning."

Mose had always been the only one of the sons who could reason with Levi, the only one who had ever been known to stand up to him and not lose badly. Levi Mullet was the master of his house and he tolerated no insubordination; however, Mose knew how to talk to him, when to be deferential and when to stand firm. A truce of some kind existed between them that no one else understood, let alone enjoyed, but it was a fragile truce and Will knew it would not stand this test. Even Mose couldn't mend this.

"No," he said, and he felt Helen's hand soft on his forearm. He swallowed hard and reached for the keys in his pocket. "No, I got what I came for. I have his answer. I think it's better if we just go now."

Twenty minutes down the road Helen turned around and peered into the back seat to see about her children. Softly, she asked, "Where are we going?"

"Millersburg." He said it in a way that made her turn away and leave him alone.

White-knuckling the steering wheel, Will's thoughts turned inward and his memory dragged him back inexplicably to a conversation he'd overheard one night in the crew's mess on the Liberty Ship in 1945. One of the seamen, an old sailor who had survived many crossings of the

North Atlantic, had talked often about good men lost on both sides, merchant marine and submariner alike. He spoke with a hard-earned empathy about what it must be like for a man to be robbed in an instant from the shattered hulk of his ship and left to drift, to flutter softly down, as unmindful of his own weight and posture as a leaf, to be torn forever from the grasp of sunlight, and fall for hours—perhaps days—down, and down, and come to rest delicately in a silent puff of silt at the cold bottom of darkness itself. Will hadn't entirely understood the sentiment at the time. He understood it much better now.

There was no pay phone at the gas station by the main intersection in Millersburg, but they let Will use the old box on the wall behind the register, where he rang the operator and somehow managed to get through to Tobe's house. Tobe lost his composure, actually broke down and cried, when he heard Will's voice.

"I thought you were dead," he gasped.

They were waiting in the yard when Will's car pulled up, Tobe and Sylvia and their baby girl, and Will found the celebration he had dreamed of with his father. The fatted calf consisted of steaks cooked on a brick grill that Tobe had built in the backyard.

Sylvia was a lovely girl, possessed of that shy innocence unique to Amish girls. When she and Tobe married he refused to go back to the Amish, yet he didn't have the heart to force her to entirely leave the lifestyle behind, so they met each other halfway and became Mennonites. He would be able to drive a car and their house could have electricity and a telephone, but he would still wear a short beard and she would still wear a covering. In the end, she had to admit it was nice to be allowed to wear dresses of bright floral print instead of the dark, solid colors of the Old Order.

Tobe had grown an inch or two—he was the same height as Will now—and filled out. He'd taken a job as a cabinetmaker in a local shop and made pretty good money. In his off-hours, with his own two hands, Tobe had built a modest house on his own little parcel of land, doing everything himself, from digging the foundation to laying the brick. They were a handsome couple, she with her dark blond hair and demure smile, he with his crop of wavy brown and that ruddy, devilish grin. The baby girl, Hannah, had a thick head of blond curls. Tobe worshiped her.

Tobe won the heart of Welch and Riley by taking them out back while he was cooking the steaks and showing them the dog pen where he kept a pair of prize beagles—his rabbit dogs, Butch and Thelma.

"Thelma will have puppies someday," he told the boys. "Maybe your dad will let you have one." Instantly, he became their hero.

After dinner Tobe and Will left the women to clean up the kitchen, bathe the babies, and talk. Tobe took him out back to show him the shop he was building.

"Seems kind of big," Will said, his voice echoing in the empty building as Tobe plugged in a string of bare light bulbs. Tobe had poured the slab, built the frame, roofed it, and nailed on the siding, but apart from an assortment of toolboxes the interior was bare.

"Yeah, well, I don't want to spend my whole life making somebody else rich," Tobe said. "I plan to set up my own cabinet shop."

Will nodded his approval as he lit a cigarette. Tobe proudly showed him where he planned to put the table saw and planers, lining them up with windows on both ends to make it easier to handle the longer boards. Tobe had grown up. He was going to be all right.

Will didn't say much while his brother laid out his grand plans for the shop. Tobe read his mood easily, and apparently figured out the reason for it.

"Shame about Dad," Tobe said quietly. "He can be a tough old goat when he wants to. Still doesn't have much to do with me, but then he never did."

"Did they ban you when you came back?"

"No, but then I never was baptized into the church like you were. For a while there Dad wouldn't let me in the house, but when we joined the Mennonite Church, he sort of forgot about it. I don't think he ever took me that serious to start with, and all I did was run away for a while. Dad never expected much out of me. But you!—that was another story. Anyway, he doesn't have a constant reminder with me the way he does with you. Did you have any trouble at Clara's?"

Will shook his head, blew a cloud of smoke. "No, everybody was pretty decent to us. Of course we weren't there at mealtime. Clara was a little stiff, maybe. She didn't say much. She acted kind of funny, especially when the kids were around, like she was afraid, or..." He paused mid-sentence as something Tobe had said came back to him. "What do you mean, 'constant reminder'?"

Tobe was sitting on the lid of a toolbox the size of a desk. His eyebrows went up in surprise at the question.

"You mean you don't know?"

Will shook his head. "Know what?"

"Nobody told you?"

"Told me what?"

"About the girl."

"What *girl*? What are you talking about, Tobe? Just say it."

"Oh boy." Tobe raked a hand through his hair. He rose wearily from the toolbox and walked away from Will.

Will dropped his cigarette butt, ground it on the concrete.

"Maybe I better just start at the beginning," Tobe said, leaning his palms against the bare studs of the wall, pushing against them as if he were inspecting the framing. "Oh boy. I can't believe they didn't tell you about Mattie." When he turned around, his eyes were hard and serious.

*So that's what this is about.*

"No," Will said. "Nobody ever mentioned her, and I wasn't about to bring it up either." He fidgeted for a moment before he explained, "Helen doesn't know."

Tobe sighed, glanced at him twice as if to make sure he was serious, then shook his head and said, "Well then, I guess it's up to me." There was a heaviness about him. "Mattie's dead, Will. She died in childbirth."

Will's knees almost buckled. The concrete slab seemed to be moving beneath him as his hand fumbled for another cigarette. He lit it and took a shaky drag before he managed to push out a single word.

"Mine?"

A deep compassion came over Tobe's face. He placed a hand on Will's shoulder and squeezed gently. "Aw, no, brother, no. It wasn't your baby that killed her, Will. It happened two years later."

"So . . . she got married?"

"Oh, yeah. After she had your baby she was in kind of a hard way, having to live with her father and all. So the first time she saw a way out, she took it."

Will nodded. "I can understand that. Old Gideon was almost as crazy as our own father." He'd thought about it enough—what it would be like for Mattie after he left. Living in Gideon's strict Old Order house with an illegitimate baby, life would have been unbearable.

"She married Simon Schlabach," Tobe said.

Will mouthed the name slowly, confused. Maybe there was another Simon Schlabach. The name was not uncommon.

"Clara's husband?"

"He is now. Mattie died having his baby, a couple years after you left. They couldn't stop her bleeding. They said later even a doctor couldn't have done anything."

Pictures of Mattie flashed across his mind, laughing, crying, breathless with excitement, bright with wonder. He could hear her voice as plainly as though she were standing next to him, that odd way she had of rolling her *R*s. He had teased her about it, and now he could feel, actually *feel* the sting of her pinching the back of his arm. He rubbed the place with his fingers while shouts and whispers rained on him, pummeled him, slapped him.

All this time he had avoided her memory, pushed it away, shunned and silenced it. Until now. Now her face, her voice, the feel and smell of her leaped at him and pressed upon him until he feared he would cave in. Mattie had cared about him, and he about her. He still could not entirely understand all the wrong choices he had made, and how they had led to him standing in Tobe's shop hearing about her death as if it were an old newspaper story. Mattie had been vibrant and alive. She had cared for Will Mullet. Now she was dead, and he could see her eyes in front of him, accusing. It had not been his baby that took her life, but if he had stayed would things not have been different? Would she not perhaps have lived? Would she not perhaps be alive and rolling her *R*s that funny way even today? It seemed there would be no end to the chain of troubles he had caused. Then it came back to him, as out of a haze, that Tobe had started the conversation by mentioning a girl. Another thought forced itself upon him.

"Mattie's baby," he said, "the first one, the one that was . . . mine."

Tobe nodded. "A little girl. And yes, she's still with Simon. Clara knew about her. That was why she married him—or part of it, anyway."

The end of Will's cigarette quivered, brightening as he took a drag.

"So that's why Clara acted so funny toward me," he whispered. "I thought it was only that she was surprised to see me alive."

Clara was raising his child.

His mind's eye raced through mental snapshots of a dozen girl children he had met that afternoon at Clara's house. He had long since done the math, and already knew that the child would be almost eight years old now, wherever it was. Always in the past he had managed to reduce the baby to an *it*, an abstract, a mere idea. Now Cassie's face came back to him, an impish gleam in bright blue eyes. Will's eyes were blue, and Cassie was the right age. But what was it that she said?

*"I told her you're not her uncle. Katie is Dad's girl, and I am my mother's."*

*"Katie is Dad's girl."*

Simon Schlabach's daughter, but not Clara's. Katie, too, was almost eight.

Will's hand, with the forgotten stub of a cigarette in it, went to his forehead and made a little up and down motion.

"Does she have a mark—here? An angel's kiss?"

Tobe smiled, for the first time. "Yes, that's her. Cute little thing. Kind of shy."

Will nodded mechanically, and his voice came out in a raspy whisper. "Katie. Her name is Katie. She hid in the loft all afternoon, upset because I'm not her uncle."

## CHAPTER 19

*January 1985*

Riley returns to Will's table in Yoder's Kitchen, trailing the odor of cigarettes. He tastes his coffee, wrinkles his nose. "Cold," he says, and shoves it away.

Startled by the thirty-five-year-old Riley in front of him now, Will returns too, though no one knew he was gone. He rises, glancing at his watch. The ladder-back chair groans against the tile floor as he slides it under the table. He takes out a wallet worn shiny from long use and leaves a tip.

Riley browses a rack of glossy paperbacks about Plain Folk while Will pays at the glass counter near the door and takes a toothpick from the lidless glass salt shaker by the register. As he starts for the door their waitress waves goodbye from across the restaurant. Will waves back, noting that the angel's kiss has faded. He stops with his hand on the door, turns and goes quietly back to his table and doubles his tip.

Snowplows have scraped all the roads by now, scattering sand and salt on the hard-packed skim. In Amish country the paved shoulders of the roads are very wide and set off by a solid white line so that horse-drawn buggies, hacks, and wagons can peacefully coexist with much faster moving cars and trucks. When the roads are clear the shoulders are littered with horse droppings and bits of hay, but for now, until the plows can make another pass, a deep bank of cast-off snow blocks the shoulder, forcing buggies and automobiles to share the lane.

Riley and Will aren't even out of Winesburg before they're held up behind a buggy. Through the undercarriage they can see the horse's feet clipping briskly along, yet even a fast trot is a slow crawl for an automobile. At the wheel, Riley leans left impatiently. A sparse but endless line of cars crawls toward him in the other lane so that he can't pass. He's trapped. Huffing, he drums on the steering wheel with his fingers.

"It's all right," Will says. "We've got all day."

Riley settles back, stiff-arming the wheel, and regards the buggy with something approaching contempt. "I ought to blow the horn at him," he says. "Let him know I want by. Maybe he'd pull over and let me pass."

"He's not interested in holding you up," Will says. "He'll pull over as soon as he gets a chance, unless of course you blow the horn at him. He's Old Order. Start honking your horn at some Old Order grandpa and you're probably going to see his stubborn side."

Riley frowns. "How do you know he's Old Order? You can't even see the guy."

Will is constantly surprised by the things Riley doesn't know. "It's the buggy. He's got hard wheels—no rubber around the rim. And there's no blinker light, no reflectors or anything. No mirrors on the sides, and no rear window."

"I see. So he's Schwartzentruber?"

"Well, no. Schwartzentruber is conservative, but some are even stricter than that—sort of Orthodox Old Order. Notice he doesn't even have the little window in the back? Another *nuddleroller* quirk."

"Nuddleroller. What's that?"

Will winces a little, already wishing the word hadn't slipped out. "It's a disparaging term we used when we were in school, a dirty name for the really Old Order kids. Means 'dung roller.' They used to come to school barefooted—well, we all did until after frost—but some of the real orthodox didn't believe in wasting a lot of time bathing. Everybody had to do morning chores back then, but most of us washed the barn off our feet before we came to school. For whatever reason, they didn't, and that's where the term came from."

A wry grin grows on Riley's face. "Wait. Now I'm confused. I always thought there was just Old Order and New Order, and Schwartzentruber was another name for Old Order."

"No, Schwartzentruber is just one *kind* of Old Order. There are different sects."

"And they look down on each other—have nicknames for each other and stuff?"

Will scratches his head, winces again. "Truth? Yeah. I guess everybody needs somebody to look down on. Adults are too polite, I suppose, but when we were kids we were about as cruel as any."

"So, where do all these different sects come from? I mean, what are they based on? Rubber wheels and reflectors?"

Will chuckles. "Well, yeah—that and a million other things. Every church covers maybe ten or twenty families, and their bishop says what goes in that district, so you get little variations in the rules from one place to another. Sometimes one of the ministers or deacons takes issue with the bishop over the rules, and then like as not he'll end up joining another district or starting a new church."

"Get outta here! You mean to tell me they'll bust up over rubber on buggy wheels?"

"Sometimes. Or the color of the roof. There's a bunch in Pennsylvania with yellow tops on their buggies. There's also white, gray, brown. You can tell who belongs to what church by the color. There's another sect someplace whose buggies are shaped a little different. And that's just the buggy rules—wait till you get into clothes. There's one group where the men only wear one suspender, and another where they don't wear suspenders at all. I remember once, a church split up over a washing machine."

Riley raised an eyebrow, looked sideways at him. "Amish don't *have* washing machines."

"Oh yeah, some of them do. Sears used to make an old wringer type washing machine with a gas motor underneath, like a lawn mower. Put gas in it, give the cord a yank, and off you go. Of course, none of the Old Order would allow that—it was Worldly because it had a motor built into it. But then they found out that Sears also made a machine with just a pulley underneath. You could buy a separate gas motor, set it on the ground next to the machine, hook a drive belt to it, crank it up, and still have a powered washing machine without the built-in motor. Some of them thought that was okay, but the bishop said it was Worldly, so they had a big fight and split up over it."

Riley snorts with derisive laughter. "I guess when you get right down to it, they're as goofy as anybody else in the religion business. Not a bit of difference."

Will doesn't take the bait. There was a time when he would have fought back over a cheap shot like that, but not now. This is the one useful thing the counselor has taught him. Riley doesn't start arguments in order to win them, although he'll try to do that too. What he really wants is to provoke anger, mostly just to prove to himself that he can. This was tough for Will to grasp at first, that somebody might actually start an argument for some purpose other than proving a point. *"It's a control issue,"* the counselor had said. *"He just wants to get a rise out of you."*

Will nods toward the buggy jostling along in front of them. "You don't think that's *different?*"

"Well, yeah, of course the whole horse and buggy thing is different— at least on the surface. But underneath all that they're just like the church people I grew up with. It was all about rules and regulations—who was wearing their hair too long, or their dress too short, or listening to the wrong kind of music. Bottom line, people just can't agree on anything."

"I guess that's true enough," Will says. "Put six Amish in a room, ask them a question, and you'll get eight different opinions."

"Right. That's why there are a thousand denominations out there. It's just that somehow I thought the Amish were different. They always seemed so . . . *pious.*"

Will smiles at this. "Growing up, I never thought of them as pious. They don't see themselves that way. That would be arrogance to them."

The surrey in front of them finally veers into the entrance of a gas station to allow the long line of cars to get by. The grandpa peers out from under a wide black hat as they pass, his white beard spilling like a waterfall down his chest.

Will explains some of the traditions while Riley drives. Riley knows almost nothing about the Amish, but they never did talk much and it suddenly dawns on Will that Riley hasn't even visited Amish country in a very long time.

"When's the last time you were here?" he asks.

"Let's see." Riley has to think about it for a minute. "I believe I was twelve. That would make it twenty-three years."

They are passing through an evergreen forest, a dark sea of pines bent under the weight of snow, profoundly still. More and more these days Will is confronted with the far-reaching consequences of his past. This one catches him by surprise.

"Twenty-three years?"

Riley nods. "*Tempus fugit,* doesn't it? Yeah, I was just a kid."

The rift between them is even wider and deeper than Will thinks, but if his own father taught him anything it was that a field untended was a field lost. He feels old. He knows, too well, how the years can fly past like a flock of birds.

## CHAPTER 20

*October 1951*

On the drive south from Ohio the remains of Helen and Will survived in separate little isolated cells. He knew what troubled her. She was, after all, a simple country girl who had been hauled away from home to bear children in faraway countries in the shadow of enemies, and then subjected to a series of thunderbolts no human could be expected to weather without injury. Worst of all, he had told her so many lies that she wasn't even sure of her own name anymore.

Will was aware of these things—painfully aware—but his mind was full of its own troubles. While Helen's heart yearned for the solid footing of the good red Georgia clay and the haven of her mother's front porch swing, he brooded over his own losses. He said not a word as his thoughts railed against the injustice, the stubbornness, the intractable judgmental nature of the Amish. He thought of a million things he might have said to his father that night, things that might have turned him, or failing that, stabbed back at him. He hadn't said them. He hadn't even the presence of mind to think of them at the time, and the door had closed on him while he stood there as stunned and stupid as a mule in a downpour.

The worst of it was that his father was a good man, honored by his family, respected by the church, and looked up to by the farmers. Digging into his box of childhood memories Will unearthed vision after vision of his father as a tower of strength and a bastion of righteousness. There were days in the early winter, around the first snows, when Levi would hitch up a wagon and take Will and Tobe out with him, just the three of them, bundled against the cold, to cut up a dead tree for stove wood. Even now he could see his father's hands, hard and sure, hefting an ax with a powerful confidence and sinking it deep, the air ringing with solid strokes and the chips flying. Will and Tobe would drag the smaller limbs to the fire as Levi sliced them free, and when the limbs were gone, Levi would bring out the two-man crosscut saw to divide the trunk into lengths that would fit into the stove. He would man one end of the saw alone, and his two small sons would push and pull together at the other end. Then he would split the wood while his sons loaded the wagon. There were moments when they would take a break and sit on a log beside the fire together, Levi and his boys, and Levi would pull a bag of walnuts from his pocket. He would press two of them together between his iron palms until they cracked and then hand them to his sons.

Levi Mullet was a model of patience in those days, showing his sons how to lend themselves to the rhythm of another, teaching them the harmonies of life and work. Sometimes it would snow, and Levi would serenely ignore the collecting of flakes on the wide black brim of his hat. The boys took comfort in the sight because it seemed even the weather was no threat so long as their dad was there.

These were the childhood memories fixed in Will's mind, little snapshots of Eden—the hiss and crackle of the fire, the veil of woodsmoke hanging in the gray winter afternoon, the redness of his father's cheek, the look of contented concentration on Tobe's young face as he picked walnuts from the shell, the snuffling and stamping of a draft horse. All of it together added up to a kind of security that only a father could offer, a warm certainty that all was well on the earth. All was as it should be.

Will had no choice now but to hate that man, for if Levi was right in his judgment of his son then life was not worth living. There could be no middle ground. In the end it was mere self-preservation that taught him to hate that which he could not change.

By the time he drove across the Georgia line Will had bricked a formidable wall between himself and Levi Mullet. It wasn't that hard. After all, Will didn't need his father. He'd proven it in the years he'd been gone from home, proven that he could take care of himself and his family just fine without help or interference from Levi. There was great security in the Army.

But Helen had arrived at some conclusions of her own.

"So, what do you plan to do now?" she asked, too calmly.

Will glanced at her and caught the slight narrowing of eyes, the set of the jaw. He could see lines forming, battle flags unfurling in the breeze.

"I'm not sure," he said. "They won't issue my orders until I reenlist, but the rumors have been flying around for a while. Things are getting pretty heated in Korea. I think that's where they'll send me next." He glanced at her and saw that her lips had retracted. "But it'll probably only be for a year," he added.

"So, you'll be leaving us here?"

"Yes, I suppose—if I have to go. It's a combat zone. You can't take family. But it's not definite yet so don't worry, I'll get you set up here before I leave."

She took a deep breath, stared out the window. A red barn drifted past with a big *See Rock City* sign splashed against a black roof.

"No," she said, and just like that, her mind was made up. "I've been through enough, Will. I won't have it."

He lit a cigarette, cracked the window, kept his eyes on the road. "Babe, I don't know for sure if that's what'll happen. Maybe they'll send us someplace else. Alaska would be nice, or maybe Okinawa. You can take family to those places."

"They'll send you to Korea," she said flatly.

He nodded. "Probably."

"People are getting killed over there," she said.

"Right, and it's partly because of that that I have to go. I can't try to get out of it just because it's dangerous. It comes with the job. Somebody has to go. What makes me better than the next guy?"

"All right," she said calmly, and shrugged. "Go ahead and go to Korea if you want, but I won't be here when you get back."

"I'm in the Army, babe. You know? They don't ask me where I'd like to go. I was a soldier when you married me, and you knew what that meant."

She wheeled on him then, with fire in her eyes. "Will McGruder, or whoever you are, if you're trying to tell me I knew what I was getting into when I married you, you better think again. That dog won't hunt. What I married was a sackful of nickel-plated lies, and it's high time we got some things ironed out! I'm in Georgia now," she said, jabbing a forefinger into the seat. "I may not know my own name but I know where home is, and I'm home now. I'm not leaving, and neither are my kids. If you go away again, you go alone. For good."

"The Army doesn't give me a choice," he said weakly.

"Then get out of the Army." She crossed her arms and sat back. The discussion was over.

They spent that night in a swaybacked bed at Welch and Erma's house, the boys sleeping on a pallet on the floor in the same room. Helen didn't tell her parents anything, never let on that her marriage was teetering on the brink, or mention that her husband was an impostor. It was his move. She would wait and see.

He lay awake most of the night listening to the rasping of cicadas in the cotton fields, thinking. The events of recent days had left him reeling like a punch-drunk prizefighter. His father's cold dismissal, the news of Mattie's death, his daughter being raised by his own sister, and now Helen's ultimatum.

Long before the birds announced the coming of day he had made up his mind about Ohio. Already he had reduced his former life, along with his former family and all the pains and longings and regrets they entailed, down to one word, three short syllables: Ohio. It was a kind of mental shorthand that enabled him to put the whole tangled, painful mess into one neat file and address it with one simple solution.

He would stay out of Ohio.

He didn't need his father's approval. *Approval.* He couldn't even think of the word without a cynical chuckle. He'd *never* had his father's approval. The man was impossible to please. Will Mullet had been, in his father's estimation, self-serving, incompetent, and thoughtless. And wanton—let's not forget wanton.

Will Mullet had never done anything right, but Will *McGruder* had married, fathered two sons, lived through a war and made the rank of sergeant completely on his own. Will McGruder didn't have a father, and didn't need one. Best to just let Levi Mullet go. Will could keep in touch with Tobe by mail, and the last thing he wanted to do was interfere with Clara's raising of Katie. He would leave the girl alone. It was probably the best thing he could do for her. Maybe someday, when she was older, when she understood grown-up things, when she could handle the truth, then he might tell her.

He couldn't think of a single reason to set foot in Ohio ever again. They were the Levi Mullets. They were Amish. His name was Will McGruder, and whatever he was, he was not Amish. He wasn't sure he ever had been. He would not go back.

Helen's ultimatum was another matter. She was forcing him to choose between his career and his wife, and he was shocked to find the choice so difficult. It seemed unfair, somehow, because he knew that Helen, in her own way, was exacting punishment from him, making him pay for lying to her. As if he had planned it. The Army had been good to him, and he had been good to the Army. Best of all, he never had to make a decision about anything above his pay grade. In the Army the rules were all laid out—everything was clear and well-defined. For a kid raised under Amish law and disciplined by the stone hand of Levi Mullet, the Army was a natural fit. Only thirteen more years and he could retire, still young enough to start another career. He could even go to school if he wanted, and the Army would pay for it.

If he walked away from the Army now, he walked away with nothing. Yet Helen left him no choice. He would not abandon another entire life, another whole identity, and divorce was simply not part of his thinking. Will McGruder had vowed to remain married for life, and a vow was a vow. He had also promised to provide for his family, and whether he liked it or not he would now have to find another way to make a living. He'd always been good with his hands, but he had no marketable skills that he was aware of, and no education. In civilian life he felt sure he wouldn't find much demand for a Sherman tank mechanic, and the pittance he could earn as a migrant farm worker would never be enough to feed a family of four.

Lying in the swaybacked bed and staring at the shadows in Welch and Erma's extra bedroom he decided he would go to Atlanta and look for work—any kind of work. It seemed to him that the outcome of his search would determine the course of the remainder of his life. His future lay hidden behind a veil of chance, a condition that worried and frightened him until he looked back and realized that it had always been so.

The next morning he dressed in civilian clothes, tossed an overnight bag in the car, and told Helen he was going to Atlanta.

"Fine," she said, and stopped there. She would wait and see.

As he neared the city his mind took him back to the year he had spent there before, an angst-ridden year that he now came to see, in contrast to his present lot, as a carefree, happy time. His thoughts turned to Barefoot, and he suddenly remembered. If Barefoot still lived in Atlanta he might have an idea where to find work.

He found a scrap of yellowed paper in his wallet with Barefoot's old phone number on it, and when he got to the city limits of Atlanta he called. Barefoot's mother answered the phone. Jubal didn't live there anymore, but she gave Will the name of the place where he worked.

He looked up Stanford Construction in the phone book. The girl who answered didn't know any Jubal Barefoot, but it was a big company. When she checked the records she found that he was indeed employed by Stanford. He was working on a highway bridge over the South River.

Will found the jobsite easily enough. It was at the bottom of a pretty little forested valley out in the country south of town. In the bottom of the valley the D.O.T. had raised up a bed for a new road right beside the old one so the new bridge could be built without shutting down the highway. Will pulled off the road, eased between the sawhorses, and parked in the gravel next to a brand-new Ford with New York plates.

The bridge was almost finished, and as Will approached he could see they were pouring concrete for the road surface. A crane sitting at the near end of the bridge lifted a huge funnel-shaped bucket from behind a concrete truck and swung it out, lowering it expertly in front of the screed and swinging it gently into the hands of the tall guy in the rubber boots. Moving with the bucket across the slab in a kind of dance, the tall guy tripped the handle and spread a yard of wet concrete in precisely the right spot and then let go and waved off the bucket, all in one smooth motion. Three other guys started spreading out the new ridge of concrete, knocking it down with shovels to make sure it didn't overwhelm the mechanical screed scissoring back and forth and leaving a smooth, level surface in its wake. When the tall guy turned around, Will recognized his profile, even from a distance. That nose. Barefoot looked almost as silly in a hard hat as he had in an Army helmet.

Bypassing a storage shed and what looked to be a crude office shack, Will walked past the crane, past the concrete truck with its churning load, and went straight out onto the bridge, picking his footing carefully on a crisscross mat of reinforcing rods. By the time Will reached the place where they were pouring concrete Barefoot had gotten distracted by some guy with neatly parted hair. It was pretty obvious the guy didn't work here; he was wearing street clothes, no hard hat, and his hair was slicked down like a movie star's. Will stopped short and waited for Barefoot to turn around.

"Yeah, I got tons of experience," the slick-haired guy was saying. His porkpie hat sat on the very back of his head and he kept his hands in his pockets. He talked fast. "I got eight years building bridges up in N'York— all kinds'a bridges. You ain't *got* a man with more experience than me. You name it, I can build it. I could run this crew in my sleep."

Barefoot nodded appreciatively, but before he could answer the shadow of the concrete bucket passed over him. Somebody whistled and he turned around to catch it, guiding it in for another pass in front of the screed. When he let go of the bucket he saw Will, and his whole countenance changed.

Barefoot let out a whoop and almost fell down as he slogged through the wet concrete, then he almost tripped again rushing across the woven mat of reinforcing rods in his clumsy rubber boots. He nearly lifted Will off his feet in a wild hug.

"What are you doing here?" Barefoot asked, a wide grin on his face. Slick Hair fidgeted, waiting for a break in the conversation.

Will glanced at Slick Hair, shrugged. His first thought had been to tell the truth and see if he could land a job, but he didn't want to cut in on the man who got here ahead of him.

"Oh, I was just in the neighborhood and thought I'd look you up," he said.

Slick Hair smirked, shifted his weight, jiggled the keys in his pocket until Barefoot noticed him.

"Oh, hey! This here is my old Army buddy, Will McGruder," Barefoot said.

Slick Hair pulled his hand out of his pocket to look at his watch and said, "Yeah, that's nice, pal, but I got places to go and people to meet. You want to tell me where to go to get signed in?"

"Why certainly, sir," Barefoot said, and a tone of sweet Southern politeness crept into his voice. Will recognized the tone. Helen had taught him to be wary of it. "I'm sorry, it was rude of me to keep you waiting. Fact is, Shorty told me just this morning he's looking to hire one more good man, so if you'll just go right over there to that shack—the one with the little window and the—"

"Yeah, yeah, I seen the shack," Slick Hair said, already moving, picking his footing across the grid of rust brown reinforcing rods.

"He's in there doing timecards right now," Barefoot called after him. "You'll like Shorty—he's a real nice fella! Just go right on in and tell him I sent you!"

Already nearing the end of the bridge, Slick Hair threw up a hand in acknowledgment without looking back.

The bucket swung in again. Barefoot caught the handle and steered it deftly into position, dumping a cubic yard of concrete in front of the screed. When he let it go he turned back to Will, and his expression changed.

"So what are you *really* here for?" he asked. "I'm real glad to see you, Will, but you had to go to a good bit of trouble to find me way out here on the job. It's been what, six years? If you just wanted to catch up on old times you could have called me at home in the evenin'." He scratched his cheek, studied Will's eyes. "You're looking for a job, aren't you?"

"Well, I . . . uh, tell you the truth, I was thinking about getting out of the Army. I don't know too many people in the real World, so yeah, I thought maybe you could give me some tips about where to find work."

"Well, why didn't you say so, buddy? You can work here!"

"Me?"

"Why, yeah! I never seen anybody work harder than you. It'll be a hoot! You and me together? We'll move mountains!"

There was a flash of light in Barefoot's words. Will hadn't expected it to be this easy. He had come here chasing the thin thread of chance, doing the only thing he could think of to do. Now, with his open friendship and unflinching confidence in Will's worth, Barefoot held out a strong hand. Will would take hold of it if he could.

He looked back at the little office shack. Slick Hair was trotting up the steps, opening the door. "Well. Looks like I got here too late. I heard you say you only had room for one more man."

"What, *that guy?*" Barefoot shook his head. "He won't get the job."

"Are you kidding? With his experience? How could they not hire him?"

Barefoot's face scrunched up and he chewed a corner of his lip. "Well . . . call it a hunch. Anyway, you don't need no experience to work here. It don't take a genius."

The door of the shack burst open and Slick Hair came flying out as if he'd been launched from a catapult. Thrown clear of the steps, he hit the dirt like a bag of flour, sending a fine cloud of dust puffing out from around him. He rolled over and sat upright just in time to catch the hat that sailed out the door after him. A stocky little man in khaki work clothes stormed out and stomped down the steps, slamming the door and jamming a hard hat on his head without so much as a backward glance. Slick Hair let him pass before dragging himself up out of the dust and shuffling off toward his car.

Barefoot removed his hard hat and held it solemnly against his chest.

"'Pride goeth before destruction,'" he said, "'and a haughty spirit before a fall.'"

The man who had tossed Slick Hair came straight up onto the bridge. He was short—not much over five feet tall—but beefed up like a weight lifter. He carried his elbows high, and his movements were tight and quick, like a man spoiling for a fight.

"That's who you need to talk to, right there," Barefoot said, reaching up to catch the incoming bucket. "He's the foreman. Name's Doug. Now you be careful what you say to him, you hear? He's a ornery little banty rooster, and he's real sensitive about his height."

Will liked building bridges and he liked working with Barefoot. Stanford Construction made up for light wages by working long hours and paying overtime for everything over forty, an arrangement that ultimately worked in the company's favor by penalizing a man who laid out or came in late. Any hours he missed came out of his overtime pay. Missing a day's work meant losing ten or twelve hours of overtime, depending on the season. In the wintertime the crew worked ten hours a day; in the summer, twelve. There were no paid holidays or vacations, no sick days. But the work suited Will. It was steady and hard and honest, and there was never too much thinking involved. In fact, thinking was discouraged. The least little decision was always deferred to the foreman.

Will enjoyed working outside in the weather, even in the winter, which was mild compared to what he'd grown up with in Ohio. Once the sun got above the trees the temperature rarely stayed below freezing, and anytime he started thinking it was cold he had Barefoot there to remind him of the winter of '44 in Europe.

Still, the pay wasn't much, and Stanford Construction didn't provide housing like the Army had done. Will rented a duplex in College Park, a suburb on the south side of Atlanta—three small rooms and noisy neighbors, but it was the best he could do on a laborer's wage. A kind of uneasy truce existed between him and Helen in those days. Neither of them liked where they were, but they tried not to blame each other for it.

CHAPTER | 21

*October 1951*

O nce they had moved into the tiny duplex in College Park, Helen started going to church. It puzzled Will until he listened to what Helen's mother had to say about some of her neighbors. If you had small children in the South you were expected to take them to church. People who didn't go to church were heathens to Erma, and people who had small children and didn't take them to church were "white trash." Church was part of Helen's fabric, though she said little about it while they were in the Army and away from home. In Germany she had gone to services on the base once or twice but quickly lost interest. She said they were too nondenominational to have any meaning. Will didn't argue, but he could remember services during the war in bunkers and bomb-damaged chapels where men from all faiths crowded together—Jews, Gentiles, Catholics, Protestants, and more than a few agnostics—all clamoring in foxhole earnestness for the briefest glimpse of God.

When she started going to church Will stayed home, refusing to be shamed into going with her. He hadn't been on speaking terms with God for a long time, and he saw no point in pretending. He expected an argument out of Helen, for this was surely another of those little places where she would try to exert control, but she never pressed the issue at all. She simply got up on Sunday morning, dressed herself and her boys, and quietly went to church.

He had driven a wedge between them when he told her the truth about himself, and she had hammered it in deeper when she forced him out of the Army. They remained civil to each other, as every day Will went off to his job and Helen turned to the raising of their children, and slowly they let each other drift away. With her taking the kids to church and never once pressuring her husband to join them, Will knew that another part of her had ceased to care. After a month of this, however, he got dressed and went with them. It was foreign to him at first, but he settled quickly into the routine. The rituals were different from those he had grown up with, and yet they were the same. Ritual is ritual. Though the people in the church didn't dress like Amish people, they still had rules, and they still dressed like each other. The men wore suits and ties instead of plain clothes. Women's dresses were short—nearly up to the knee—and while they didn't wear a covering like the Amish, most of them went to the beauty parlor on Saturday and had their hair tamed and starched and molded in such a way that they all looked the same from behind. The pews had backs, and they were bolted to the floor, not all that different from the collapsible benches of Will's childhood. The preacher thundered in English instead of Dutch, but the thunder sounded pretty much the same.

In the end he saw nothing new in this church, heard nothing he had not heard before, only he sensed a change in Helen. They never discussed it, perhaps for fear of doing damage to the bridge they were building. Still, her attitude toward him gradually softened. It seemed a fair trade to Will.

Going through the Sunday morning ritual was only a small kind of work, and if it helped mend things with Helen, well, he could do that.

After a year of attending Helen's church Will decided to have himself baptized. They asked him a lot of questions and he answered them. They wanted to know if he believed that Jesus was the Son of God who died to save him from his sins, and he answered honestly, "Yes." They asked him why a man should be baptized and he told them, "Out of obedience." They asked more questions and he gave the right answers, but they never once asked him if he actually thought any of this would do him any good. If they had, perhaps he would have thought it over and concluded that it had already done his marriage good, and he would have answered honestly, "Yes."

But they never asked him.

It was then, while they were living in the duplex, that Riley finally started to talk. That event—and an event it was, since Riley waited very late to do it—was memorable mostly because he never went through any baby-talk stage. He talked in whole sentences from the start, as if he had studied speech until he got it down cold before he would even attempt it. His very first words—which rolled out with an astonishing clarity while his mother was struggling to fit a lid onto a sippy cup—and which caused her to drop the cup—were, "I don't need that."

It would be years before they figured out that this was just Riley's way. He would study a new venture until he knew all there was to know about it before he would attempt it. Helen always believed he was just cautious and thoughtful, though Will grew to see it differently. Will knew. It was pride. Riley refused to be second best at anything. He wouldn't stick his toe in the water unless he could be the fastest swimmer in the pool.

The bridge crew moved from one place to another, starting another bridge as soon as the last one was finished. Atlanta was growing, the roads were expanding and there looked to be no end of bridges to build. Will was happy in his work. He liked the sun on his back, the wind on his face, and the feel of steel in his hand. He learned quickly how to tie steel, how to build a concrete form, how to read a print, set a footing, pour concrete, and operate a backhoe. Within a year he had learned most of what he needed to know to build bridges. Barefoot was right; it didn't take a genius.

Barefoot never did like Doug, the banty rooster foreman. Doug was one of those old-school tough guys who carried a stub of a cigar in the corner of his mouth and thought he had to prove himself against everybody he met, every day of his life. He had a million arbitrary rules and regulations, mostly in his head, and he threatened to fire somebody at least once a day. He gave his men thirty minutes for lunch, then allowed one ten minute break in the morning and another in the afternoon. Early on, Will figured out what sort of guy Doug was when he fired a man for sitting down during his coffee break. Doug was old school: they weren't getting paid to sit down, even on break. Will steered clear of him. He simply learned Doug's rules and then didn't break them, no matter how trivial. It was Doug's little kingdom, and although it seemed silly to treat grown men that way, it was no great inconvenience for Will to drink his coffee standing up.

Doug never trusted anybody with a decision. If a man could see two ways to do a thing he would automatically stop and go find Doug to see which way it should be done. Will didn't particularly care, but Barefoot did. Doug's obsessive dominance, his insistence on controlling the smallest decision, grated on Barefoot. More than once, when Doug was on a rampage about something or the job was running behind schedule, Barefoot could be heard muttering that there was a better way to do this. Barefoot persisted in calling him "Douglas" because he knew he hated it, and it was the most irritating thing he could do without getting fired.

But Will could handle it. He'd seen worse. Doug's pettiness and ceaseless carping reminded him so much of his father that he sometimes joked with Barefoot that Doug made him homesick.

It wasn't the job, it was the duplex that drove Will crazy. His home was becoming something foreign to him—a strange, tight little place littered with Tinkertoys and bicycles and noisy appliances.

They bought a television. Everybody else on the street had one, Helen said, so they had no choice. In the evening, after supper, Will would go outside and find something to do in the yard to get away from it. He didn't own the duplex; he was a renter. The yard around it was not his, and the work he put into it would not profit him, yet he worked on it ceaselessly. As long as there was light, and sometimes even when there wasn't, he worked in the yard of the little duplex, cutting, pruning, planting, fertilizing, watering—anything he could find for his hands to do until bedtime, partly to escape the sight of his sons gawking like a nest of baby birds in the glow of that strange box, but partly because something in him longed for a place with enough room to grow a few rows of corn and potatoes.

The second summer in the duplex Will planted a little garden in the backyard. It was a postage stamp plot, with barely enough room for a couple of tomato plants, a few squash, and some pole beans. He kept having to cut the squash back to keep it from crawling through the privacy fence into the neighbor's space. It was too small to produce a useful store of vegetables. The main thing Will's garden accomplished was that it clarified his thinking and hardened his resolve. He finally understood just how important it was for him to find a way to acquire a piece of land. With two growing boys in the house he could only manage to put five dollars a week into savings—not enough to build a down payment. Something would have to change. He contemplated taking on a second job.

As it turned out, it was Barefoot who made the change. Will really didn't have much to say about it. It happened very suddenly—a bolt out of the blue. They were eating lunch underneath the bridge that day with a bunch of other guys, and things didn't really seem any different from any other day. Barefoot, as usual, dominated the conversation. He was a little put out with Douglas about something that had happened that morning.

One of the new hires, a kid they called Harm—his name was Hiram, but he pronounced it Harm, so that was what they called him—was carrying a sheet of plywood over his head, walking a twelve-inch I-beam out to the middle where they were forming up the top of the T, when the wind gusted and snatched at the plywood. When Harm started to lose his balance he let go rather than take a nasty fall. Anybody would have done the same, and everything would have been all right if the wind hadn't caught the sheet of plywood on the way down and sailed it like a swooping kite straight into the back glass of Doug's company truck, forty feet downwind. Nobody was in it at the time—the only damage was to the truck—but Doug fired Harm anyway.

"It's not like he *meant* to hit the truck," Will said.

Barefoot was sitting on a wire spool unpacking his lunch and spreading it out. "If he'd been trying to hit it he couldn't have done it in a hundred years. But if he was gonna mess up a perfectly good truck, why, it's a cryin' shame Douglas wasn't in it."

Will laughed, unwrapping the wax paper from the edge of a ham sandwich, recalling the sight of the full sheet of plywood punching through the window and knifing into the dash.

"He couldn't have hit it any straighter. It went through there like a guillotine blade." Will made a little slicing motion with his sandwich.

"Now there's a thought," Barefoot said, pensively. "Get rid of Douglas, maybe they'd move me up to foreman and then things could make sense around here for a change." He started to take a bite of his sandwich, but stopped. He stared off into space for a minute, then dumped out his tea, packed his entire lunch back into the steel lunch pail, and latched it. Rising, he hitched up his pants and took off up the hill toward Doug's office.

One of the guys watched him go, then turned to Will. "Where you reckon he's goin'?"

Will finished chewing, swallowed, took a sip of tea. "Judging by the smile on his face I'd say he's going up there to kill Douglas. He's been wanting to do it for a long time."

Five minutes later Barefoot came back, whistling happily. "Pack up your stuff, Will. We just quit."

He was serious. It was an epiphany, he said—the pieces of a plan had all fallen into place in his mind in one bright flash of inspiration, and in typical Barefoot fashion he had acted on the impulse before the fire in his belly had time to cool. His grandfather had died the year before, leaving his father a huge chunk of land which he had recently sold for a small fortune. Barefoot's father had no idea what to do with money—he'd never had much of it—so he had bought a new truck and put the rest in the bank. The money was just sitting there waiting. And when Barefoot heard himself say that things would make sense around here if he were in charge, he realized all of a sudden that he meant it. He really did know how to build a bridge and how to manage men. It all made sense. It had the ring of truth to it, of destiny.

It was a measure of Will's faith in Barefoot that he didn't say a word. He just packed up the remains of his lunch and followed.

## CHAPTER 22

*November 1953*

In all his experience with the Army, and in the year he'd migrated south working the crops, Will had never encountered a foreman, an officer, or a farmer who ran things the way Barefoot did. Even Abel Elliot, though he looked on Will like a son, had kept a close watch on him. Barefoot did not.

"I don't have time to bird-dog my men," he told Will. "I figure if I hire the right people to start with, all I gotta do is keep 'em supplied. If you got the right horse you never have to go to the whip."

"Fine for horses," Will said. "People, you can't trust."

"Most of 'em, you can. People generally *want* to do right till they find out you don't trust them. If you want a man to be trustworthy, trust him."

"Good way to get burned."

"Yep. It's also how you find good men. It just takes a little patience, that's all."

The postwar boom hit the Atlanta area hard, and within a year Barefoot Bridge was running two crews. Will ran one, and Barefoot hired an old hand away from Stanford to run the other one. Barefoot personally kept both jobs supplied with material, plus he did his own estimating and bidding on new work, so he only spent a couple of hours a day in the field.

His philosophy was radical, his results miraculous. Barefoot behaved as if he was a low-level employee, and somehow this made his employees behave as if they owned the company. There was no turnover; when Barefoot hired a man and trained him, he stayed. The guys on the job worked harder than they ever had in their lives, and applied themselves in ways they had never done before. Barefoot made it clear that he trusted every man on his job and expected every one of them, as far as his experience allowed, to make his own decisions. No more wasting time hunting down the boss for unnecessary instructions.

"If you know what to do, then do it. If you know what you need, go get it. Make a mistake and we'll fix it, and there won't be no finger-pointing or threatening either. It's cheaper to fix a mistake every now and then than to have a whole crew workin' at half speed," Barefoot said. If a man got sick, Barefoot paid him until he got well, and the men were so grateful they didn't get sick. It was said that if a man laid out on one of Barefoot's jobs you'd likely find him in the hospital. If they hired a guy and he turned out to be a slacker, the other men ran him off. Men who had been slackers with other companies worked hard for Barefoot, even when nobody was looking.

Barefoot Bridge quickly built a reputation for finishing jobs ahead of time and under budget. The company made money, Barefoot made money, and his men made money. In his first year as a foreman with Barefoot Bridge, Will's Christmas bonus was enough to make a down payment on thirty acres of land out in the country south of town. He had lived in the cramped little duplex for almost three years, scraping against his boundaries like a caged animal and listening to his neighbors fight on the other side of a thin wall. He couldn't take another year of it. As soon as he could he bought a used house trailer and moved his family down to "the farm."

Even with the raise Barefoot gave him, Will couldn't afford to build a house until the land was paid for, so he found a thousand ways to improve the place without spending money. He marked off a huge garden plot and worked it as if his family would starve without it, tilling the soil by hand and planting long rows of corn and beans and peas and potatoes and squash and tomatoes. He grew more than they could eat, more even than they could can or freeze, but it didn't matter. They ate what they could, gave some away, sold some, and Helen canned the rest. Helen taught him the joys of a sandwich made from a homegrown tomato so big that one slice covered the bread, and so ripe that he had to stand over the sink to eat it. In the summertime he would come home from a hard day on the bridge and go straight to his garden, where he would weed and water and prune—and pick whatever was ripe until the light failed and he could no longer see to pick. He planted pecans in coffee cans, and through the winter lined the windows of the trailer with seedlings. Come spring, the pecan seedlings lined the driveway.

In the wintertime he didn't get home until dark every day, but on weekends he would go to the pine grove on the back of his land, cut sawtimber, and then use his truck to drag the logs up near the house trailer. He rigged a few lights out back so that in the evenings, as soon as he had finished supper, he could put on his coat and go out to trim logs. Squaring the great pine logs by hand with a broadax, he nicked each side at precise intervals the width of his wrist and then sliced off the nicks to leave a smooth, flat side. He laid out a nice level lattice of slats, stacked his finished timbers on them and then wedged them tightly against each other to prevent warping. He shaved the bark and set it aside for the flower beds in the spring.

It was a good time, a busy time, a time of forgetting. Yet there were winter evenings when the cold crept into him and he would build a small fire, feeding it with trimmings and slabs. Sometimes he would take a break to stand by the fire and warm his hands and smoke a cigarette. In the fierce lonesome pride of those still moments in the firelight, surveying his property and the lit windows of the modest mobile home where his own small family lived in relative comfort, fed by the produce of his own two hands, he could not keep his father out of his mind. Even then, a thousand miles and a thousand light-years away from Levi Mullet, sometimes Will gazed into the fire and saw before his face the flame of a single match flickering in the breath of his father's condemnation. Even then some small part of him understood that it was no slavish ambition that drove him to work so hard, but a deep and festering need to prove something. "I'm still alive," he would whisper as he flipped a cigarette butt into the embers, then he would tug his gloves from his coat pocket and go back to work.

By the end of the first winter he had squared and cured enough timbers to begin work on his barn. He made no drawings or sketches. So clearly could he see the vision of his barn that he could count the beams in his head. He knew how many he would need, what girth and what length. When he had stockpiled what he needed he sold off the remainder of the sawtimber in the pine grove, took the money to an auction and used it to buy an old tractor with a cutting harrow and a bush-hog.

CHAPTER | 23

*July 1957*

As soon as Will paid off the land he took out a permit to build a
house, then borrowed a backhoe from work and dug his own
footings. He chose a site on a little rise in the pasture where two spreading
live oaks shaded the southern exposure, a perfect spot. As was his way, he
would do it all himself. What he didn't know about building a house he
would learn as he went, from books or from friends.

He started building with whatever materials he could buy out of
pocket, figuring that if he worked alone he couldn't go any faster than his
budget allowed anyway. His Amish blood balked at the notion of a mortgage until the framing sucked his savings dry. Even then he chose to borrow what he needed from Barefoot, whose bridge company was running
four crews and making more money than he could spend. Barefoot said
he was happy to loan Will the money interest-free because it would keep
Will beholden to him. It may have been the greatest tribute that Will
could offer a man that he didn't mind being beholden to Jubal Barefoot.

He'd kept in touch with Tobe over the years, writing letters three or
four times a year. Early on Tobe had pestered him to come up for a visit.

He refused, and eventually Tobe stopped asking. Tobe wanted to know all about the house, and Will kept him posted on the progress. As soon as it was framed and roofed and all dried in, Tobe insisted on building the cabinets. Will sent him the dimensions, and in the summer, when the kitchen walls were ready, Tobe and Sylvia and the girls loaded a utility trailer with cabinets and tools, hitched it behind his brand-new '57 Chevy, and came down to Georgia for a good long visit.

It had been almost six years, and Tobe's letters had been Will's only contact with Ohio in all that time. He didn't realize how badly he had missed his little brother until Tobe rolled up in the yard with Sylvia beside him and two little girls in the back. Will was on an extension ladder at the time, nailing up gutters. When he saw the car and trailer coming up the drive he got so excited he rushed down the ladder, missed a step and fell sprawling in the front yard, then jumped up and *ran* to meet the car.

It seemed to Will that he had lowered his head in concentration for a little while—where had the time gone?—and when he looked up, Tobe's infant girl, Hannah, had been replaced by a six-year-old streak of light who ran everywhere she went, trailing laughter like a comet. Rachel, a four-year-old clone of her sister, was still attached to her mother's skirts. At first she only peeked out with wondering eyes from behind Sylvia, watching her sister cavort with Welch and Riley as if she'd known them all her life, but by evening she had joined the fray.

The two girls arrived wearing nice new print dresses down almost to their ankles, hair pinned neatly into a bun under a downsized Mennonite covering at the back of the head, but the next morning they turned up for breakfast wearing hand-me-down T-shirts and jeans from the bag of stuff the boys had outgrown. Wavy, corn-silk hair that had never known scissors spilled over the girls' shoulders, liberated. Helen and Sylvia exchanged a wry, conspiratorial grin. They were breaking rules, but they were a thousand miles from watchful eyes. Even Sylvia let her hair down.

Unloading the cabinets from the trailer, Will paused as he passed by Tobe's new car and took time to admire it. It was shiny and new and flashy with its eggcrate grill. Apart from an impressive amount of gleaming chrome, the car was solid black from top to bottom, and yet something about it looked odd. There was a fingernail scratch on the roof, and white paint showed through the scratch. Will leaned in for a closer look and ran a finger over the scratch. His finger came away with flakes of black on it. Looking closely at the top of the car he saw that it had been painted over, and none too professionally. There were drips and runs.

He frowned. "Tobe, did you paint this?"

Tobe grinned sheepishly. "Oh, yeah, well, just the roof, you know. They made me. We can't have a white roof."

The Mennonite order to which Tobe and Sylvia belonged allowed their people to own a car, but it had to be black. *Solid* black.

"You mean to tell me when you bought the car it had a white roof and they made you paint it?"

Tobe nodded. "I just bought it a couple weeks ago. It was so pretty I thought maybe they wouldn't say anything, but they did. I didn't want to put it in the shop because I was afraid it wouldn't get done in time for this trip, so I had to spray it myself. After we get back I'll probably get somebody to do it right."

Will chuckled. "The more things change, the more they stay the same," he said.

It was a grand week. The kids kept themselves busy picking blueberries, chasing lizards, dropping ants in doodlebug holes in the barn, and playing in the creek that ran through the back of the property. Sylvia and Helen gabbed like sisters, picking and canning what seemed like a truckload of beans and peas, while Will and Tobe wrought miracles on the inside of the house.

They stained and varnished the cabinets on sawhorses in the barn. The varnish needed to cure for a day, so Sylvia and Helen talked the men into taking a day off and they all went up to Stone Mountain for a picnic. By the end of the week they had hung the kitchen cabinets, varnished the remainder of the hardwood floors, and laid the linoleum in the kitchen. Will and Tobe worked together in that rare union that exists only between brothers and the oldest of friends. Will would not speak of it—there were no words—but it nearly broke his heart. He had almost forgotten what it was like to have a brother.

In the evenings Will took Tobe around and showed off his place—the new barn, as yet unoccupied, the fence he was building, the lean-to chicken coop he had thrown together out of scraps against the end of the barn, the rows of blueberries, and the scuppernong arbor down near the pasture fence. He talked of his plans for a few cattle and showed Tobe the narrow place where he thought he might be able to bulldoze an earthen dam on the creek to make a fine little catfish pond.

The evening before Tobe was to go back home he and Will took a stroll out off the property to look over the surrounding countryside. They followed the dirt road in front of the house to the south for a few hundred yards to a place where the road turned aside and left them at the corner of a hundred-acre field. The field belonged to the Kilgore clan, and had been in their family for generations. Old man Kilgore used to grow cotton here, but he'd been dead for a long time and so the field lay fallow now, leached by years of runoff and stunted by drought so that even the weeds didn't grow very high anymore. His heirs planted thousands of pine saplings along the edge of the field and left them to grow up dense and untended, choked with blackberry brambles, a forbidding hedge punctuated here and there by the worn pathways of rabbit, raccoon, and possum. On a summer evening the air was heavy with the cloying scent of pine and the drone of cicadas.

Over time, the place where the field met the pine thicket had become a dumping ground where the flotsam of a wasteful civilization washed up, as if on a night tide. Along the edge of the field Tobe stopped often to poke at things with his foot—a red beer can sun-bleached to a dull pink, a lonely shapeless brown shoe, a pair of frayed tires brimming with brackish water and mosquito larvae. Farther along, the debris got bigger—the rusted-out hulk of a washing machine, a disemboweled mattress, a faded sofa impaled by a cracked wooden oar someone had jammed into it like a mast, canting ten degrees to port.

They walked a little farther and Tobe stopped to poke at a rusty galvanized wash tub full of weeds. He gave it a little kick and sent a swarm of grasshoppers buzzing off to look for a new home. A weather-gray oblong wooden box in the bracken caught his eye and he carefully parted the thorny blackberry stalks to look at it.

He smiled. "A rabbit box," he said. "Some farm boy must have forgot where he put it."

Will pressed the blackberries aside with his boot and stepped in for a look.

"The trap door is closed. Looks like he caught something." He reached down and slid the wooden door up from the front of the box, revealing the narrow interior. A dry tuft of rabbit fur rolled out, lurched on the breeze and caught itself on a briar. Leaning further, he could make out the shapeless, long-dead remains of a small rabbit bunched in the back of the box.

"I guess he never came back to check. Shame," he said, and slid the door back down.

Tobe eased out of the bracken and continued on his meandering course, a new sadness in his eyes. He was a born rabbit hunter; he would kill a rabbit, but he would not waste one.

The light wind that had blown all afternoon dwindled as the sun dropped below the treetops. Tobe was quiet, wading through the field chewing on a long straw he had plucked as he walked. The trapped and forgotten rabbit had said something to him, and Will waited to see what it was.

Finally, Tobe spoke. "So, when are you going to come up to Ohio for a visit?" The sadness in his eyes came out in his voice as if he already knew the answer.

Will sighed, squinting into the setting sun. "I guess I'll have to start watching the weather on TV," he said, and then ducked his head and moved on. He felt Tobe staring at his back.

"Why?"

"So I'll know when hell's going to freeze over," Will answered.

Tobe thrashed through the weeds until he caught up. "You'd walk away from your whole family forever because of Dad?"

"Dad, Mattie, Katie—take your pick." Then he let out an exasperated sigh and puffed, "*Yes*, because of Dad. The man hates me."

"You haven't seen him in six years. Things change."

"I didn't see him for *eight* years before I went home the first time, and it didn't turn out so good. The man hates me."

"Hates you. *Pah!* There are worse things than hate."

"I'm not going back, and that's the end of it."

"No, that's not the end of it. You're right, he hates you, but that's not the end of it. He still grinds his teeth when he thinks about you, every day. Every day, Will. He thinks about you *every day*! No man spends fourteen years being mad at somebody he don't care about."

Will walked on in silence for a little ways, the scent of a burning match seeping from his memory.

"Yeah, well, I gave him the chance to say how much he cared, and he said his piece. I think he made it pretty clear."

Tobe snorted. "You think he would say it? You ought to know our father better than that. He's Levi Mullet—he's got to be *right*. If it meant the end of the world he'd have to be right, yet."

An old anger flared inside Will, welled up so that he felt the pressure of it behind his eyes and along the edges of his ears.

"How is he *right*? How is it right to allow bundling and then condemn the ones who get in trouble with it? If you give a teenage boy a bottle of liquor and a car, are you *right* to disown him when he has a wreck?"

Tobe shook his head. "Right, wrong—I don't know these things. I don't really think any of us is right, but I think if you stay mad because of what happened, then you're no different than he is. You're judging him, too."

Will turned his back and walked away. They were nearing the far corner of the field where a patch of English ivy encroached from the shadows under a stand of massive white oaks. The home that had been here years before had burned, leaving only a chimney rising like a gaunt gravestone among the trees. Will saw something in the ivy a few yards away, curved pieces of steel standing in a row, like ribs. Stepping high, he waded in to look at it and found a busted old spring-toothed plow.

Tobe came up behind him. "You can't just let it go like this, Will." He spoke quietly now, a small voice in the fading light.

Will didn't answer right away. The plow at his feet must have been twelve feet wide when it was in one piece, but now it lay piled upon itself in an awkward way that made it hard to measure. Great spring-steel tines curved upward to end in spade-shaped teeth that once scratched miles of furrows in the earth like a giant claw.

"Why not?" he finally said. "Why shouldn't I just let it go? I'm doing okay so far. Besides, what did *you* ever get out of going back home? He didn't exactly welcome you back with open arms, did he?"

Tobe took a moment to answer. He wasn't used to thinking things out.

"I'm not sure," he said quietly. "But I know I had to go home. I *had* to. I couldn't stand being without a name, without . . . boundaries. I had to be attached to something, to *come* from something. I can't explain it right because I just don't have the words like some people, but I know when I was out there like you, I could have been *anything*, and it would have meant nothing. It was like being alone in the middle of an ocean. How do you know who you are, or what you are, or how big you are, if you can't see anything but yourself?"

Will rocked one end of the broken plow with his boot and there was a protest of anguished metal as the pieces ground against each other. In Will's mind, Tobe had always been the good-natured oaf. Now his mind would have to be rearranged, because Tobe's simple words revealed a piercing wisdom.

"I had to have something to measure myself against, even if I came up short," Tobe said, chuckling. "If the Old Man is hard, well, I guess I can live with that. But, Will, *everything we are* comes from there. You can't just let it go."

The vines had nearly claimed the plow. The once proud steel was pitted and flaked and brittle, coated with rust the texture of dry coffee grounds. It was easy to see what had killed it. A thick steel pipe ran through the center of it like a spar, holding everything together until it buckled and broke, right in the middle. The plow could have lost any other part and still functioned, however poorly, but when the thing that held it together failed, it wasn't a plow anymore. It was scrap iron.

"All right then," Will said. "All right. I'll try."

He returned to Ohio in the fall, just before Thanksgiving. He would have gone sooner or later anyway because he said he would, and his word had made it law in his own mind. He would try. But he had used up his vacation while working on the house, so he figured they'd wait until the following summer to make the first trip, after the boys were out of school. His plans changed when the phone rang at midnight and Sylvia said, in a hoarse whisper, for a whisper was all she had left, "Tobe is dead." There had been an accident, she said. Hunting. In a voice wrung dry by shock and grief she gave scant details. Tobe was following his dogs up a steep bank at the edge of a wood, a log broke loose and rolled over him, and now he was gone.

CHAPTER | 24

*January 1985*

T his is it," Will says, as soon as they top the rise and the Mullet farm comes into view. He has had to direct his son at every turn. Riley has no idea where he is.

The car slows, turns in. The driveway has been shoveled down and packed hard, so there is no crunch of gravel as Riley eases up between the main house and the smaller *dawdi haus* Levi built for himself when he sold Mose the farm. There are already a few cars and several large vans parked beside the driveway beyond the barn. Riley finds a spot and pulls in. A Haflinger colt peers over the pasture fence at them for a moment, then tosses his blond mane and trots off down a trail he has packed in the snow. There are more buggies than cars, lined up on the slope beside the barn wall with their shafts resting on the ground, waiting. The horses have been unhitched and stalled.

"He'll be in the dawdi haus," Will says. This day will be given to visitation and viewing in the dawdi haus, and the funeral tomorrow will be held across the drive in the much larger main house. Maybe it's because of Riley, whose nervous glances give him the uncertain look of a man dunked suddenly into a foreign culture, that Will has become keenly aware of everything in the moment. Coming up the drive he has already seen that the front porch and walk of the dawdi haus are cleared of snow, but the door is closed and there is no place to pile boots and coats. Such things would have been thought about. Plans would have been made. The family will have made arrangements for the large group of people they know are coming, through bitter cold and snow. If there is no provision at the front door for the wiping of feet and removing of boots, then Will knows the entrance will be found in the back of the dawdi haus. He doesn't know whether it is tradition or common sense that shows him these things, or if it even matters. To an Amish mind, tradition is the wife of common sense.

The first thing he sees out back is a rented Jiffy Johnny standing well out from the house. Mose and his family still don't have a toilet in either of the houses, but they know there will be a crowd here over the next two days, so they have made provisions. A tent-like structure runs out twenty feet from the back door of the dawdi haus, blue plastic tarps lashed to pipe. Inside it, tables line the temporary walls, piled with hats and coats. A long row of galoshes rests underneath, accounting for the smell of manure in the air. A rubber mat has been rolled down the aisle, and a thick rug lies before the door.

The tarp walls heave and luff in a light wind, softly—*flup*. A bright sun floods the space with blue light. There are a half-dozen people in the makeshift vestibule, all middle-aged couples, bearded men and bell-shaped women. Will cannot tell at first whether they are coming or going, taking off coats or putting them on, for they stop what they are doing when he and Riley come in, and stare at him. He pumps each hand once, and greets them in Dutch. He recognizes one of them, a cousin, and stops to make small talk for a minute. They exchange *"Wie gehts?"* and Will learns that Reuben, the cousin, has bought a farm down off of Carr Road, near the old Byler place. Through it all Riley remains silent, watchful.

Inside the house the air is close and too warm, overlaid with the petroleum residue of kerosene lanterns and oil lamps. Every room is lined with benches, and the benches are lined with people. Everyone is talking, low voices mingling into a general buzz. The large kitchen has been cleared of table and chairs to make room for more benches, and the young ones have gathered there—teenagers and the unmarried—boys on one side, girls on the other. The boys are wearing their Sunday-best black and white, with vests. The girls look the way they always look in public—trim and neat, hair precisely parted under the stiff white covering, capes crisply pressed. Will waves and smiles at them, and many of them return the gesture with an unfeigned gladness he doesn't see among teenagers in the World these days. He recognizes most of them, the grandchildren and great-grandchildren of Levi Mullet.

A path has been left open into the next room, which is warmer still. The wood stove throws off too much heat for such a small house with so many people in it. The grown-ups have gathered here in the living room, and it is a social time. Most are sitting on the benches, but it's not the stiff-backed, attentive, Sunday service kind of sitting. They move and talk, turn this way and that, get up and go across the room to speak with someone, and yet they keep the loose order of the benches and keep the women mostly separate from the men.

He looks everywhere, but Clara is not here yet, nor any of her daughters. Two of his younger sisters have come—Ada Mae and Amanda. Alma lives in Montana and couldn't get here because of weather. Will's mother bore Mose, Clara, Will and Tobe, in that order, before she died.

The others are all Elizabeth's children. The younger girls are Will's half sisters, Elizabeth's daughters, too young to remember when he lived in the same house with them. He knows them mostly from visits in recent years, and they seem more like cousins than sisters. He speaks to each of them, but in the end he is still looking for Clara.

Nor does he see Mose, though the younger brothers are present. They too are half brothers, and old enough to share some memories with Will. One by one they spot him, rise from their places and, smiling, come to greet him.

Daniel, ever the silent one, pumps Will's hand without a word and turns to Riley. Now in his late fifties, Daniel has aged into a dignity he did not possess in his youth. Like Mose, he is taller than the others. His beard is long, his hair thick. The gray in his hair complements his deep blue eyes. The crescent shaped "donkey scar" from his childhood still puckers the skin above his left eye, distorting the eyebrow slightly. Will can see from Daniel's expression that he doesn't recognize Riley, so he introduces them.

Daniel nods. "Long time," he rumbles, pumping Riley's hand firmly, once.

Ben and Samuel are more gregarious, even now aware of their position as the youngest, the mischief-makers of their generation, but for now they are on their best behavior. Shorter even than Will, their diminutive size only adds to their impish reputation. They look alike, except that Ben has put on a few pounds around the middle from working in an office. They ask after Helen and Welch, and when Will explains about the winter storm they want to know all about the weather along the route.

"There was a lot of ice on the trees coming through Kentucky," Will says. "Power lines down. Lights out everywhere."

His brothers nod gravely, faces lined with real concern for thousands of people without electricity in the bitter cold, even though a power outage is a nonissue among the Amish.

Will remembers an ice storm when he was little, and the aftertaste is one of awe and beauty. The glazing of the trees posed no threat, except maybe to a fence here and there where a limb might crack and fall from an overburdened pine. The earth was merely trying on a different suit of clothes—a very fancy suit. He remembers going out with his father to check the fence line, riding high on Levi's shoulders, and the memory sparkled like a moment from a dream.

Mose appears suddenly from the bedroom on the right and comes straight to Will. By now Will has figured out that the bedroom is where his father's body lies.

"Will, I'm sure happy to see you," Mose says. "Riley, I heard that you were driving up with your dad. Helen called the neighbors' house last night, and sent a message she was sorry she couldn't be here. It's good what you are doing, helping your dad make the trip with the bad roads and all."

Riley smiles awkwardly and shrugs it off.

Mose's beard has finally gone solid gray, though his face is perhaps redder and ruddier than ever. His shoulders are still broad and strong, despite his being sixty-five, and he still has that twinkle in his eye. "Well, come on then. You'll be wanting to visit Dad."

Mose leads him into the bedroom where their father's body lies. The curtains are drawn and the room is lit by kerosene lamps. Levi's remains are not in a coffin yet. That will come tomorrow morning. For now they have removed the bed and built a waist-high bier of planks in the center of the room, covering it with a navy blue sheet that swags to the floor.

Levi, dressed in a simple white shirt and black coat, is stretched out on the makeshift platform with his hands folded on his chest. A blanket covers him from the waist down.

Mose and Will stand on opposite sides of the body, and Will is there for a minute before he becomes aware that it's Daniel standing beside him, and not Riley. Leaning back to look around his taciturn brother, Will sees that Riley has chosen to remain in the living room talking to Ben and Samuel, his hands in the pockets of his coat. Riley is still wearing his coat despite the stifling warmth in the dawdi haus, and he remains standing. He glances into the bedroom once, briefly. Will wonders if Ben and Samuel see the hint of fear in Riley's eyes.

Levi seems so small now. He looks like a wax figure. Even his hands could be wax hands with makeup on them. Mose fusses with the black coat, picking away a piece of lint and straightening the sleeves at the wrists. The shoulders of the coat seem tented, hollow. Levi's face is smooth and unreal, most of the wrinkles having fallen out of it so that it looks waxy like his hands. His face—that's the thing. The shrinking of muscle and bone in old age and the wasting of his body by disease—these things are to be expected. But no matter the weather, Levi Mullet's face had never, ever, been slack.

CHAPTER | 25

November 1957

I t rained the morning of Tobe's funeral. A close, malignant sky
dumped a cold flood on the drab November landscape. Will leaned
forward trying to see between slaps of the windshield wipers while a radio
commentator voiced shrill warnings about the Red menace. The Russians
had successfully launched a dog into space on Sputnik II and the day was
not far off, the commentator said, when they would aim an atomic missile
at the Capitol rotunda. Helen turned off the radio.

They arrived late to the Mennonite church building where the funeral
was held, to avoid the inevitable controversy over where they should sit.
They slipped in and sat on the back row. When it was over they were the
first ones out the door. At graveside the rain and the umbrellas gave Will
ample separation from his brothers. Throughout the entire funeral he
managed, somehow, to be there without being there.

Later, he drove over to Sylvia's in a drumming downpour that forced
him to go slowly, for he could see only a few yards ahead. It occurred to
him then that driving through a downpour somehow defined his very life,

and Tobe's death served as a jolting reminder that he had *never* been able to see very far ahead.

Apart from whatever she whispered to her daughters as they came, often, to hold on to her the day of the funeral, Sylvia didn't say three words. But the next day she invited Will and Helen and the boys for lunch, then held her head up and told them in a clear voice that she would be moving back home. She had spoken to her father, and he had promised to take care of her and her daughters. With Tobe gone, she had no way of making a living. Oh, she could clean houses or take in laundry, but with two girls to feed she knew she could never keep up the mortgage or the utility payments on the house that Tobe had built for them. So her father had offered her a place to live and a way to work and eat and dress her daughters, if only she would return to the Old Order church.

Sylvia had consented. She would sell the house and the car, and she had already arranged for various of Tobe's friends to come by in the next day or two and make offers on his tools and his guns. She asked Will to stay long enough to supervise the selling of Tobe's things because he would know better what they were worth.

He did as she asked. It was the least he could do. Helen hovered over Sylvia and took care of Hannah and Rachel as often as they'd let her. Will spent most of the next couple of days in Tobe's shop dealing with men who stopped to buy what Tobe had left behind. He prepared himself to argue with some of them—he would not sell his brother's things too cheaply—but it turned out not to be necessary. Most of the men who came to buy had been friends of Tobe and Sylvia, and Will found himself in the awkward position of wanting to tell one or two of them that they were offering far too much. Most of the tools in the shop sold for three times what they were worth.

Tobe had kept his guns in a locked cabinet in his shop, and Will sold these as well. Tobe's favorite shotgun, an old double-barrel 12 gauge he used for rabbit hunting, went for four hundred dollars. Will held the gun, fitted the stock to his shoulder and sighted down between the barrels, broke it open and held it up to the light to look through the spotless chambers, and almost decided not to sell it. The gun wasn't worth four hundred dollars—it wasn't worth half that—but it was Tobe's favorite gun. Holding it brought back memories of hunting with their father when he and Tobe were small. Levi only owned one shotgun, and he never owned a bird dog because he said it didn't earn its keep most of the year. Come pheasant season, Levi would walk the fields with his shotgun at the ready while various of his sons circled like dogs through hay and heather, trying to kick up pheasants. From the time they were very small Levi taught his sons to sing out when a hen burst from hiding so he could check his fire. By law, he was only allowed to take male pheasants. There were times when he shot the hens anyway, and then blamed it on his boys, saying they were too slow in singing out. But as they grew accustomed to the hunt they noticed that Levi only took hens late in a luckless day, when there were no pheasants in the bag. It seemed the law was malleable when it came to feeding a family.

Will didn't have four hundred dollars to buy Tobe's shotgun, and Tobe's wife and kids needed the money. Reluctantly, he parted with it.

Tobe was present in a million little ways. Will saw him everyplace— in the wooden handle of a miter saw worn to a burgundy sheen from long use, in the haphazard drawings and indecipherable figures scratched on scraps of paper and stuffed into a desk drawer, in the faded sepia picture of Tobe grinning into the camera with his shotgun on his shoulder in a field someplace, at dusk.

The picture conjured Tobe's voice from another field at dusk.

*"You've got to try, Will."*

"My no is no, and my yes is yes," Will said, out loud, to the picture. "I said I would try. I will try."

The next morning he left Helen and the boys at Sylvia's and drove over to his father's house alone. Apart from the odd glimpse during Tobe's funeral, he had seen his father precisely once in fourteen years—the night of the match. His father had caught him off guard that time. This time would be different. This time he would go to his father to pay his respects and nothing more. Gone were the naïve expectations of the prodigal returning with hat in hand, all full of apology and hope. Gone were the illusions that his father would welcome his wife and children into the clan, different though they may be. Gone was the childlike dream that something in his life and accomplishments might be worthy of a pat on the back from his dad. Gone was the child.

There had been a hard white frost that morning—a killing frost, the first of the year—but the sun had melted it and by midmorning the temperature climbed above fifty degrees, a fine autumn day. Pulling in, Will could see two boys, probably his nephews, unloading green cornstalks from a wagon near the silo and feeding them into the big steam-driven chopper the family shared with a co-op—making silage. The boys stared for a moment, waved, and went back to work.

He parked the car and walked to the back of the barn, looking out over the fields. A large box wagon sat on the edge of the cornfield about halfway out, hitched to a team of Percherons who nuzzled the ground between the shocks, looking for stray ears. From such a distance he couldn't be sure, but it looked like Ben and Samuel and another man bending between shocks the color of dry wheat, pitching ears of shucked corn into the stake-side wagon. The two horses stirred, all on their own, without anyone touching them or the check lines. They leaned patiently into their load and pulled ahead fifteen or twenty feet, then stopped. A small pride welled up in Will when he saw that—just that one little thing—because he remembered. The workhorses were so well trained they could be started and stopped and held in place with nothing more than clucks and whistles. He was twelve the first time his dad turned him loose by himself to cultivate a cornfield with a team of Belgians even bigger than these massive white Percherons.

"They need to keep them horses out of that corn," a deep voice said from behind him.

Mose had come out from the barn, dirty and sweaty from his labors, his shirttail out. His face had widened and leathered a bit, but it was the same old Mose.

"I been gettin' the barn ready for winter," he said, offering a grimy hand. His gaze returned to the wagon in the cornfield. "I told Ben and Sam not to let them horses fill up on that corn. Too much moisture in it yet. Cows can eat it okay, but the horses don't know when to stop."

Will nodded. Mose knew why he was here—it was in his eyes. Will said nothing, and waited.

"I seen you at the funeral," said Mose. "You know, you coulda mebbe come up and set with your brothers—what's left of 'em. Bench seems a little bit long now, without you and Tobe."

Will pondered this. "I just didn't think it was a good time to try and . . . uh, you know, with Dad there and all."

"I'm thinking you should go and talk to him. He's in his cobbler shop." Mose glanced over his shoulder toward the corner of the buggy shed. "He fell off the thresher a couple years ago and busted his knee up pretty bad.

Not much use in the field anymore, so he took up fixing shoes to keep his hands busy. Jemima Hostetler's in there right now, but she won't stay long. If you wait till she's gone, why, mebbe you could catch him in there alone."

Mose owned a knowledge of his father that no one else could approach, and it was a plain fact that he wouldn't plant seed without first preparing the ground. If Mose was prodding Will toward his father it meant he had already spent some time softening the old man up for just such a moment.

"Okay," Will said. "I'll give it a try."

He found Levi's cobbler shop in the corner of the buggy shed, with windows on two sides and glass panes in the top half of the door to let in plenty of light. Will hadn't noticed it as he drove by because of the solitary buggy blocking the view from the front, a black standard-bred horse tied to the hitching rail. Through the window Will could see Mrs. Hostetler's back, and he could tell she was talking. She was always talking. He remembered Jemima Hostetler from when she was a girl, nine children and a hundred pounds ago. Her last name was Weaver then, and she was the biggest gossip in six counties, even before she was married. On an impulse, he decided to go on in.

It was a stroke of genius, making his entrance while Jemima was there. Levi would be forced to control his temper and mind his words. Levi and Jemima faced each other across the worktable, both of them in line with the door, so that Levi couldn't see him at all until he had stepped inside and closed the door. Will went quickly to the far end of the long worktable and pretended an interest in the shoemaker's tools he found there.

Jemima and Levi paid no attention to him at first because they were busy glaring at each other over the pair of shoes sitting precisely between them on the worktable. If they glanced at him at all, they didn't recognize him. Morning sunlight angled sharply through the window, falling on the shoes and on Levi's gnarled hands.

Jemima clutched her change purse at her ample waist and spoke to Levi in Dutch. "Still, I don't see why I would pay that when it's more than these old shoes are worth. For that, I could almost buy new ones."

Leaning on his palms on the edge of the table, Levi tilted himself a bit farther toward her and said, "Do, then. Go and buy some new shoes for five dollars. And when you find them, let me know where they are because I want to buy some too!"

"These aren't worth five dollars." Jemima's bottom jaw protruded just a bit, and her eyes widened in outrage as her fists closed tighter on her purse.

"They are now. They have new soles on them—just like you *asked* me to do!"

"Well, you didn't tell me it would cost five dollars!"

"You didn't ask me that. You just said put new soles on them."

"I won't pay it."

"Then you won't have your shoes back."

"Well then, Mister Mullet, you can just keep these old shoes yourself until you change your mind."

Will could tell she wanted to add "You old mule!" though she didn't say it. She thought about it, but it was at that point that she and Levi began to feel uncomfortable arguing in front of the English man who had come in without saying anything and now stood waiting at the other end of the worktable. They both turned and stared at Will.

It took her a few seconds to recognize him, and when she did she gasped.

"Ohhh!" she cried, pointing him out with a wagging finger as if Levi were blind, "Will Mullet! Levi, that's your son, Will! Oh, my! How long has it been?"

As quickly as Jemima's face had flown open, Levi's closed. He regarded Will with thinly veiled contempt.

"Well," he said, "his name is Will, anyway. You got that much right."

His tone was unmistakable. Jemima glanced from father to son and back, and then her smile disappeared and her head dropped. She was a member of Levi's church, and Will Mullet was banned. She wasn't even supposed to be speaking to him. She started to say something to Will, then to Levi, but in the end she swallowed it all and said nothing. She lowered her eyes and quietly let herself out, leaving the shoes on the table and her money in her change purse.

Levi picked up the shoes, turned about and put them high on a shelf behind him. When he turned back to the table he didn't look at Will. His mouth hardened into a narrow line, and his black eyes stared at his fists on the edge of the table. His chin moved slowly, side to side, the movement accentuated by the wagging of his beard.

*"Du bist faflucht!"* He spat the words at his clenched fists—*You are cursed!*

Will's fingers picked through the tools on the table—gouges, punches, a couple of edge irons and curved sewing awls, a half-moon knife—all with good stout handles of maple and rosewood. Levi Mullet always invested in good tools, made to last a long time. He did nothing in half measures.

"It's been fourteen years," Will said, his voice even and calm. "I thought maybe we could at least speak to each other."

Levi raised his eyes then, and they burned. "Would we have something to say to one another? What has light to do with darkness?"

Will picked up an awl, the handle burnished from long use, and jabbed it absently into a little triangle-shaped scrap of leather on the table.

"Blood is blood," he said softly. "I'm still your son, no matter what the church says."

"A question is in my mind." Levi's face shook with suppressed rage. "Was it the church that changed your *name*?"

Will twisted the awl, boring a little hole through the scrap of leather. He had stopped trying to meet his father's glare.

"Okay," he finally said, nodding slowly. "I know I've done wrong, and I deserve whatever you have to say to me. I can't fix any of it—not one little bit. I can't undo anything, and believe me, I've carried my sins long enough to know the weight of them. But listen. You can go on and live your life minus a son because you have plenty of sons—"

"Not so many now, because of you," Levi said, and it hit Will suddenly that Levi blamed him for Tobe's death. He would never come right out and say it, for it would be presumptuous, but in Levi's mind it was perfectly plausible that God would strike down a wayward son, and he had always believed that Will led Tobe astray. Levi's only question would have to do with God's choice of wayward sons.

Will stopped twisting the awl, laid it gently on top of the leather scrap, and looked up to meet his father's eyes.

"Well, I have only one father. You can say what you like about me— *do* what you like—but I won't run away anymore. I'm through running away. All I can say is I'm sorry for what I've done."

Levi's lip twitched. His eyes flared.

"Talk," he said. "Chust talk. Words, from a boy whose god is his belly.

If I wanted to know the truth about a man, why, I'll watch to see what he does."

The stone denial in Levi's face told Will that further conversation was useless. Deciding he had already said what he came to say, he reached for the doorknob and then turned to look at his father once more.

"I'll be coming back," he said. "I want you to meet your daughter-in-law and your grandsons. They're good people, no matter the company they keep. Not now, I guess, because I'm sure you'll need some time to get used to the idea. But I'll be coming back."

Levi would say nothing else. Will closed the door softly and walked away.

Mose was waiting for him, leaning against the car. "Must not have gone too bad," Mose said. His wide hat tilted and he stared at Will's neck. "I don't see any tooth marks."

Will smiled a sad little half smile and looked back over his shoulder. "He really hates me."

Mose smiled too, and there was weariness in it. "Ja. So I'm thinking there's still a little hope."

"Yeah, that's what Tobe said." Will wondered if his older brother had come to the same understanding on his own or if his younger brother had given it to him. He missed Tobe terribly. Three days, and he was only just beginning to probe the edges of the hole torn in his heart by his brother's death.

"Let's go inside the house," Mose said, glancing sideways at the cobbler shop. "He won't come out now until you're gone, so I'm thinking mebbe this would be the time to go and say hullo to Elizabeth and the girls."

CHAPTER | 26

January 1985

Standing beside their father's body in the bedroom of the dawdi haus, the brothers talk for a bit. Mose and Daniel relax in Will's company and begin wandering down old rabbit trails, talking in subdued tones as if the old man is merely sleeping and they don't want to wake him. Yet there is a liveliness in them. They will not be loud or boisterous, but neither are they morose. They have done all they can and therefore have nothing to fear, nothing to be ashamed of.

It strikes Will that the laws and rituals his brothers have observed with such diligence all their lives shine with purpose in moments like these. They are connected somehow to a greater truth, and they know it in their bones. They know that a man should not grieve overmuch, for that is a complaint against God. Nor should he forget the task at hand, for that is unfair to his brother. They will bury their father with dignity and dispatch because it is their proper duty, and they will teach their sons how to do it because the day will come when the task will fall to them.

Will remains beside his father's body only for a little while, glancing often toward his son in the next room. Riley's lofty cynicism and incisive wit are useless here. He seems as fragile as a bird in the company of these cast-iron people, as frail as Naomi.

"Where is Naomi?" Will asks suddenly. Something had been nagging at him since he arrived, though amid the storm of faces and memories it simply has not crystallized until now that he has not seen his stepmother, Levi's third and last wife. Levi married her in his seventies, a year after Elizabeth died, and moved off up to Geauga County to live with her.

"Oh, you didn't hear?" Mose's eyebrows go up. "She had to go home yesterday to see her heart doctor. She hired a driver to bring her down then, but he couldn't get out—the snow was too bad up there. This morning he made a go at it but ran off into a ditch and broke something under his van, so I don't know if she can find somebody else yet."

Will likes Naomi, always has. She's just a tiny sweet bird of a woman with a little chirp of a voice. She looks like Whistler's Mother.

"I don't have anything planned this afternoon," he says. "I could drive up and bring her down myself."

"Oh, no, I don't think you should go all the way up there, Will. It's eighty miles."

Will shrugs. "You don't need me here, and I don't have anything else to do. I'd like to go. Make myself useful."

"But they'll have another van before morning, for sure," Mose says. "The rest of them will want to be here too."

"They can still do that, but you know she'd like to be here now. She was his wife."

Mose finally gives in. He nods to Daniel, nothing more, and Daniel leaves. He'll take a bicycle down to the neighborhood phone shack to call a neighbor of Naomi's and relay the message.

While he's waiting Will goes out to mingle with the rest of the family, and he drags Riley into the corner to see his younger sisters. They have not seen Riley since he was a child—no one here has—but like everyone else they want most of all to tell him what a fine thing he has done, bringing his father all this way in bad weather. Riley shrugs it off. He doesn't really know what to do with a compliment. He doesn't hear many of them.

Samuel, Will's youngest brother, comes in from the kitchen with news. He finds Will and says, "One of Clara's boys is here and he told me Clara can't be coming until later. Katie might not make it at all, but she'll probably be at Toby's tonight. Me and Ben are coming too, I think."

Toby is Tobe's son—the one Tobe never met, born months after his father was killed in the hunting accident. He has a wife and child of his own now, along with a little plot of land containing a small house and the mobile home Sylvia lives in. Toby is Will's host while he and Riley stay at Sylvia's, but Will hasn't spoken with him since he called two days ago and made the arrangements to borrow the place.

"I haven't been invited to Toby's," Will says.

Samuel grins. "That's chust what I'm doing now. He told me to tell you to come at six-thirty for dinner."

Despite the circumstances, Will finds he is enjoying himself, hanging around talking to his brothers and sisters, nieces and nephews. It's clear that Riley isn't enjoying himself at all. He is edgy and uncomfortable around these people, and after a while he disappears.

Daniel comes back from the phone shack and finds Will. He's still puffing a little from the bicycle, and the cold air is still rolling off of him as he says in his blunt way, "You can go get Naomi if you want to. I talked to her neighbor and she said Naomi is there yet. She's gonna go up and tell her you'll come."

Will finds Riley out back by the Jiffy Johnny smoking a cigarette and staring at the horizon. When he walks up, Riley glances over at the plastic outhouse, blows a cloud of smoke and says, "I don't see how they live like this."

Will doesn't argue. He knows Riley's moods well enough to know that what's building inside him won't be pleasant.

"We can leave now," he says, and then explains about Naomi.

On the way to the car they pass by the buggy shed and Will stops. He doesn't say anything, he just stops in his tracks and stares at the door of the little shop in the corner of the building. He can see through the windows that what used to be a cobbler shop is now a tool shed, which explains why the walk is cleared right up to the door: they needed the shovels this morning. There hasn't been a cobbler shop here in ten years, not since Levi moved up to Geauga County to live with Naomi at the Kauffman farm.

"What?" Riley shivers slightly. It's cold out, and he's ready to get in the car and crank up the heater.

"Nothing. I was just wondering . . ." Will bites his lip. Surely not. "Hang on a minute," he says, starting for the door of the shop. "I just want to check something."

Riley follows him in. The oil and leather scent of the old cobbler shop is gone now, replaced even in dead winter by the dusty wasp-nest smell of a tool shed. Leaning in the corner of the room is a dense forest of cutting tools—double-bit axes, broadaxes, bush axes, pickaxes, splitting mauls, post-hole diggers—and an assortment of rakes and shovels hangs from a row of pegs. The worktable and all the cobbler's tools are gone without a trace—on an Amish farm a space like this will not be wasted—though the old shelves still stand against the back wall. The shelves are lined mostly with buckets and boxes of nails and screws, and various junk boxes containing bits of hardware, hinges and hasps.

Will reaches up to the top shelf and feels around behind a ten-pound bag of rock salt.

"What are you looking for?" Riley asks, but his question is answered when Will pulls down an old pair of shoes.

He holds them in the light from the window and blows off the dust, then swipes at the uppers with his fingers. They are clunky-looking black high-top shoes with flat heels, and they look to be fairly large for a woman. He turns the left one upside down and shakes out what appears to be a long-deserted mouse nest.

"Looks like they've been there awhile," Riley says.

Will gazes at the ceiling for a second, thinking.

"Twenty-eight years." He reaches into his back pocket, but then he remembers. "I left the last of my small bills for a tip this morning. You got a five?"

Riley snorts, pulls out his wallet. "Maybe. Just out of curiosity, what are you doing?"

"What does it look like? I'm buying a pair of shoes."

Riley points to the cracks in the leather. "They're dry-rotted. And ugly. I've got a ten."

Will shakes his head. "No, I need a five."

"Here. I got five ones."

Will takes the bills, folds them and slides them in behind the bag of rock salt on the top shelf.

Riley is laughing now. "I think you've lost your mind, Pops."

Will winks at him, tucks the shoes under his arm. "You think? How much are new soles worth these days?"

It's good to hear his son laugh, though it causes a twinge in Will's patched-together heart. The sins of the fathers are indeed visited on subsequent generations, he thinks, as his mind slips back into the past. What he knows now to be a hereditary anger born of a hereditary disapproval has caused him to lose great chunks of his son's life in precisely the same way he had lost great chunks of his father's. While he and Riley have never been close, they have not always been enemies. He didn't see it coming at the time, but the crack between him and his son started at Clara's house when Riley was seven, the first time Will's family saw him openly shunned. The incident emerges from his memory like a ship from the fog.

## CHAPTER 27

*November 1957*

Will took a step toward his father in the cobbler shop that after-noon, and it felt like a victory. Maybe Tobe was right, and hatred really was better than indifference.

Buoyed by success, however thin, he left his father's farm thinking of Katie. He had pictured her face every day for six years, the bashful face of a girl-child with an angel's kiss on her forehead. His daughter. Helen still didn't know about Katie, and he saw no reason to tell her even now, but he longed to see the girl. He had no other thought, no other design than that—just to see her, to know what she looked like now—and he convinced himself that it would be all right. Enough time had passed that he could now take his family and pay another visit to Clara and Simon's house. Clara was, after all, his sister, and apart from a distant glimpse at Tobe's funeral he had not seen her in six years.

Clara and Simon still lived on the old Coblentz place, except now there were twelve kids, some of whom had grown big enough to help Simon wrestle a living from a marginal strip of land. The house and outbuildings looked no better than they had six years earlier, still in need of paint.

Will loved this time of year. The crops were mostly all in and safe from harm, the garden finished, the winter's provisions laid by, the leaves of the trees down and raked and burned, the silo filling, and shucked corn drying in the crib. Smoke curled contentedly from the chimney. In late autumn, when the air turned crisp and clear and the summer's work was done, there came a time of reflection, a satisfied pause before the cold reality of winter set in.

Helen tensed up when they pulled into Clara's drive. She hadn't forgotten her last visit, how she had been trapped in a room full of prying eyes and peppered with relentless questions. She relaxed a little when she saw that there was no line of buggies parked in the yard this time.

Someone must have seen them coming because children went scurrying to round everybody up. By the time Will and Helen and the boys had parked and gotten out of the car most of Clara's family was there to meet them in the front yard. Kids came running around the corners of the house, boys clutching hats to heads and girls holding broad skirts up off the ground, flocking to their mother. Clara smiled, drying her hands on her apron and looking like a postcard of an Amish mother. Simon came last, probably from the barn because he was still wearing his rubber boots. The kids lined up in order of age as if it was some kind of drill, which, as Will recalled from his own childhood, it was.

It seemed a bit formal, sidestepping down the line shaking hands with each family member, but it had been six years, so a little formality was appropriate. He knew Katie immediately, though the angel's kiss had faded. She stood beside Cassie—a brace of fine healthy girls just starting to fill out—and Will moved past them quickly. His eyes might have stayed a second too long on her forehead when she blushed, but he was sure Helen didn't notice. Helen also didn't notice Katie's uncanny resemblance to Will, or if she did she saw it only as a genetic accident. Will was watching. Helen moved past Katie quickly enough to ease his fears, at least for now.

Simon's hair was turning gray where it hung over his ears. His face had grown frown lines and crow's feet. He was still odd, saying nothing much beyond hello, yet staring, always staring with those bug eyes of his. Clara had put on a little weight, but then she was thirty-six years old and had borne ten children. She seemed cordial enough, and made all the standard comments about how much the boys had grown; however, whenever she looked at Will he thought he saw a hint of something approaching suspicion in her eyes.

Once the formal introductions were over, everybody scattered, Welch and Riley running off with a clutch of barefoot boys in the general direction of the creek, Helen into the house with Clara, and Will off with Simon to admire the two hogs he had penned up for fattening.

Though endless, Simon's questions were innocuous enough. He had a way of leaning a little too close and staring a little too intently.

"So how is it, living in the city?"

"Well, I work around the city, but I don't live there. I live on a place a lot like this, only smaller."

"You got a television?"

"Oh yeah. The kids watch it all the time. I'm kind of busy."

"What kind of stories do they have on that television?"

Simon pressed hard enough so that Will thought more than once about telling him to back off, yet even in private, Simon never mentioned Katie. He could not have forgotten it. He avoided the subject intentionally and focused instead on indulging his almost fanatical curiosity.

They hadn't been there an hour when Simon looked up toward the house as if he'd heard someone call, and told Will it was time for them to go wash up for dinner. A tingle ran up Will's spine as he realized what he had let himself in for, only it was too late. There was nothing to do now but tough it out.

Clara had laid out a feast. The dining room was four windows long and they needed every inch of it for the plank table running the length of the room. Simon's two children, plus Clara's two children, plus the eight they had together made an even dozen. While Helen had insisted on helping, she hadn't taken into account the flock of stair-stepped girls swirling around the kitchen at mealtime. In the end it was all she could do to stay out of the way while they set the table and loaded it down with bowls of roast beef and gravy and corn and squash and green beans and potatoes. Amid the bustle, she hadn't noticed one of the girls setting up the little folding table in the corner.

"Whew, this is a lot of food," she said. "Y'all eat like this all the time, or is Third Army coming for dinner?"

Clara smiled, and there was a distinctly Amish humility in it. "God has blessed us," she said. "We are always happy to share His gifts."

Simon bade Helen sit at the other end of the table, opposite his position at the head, and her boys were seated at her flanks. A single bench ran down the side of the table nearest the window, and all the middle-sized kids sat there, shoulder to shoulder. The bigger kids sat on the other side in cane-bottom chairs like the grown-ups. Some of the older girls held the smaller children on their laps. Amid the confusion of seating such a crowd at the long table, Helen had settled in before she looked around and saw that Will was still standing in the shadows.

"Wait," she said. "There's no place for Will." She gripped the sides of her chair and started to scoot back, but Will shook his head and motioned for her to stay. An awkward moment followed as Clara averted her eyes and Simon waited to see if Will would explain, or if he would have to explain it for him.

Will pulled the chair out from the little table in the corner and said, very quietly, "I will sit here."

Only then did Helen notice the single place setting on the folding table, along with the miniature bowls of roast beef and corn and squash and green beans and potatoes that had been arranged there. Will saw the look of indignation in her eyes, her mouth falling open to protest. He heard the sound of trumpets, saw the battle flags unfurling in the breeze and feared for the coming storm, yet Helen hesitated, looking from Simon to Clara and then back to Will without firing a shot. She hesitated, he knew, because she was a long way from Georgia, in a strange place, among people whose customs she did not understand. So when she looked to her husband and he gave her a grave little shake of his head, it was enough. Stunned and confused, she retreated and waited to see what would happen next.

All eyes turned to Simon, who bowed his head. Again Will held his breath, fearful of an outburst from one of his sons, for he had forgotten to warn them that the Amish do not pray out loud when they bless the food. Thirty long seconds of silence ticked by. The end of the blessing was marked only by a general rustling of bodies and the rattling of dishes. Clara and Simon's kids attacked the platters as though it were a competition.

It was a quiet dinner. Simon and his kids ate with a businesslike intensity. Talk could wait. Will sat in his corner eating in silence because he didn't want to call attention to himself. Best to let it blow over. Helen picked at her plate, and she too remained silent because she was lost in this place and did not know what to say. Once, she told Welch to get his elbows off the table and Riley not to talk with his mouth full.

Clara sensed their embarrassment—surely she had expected it—and kept her own head down. Will couldn't tell what Simon was thinking. Simon stared a lot. Once or twice Will stole a glance at Katie. She behaved as any thirteen-year-old girl would, sharing the occasional whispered secret with Cassie and firing stern looks at a pesky younger brother, but when she looked at Will there was nothing in her eyes to even hint that she knew he was her father. He was sure she had not been told.

He might have been able to slide by. Everything might have turned out all right if it hadn't been for Riley. Even Helen, after a little cultural indoctrination from Will, probably would have eventually come to understand the banning, even if she didn't agree with it.

But Riley noticed his mother's uncharacteristic silence and downcast eyes. He was only seven years old then, but he was unusually bright and perceptive for his age. Then Helen snapped at him when he wouldn't quit trading elbow jabs with Mahlon. She never snapped, especially in somebody else's house. Finally he looked over his shoulder and watched his father for a moment, eating dinner by himself at the little card table in the corner, and he knew his father was being punished. He had done enough time alone in the corner to know what it meant. Here Riley was only a child, and his father practically Superman. His keen little eyes saw Will's aloneness and Helen's sadness, and he knew that one was the product of the other. He turned sideways in his chair and stared at his father.

"Is Daddy in trouble?" he asked.

Helen's mouth fell open, but she was at a loss. She looked helplessly at Will, then at Simon, then turned back to Riley and said, "No, son. Everything is all right. Turn around and eat your supper."

Even at seven, Riley knew a lie when he heard one. Everything was not all right. He stared at his father for a few seconds. Without making a sound, he swallowed, his eyes filled and his chin quivered. He turned slowly about in his chair, but he didn't look up again, nor did he answer Mahlon's elbows. And he refused to eat another bite.

There was no relieving the tension after that. They made excuses about having to go visit other relatives and left right after dinner.

Helen was furious, and the whole episode gave Will a strange sense of déjà vu. Twice in fourteen years he had gone to see his sister, and both times he had driven away at dusk with Helen thin-lipped and fuming.

"What, exactly, was *that* all about?" Once out of sight of the place, she let it all out.

"It's the ban. I think I told you I was banned, babe."

"You never told me they'd shove you in a corner like that. It was all so . . . *cold*. What else do they do to you?"

"Well, let's see. They won't buy anything from me, or sell anything to me. They won't accept a gift from me or eat food that I've provided. Oh, and they won't ride in a car with me either."

"All of them? You mean *none* of your folks will eat with you?"

"I don't know. Sometimes it sort of depends on who's looking, you know? Take Mose. If Dad wasn't there, Mose wouldn't observe the ban, I'm sure of it."

"Your own *father* won't eat with you?"

"Well, of course not. I mean, he's the main one. He's the head of the family—sets the tone for everybody."

She stared straight out the front of the car for a while. When she finally spoke, she said, "It's not right. I'm sorry, I don't care how old the custom is. I don't care if it goes back to Adam, it's not right. There was a family of coloreds lived on the farm next to us when we were little, and we grew up playing with their kids. They were decent, hardworking, honest folks. Daddy and Mister Lem used to swap out work all the time, and Daddy thought the world of him. Sometimes I rode into town in the back of Daddy's pickup, and I remember once he took Lem with him. While we were in town it got to be lunchtime and I was real hungry. There was a little restaurant in town and I pestered Daddy to take me and Mister Lem in there for lunch, but Daddy wouldn't go in there because if he did Mister Lem would have to eat in the kitchen. He told me if they were too good for Mister Lem they were too good for us."

She slid over next to Will, took his arm and said, "We won't be eating at your sister's house anymore. I guess we can still visit if you like but we won't be staying for dinner. If they're too good for my husband, they're too good for me."

Her loyalty warmed him, but he could see there was going to be a problem.

"All right," he said. "That's fine for Clara's, and I appreciate it, but you're just going to have to put up with it at Dad's house."

She backed away a little in shock. "If you think I'm sitting through that again at your Dad's house, you're going to have to give me a real good reason. I'd just as soon skip it."

"No. I'm afraid we can't just skip it."

"You mind telling me why?"

He shrugged. "I know how my father thinks. If you got punishment coming you take it like a man, you don't dodge it. There's a place I have to try and get to, and this is in the middle of the road, babe. Things will never change between me and my father until I face up to the punishment."

She shook her head in disbelief. "Well, I don't like it. It's not fair. They talk all the time about Amish who left the church. I know for a fact, there's lots of them. They can't possibly treat *all* of them like that."

"No, it's not all of them. Just the ones who left after they were baptized into the church. Like me. They say nobody that puts his hand to the plow and looks back is fit for the kingdom of God."

It sounded solid. It was even true, as far as it went; it just didn't happen to be the *whole* reason he was banned. He thought for the briefest moment that he might tell her the truth about Katie, but Helen was a Southern girl with a Southern girl's inviolable sense of chivalry. Will's ostracism at dinner had violated her most deeply held tenets of fairness and loyalty, and for the first time in years she had come down entirely on his side. He wasn't about to mess that up by telling her the truth.

He regretted the choice soon enough. For less than two weeks later he came home from work one evening to find Helen sitting at the dining room table with a letter in her hand. She was crying. It was clear from her red, swollen eyes that she had been crying for some time, and as soon as he saw her, he knew he was in trouble. He put his lunch pail on the table, waited.

Her fist tightened, and the letter, written on a child's three-hole notebook paper, scalloped like a seashell.

"This is from Clara Schlabach," she said, her voice a hoarse whisper. "Your sister. Let me read you a little of it. '*I don't know what is in your mind to do with Katie, but I know you must not take her from me. She is mine. I have raised her. You must not even tell her. I have gave much to cover your sin, and I would not let you ruin it now. Leave her be.*'"

She laid the letter down and pressed it to the table with her fist.

"We've been playing this game too long," she said softly. "Now you're going to sit yourself down at this table and talk to me, mister. You're going to tell me the truth for once, you no-good, low-down, lyin' piece of Yankee trash, and you're going to tell me all of it or I'm gone. You're going to answer every one of my questions, and if you lie to me, or if you hold anything back, I'll know it. I promise you, it'll be the worst mistake you ever made." Her red eyes flitted to the letter under her fist and she added, "Almost."

And so he told her. Then, in the aftermath of his confession it came to him that the truth, if indeed it ever made a man free, must have done so under very strict conditions. It must have been that the truth would make a man free if he turned to it willingly and embraced it like a friend, but when the truth had to hunt him down and handcuff him and force a confession out of him it was far more likely to throw him in prison afterward.

She didn't speak to him for two weeks, and he felt the whole time like a man waiting for the jury to come back into the courtroom. Even then she never rendered a clear verdict apart from the fact that she would not leave. She meant what she said: she would have left him immediately and forever, and she would have taken the boys with her, if he had held anything back this time. But he hadn't. It was almost as if he had tricked her, giving in and telling her the whole truth in the face of her ultimatum, because it left her honor-bound to stay with him no matter what.

In the end he slowly realized there was nothing she could do to him that he could not wait out. His life had taught him patience, if nothing else.

CHAPTER | 28

*January 1985*

Levi hasn't lived at the old farm in ten years, but Will can still feel his presence about the place. Mose has been master of house and land for a generation. He will soon turn the main house over to his son and retire to the dawdi haus himself, yet the farm still feels like Levi Mullet's farm. Will knows it is only his memory talking. The sons of Mose would no doubt see their own father imprinted in the place and on themselves.

He sees two of his nephews, Mose's younger sons, hauling a plank table out the back door of the house to store it in a shed someplace, making room for the funeral tomorrow. The church wagon sits waiting nearby, a completely enclosed weatherproof trailer made to hold fifty or sixty collapsible benches and the box of books used in church services. Half of the benches are in the dawdi haus now, but by nightfall they will all be set up in the main house, ready for the funeral. It's only work, and there are many hands.

Will takes the wheel and backs the car out carefully, threading between a crowd of parked buggies and easing back down the driveway between the main house and the dawdi haus.

"Whew," Riley says, shaking his head as they pull out onto the highway. "Back into the *real* world, finally."

Will answers only with a wry smile. He doesn't have to think too deeply to know which world is best described by the word *real*, but he also understands that "the real world" is a matter of perspective. His sons taught him that in the sixties.

*The sixties.* Will remembers the decade as something other than what a calendar would have him believe. The sixties wasn't a decade at all; it was an era, a tectonic shift in reality itself. The era started, as everyone seemed to understand, with a nation sitting lost and breathless in front of a box, watching black-and-white moving pictures of a president's wife scrabbling on a trunk lid for pieces of his head, and it ended with the same nation torn, bleeding, lost and cynical, watching another president resign his office on live TV, in color, while disillusioned American soldiers lost a war that wasn't a war. It was a time of impossible extremes—hedonists dancing in the mud at Woodstock while astronauts walked on the moon. As a boy, stuck in the strictures of the Amish, Will had longed for change, had desperately wished that his world would at least change its clothes now and then. He had not wanted, nor anticipated, that the World might fling away its clothes entirely and run shrieking like a herd of possessed pigs into the sea.

*June 1959*

He never quite knew whether he did it consciously or unconsciously or whether it even mattered, but after Helen found out about his illegitimate daughter, Will took a renewed interest in church work. When the neighborhood started to grow and the church decided to add a new building for Sunday school space he borrowed machines from Barefoot Bridge, graded the site, and dug the footings. While he might not be the sort to teach Sunday school, surely he could help construct the building. For the better part of a year he was up there almost every evening, working.

The new and improved Will McGruder made such an impression on the pillars of the church that somebody nominated him for deacon. But when they read the short list of names to the congregation at the Wednesday night business meeting and asked if anybody knew of any reason why this man shouldn't be considered, Helen raised her hand to object. She gave no explanation at the time. None was needed. Nobody was going to vote for a man whose own wife objected. She was bound to know something they didn't. When they asked Helen about it later, she said she voted against him because he wouldn't quit smoking. It was a foul habit, she said, the sort of thing done by tattooed men in pool halls and bowling alleys. Smoking was only one step short of drinking, she said, good enough for Humphrey Bogart maybe, but unbecoming for a deacon in the church. Her remarks puzzled the stalwarts of her little country church because she was ahead of her time. Smoking had not yet become a sin, and in those days the front steps of the church were littered with cigarette butts from where deacons had slipped out while they were waiting to take up the offering.

Will knew. The real reason she had voted against him was Katie. There was a balance sheet in Helen's head, and sometimes it demanded a pound of flesh. Though he was sure now that she would stay with him for life, her loyalty would not always come without a price. Once she got her pound of flesh she was satisfied. She settled back into herself and began to view her besmirched and properly chastised husband with a new and grand benevolence.

On their next trip to Ohio, Helen went armed with the truth—armed to the teeth with it. It seemed to Will that if the truth were bullets she would have been wearing bandoleers over both shoulders like one of Pancho Villa's men. Now that she knew the entire story, she would go to Ohio and get this whole mess straightened out once and for all. Her mill ground slowly, but it ground exceedingly fine.

As for Clara and Katie, Helen said, she and Will would honor Clara's wishes and tell the girl nothing. For now. Katie was already fifteen years old and would be an adult before long. When Katie turned eighteen Helen figured they could bring the question up for further review, but in the meantime it seemed best to do as Clara asked and keep quiet about it. Besides, Welch and Riley didn't know. They were too young to understand such a thing, and if she told them they'd just blab it all over church and ruin the whole family's reputation. There was no sense in that.

"Your problem is your father," Helen said, with authority, and went on to explain how, now that she knew the whole story about Will, it was perfectly plain that most of his quirks stemmed from the disapproval of his father. Once she held Will's behavior up to the yardstick of his past it all became clear to her.

"Well, *of course* you only say two or three words a year—it makes it a lot easier to remember what lies you've told. And *of course* you don't spend time with the kids—your father didn't either. And *of course* you're ill-tempered—I would be too if my father hated me."

Helen devised a plan. She only wished Will had come to her with the truth years ago because *of course* a Southern girl would know how to handle an irate father. They were raised to it. Will protested mildly, pointing out that Helen was not given to pretensions; she was nothing like Scarlett O'Hara. Helen countered that, yes, she had been something of a tomboy, and in her childhood had been known to beat up girls who batted their eyelashes to get what they wanted, but that didn't mean she didn't know how to do it. She was a Southern girl.

"It's like boys and baseball," she said. "Some are better than others, and some are naturals, but when it comes right down to it they all know how to play the game." She would charm him, she said. Levi wouldn't stand a chance.

"What does he like?" she asked one evening as she stirred a pot of black-eyed peas with a wooden spoon.

"Nothing. He doesn't like anything." Will had just come in red-faced from the garden and sat down at the kitchen table with a glass of iced tea. "Except work. Now there's an idea—you could plow a field for him."

"You're not helping. Didn't you ever see him love something? Did you never see his eyes light up?"

Will pushed his cap back, gazed out the window for a minute. "Yeah," he said. "Cake. He loves cake."

And so a coconut cake was conceived, a peace offering fit for a pharaoh. She made it from scratch, from an old family recipe, mixed it up by hand and baked it to perfection, then iced it, covered it with fresh coconut and carefully placed one maraschino cherry precisely in the center. She pinned the layers together with toothpicks and put it in a covered cake tin and borrowed a cooler big enough to hold the cake tin, then made Will drive all night because she was afraid the heat of the sun on the trunk would curdle the icing.

Somewhere in Tennessee in the middle of the night, after Helen and the boys fell asleep, Will started to nod. After he nearly dozed off a time or two he turned on the radio to keep himself company. He could find only one station still on at that time of night—a little backwater country station. In between Marty Robbins and Patsy Cline, the disc jockey, apparently figuring nobody was listening anyway, griped about the absurdity of making states out of Alaska and Hawaii. "Salmon crunchers and hula dancers," he said. "They don't live here and they don't think like us. They don't belong, and we don't need 'em."

"Ike knows what he's doing," Will muttered, and snapped off the radio. It was as good as a cup of coffee. He had served under Eisenhower, had watched good men die carrying out the man's orders, and he didn't take it lightly when somebody questioned the commander in chief.

He had the blackness to himself, winding through the hills of Tennessee and Kentucky with his elbow hung out the window and the wife and children asleep. It was in such moments, following a moving pool of light through endless darkness, that he sometimes let his earthbound mind drift free so that he could see himself from the outside. He was a halfway man, he thought, at that very moment halfway home, and in the larger moment halfway through his life—a life defined by half-truth. Leaning toward the open window to catch a bit of the night wind, he ran a hand over his head. Even his hair was half gone. He said half a prayer to half a God, and held out half a hope. Perhaps he would only be condemned for half an eternity.

Helen organized her campaign against Mount Levi with the steely-eyed calm of a seasoned general. She spent the last hour of the drive twisted around with an elbow hanging over the seat, instructing Welch and Riley in great detail about how to conduct themselves like gentlemen. She made sure they had on their best clothes, shirttails tucked in, hair slicked down, pants zipped up, Sunday shoes shined. She licked a thumb and rubbed a peanut butter smudge from Riley's cheek.

When they arrived, she put on her brightest smile to go with her brightest dress and her new shoes. Levi was there, lined up at the head of his family in the shade of a silver maple that had been a mere sapling when Will left home.

Will caught the slight wink from his older brother and knew that things would be all right, at least for the moment. Mose, as usual, had prepared the ground with his father as well as could be expected. Levi even smiled at Helen and the boys, who had, after all, done nothing to offend him. He said hello to Will and shook hands stiffly, as if it pained him. It was the first time Will had actually touched his father in over sixteen years.

And then Levi promptly ignored him, although he took what appeared to be a grandfatherly liking to Welch and Riley, teasing them about their ages, about the girlfriends they swore they didn't have, and introducing them personally to a couple of his more outgoing Amish grandsons who, as soon as was proper, whisked the boys away to swing on the ropes in the haymow.

Helen, after retrieving her prize cake from the trunk of the car, went into the house with Elizabeth. The flock of kids had vanished. Mose and Will and Levi found themselves alone with each other in the yard, an awkward silence hanging between them. They crossed their arms and looked around, kicked the dirt a little. Finally, Mose and Will started to talk at the same time. Mose gave ground.

"I was just going to say it looks like you're a little behind on the hay," Will said.

"Rain," Levi answered. "Last week it didn't rain since Monday, and then it rains three inches in three days. The almanac says the moon changes to last quarter tomorrow with windy and clear, so maybe then. We'll see."

"Mose tells me you don't work the fields anymore, though. Is that right?" He knew the answer. He remembered the conversation with Mose year before last, but Levi granted him only a grudging nod and looked away.

Mose's eyes roamed, looking for something to fill the silence. "We left our martin houses down last week and they all had nests in 'em. Lots more eggs in the nests this year too," he said.

"I think it's chust our birds are getting older and laying more eggs. The younger ones don't lay so many," Levi said.

It was subtle, the way the conversation went, but Will saw the pattern. Levi was establishing ground rules about what he would discuss and what he would not. He would talk about the farm, or the weather, or the birds—the small talk he might discuss with any outsider—as long as Will didn't get personal. Levi wasn't going to answer any question about himself, period. They walked around for a bit, Levi hobbling noticeably on his bad knee.

Will could still read the farm. The peas were ready, and the sweet corn was just beginning to tassel and make ears.

"It's been so wet there's a lot of corn probably won't get planted now anymore," Levi said.

Will shaded his eyes, looking down the valley toward the far edge of the pasture where grapevines grew wild up the sides of the trees.

"Remember that yearling colt that got hung up in the vines and choked himself to death?" he asked absently, but before he finished speaking Levi had turned back toward the house as if he hadn't heard.

Will and Mose glanced at each other. Mose sidled close, his hands clasped behind him, and whispered, "He blamed you for that. He hasn't forgot."

"I plowed that day," Will said. "From sunup to sundown. The one day I don't go by the pasture and check on the horses, that's the day the colt decides to hang himself."

Mose smiled patiently. "You think that colt got himself twisted up in those vines chust so he could get you in trouble?"

Will's face hardened as the anger welled up. "I think it wouldn't have mattered what I did. What are the chances I would have been there at just the right time? I think if it hadn't been that, it would have been something else. My problem is I'm not perfect."

Levi was hobbling toward the barn. Mose and Will followed along behind, hanging far enough back to be out of his hearing. "I promised Tobe I would try," Will said. "I didn't promise to succeed. I'll come here and visit our father and pay my respects. If that's not good enough, well, why should it be? Nothing I ever did was good enough."

Dinner at Levi's was nearly the same as it had been at Clara's—a big meal laid out on a long table, the middle-sized kids down one side on a bench and everybody else in sturdy, simple chairs. Elizabeth arranged a small table in the corner for Will, and this time Helen helped.

Helen was prepared this time. She had explained very thoroughly to the boys that their father would be dining at a separate table. It was all right, she told them, just something he had to do to get back in the good graces of his father. A kind of penance. Welch and Riley understood. At eleven and nine, they were practically grown.

Will had never seen Helen turn on the charm the way she did that day, all girlish and helpless and laughing at whatever anybody else laughed at. He watched her. He understood the Amish sense of humor, but he also knew that it was very different from the Southern sense of humor, and half the time Helen didn't know why she was laughing.

She laughed anyway, and he enjoyed it.

Helen had put on a little weight in her thirties—not a lot, but enough so that, combined with the teased, rounded hairdo, she looked more like a mother and less like the slip of a girl he had married. She had changed, but when she laughed he could still see the girl. She was still in there, and he found it comforting because he knew that if he could see the girl in her, she could still see the boy in him.

Even more impressive was the fact that Levi actually seemed to like her. He went out of his way to tease her, and so did Mose. Helen's Southern girl charm seemed to be working. It appeared she had gained an easy acceptance with Levi, and Scarlett O'Hara moved up a notch in Will's estimation.

Levi's dinner table was even more crowded than Clara's had been. Besides Levi and Elizabeth there was Mose and his wife, quiet Daniel— he of the donkey scar—Levi's two remaining unmarried daughters, and Mose's nine children. And this time, since she knew what to expect, Helen kept a lively banter going during the meal so that it seemed she barely noticed her husband sitting in the corner at a table by himself.

Dinner flew past, and Helen's big moment came. Will watched her face, saw the catlike smile of anticipation as three of the older girls got up and went to the kitchen to bring back dessert. He saw the triumph on Helen's face when young Mary came through the door with her coconut cake. He saw radiance fade to puzzlement as Mary trooped right past the big table, all the smaller kids following the dazzlingly white cake with their eyes. And he saw the look of utter shock and dismay when Mary placed the whole big coconut cake gently on his little table off in the corner.

Helen turned sideways in her chair, her mouth hanging open. She sat that way for a minute, then stared down the length of the table at Levi.

Pointing at the cake, she said, "Y'all aren't gonna eat that cake?"

The two other girls had followed Mary into the room bearing freshly baked cherry pies, and were setting them down on the long table as Helen spoke.

"We have cherry pie," Levi said, stone-faced.

"But I went to a whole lot of trouble to make that cake, just for you. You've got to at least *try* a piece of it." She was on the verge of pleading.

"We will have the pie," Levi repeated calmly. "Y'unce can eat the cake if you want to."

"But *why?*" she demanded, beginning to lose control.

Levi leaned forward, placed his palms on the table. "Because it is—" he stalled out, clearly trying to translate something he knew very well into a different language—"*Ein greuel,*" he mumbled, and then said, "Abomination. The sacrifice of the wicked is abomination unto God. We will have none of it."

She jabbed a finger toward her husband. "*He* didn't make that cake! I DID!"

Levi's head tilted slightly and he asked, very calmly, "But who bought the flour?"

The crowd, for it was a crowd, had fallen utterly silent, two rows of heads turning back and forth between Helen and Levi as if they were watching a tennis match.

· Helen sat back, defeat written on her face. She shook her head. "I just don't understand it. This man is a Christian. He's been baptized. He's a changed man."

"A question is in my mind," Levi said evenly. "He was baptized one time before. Did it change him *then?*"

Will could see her eyes narrowing. "Mr. Mullet, this is your own flesh and blood," she said, knifing a hand on the tabletop. "Yeah, he did wrong, but that was a long time ago. He told you he was sorry, and he meant it."

Levi looked down his nose at her.

"Words," he said.

Frustrated, Helen rolled her eyes and waved her hands in the air. "But he was practically a *deacon,* for cryin' out loud!"

Levi folded his hands and refused to answer.

It was then that Will saw the other side of Scarlett showing through Helen's eyes. She said nothing else, but there was a purely Southern petulance in every move she made as she shoved her chair back and got up, holding her head high, went over to Will's table, hacked out four obscenely large hunks of coconut cake and plopped them down on her family's plates. Welch and Riley caught on to her game too, making a great oohing, aahing, lip-smacking fuss about how delicious was their mother's cake. Will saw the mischief in their eyes, the stolen glances, and knew that Helen's cake was made all the sweeter for his sons by knowing they were being watched by a whole tableful of kids who couldn't have any.

And so, because of Helen and her coconut cake, a strange kind of competition was born. Once the battle lines were drawn between Helen and Levi—the irresistible force and the immovable object—Will became almost a spectator, an afterthought, a judge by default over a bizarre contest of wills.

The following summer they went to Ohio in the first sweltering week of August. A busy time for the Amish, the wheat and spelts were all done and the oats about ready to cut and shock. Helen made it a point to concoct the most elaborate, beautiful, mouth-wateringly tempting dessert known to man and carefully transport it over a thousand miles to Levi Mullet's house, just so they could eat it in front of Levi's family. She brought enough for everybody—more than enough—and she made it a point to offer it to them, even after it ended up on Will's table.

When Helen unveiled her Strawberry Banana Suicide Cake and forced Levi to reject it in front of—and on behalf of—a dozen kids, she thought she had won. Again. But she hadn't taken Elizabeth into account. Will's stepmother was rarely outwitted and never outworked. Elizabeth had endured the embarrassment the summer before. She would not suffer it again.

"Would y'unce like some ice cream with your cake?" Elizabeth asked sweetly. And then her daughters started bringing in the homemade butter pecan ice cream, made that very morning with fresh cream straight from the barn and pecans that Helen herself had brought all the way from Georgia as a peace offering. Three of Elizabeth's grandsons had turned cranks on the oaken buckets for an hour out in the buggy shed, and three gallons of ice cream had sat unnoticed, iced down and firming up in the summer kitchen for the last forty minutes. Elizabeth smiled innocently, not a trace of pride as she set heaping bowls in front of Helen's boys. Helen saw through it immediately. Elizabeth couldn't possibly have owned three ice-cream freezers—she had to have borrowed at least one of them ahead of time. It was premeditated.

The scoops were firm and round, just starting to glaze and form little drops at the edges. Welch and Riley took one look at their mother, shoved her Strawberry Banana Suicide Cake aside, and dove into the ice cream.

## CHAPTER 30

*July 1962*

A new belligerence invaded the McGruder household in the early sixties as Welch began staking his claim to manhood, and Riley—well, Riley discovered Emerson and Thoreau and became, naturally, a majority of one. He had always marched to a different drummer. When he turned twelve he started making his own beat.

Will, for his part, thought everything was progressing nicely. Levi had relaxed toward him in some ways. He still wouldn't engage in any sort of personal dialogue, but he had become almost comfortable in Will's presence and didn't object when Will was included sometimes in casual dinner conversation from across the room. Will imagined that getting back in his father's good graces was simply a slow, painstaking, incremental process, rather like taming a bear. A little bit of trust at a time. In the end, it was all just work.

But his sons saw it differently. They had no history with Levi Mullet. He had only recently become a grandfather to them, and even that relationship was a little stiff. He took them for buggy rides sometimes, and that was about it. They didn't mind his Amishness as long as they weren't bound by any of it. They didn't mind Levi's clothes or his beard, and they rather enjoyed having a dozen cousins, a barn, a huge farm, and an endless supply of livestock to play with, though they said their grandfather smelled funny and they didn't like having to use the privy when they were at his house.

The only thing that really bothered them about Levi was when he would occasionally take little cheap shots at their father. It seemed that at least once every time they were around Levi he made it a point to pronounce their father cursed, or mention how he had "gone to the dogs," or slip a snide remark into casual conversation about how God is not mocked and a man's sins would surely find him out. He always delivered such nuggets with a knowing glance toward Will. As far as Welch and Riley knew, their father's only sin was that he ran away from home when he was nineteen, and after seeing how Levi treated him, their only question was, "What took you so long?"

They made no secret of their feelings, at least when they were alone in the car with Will and Helen. But Will told them these things were beyond their reckoning and the best thing they could do was to keep their opinions to themselves. Amish kids, much like Amish wives, were meant to be seen, not heard.

"But we're not Amish," Riley said.

"When in Rome," Will answered, glaring at him in the rearview mirror.

The gap between father and son widens slowly most of the time, like continents drifting apart, so that neither of them notices it until one day they look up to see each other from across a gulf they can no longer leap, and so come to know each other, for the first time, as foreigners. The crack that had opened between Will and Riley might have been traceable to Clara's house, when Will was shunned in front of his boys and they first saw him as fallible and human, but even then he might have repaired the damage if he had understood it—and if he had understood his sons. There was a moment when his sons tried to bridge the gap, and Will, because he did not understand their intentions, stopped them.

It started innocently enough. They were having dinner one night at Levi's, Will seated in his private corner and everybody else at the plank table near the windows. The boys had helped pick blueberries that day from a row of bushes on the south side of the buggy shed, and Welch now asked Levi how long those bushes had been there. Levi's beard and what was left of his hair had gone entirely white, and he had taken to wearing square reading glasses at the dinner table. If he hadn't shaved off the mustache it could have been Santa Claus sitting at the head of the table with a fork in his hand.

"Let's see," Levi said, scratching his chin through his beard. "I put those bushes in the ground about the time your dad went to the dogs, so I'm thinkin' it's been about nineteen years."

Will was pretty sure Welch didn't instigate the little rebellion. Welch never started anything, though he wasn't above joining in once Riley picked a battle. Riley must have conveyed something to him across the table because Welch slid his chair back first, then Riley stood up with him. They gathered up their plates and took a step toward Will's table.

"Where are you boys going?" Levi demanded.

The brothers stopped and looked at each other, then at Will, who had frozen, not sure what was happening, and then back at Levi.

"We're going to sit with the dogs," Riley said, and then added, with a little too much emphasis, "*sir.*"

Levi had put down his fork and was staring hard, not at the boys but at Will. As if it were *his* mutiny. Only his jaw moved, still grinding some little something between his teeth. An electric tension connected three generations in that moment, carrying a clear message from Levi to his errant son, and through him to *his* errant sons: *This is my house, and in it I will not be slighted.*

Will had no choice. There was nothing else he could do without giving up the meager acceptance he had worked so hard to achieve. He gave his sons his best *don't mess with me* glare, and pointed.

"Sit. Back. Down."

Riley stayed where he was for a long moment. Perhaps too long. Will was prepared to get up from his little table and confront him physically, but at the last second Riley broke the stare and turned away. Both boys returned grudgingly to their places and said no more. There was hardly a word spoken by anyone after that.

Will wasn't entirely sure what had happened, even after it was over. It seemed his sons had mounted a little rebellion of sorts, and he was forced to have to put it down. But something else happened. He had looked into Riley's eyes as if they were literally a window on his soul, and he could have sworn that just before Riley turned away, something in there ripped.

Riley had been a problem child from the beginning, not because of his attitude—that came later—but because he was cursed from birth with an incisive intelligence. It was puzzling at first, then cute, then promising, then frustrating. He was different from his older brother in nearly every way. If Welch was tenacious, Riley was analytical. When Welch got his first bicycle he climbed on it immediately, pedaled six feet and fell over. Then he brushed off his skinned palms, got back on the bike, rode six more feet and fell over again. He repeated the same pattern for two solid days without complaint, blowing the knees out of two pairs of jeans in the process, but at the end of two days he had stopped falling down. He learned by trial and error.

Riley, on the other hand, when they gave him a bike for his fifth birthday, pushed it to the side of the garage and parked it. Welch begged him to ride with him, yelled at him, called him chicken, then went back to pleading with him, but Riley wouldn't get on the thing. Instead, he spent the better part of two weeks sitting quietly with his arms around his knees watching his older brother ride. Helen noticed that he would stop whatever he was doing whenever Welch got on his bike, and watch. Occasionally he would ask a question, but the riding of a bike is not something one boy can explain to another. A few times Riley rolled his new bike out and walked it down the drive, testing the weight and balance, spinning a pedal with his toe, but he didn't get on it for two weeks. When he finally decided he understood it, he got a running start—the way he had seen Welch do—planted a foot on the low pedal, swung a leg over, and stayed up. He wobbled a little at first yet never fell. Before the week was out, Welch couldn't outrace him. That was Riley's way.

Helen bought books for him, and when he started asking questions about the words, she bought alphabet books and taught him how to read. In a matter of weeks he was reading on his own, two years before he was old enough to go to school. Within a couple of months he was correcting Helen's pronunciation, and before the year was out he had stopped asking her to read to him. He could do it himself, thank you.

Riley had problems in school right from the start. Teachers said he didn't listen, and the times he did listen he invariably argued with them. After several conferences during his first three years of grammar school, Helen concluded that his teachers disliked him, not because he argued with them, but because he usually won. His grades were good, though not spectacular, and the teachers' comments on the back of his report card were remarkably consistent: *Riley is a bright boy and could be an excellent student if he wanted to be.*

They were right. He was, in fact, an excellent student of whatever he wanted to study. Math intrigued him, so he borrowed Welch's textbook and learned algebra two years before he had it in school. He devoured books, but only the ones he wanted. He never bothered with what English teachers tried to tell him to read. And he remembered most of what he read. He became a harsh critic of fiction, mostly because his innate skepticism wouldn't allow him to suspend his disbelief—ever.

When he was in the seventh grade, thrust into a cauldron of pubescent boys marking boundaries and establishing pecking orders, Riley got kicked out of school for fighting. By then Will had pretty much given up the raising of his sons. But this was a serious offense, a whipping offense. Helen handed the matter over to him when he came home from the bridge that day.

"I didn't start it," Riley said, one eye swollen half shut. "It was Greenberg."

Even Will knew the name. Greenberg was a big dumb kid who liked to throw his weight around. His name was synonymous with fighting.

"What did you say to make him mad?"

So Riley told him. The argument had started in gym when a couple of older boys who had seen *The Invisible Man* fell to speculating about what they would do if they could turn themselves invisible. Greenberg mentioned the girls' locker room, a suggestion that met with approving snickers until Riley, who up to that point had remained on the edge of the conversation, told him it wouldn't do him any good. Falling ominously silent, Greenberg demanded an explanation.

"I just pointed out the obvious," Riley told Will. "I informed the moron that vision is the processing of reflected light. If he's invisible, so is his retina, and without an opaque retina he'd be blind." Riley was still sneering, even with his own vision somewhat impaired as a result of his attitude.

"Did you call him a moron?"

"No, I called him a dolt."

"A guy doesn't like being called a dolt in front of his friends, especially if you prove it to them."

Riley got his whipping, but it didn't have any effect that Will could see, apart from driving him a little further away. He reacted not at all, his usual insolent defiance.


It was in the early sixties that the great ribbons of interstate highways began wrapping their tendrils around and through Atlanta. Barefoot, whom Will believed was the luckiest man he'd ever known, found himself and his bridge company, as always, in precisely the right place at the right time. It was then that they began working twelve-hour days whenever the weather permitted.

Will was glad to get it. The one thing in the whole insane, madly rushing World that didn't change—never changed—was his job. The dimensions of a bridge might change, but the task was always pretty much the same. Dig footings and pour columns, build headers over the columns, swing the long main beams into place across the headers, frame and fill the spaces over the headers, then form and pour the surfaces. It was hard work tying steel and pouring concrete all day long, but hard work was Will's salvation. A man could shout down his past with the scream of a circular saw or the roar of a heavy diesel. He could sweat out a kind of penance under a merciless sun and find comfort in the company of other failed men. He could even dredge a tangible pride from looking back at the end of a long day and seeing hard evidence that he had been there, that he had made a difference.

The summer Welch turned fifteen he went to work with Will on the bridge crew. They didn't make a trip to Ohio that summer because there was simply too much work to do. They were building bridges for I–75 and were behind schedule because of the rain.

The next year Will and Helen made the trip, but the boys stayed home. Welch wanted to work because he had just turned sixteen and he wanted to try to earn enough money that summer to buy a secondhand car. Helen decided that Riley, at fourteen, could take care of himself during the day. Will had not forgotten the incident at Levi's on the last trip—the mutinous glare, the silent clash of wills. Something in Riley had gone away then, and hadn't returned. Maybe it would do the boy good to stay home by himself for a few days. Maybe he'd grow up a little and learn to take care of himself.

On the long drive up to Ohio Will discovered another reason behind Helen's willingness to leave her boys at home: Katie. Katie had gotten married and left home, which changed everything. Ever since the shunning at Clara's, Will and Helen had made it a point to stop by for a brief visit anytime they were in town, but they never stayed long and never, ever, stayed for dinner. They were always very careful not to say anything about Katie, not just for Clara's sake but also because Welch and Riley didn't know.

But Katie's marriage changed all that. Now, without the boys in the back seat listening, Helen was able to talk out her feelings the whole way to Ohio, and by the time they arrived it had been decided. It was time for

Will to tell Katie the truth. It would be difficult. Twenty years of passive denial would not make it easy for him, but Helen felt he owed it to his daughter.

Helen stayed behind at Sylvia's while Will went to see Katie. She and her new husband lived on a little farm not far from Clara's house—not a big place, but Will's eye said it was a fine, rich piece of bottom. Katie's husband was sitting up in the seat of a grain binder behind a team of four big, healthy Belgians, cutting a neat six-foot swath in waist-high hay and spitting loose piles out the near side. When he spotted the car he halted the horses, jumped down off the seat and strode across the field toward the house with the lively, earnest step of a newly married young man who wants to know what some Englisher is doing in his yard. Will had not met Reuben Kurtz before, having stayed away from the wedding because it just would have been too awkward. Too many people knew. Reuben was a big boy, and he crossed the open field rapidly with his long strides.

"What can I do for you?" he called out as he crossed the line between cut field and grass yard.

Will smiled and waited by the car. Reuben's ruddy face was ringed by a thin red beard and topped by the wide, flat-brimmed straw hat common to farmers in the summer. An ambitious twenty-four-year-old, he had purchased the farm and got it running well before he asked Katie to marry him.

"That's a fine team of horses you've got there," Will said.

Reuben crushed Will's hand with a solid one-pump Amish handshake. "Och, only two are mine. The other two belong to my brother. He'll use 'em to bring in his hay when I'm done." His eyes showed no sign of recognition.

"I'm Katie's uncle Will. Do you think I could talk to your wife?"

Reuben's eyes lit up, and there was no guile in his smile. "Oh, ja! It's good I finally get to meet you. Katie's out back hanging up clothes. Today is washday."

"Of course. It's Monday. How could I forget?"

Katie was busy hanging laundry on the line and didn't see them coming. When Will spoke she gave a little startled yelp and snatched a handful of clothespins from her mouth. Her angel's kiss flashed briefly above an embarrassed grin as she reached to shake Will's hand. She didn't know what to say, and neither did Will so long as Reuben stood next to him. The three of them made awkward attempts at small talk. How's the family? How do you like married life? But it seemed hollow and transparent, and Will could not sustain such chatter for more than a sentence or two. He wanted to talk to Katie privately, but he knew no way to suggest such a thing to her husband. Fortunately, Reuben seemed suddenly to notice the awkward silence and he excused himself, saying he needed to get back to his grain binder before the horses ran off with it.

Katie had stopped hanging clothes on the line. She stood facing him quietly, respectfully, her hands folded loosely in front of her. Now that he was alone with her and keenly aware of her full attention, Will became self-conscious and tongue-tied. He had spoken to Katie often over the years, but always in the company of other people—usually a good many of them—and always as an uncle to a niece. This was different.

"I wanted to, um . . ." he started, but trailed off. She seemed to sense his unease, though her calm demeanor gave no hint that she shared it, and turned quietly back to her work. She bent down and uncoiled a long, full dress from her basket, shook it twice and pinned it to the line. She had diverted herself on purpose, he was sure of it, to give him a chance to say what was on his mind.

"Katie, you know that your mother died when you were very small."

She nodded without looking at him, and mouthed a faint "Mm-hmm" as she plucked a clothespin from her lips and pinned the other shoulder of the dress. A light breeze stirred the row of clothes on the line. A bed sheet hanging right beside him twisted and luffed, tossing him a faint whiff of wet laundry soap.

"And I guess you probably know that Simon was not your real father."

She bent and plucked a very long pair of trousers from the basket, giving him a glancing nod as she shook them out.

"I just . . . I thought you should hear it from me. Katie, I'm your father."

"No, you're not my father," she said, taking the last clothespin from her mouth and pinning the other corner of the trousers to the line. She moved the basket sideways with a bare foot, then shook out another pair of trousers. She did not look at him. Her face, as far as he could tell, was expressionless, although he noticed that the angel's kiss fairly glowed.

"Katie, I'm sorry. I know it must be a shock to you, but the truth is, Mattie, your mother, and I—"

"I know this," she said, and yet the look in her eyes was one of puzzlement, as if she understood his words but not his reasoning. She dug some clothespins from the bulging pocket of her apron and continued hanging clothes.

"I have known for years now," she said. "You can't hide a secret like that among Amish women. Not long, anyway. Everyone knows. Sooner or later someone tells Cassie, and then Cassie tells me."

He wiped a hand across his mouth and focused on the clothes basket, trying to figure out what to say next. He had expected some sort of reaction—joy, tears, anger. Something. Not this.

"I would have told you years ago," he said. "Really, I would have. It's just that Clara thought it would be better if I didn't, and it seemed to me that her right was greater than my own. She shouldered the responsibility that I . . . abandoned. So I honored her wishes. I'm sorry if that—"

"But you're not my father," Katie repeated. There was surprise in her eyes, and a little smile. It was his turn to look puzzled.

"My father was the man that put food on our table and kept a roof over our heads when we were growing up—the husband of my mother, the father of my brothers and sisters, the man who told stories and played checkers with my cousins by the stove in the wintertime—*that* was my father."

Conflicting emotions pummeled him, chasing away any answer that might have gelled into words. He felt a deep sense of loss over the twenty years of his daughter's life sacrificed on the altar of a dirty secret, a twinge of anger at his sister Clara for having bound him to that secret, and at the same time a profound respect for Clara because of the sacrifices she had made in order to raise his child. Through it all he felt a surge of proud delight in the wisdom of his daughter's words, though they disowned him.

"I'm . . . sorry," he stammered. "I only meant to honor Clara's wishes."

"What's done is done," she said with just a tiny shake of the head, "and I am thankful for the life God has given me."

She went back to hanging her clothes as if nothing had happened, and something in her face and posture told him that she was telling the plain truth. She had said, quite simply, all that needed to be said. The past was the past. She did not say, nor did she mean, that no harm had been done, for great harm *had* been done. He could have been a father to her, but chose not to be. The opportunity was lost forever, swept downstream and gone, yet here she was, whole and healthy and grateful for what life had brought her.

Will had seen enough of Simon over the years, and heard enough rumors, to know that life in his house could not have been entirely pleasant, though his own scant experience with the man had revealed nothing other than a certain oddness. Whether or not he owned the right, his conscience demanded that he ask.

"How was it, really, growing up in the house of Simon Schlabach?"

She laughed. A little puff of a laugh escaped her, and she took the pins from her mouth to keep from dropping them.

"He really isn't quite right, you know, but it's not his fault. Just a couple of years ago, when I first met Reuben, there was a husking at the Weavers'. All the young folks were going to be there, especially Reuben, so Cassie and I wanted to go. We hated to ask Dad—Simon—because it was one of his bad days, but he said okay, so long as we put the blinker light on the buggy. We couldn't go without it."

Will had heard about the battery-powered blinker lights. The county had instituted the new requirement because the black buggies were almost impossible to see at night and several of them had been hit by cars recently.

"So we got dressed and hitched up the horse, only we couldn't find the blinker light. We looked high and low, but it was nowhere to be found. Always before, it was right there on the shelf above the harnesses, but not that day. When we finally figured out that Dad had hidden it from us and we weren't going to find it, we put the horse away and just sat there in the buggy in the dark, just me and Cassie."

Her eyes shined, and again she laughed at herself. "Oh, how we talked about him! We sat out there in the buggy shed and let it all go, let me tell you! We talked about all the crazy things he did to us all our lives and how we felt about it. We didn't hold anything back."

She picked up the empty basket. "After we said everything we could think to say about him he stepped out from behind the door. He was hiding there the whole time, listening."

She just stood there for a minute, absently bumping the laundry basket against her leg and toying with the dangling lace of her covering, remembering.

"But he has his good days too," she said, very softly. "Sometimes he's happy. I didn't feel too good, saying the things I said about him in the buggy shed—even though he shouldn't have been listening, and even though he punished us and stayed mad at us for weeks. I felt bad because I knew he couldn't help it. Something in him isn't right, but whatever it is, it's just *in* him. It has always been in him, and there's nothing he can do about it. Anyway, whether it was a good day or a bad day," she said, with a purposeful glance, "he was there. He was always there."

There was no anger behind her words, but they stung like hornets. *"He was there,"* she said.

*And you were not,* the silence answered.

CHAPTER | 31

*February 1968*

The telegram came on a Saturday in February, during the Winter Olympics. Will walked back to the house very slowly, reading it, and then stood in the kitchen reading it again, in shock, while Helen sat oblivious in the den, rocking and doing her needlepoint and watching the figure skaters, in color, all the way from France.

A lovely flaxen-haired girl glided regally in a long arc, the hem of her little dress fluttering in the wind of her passing, as Will read:

THE SECRETARY OF THE ARMY HAS ASKED ME TO INFORM YOU THAT YOUR SON

PFC Robert W. McGruder

WAS WOUNDED IN ACTION IN VIETNAM ON 08 February 1968. He received shrapnel wounds to the left arm, right leg with a fracture of the fibula, and abdomen causing lacerations of the small intestine and damage to the spinal column when a hostile force was encountered during a combat operation.

A Technicolor smile dazzled the watching world as spring-steel youth flung itself into the air, spun a couple of times and landed gracefully, arms out, fingers pointed, legs pumping to regain momentum.

```
PLEASE BE ASSURED THAT THE BEST DOCTORS AND
MEDICAL FACILITIES HAVE BEEN MADE AVAILABLE AND
THAT EVERY MEASURE IS BEING TAKEN TO AID HIM. HE
IS HOSPITALIZED IN VIETNAM PENDING TRANSPORT TO
WALTER REED ARMY HOSPITAL, WASHINGTON, D.C.
```

The figure skater raised her arms over her head, tightening the spin until she became a blur, and then jammed a blade in the ice to stop herself abruptly amid thunderous applause.

```
YOU WILL BE PROVIDED PROGRESS REPORTS AND KEPT
INFORMED OF SIGNIFICANT CHANGES IN HIS
CONDITION.
```

"Will?" Helen looked up, finally, and saw the telegram in his hand, the look on his face. Her needlepoint fell to the floor.

It was another month before Welch could make the trip halfway around the globe to Washington.

"It'll be all right," Will said. He had to keep telling her that. "You'll see. Once they get him to Walter Reed everything will be fine. It's probably not even all that serious—they're just being very careful with him."

It was a lie. If the Army was sending Welch to Walter Reed, Will knew it had to be serious. The Tet offensive had overloaded the system, and bed space at Walter Reed was at a premium. Only the worst cases would be sent there.

They made good time on the drive up to Washington because of the new expressways tying all the major cities together up and down the East Coast. Even so, the higher speeds and the big trucks constantly brushing past them drove Helen crazy. Helen drove Will crazy, ducking and gasping. Riley sprawled in the back seat looking out the window with his chin in his palm most of the way. Riley had finally reached the state Will had wished upon him in his childhood—he spoke only when spoken to—but it was an intentional silence, which made it even more annoying.

When they got to Walter Reed it seemed more like a macabre university campus than a hospital. Fifty years of constant remodeling had produced a vast complex of separate buildings bonded to each other by an endless maze of beige corridors and wheelchair ramps covered with beige linoleum. Everywhere, the halls were literally choked with damaged men. Young men.

Will had seen war. He thought he was prepared for what he would run into at Walter Reed, but he had not seen anything like this. He and Helen and Riley couldn't go ten feet without having to make way for a wheelchair or somebody on crutches or a pair of orderlies pushing a gurney with a topmast of IV bags. And every last one of the men was missing some combination of extremities—arms, legs, ears. The air was tinged with a distinctive smell homogenized from disinfectant and alcohol and burnt, necrotic flesh. Helen's mouth hung slightly open and her breath quickened. Riley—jaded, cynical Riley—did his best to hide the tears in his eyes.

Here, among men who had lost much in the service of their country, Will felt the presence of his second son like a ball and chain. Here, among the shaved heads of soldiers, Riley's flagrant mop drew stares. There had been a major battle over Riley's hair when he first started growing it out.

Will's own father had inspected his sons' hair to make sure it covered the ears, so it was a kind of latent defiance that made him insist that Riley's ears remain in sight. But when Helen took Riley's side, Will gave up. He stood apart from his sons in their teen years, and they grew into manhood on the edge of his vision, imprinting themselves in jerky, half-remembered flashes like a time-lapse film.

Welch had played football and hung around with other football players who kept their hair short and neat all the way through high school—the last of their generation to hold the line against the madness of the sixties. He didn't get the scholarship he had hoped for. The paper work was late in coming for his second choice of colleges, and when Welch graduated high school in '66 the draft board classified him 1-A. Rather than fight it he just went ahead and joined up. America's troops were out there trying to stop the spread of Communism, and Welch McGruder wanted to do his part. He figured he would do a couple of years in the Army and then let them help pay for his college.

Riley, on the other hand, didn't hang around with athletes. By the time he got to high school he was quoting Ayn Rand and starting to get beat up with some regularity. While other kids were arguing the Beatles versus Herman's Hermits, Riley was snubbing them all, listening to Bob Dylan and teaching himself calculus. He was always a little ahead of his time. In fact, he and his small clutch of aspiring intellectuals regarded Welch and his jock buddies with the same sneering contempt as marching bands and Miss America contestants. It seemed to Will that the minute Riley hit teenagerhood he made a list of Things To Be Held In Contempt. His parents were at the top of that list.

By the time they were in their junior year of high school, Riley and his friends had somehow become the final authority on what was "cool" and what wasn't, and their Contemptible list had grown to include pretty much everyone outside their own little clique. There were four of them in the nucleus—three boys and a stringy, dark-haired girl who might have been a deaf-mute for all Will knew—and they flitted in and out in varying combinations, riding together in whomever's Volkswagen happened to be running that day. They were the first in their class to let their hair grow to their shoulders, though Riley's dark wine-colored hair remained kinky like his uncle Mose's, and by the time it reached down to his shoulders it also reached *out* to them. He and his avant-garde friends were the first to wear love beads, tie-dyed T-shirts, and bell-bottom jeans with blown knees. Mimicking their rock-star heroes, they wore tinted granny glasses until some *un*cool people started wearing them, and then promptly abandoned them in the name of individualism. They seemed to have developed their own language, complete with an array of hand signs, and they were always either mouthing the words to a song or pounding out a beat with imaginary drumsticks or hunching over an imaginary guitar—which struck Will as particularly odd, since none of them actually owned a guitar. And the *music* they listened to! He didn't see how anybody could classify it as music. It was noise, plain and simple.

Will made them keep their noise out of his house whenever he was home, but Helen allowed it in his absence. He came home lots of evenings to find album jackets scattered all over the living room. Helen was willing to suffer a great deal in order to have Riley and his sullen friends where she could keep an eye on them. Will mostly just wondered where they got the money for all those records, and the dozens of eight-track tapes in their cars, not to mention the cars themselves, and the gas money. None of them had jobs.

Here, at Walter Reed, among hundreds of wounded young men who all looked like football players, pale Riley with his red-flag hair was a weight and an embarrassment to Will.

It took the better part of an hour to get through the red tape and find Welch's ward, a beige tunnel with a window at the far end and beige curtains between the beds. The long room had been designed to accommodate six beds. It held nine.

Welch had changed. Gaunt of face, he looked like he'd lost fifty pounds, and he hadn't been overweight to start with. There were half a dozen little white check-mark scars on his face.

Helen took his head in both hands and kissed him on the forehead. Strapped down to immobilize his back, with his left arm heavily bandaged and tied up to an IV stand, with some sort of screw contraption holding his right leg together, there wasn't much else she could do. She couldn't stop crying long enough to say anything to him. Will took his hand.

"You still got a grip," he said, and Welch smiled a little. There was a hardness in his eyes that had never been there before. He had aged.

"Doc says it may be a week or two before I can play football again."

"I'm glad to see you can joke about it," Will said. "You're lucky to be alive."

Riley pulled his long hair back from his face and glanced out toward the hallway. "Can't say that about all of 'em."

Will shot Riley a stern look, but Welch squeezed his hand.

"Riley's right," Welch said. "It's just a fact. Some of these guys would have been better off. Sometimes the field hospitals are *too* good. I heard they save ninety-nine percent of the guys who make it that far. Hang around here awhile and you start to think maybe ninety-five percent would be better."

"Well. I'm glad they took care of you." Field surgeons had removed part of Welch's small intestine and resected it—in a tent.

"And you're going to walk again, mister," Helen said. She said it the same way she would have told him to clean his plate ten years ago.

Welch gave her a tired smile. "Aw, Mom. Doc says my spinal cord is completely severed. My legs—it's like they're not even there anymore. I got nothing."

They talked for a while, and the conversation finally turned naturally to what had happened—how he'd gotten wounded.

"I don't remember, really," Welch said. "They sent us to a town called Ben Tre. They didn't even have time to learn my name—I was just 'the new guy.' I think I was in country for two days before the whole North Vietnamese Army came down on us." He shook his head. "When it looked like we were overrun, the lieutenant called in artillery on our own position. I remember hearing the incoming, but that's it. I woke up in the field hospital."

"Ben Tre," Riley said. "Wasn't that where some guy said they had to destroy the town in order to save it?"

Welch chuckled. "Yeah, I heard about that. They could've phrased it a little better, I guess."

They stayed for three days, spending as many visiting hours with Welch as they could before they had to leave. Helen wanted to stay longer, but Riley couldn't afford to miss any more school and Will had to get back to work.

If they hadn't seen Walter Reed they would never have been able to conceive of it, a place so tick-full of horror it didn't do any good to look away. Turn this way or that, and the view only got worse. They ate lunch in the cafeteria the first day, but no more, not after sitting next to a man with no jaw. The next day Helen came prepared. At lunchtime she broke out sandwiches and potato chips and had a picnic right there on Welch's bed. He was tired of hospital food anyway.

But the last day before they left, Welch had to go down for a few hours of therapy right in the middle of the day. The weather had turned downright balmy for Washington in February, so Will, Helen, and Riley took their sandwiches out front and plopped down on the slope of the grass in the sunshine.

Sitting on the grass eating peanut butter and strawberry jam sandwiches, they chanced upon a strange ritual. Right in front of where they sat lay a stretch of flat lawn big enough to hold maybe a couple of tennis courts end-to-end.

When the sun climbed above the buildings and poured down into the little flat place, patients in wheelchairs began creeping out through a side door and gathering on the lawn. Every one of them was heavily bandaged in various parts, and most were missing two legs. Some were missing an arm. Will assumed at first that they were just coming out to take advantage of a warm day and catch some sun, but they kept coming, one by one, until twenty or thirty of them had gathered in a loose cluster at the far end of the little green. They wore hospital robes over their bandages, and a good many had blankets over their shoulders when they came out.

They lined up wheel to wheel, side by side, and one of them rolled himself past the whole pack and made for the end where Will's family sat. Right in front of Will he stopped, spun his chair sideways and held up a pack of cigarettes.

Those who had lined up tossed off their blankets and dropped them carelessly over the back of their chairs. Their eyes focused on the pack of cigarettes held aloft by the starter.

The starter tossed the cigarette pack high in the air. The instant it bounced on the turf the line of wheelchairs broke more or less toward it, and a raucous outcry filled the air as the spectators tried to outshout each other. Most of the racers were new to their chairs and hadn't gotten the hang of it yet. They wobbled and jerked, veered off course and crashed into each other, but three of them did manage to break away from the pack and zigzag their way down the lawn. All three closed on the goal at the same time, pitched themselves out of their chairs and grappled for the cigarettes until one of them emerged from the pile victorious, sitting up next to his chair and raising the pack high, a triumphant grin on his face. There were hoots and high fives among the spectators, and a few bills changing hands as bets were paid off.

Slowly, the first wave straggled back out of the way to let a new race form up. The next bunch had to wait because the winner of the previous race was having trouble getting back aboard his chair, which kept rolling away from him when he tried to pull up.

Riley couldn't take it anymore and started to go help, but Will grabbed his arm and pulled him back down to the grass.

"No," he said. "Leave him alone."

One of the guys who had grappled on the ground for the cigarette pack, as soon as he had regained his own ride, pulled up behind the chair of the winner to block it from rolling back, and then reached over the seat and hoisted him up.

Riley pointed with an open hand and glared at Will as if to say, "See?"

Will stood his ground. "That guy can help him. You can't." It was a matter of credentials.

Will and Riley had watched the endless parade of mangled bodies for two days, and watched each other watching them. Neither of them said anything at first because they were overwhelmed, and they rarely spoke to each other anyway, but Walter Reed Army Hospital in the spring of 1968 was not the kind of place where a man could remain at peace with his thoughts for very long.

Another cigarette pack flew through the air, bounced on the grass, and they were *off*. More legless bodies pitched themselves into a squirming mass at the end.

"Man, this is sick," Riley said, "a pile of cripples fighting over a pack of cigarettes."

"They're not fighting for a pack of cigarettes." Will understood. He had seen the same spirit in 1944. "And it's not sick. It's heroic, is what it is."

"Heroic," Riley sniffed. He was sitting with his arms locked around his knees watching, his face hidden behind his bushy hair. Now he straightened up and leaned back onto his palms, looking at Will. "It's sad. It's horribly, tragically, gut-wrenchingly sad—and stupid. How is it heroic to get yourself ripped in half for no apparent reason?"

"They had a reason," Will said. "A *good* reason. They were defending their country. There's a price, son. Freedom isn't free." A picture floated to the front of his mind from the winter of '44—a ditch full of frozen bodies, arms and legs turned at odd, careless angles. Evil was real; it existed. And sometimes it had to be put down, whatever the price.

Riley waved loosely at the struggling mass of bandaged stumps. "They got their legs blown off *twelve thousand miles* from here! How is that defending their country?"

"You want to wait till they come here? You want to fight the communists *here*, after they've taken everything else? If we'd had that attitude in my day we'd be speaking German right now. We're taking the fight to *them*. And we're winning."

"Right," Riley sneered, as the victorious amputee held aloft a crushed pack of cigarettes. "Winning. This ain't no football game, Pops."

It was the first time Riley had ever called him "Pops," and it raised the hair on the back of his neck. Insolent punk. His own brother was one of these men. Did he think Welch had given his legs for nothing?

But Riley raged on, oblivious.

"You watch Huntley and Brinkley every night and they put the scores up—'In heavy fighting near Dung Poo today there were a hundred and thirty-seven Americans killed, five hundred and eighty-two wounded. But you oughta see the other guy—we maimed *two thousand* of them!' We win! Yippee!"

"Facts," Will said. "Numbers represent facts, that's all. You can poke fun at anything, but the *fact* is, those numbers tell a story. They tell the truth."

"No, they don't," Riley said, shaking his head. At seventeen, he was pretty sure he was the smartest man in the world. "They're television numbers. Politician numbers. Figures lie and liars figure." He pointed at the platoon of amputees dragging themselves back up into their wheelchairs. "Look at them. You don't hear about *these* guys on the six-o'clock news. All you hear is a nice clean number, and that's the lie. Brinkley says 'a hundred wounded,' you don't see *this*—you couldn't picture it in a million years. The wounded, they're the lucky ones, right? They're not dead; they can get on with their lives."

He paused for a second, squeezed his head as if it hurt, and then continued. "Yeah, right. What is it, maybe a dozen times in the last couple days we've seen gurneys go down the hall carrying guys with no legs, no arms, and no eyes? What's that guy gonna be when he grows up, huh? Second base?"

It shocked Will—the speed at which his arm flew out and back-handed his son in the teeth. The blow knocked Riley over for a second, but he righted himself, holding his fingers to his lips and glaring at Will. He pulled his fingers away to look at the blood, then got up without another word—maybe the smartest thing he could have done—and walked off down the street.

Helen would have gone after him if Will hadn't stopped her.

"No," he said. "Leave him alone."

"He turns eighteen next month," Helen said, glaring. Draft age. Her baby.

*That says it all*, Will thought. Riley's outburst hadn't come from any grand idealism but from common fear, and it was that one distinction, that little difference, which allowed Will to keep his dignity. And his anger.

"He needs to grow up," Will said, nostrils flaring.

The starter for the cigarette races was still sitting just down the hill in front of Will. He leaned to one side and dug a lighter out of the pocket of his robe, then flicked it three or four times trying to light a cigarette. He shook the lighter, cursed it, tried again. Nothing.

Will's dependable old Zippo clanged open and thumped to life. He reached over the one-armed soldier's shoulder and lit his cigarette for him, then, while he was at it, lit one for himself to calm his nerves.

"Thanks, Pops," the soldier said.

CHAPTER | 32

The blinding white landscape reminds Will to buy a pair of sunglasses when he stops for gas before they hit the interstate. Geauga County is to the northeast, not far from Lake Erie. Traffic is light. Occasionally a fine mist of ice crystals crawls across the surface like a cat's paw of ground fog, but it doesn't bother him. He has no problem driving in the daytime, though the unbroken waist-high bank of dirty snow lining the side of the expressway makes it feel like a bobsled run. The trouble comes at night when the headlights start to run together. He marvels at the efficiency of the road crews up here in this part of the country. If a foot of snow ever fell in Georgia it would take them a week to clear the roads. They aren't used to it.

Riley pulls his book from under the seat and withdraws into it. The morning must have been stressful for him. He doesn't know what to do with these people; they are utterly foreign to him, and he to them. He couldn't possibly remember much about his grandfather, but he has spent the morning trapped in the house with his grandfather's body and a hundred cousins whose names he doesn't know and whose language he doesn't speak. The counselor has told Will and Helen that Riley is fragile still, and he needs to avoid stress until he is stronger. Stress at this point, the counselor says, can literally drive him to drink. Gradually, he will build healthy methods and strategies for dealing with everyday problems, but for now the best thing he can do is escape into a book. It's far better than what he has escaped into in the past.

Will knows nothing about the book Riley is reading apart from what he has seen on the cover. He got bored once on the way up, while Riley was driving, picked it up and looked it over. On the front was an impressionist painting of what looked like a Mediterranean town on the water, done mostly in pinks and browns. The title, *Atlantis Requiem*, was scrawled in white letters on an angle across the top. The back of the book said it was a prizewinner of some kind, and there were endorsements from authors whose names Will didn't recognize and could not pronounce anyway. They used words like *luminous* and *alchemy*, and they called it "an important book." Nothing about it appealed to Will, but on the ride up to Geauga County, Riley fell into the story like Alice into the mirror.

An hour into the trip, Riley lowers his book and stares straight ahead, his brow furrowed.

"Was that a true story?" he asks, out of the blue. "About the donkey?"

"Oh!" Will chuckles. "Yeah. They were just kids. Ben and Sammy were always into something."

From a distance of more than forty years the story seems funny to him now. At the time, however, it was serious. They had nearly killed Daniel. The donkey was new and they didn't know anything about its temperament except that it was a bit wild. Levi had bought it to breed for mules. After chores one Saturday, when nobody was watching, Ben and Sammy hemmed the donkey up in the barn lot and tried to ride it. It tossed them in quick succession, so they got Daniel to try. He was a year older than Ben, a little bigger and stronger, except he was easygoing, so he often ended up playing the guinea pig in his younger brothers' grand schemes. To give Daniel an advantage, Ben hit on the idea of tying his feet together underneath the animal's belly with a short length of rope. The donkey quickly shook him off, but with his feet tied together he simply rolled around so that his head and arms ended up hanging down between four flailing hooves and the ground. By the time they got the donkey stopped and cut Daniel loose he was unconscious and bleeding profusely from several gashes about the head and shoulders. He regained consciousness two days later. He would eye donkeys and younger brothers with suspicion for the rest of his life.

Riley shakes his head. "Man, and I thought me and Welch did stupid stuff when *we* were little."

"They weren't stupid, they were just kids. Farm boys." Will doesn't know how to explain it to Riley. Underneath the plain clothes and beards and wide hats, Amish are just people, and like everyone else Riley will have to figure it out for himself.

Will stares at his son for a second as Riley picks up the book and finds his place again. His hair is short now, graying at the edges and starting to recede. The gauntness that has come upon him since his marriage and career fell out from under him would give him an almost distinguished look if it weren't for the circles under his eyes.

It seems now that Riley's collapse was inevitable: the natural end of selfishness is solitude. Will has always believed Riley was the engineer of his own destruction, but experience has taught him that all men engineer their own destruction, and it's not so simple as that. Digging through his memories in the silences of the last two days, a bigger picture has emerged. He begins to see that every man's failure dips its roots into the previous generation and drops its seeds into the next. Blame, as a wise man once told him, is the province of the innocent and the omniscient.

## CHAPTER 33

*September 1968*

Helen doted on Welch when he finally made it home from Walter Reed that fall. Welch gave Helen something too, because Riley left for college the next week and Welch saved her from having to face an empty house for the first time in over twenty years. Her sons had become the biggest part of her identity. She was, above all else, a mother. Will made the house wheelchair-friendly by building ramps on the outside and an assortment of pulleys and contraptions inside to help Welch get in and out of the bathtub or exercise his left arm to rebuild the portion of his bicep that the shrapnel hadn't ripped away. Will even traded the car for a new van with a wheelchair lift in the back.

Helen was the last one to accept that Welch would never walk again. Even then, Will knew that she privately prayed for a miracle, half believing that she would come into the kitchen one morning and find Welch standing at the sink rinsing out the coffeepot as if he had never owned a wheelchair. Welch, for his part, was a picture of grim determination. He had no illusions about walking again, for he had seen pictures of his spine and he understood from the beginning that even the occasional pains in his legs were only ghost pains—the memory of legs imprinted permanently on his neural pathways, nothing more. But he wanted his arm back. If he was going to have to drive a wheelchair he would do it with two good arms. He pushed himself well beyond the goals imposed by the doctors at the V.A. hospital, and sometimes beyond his abilities. More than once Helen found him sprawled in the yard at the end of the ramp wrestling with his overturned chair. Her strength at such times surprised her. She hoisted him back into his chair with an effortless ease. *His* strength surprised her even more—the way he fought against his weakness day after day without complaint, until inch by inch he built new muscles and forged a new reality for himself. He would simply live all the life he could with the tools he had at his disposal.

And then Riley came home on holidays giddy with the newfound sophistication of a college freshman, his hand out for more money and his trunk full of dirty clothes for his mother to wash.

The contrast did nothing to heal Will's feelings toward Riley. He didn't mean for it to happen that way, but there was Welch with his useless legs struggling to rebuild a withered arm, and here was Riley with his mouth and his attitude. Will mostly avoided him.

Will had always paid his own way, no matter what. It was a principle pounded into him from birth by the Amish. The Amish had gotten it from the earth, and from the Bible: a man carried his own weight. He worked or he didn't eat. A man, if he was a man of honor who understood Truth, would always put back more than he took, for that was his agreement with the earth, with God, with his brothers, and with his sons. He would apply whatever strength and knowledge he possessed with the sweat of his brow and the calluses of his hands, and he would leave a place better than he found it. This was not something Will thought about; it was the way he lived. So he never quite understood why Riley, who had never held a job of any kind, grated on him so. Will, whose hands loved the feel of concrete and steel and whose mind was tied to the good red earth, would simply leave the house whenever Riley started spouting politics or philosophy. He would go out and find something to do—till the garden or pick beans or tighten the cables on the scuppernong arbors or dredge the catfish pond or sling-blade the weeds on the earthen dam—to escape from Riley whenever he started blathering on about Timothy Leary's neopaganism or expounding on the evolution of graffiti as an art form.

Will did challenge Riley once, when he was parroting the latest rhetoric from some rabble-rousing leftist he'd heard speak in an antiwar rally at college.

"When did you turn into a communist?" Will asked.

Riley just laughed that arrogant Billy the Kid laugh of his. "I'm no communist," he said. "Too many rules. I think I'm an anarchist."

Will gave up. He didn't understand the things Riley said most of the time, and he figured it was probably just as well. The World was spinning completely out of control and taking Riley with it. Riley, because he was young and cocky, saw himself as master of his own fate, but Will looked at him from the distance he had made and saw a young man caught in the current like everybody else. Will began to wonder if the end-of-time prophets might be right after all. There were wars and rumors of wars, hurricanes and earthquakes and floods, men walking on the moon with such regularity that people didn't even stay up late to watch it anymore, and the Mets had won the World Series. The Second Coming could not be far away.

Riley's dark red mop of kinky hair grew on down between his shoulder blades. He kept it tied back most of the time, which gave him a vaguely Jeffersonian look until he discovered that his father hated mustaches, and then he grew a perfectly hideous Fu Manchu.

CHAPTER | 34

*March 1972*

During Riley's senior year at college, Will's stepmother died. Levi suspected a stroke. Elizabeth had collapsed suddenly while getting dressed on a Sunday morning. She was sixty-five, and had been married to Levi for two-thirds of that time. Helen tried to contact Riley, but his roommate said he was "off someplace at a rally with some girl" and he didn't know when he'd be back. Welch stayed home by himself while Helen and Will made the trip to Ohio. It seemed to Will that he spent half his life driving to Ohio to bury somebody.

It was the first time he ever saw the dawdi haus. Levi had built it across the drive from the main house, where Will grew up. It was the Amish way: when a man's sons were big enough to take over the farm, or when he became too old and infirm to work it properly himself, he sold his farm to whichever of his children bid the most for it. As part of the deal he reserved for himself a small parcel of land near the main house where he would build a dawdi haus—a one- or two-bedroom bungalow usually just large enough to accommodate himself and his wife. It was a form of retirement. The price of the farm provided him with a subsistence, and the family would look after the grandparents until they died, whereupon ownership of the dawdi haus reverted back to the farm. Levi had sold the place to Mose and moved into the dawdi haus, where he and Elizabeth had lived for less than a year when she died.

Ever optimistic, Helen thought that Will might be some small comfort to Levi under the circumstances. She said that maybe in his hour of grief Levi might lay aside his petty legalism and for once, after all these years, let his son be his son again, but Will was pretty sure Helen had no grasp of the nuances of Amish thinking. He knew, for instance, that Helen didn't understand the preacher at the funeral who pointed out, in Dutch, that Elizabeth had an excellent hope of heaven because she had in fact died while getting dressed for church.

While in Ohio, he and Helen also went to visit Katie, who had recently delivered her third child and who treated them with the same polite civility she would have shown to any of her assorted aunts and uncles. At least her husband didn't make Will eat in the corner—their family was small yet, and no one would know.

What bothered Will after he left was the marked absence of the word *grandfather*. Despite having three grandchildren, he would always be an uncle in Katie's house. His own lie had sealed the deal. It seemed like a Santa Claus kind of lie now, the kind grown-ups whispered to each other but studiously avoided in front of the children. Even children who knew better. After the lie spanned two generations it gained a measure of respectable antiquity so that even people who loved true things protected the noble lie from the ignoble truth, though Will could see that Katie would rather have had the truth for herself, and for her children. It pained her. He saw it when he was pushing her oldest boy in the tire swing out back, heard it in the way she spoke to him in the kitchen when no one else was listening, felt it in the lightest touch. She would rather have a father than an uncle, but the lie had become a kind of tradition and, being Amish, there was nothing she could do about tradition.

The day after the funeral Will and Helen stayed for dinner at the main house. Privately, Mose told Will he had no intention of banning him from the table. It was Mose's house now, and he would treat his brother as a brother. Levi was, of course, invited to dinner as a guest. No longer master of the house, he could not dictate how things would be done. The farm belonged to Mose.

But the instant Levi walked into the room, Will knew it wouldn't work. The old man stopped and took everything in. Will watched him closely and saw how the girls setting the table refused to meet their grandfather's wary eye. Then Levi turned and stared for too long and too hard at the empty corner where Will's card table should have been.

Pointing a crooked finger at Will, Levi addressed Mose in Dutch, with a commanding voice.

"Would this one be eating at your table?"

Everyone stopped what they were doing and looked at Mose.

"Ja." Mose nodded. "He is my brother."

"Then I will not," Levi said. "And the church will hear about it. A friend of the World is an enemy of God, and God does not change."

He would have done it. Levi would have called his own son on the carpet in front of the church and had him disciplined for letting Will eat at his table. Mose had made a valiant stand, but Will couldn't let him go through with it. He excused himself and left. He and Helen stopped on the way home for hamburgers at a McDonald's outside Columbus. He ate two bites and threw the rest away.

Riley's Volkswagen—instantly recognizable from the sunflowers painted across the back—was parked in the driveway when they got home, and they could hear shouting from the house as soon as they got out of the car. They found Riley and Welch squared off in the living room, screaming at each other.

Things might have worked out differently if Riley had showed up some other time—*any* other time. On this particular morning Will had just driven all night long while Helen slept in the back seat. All night he had been alone with his memories after having stood apart from the crowd like some kind of leper while they buried the only mother he ever knew. Driving south through the darkness, he thought about his ostracism at his stepmother's funeral, his humiliating retreat from Mose's house, and most of all the flashes of pain he saw in the eyes of the girl with the angel's kiss. Through the night he relived the moments, looking for answers and banging against the limits of his world like a June bug in a sealed jar.

The man who arrived home that morning was a frustrated and grievously wounded bear, and if Riley had known it perhaps even he would have had better sense than to tangle with him.

But despite his notable intelligence, Riley could rarely be depended upon for any kind of sense.

In the living room, Welch leaned forward in his wheelchair gripping the ends of the arms and screaming, "I don't CARE what you call it! You can call it civil disobedience, you can call it conscientious objection, you can call it peaceful protest, you can call it a purple plastic psychedelic cigarette machine for all I care, but I call it YELLOW!"

The Purple Plastic Psychedelic Cigarette Machine was a garage band with whom Riley had sung briefly, with predictably disastrous results. The mere mention of it usually sent him into spasms, and this time Welch had scored bonus points by eliciting a giggle from the willowy blonde watching the fight from the safety of the couch—Riley's latest squeeze. She had beads and feathers in her hair.

Riley was pointing his finger in Welch's face and preparing to launch a scathing rebuttal when he saw his father standing in the doorway. He straightened up then, nonchalantly jamming his fists into the pockets of the Army field jacket he was wearing. The stencil above the pocket said *McGruder*. Welch had given him the jacket four years ago, out of the duffel he brought home from Walter Reed. Somehow it took on a whole new meaning when Riley wore it.

"He's running to Canada," Welch said, still glaring at his brother. "And I want my jacket back."

Will said nothing, waiting for Riley to explain.

Riley shrugged and said, "They reclassified me. Took away my student deferment after we got busted last month at the Capitol. It's bogus. The whole thing's bogus, man—it was a perfectly legal gathering. The pigs—"

"Canada?" Will said.

"You know. Country to the north?"

Will's eyebrow arched.

"The country where draft dodgers go to hide," Welch spat. He was still leaning forward in his chair like a cat about to pounce.

"No, the country where men of conscience go to keep from fighting an unjust war," Riley countered. "A civilized country where they don't send soldiers to slaughter women and children." He still liked to bring up My Lai whenever possible.

"You're really going to Canada?" Will's nostrils flared.

"That's the plan, Pops."

Will pointed a thumb. "In that car?"

A nod, a shrug, a casual glance at his girlfriend.

"I paid for that car," Will hissed, "so you could go to college. Not so you could escape to Canada."

Riley's eyes narrowed. "I see," he said. "So a father's support for his kid is purely conditional, then. As long as I do what *you* would do, make the same choices *you* would make in every situation, you'll be my father. If not—" he chuckled then, and contempt dominated his voice—"you cancel the check. Well. Maybe you're right, Pops. Maybe I should honor my father's convictions. Like you did."

Everything happened too fast. Welch had crept closer while Riley was distracted, and now he seized the arm of the field jacket. Riley thrust a foreleg under the wheelchair and tried to rip himself away, but Welch, whose arms and hands had grown very strong from their taking over the work of his legs, held fast. Will's rage boiled over and he completely lost control. Later he would remember the wheelchair tipping over with Welch still clinging to the olive drab sleeve, Riley swinging a fist and peeling out of the field jacket, the girl screaming and tugging at him. And Will would see himself, as from a distance, going through the door with Riley clamped helpless in his arms, feet flailing, shouting curses. Though four inches taller and twenty-five years younger, Riley became a twig in the hands of a man who had worked hard all his life. Will burst through the storm door, tearing it off its hinges, then took a few running steps and hurled his son bodily into the driveway in the general direction of the Volkswagen.

Breathing heavily, glaring at Riley, he pointed to the car.

"Take it," he snarled. "Take it and don't come back."

The willowy blonde with the feathers in her hair helped Riley to his feet, and then the two of them tore off down the driveway in the sunflower Volkswagen. Riley's arm was out the window waving a final fare-well with his middle finger.

Helen watched him go, then plunked herself down right there in the driveway with her fingers entwined in her hair. There was nothing she could do but grieve.

A shudder ran up Will's spine as the shadow of a memory passed over him, uninvited. It was an old memory, more of body than mind, a flash of déjà vu from his arms and chest as he stood there trying to catch his breath after the exertion of wrestling the weight of a larger man out of the house and heaving him into the driveway. He shied away from the sight of his distraught wife and stumbled back toward the house, haunted by the face of Mikhail the Russian and filled with a terrible sense of fore-boding, a premonition that he would live to regret this day as deeply as he had that one.

Riley didn't write, didn't call. He disappeared from their lives without a trace.

But life went on, and the meltdown in the living room that day seemed to awaken something in Welch. He'd been brooding in his par-ents' house for four years, and while he had regained the strength in his arm he had reached a plateau where he simply didn't know what to do next. He had become stagnant, unable or unwilling to shove himself back into the mainstream of life until Riley came and stirred things up. Not long after the big fight with Riley, he bought his own van, with hand controls on the column and a wheelchair lift in the side door. To celebrate his independence he took a job in the local hardware store, which, com-bined with his disability check, resulted in a decent living.

Then he met a girl at church who didn't seem to mind that he was in a wheelchair. A shy, fragile girl with blue-white skin, wispy pale blond hair, and light gray eyes, Sandy did not trust most men but she felt safe with Welch. They understood each other. In tune with her reticence, he waited for her with a light touch and infinite patience as if he were taming a wild bird. When he and Sandy married they bought a house and got on with their lives.

Will was proud of Welch. Welch was a picture of courage.

CHAPTER | 35

*May 1977*

Will stood at the edge of a half-built bridge with his arms crossed, gazing down the long scar of a valley beneath him where bulldozers and great yellow earthmovers grunted and belched and shoved tons of red clay this way and that. It was midmorning of a cool, clear day in late spring after a weekend of hard rain. Banks of mimosa fronds cascaded from the tree line, drunk with rain and just beginning to put out salmon pink blooms. From behind him came the jangling, stomping, raucous noise of his crew laying out a grid of reinforcing rods, chairing them up, tying them down. Concrete would come after lunch.

"Cup of coffee?"

Barefoot had arrived, as he always did on Monday morning, to see what Will's crew needed for the week ahead. As usual, he brought coffee from the nearest Dunkin' Donuts. Cream, no sugar.

Will peeled the top from his styrofoam cup, took a sip, shook his head.

"You know, Barefoot, I don't think I'm ever going to understand you," he said. "What are you worth now, a couple million? And you're still bringing me coffee, still trucking material out to the jobs like some rookie gopher."

Barefoot smiled. "Sneaky way to bird-dog my crews, ain't it?"

"If it was anybody else I might believe that, but I've known you too long. The truth is, you're the most unorthodox man I've ever met."

It was true. Will had watched for years while Barefoot took the role of a helper to everybody in his company. In twenty years he had become the biggest bridge contractor in Atlanta, and he'd done it in a uniquely Barefoot fashion. Uncommonly generous with his men, he gave them free access to his storage warehouse, a vast uncatalogued scrapyard full of lumber, bar joists, structural steel, earthmoving machines, and electrical equipment. They all saved a fortune in material when they built a house. If there was concrete left over after a pour, Barefoot would let one of his men go home and pour a section of driveway with it rather than dump it out. If a man needed money beyond his paycheck Barefoot loaned it to him, interest free, and most of the time they even paid it back.

"Yeah," Barefoot said. "I guess I do things a little different. But you have to understand, Will, conventional wisdom is foolishness. The whole world has got it all upside-down, and in an upside-down world you can never have too much unorthodox."

Will shook out a cigarette to go with his coffee. Weekend rain had turned the whole valley to a quagmire, and one of the bulldozers had sunk up to his belly pan in it. The big machine rocked back and forth, raising and lowering his blade, twisting and turning and pouring out black smoke, but everything he did only buried his tracks deeper. Will blew a cloud of smoke, watching as an earthmover eased up against the back of the bulldozer and tried to push him out of the hole he'd dug for himself.

"You should tell that to my old man," Will said, flexing his left shoulder against a deep ache. "Now *there* is an orthodox man."

Barefoot stared at him for a second. "You're going up there again? I didn't realize it was that time of year already."

"Next week."

"So, you going up to the new place?" Barefoot asked. A year after Elizabeth's death Levi had remarried and moved up to his new wife's place in Geauga County.

"Yeah. It'll be a little strange. I was never sure if Dad was part of the farm or the farm was part of him. It's hard to think of him separate from it, you know what I mean? Then again, it's probably just as easy to be a stubborn, judgmental old mule in Geauga County as it is in Apple Creek."

"Then why do you keep going back? You told me yourself you couldn't please him, even when you were a kid, *before* you messed up. What makes you think you can please him now?"

Will shrugged. "I probably can't, but I promised my brother I'd try. Tobe was right. A man needs somebody to measure himself against, even if he comes up short." He still didn't entirely understand it, but after all these years he knew better than to fight it. For whatever reason, he knew Tobe was right. He would have his father's blessing if it took the rest of his life.

He propped his cigarette in his mouth and worked his left arm in a circle. The earthmover was stuck too, now, and another bulldozer had arrived to push against it. It was a sight, the three giant machines all in a row, bumping against each other and shuffling their feet in the mud. The pain in his shoulder was getting worse.

"Bursitis," Barefoot said, watching Will work his arm. "You're gonna have to slow down, old man. Wouldn't want you to fall and break a hip."

"It was that sledgehammer this morning," Will said. "I just need to loosen it up." He flexed his left hand. "Must have pinched a nerve in there. Got needles in my fingers."

A fourth bulldozer had joined in the dance and he, too, was about to be stuck. Something about dancing bulldozers struck Will as really funny, and he started to make a comment when a searing pain locked his jaw and it came out as a dull grunt. The cigarette tumbled from his mouth. The pain from neck and shoulder merged and forked downward into his chest, intensifying, drawing his whole body into itself. His fist clenched, the styrofoam cup crumpled and coffee spattered his boots. His chest caved in and his left arm clutched his ribs.

"Will?" he heard Barefoot say, but he couldn't see him.

Awareness came to him several times over the next few days, but in varying degrees, and slowly. It began, always, with voices. Whatever dream he was in would skip and tear and then fade completely, replaced by bloody darkness like looking at the sun through closed eyelids. And voices—the sound of many people talking, like a crowded lobby before the theater opens.

A single voice called to him, faintly at first, above the tumult, and then more clearly. A little hole full of reality opened in front of him, and Helen's face appeared in it.

"Will?" Beyond her face the world was white.

Pain. Reality brought pain. In his throat, in his chest, everywhere. Pain. Sleep.

"Will?"

He opened his eyes again. Helen. A bit clearer this time.

"Will, look who's come to see you!"

He turned his head a few degrees. A man's face, a mustache. The mustache was melting, running down past the corners of his mouth and hanging off of his chin.

"What's up, Pops?"

Riley.

Sleep.


Several hours later he awoke again, and this time he swam all the way up to the surface. Much of the pain came from the breathing tube in his throat, which they mercifully removed shortly after he woke up. Helen was there by his bedside, and the first words out of his mouth were, "Was Riley here?"

She nodded, smiled. "He'll be around for a few days. He's here with his . . . wife, and their daughter. We met Genevieve once before but, uh, we never got her name. You know."

He knew. The blonde with the feathers in her hair. Helen had pronounced the name the French way, and it struck Will as an extraordinary concession for a Georgia girl who would normally rather die than attempt a foreign pronunciation of anything. Not that she couldn't. It was just a point of honor in the South not to try. The pronunciation alone was enough to tell Will where Helen stood: She was making every possible concession to patch things up with Riley and his . . . wife.

"What's he doing here?" Will asked. It had been almost five years since he threw Riley out, and there had been no word the entire time. It struck him as too much of a coincidence that Riley would show up now, at his deathbed.

Helen took his hand, stroked it with her thumb, kept her eyes there.

"He called me a few months ago," she said. "Right after Jimmy Carter signed the amnesty thing. I didn't say anything then because I didn't want . . . I didn't know how you'd react, so I just . . . you know, kept quiet. They live in California now, and they were planning on coming here pretty soon anyway. Aw, Will, just wait till you meet Sky—our grand-daughter. She's precious."

"Am I going to live?" he asked. He really didn't know, and if the pain in his sternum was any indication he would have guessed not.

"It looks like it. For a while there it was . . . we didn't know. They did something called a coronary bypass—I still don't understand it, but Dr. Naidu says you'll be okay. He says I got to learn how to cook all over again, and you can't smoke anymore. One cigarette and you're a dead man."

"Really?" He'd heard all the noise from the medical establishment in recent years, but only half believed it. Not that long ago all the cigarette ads on TV said smoking was good for you. Now all of a sudden it was lethal.

"He said one cigarette is enough to kill me?"

"No, he said stop smoking. If I catch you with a cigarette I'm gonna kill you myself. I'm not going through this again."

It moved him almost to tears. The look in her eye when she threat-ened him spoke of a deep and terrible fear, and the fear spoke of a deep and terrible love.

Riley paid several visits to Will's room that week. He looked different. His hair wasn't out to his shoulders anymore. He'd gotten it styled down to a sort of short Afro. In concert with the garish mustache and the plaid, wide-lapel sports jacket, it gave him a very California look. Very mod. Genevieve wasn't a bad sort now that she'd become a mom, and Sky was a pure delight. A two-year-old terror with her dad's frizzy cordovan hair, she was endlessly inquisitive and drove the nurses crazy with her grabbing things.

Riley had become independent. Through five years of exile he had proven to himself that he was his own man, and now he approached his father with the air of an equal. He made no mention of the battle of the field jacket, nor did Will, though Helen said privately that Welch still wouldn't have much to do with his brother. With five years of silence and a heart attack between them, Riley and Will managed to reach an agreement without ever actually talking about it: They would simply let the past be the past.

Riley talked almost too frankly about his amnesty, and Will found it surprising that he bore no hint of shame for what he had done. He obviously considered the president's amnesty to be the natural and proper correction of a wrong that had been committed against the whole society. Will said nothing. The doctor said anger was bad, so he suppressed it.

Riley also talked endlessly about his work, and it made his eyes light up every time. While he was in Canada he'd gotten a mail-order kit for building some kind of little computer, and not only did he learn that he was a fair hand with a soldering gun but he discovered he had a natural gift for visualizing his way through a labyrinth of miniscule chips and circuit boards. He had friends in all the right places, and as soon as amnesty came through he went straight to California, to someplace he called Silicon Valley.

"You wouldn't believe it," he said, beaming. "My friend Chan got me into this think tank at Peltzer Semiconductor and, man, you just wouldn't believe it. We're making *crazy* money, and all we do is play. Seriously, it's like play. We're like the problem solvers for this next-generation game system, right? So we come up with a display chip for a new TV interface adapter and the suits are, like, 'FAR OUT!' I'm telling you, Pops, it was a piece of strudel, and they think we're, like, *geniuses* or something."

"And what you're doing is all for some kind of game?" Will was sitting up in his hospital bed with his hands folded in his lap. As usual, he didn't follow much of what Riley said.

"Yeah! A cartridge system, if you can believe it. It's the coolest thing to hit this country since . . . *ever,* and we're all going to be millionaires, you'll see. We're going to rule the world."

Will said nothing. It made no sense and nothing was likely to come of it, but he was in no position to argue with Riley, so he said nothing. He wouldn't say it, but deep down he thought the best news he'd heard from Riley was that he lived three thousand miles away.

Riley went home the next day—back to California, to "work." Welch wheeled himself in right after Riley left, and he seemed unusually cynical. He kept making little snide remarks about Riley's bloodshot eyes, and noting that his clothes smelled like burnt rope. Will didn't know what he was talking about—or want to, frankly. He was just glad to be alive.

CHAPTER | 36

*May 1977*

The day after he got home from the hospital Will insisted on getting up at five o'clock and getting dressed. Helen rolled her eyes and muttered an oath or two but she helped him get his clothes on. Incredibly stiff and sore, he couldn't bend far enough to put on pants, let alone shoes and socks. Since she was up, she went to the kitchen and started the water for a pot of oatmeal—the first of many. Later in the day, after she gathered the eggs, she called Eloise Crump and sold her the laying hens. All of them. Dr. Naidu said eggs were no good for Will's heart.

She wouldn't let Will do anything. *Anything.* Fortunately he had gotten the garden all planted before the heart attack and there was plenty of grass in the pasture for the new beef cattle he was raising, so he could afford to take a little break. But Helen wouldn't let him do *anything.* He tried to sneak off from his rocking chair on the porch a time or two, just to walk around the property and see how everything was going, but Helen always caught him before he got fifty feet and made him come back. She wasn't taking any chances.

After a week they took their case before Dr. Naidu and he sided with Will, giving his blessing for Will to walk as much as he felt like walking.

Barefoot came by to see him one evening after work. He found Will sitting in a lawn chair at the edge of the catfish pond in the shade of a poplar tree with a cane pole in his hand.

"I want you to kill me," he told Barefoot. He nodded toward the pond. "Weak as I am, you could probably pin me down with one hand. Just hold me under till I quit wiggling and the bubbles stop coming up. It's your fault, you know. You could've let me die that morning on the bridge, but no, you had to put me in the back of a truck and do CPR all the way to the hospital. Now here I am stuck at home with Helen the Hun. I can't go anyplace, can't work, can't smoke, can't eat anything—no salt, no bacon and eggs, no fried chicken, no pork chops. I'm living on rabbit food, if you call this living. Kill me now."

"Nope," Barefoot said, lowering himself to sit on a rock. "You brought this on yourself, Will, so just shut up and take your medicine like a man. Besides, you'll be ready to go back to work in a week or two, I can tell. Anybody that can gripe like that is pert' near well, if you ask me."

"You tell him, Jubal. He won't listen to me." Helen was the only one who ever called Barefoot by his first name. She had come up behind them with two glasses of iced tea. She handed one to each of them.

Will took a big slug and spit it abruptly into the pond as if he'd gotten a mouthful of kerosene.

Barefoot's prominent Adam's apple bobbed a couple of times as he took a long pull, then he smacked his lips and said, "Thank you, ma'am. Will, there ain't nothin' wrong with this tea."

Turning back toward the house, Helen glanced over her shoulder and said, "There's *sugar* in yours, Jubal."

Will sat his glass on the ground next to his lawn chair and frowned at the bobber.

"See what I mean?" he said.

Barefoot wiped his mouth on his sleeve and answered, "That woman's the best thing ever happened to you."

Will couldn't argue. "One of the *two* best, anyway." He meant Barefoot. It was as fine a compliment as either of them would ever actually put into words, though a thousand unspoken expressions of trust had passed between them over the years.

"Well," Barefoot said, and then stopped. He didn't know how to answer such a thing.

"I've been thinking," Will said. He stared stone-faced at his bobber. "You know how they say when you die your whole life flashes before your eyes? I've seen quite a bit of my life lately."

"You're not dying," Barefoot said.

"We're all dying, but that's not the point. You just don't really think about it until . . . until something happens."

"Now you're gettin' all philosophical on me. I hate when you do that."

"I don't remember ever doing it before. How long have we known each other? Thirty years?"

Barefoot scratched his chin, screwed his face up. "Thirty-three, if I remember right."

"And in all those years have we ever really talked about what we believe?"

"In words?" Barefoot asked. He drew his long legs up and folded his forearms across his knees.

It was a good question. A *really* good question, and Will would save it for later.

"What are we here for?" Will asked.

Barefoot's mouth twisted. He stared at Will's bobber. Both of them sat motionless, staring at the little red and white plastic ball. Barefoot didn't much like to talk about what he believed. He preferred to leave the other guy a little space.

"To catch fish?" he finally offered.

Nothing moved except Will's wrists. The long cane pole tilted slowly upward and the bobber jiggled clear of the water. Two feet more and a lead split shot the size of an English pea appeared, swinging side to side, and a foot below that a shiny fishhook danced. There was no bait on the hook. Will held it there for a second while they both got a good look at it, and then lowered it gently back down into the water.

"What do I know? I build bridges," Barefoot said.

"You know plenty. You know something not many people know, but I can't figure out what it is. I've been watching you for ... thirty-three years?—and I still can't figure it out. I'm not even sure you *know* you know it, but you do."

"I don't even know what you're talking about. Can you give me a hint?"

"Wish I had a cigarette," Will said absently. "Helps me think. All I know is work. Need money? Get a job. You want a barn? Cut some trees and go to work. Want vegetables on the table? Get a shovel and plant something. Work is the answer to everything. Always has been."

"Nothin' wrong with work," Barefoot said.

The aluminum frame of the lawn chair screeched as Will leaned forward and propped his forearms on his knees. He didn't look at Barefoot because what he was saying was deadly serious and it helped not to make eye contact.

"But then one day you wake up in the hospital and it hits you all of a sudden that all the stuff you think you're accomplishing doesn't mean as much when you're looking back as it did when you were looking forward."

He stopped talking for a minute and wiggled the cane pole as if he expected something to bite a bare hook.

"You remember that stupid question Harm used to pester everybody with? The thing about the bus?"

Barefoot chuckled. Harm had been working for him from the beginning, same as Will. "Yeah. A bus with nine people on it stops and picks up two, lets off three. That one?"

"Right. And he goes through a bunch of stops, adding, subtracting, and everybody sits there counting fingers, trying to keep up with the total."

"And when it's over he says, 'How many stops did the bus make?'"

Will chuckles too. "Yeah. Old Harm. He never gets tired of a joke. But what if it's like that when you die? What if you get to the end of your life and find out you used up all your time getting ready to answer the wrong question?"

A shrug. "How you gonna know?"

"Exactly. That's what I thought about when I was laying up there in the hospital. What does God want from me?"

"Way over my head," Barefoot said. He picked up his glass of iced tea, which was about half empty, and Will's, which was nearly full, and proceeded to pour them back and forth into each other, mixing them. "Helen makes her tea way too sweet for me," he said. "Don't tell her I said that."

Will took his glass back, tasted it.

"Much better," he said, then drank some and sat the glass carefully on the ground. Odd, though. He knew for a fact Barefoot liked Helen's too-sweet tea.

Over the next few weeks Will regained a lot of his strength and put some of the color back in his cheeks. By gradually extending his walks, before he knew it he was covering miles. More than that, ranging alone about the farm and surrounding countryside somehow helped him to think.

One particular morning he wandered down to the creek on the other side of the Kilgore place thinking of the conversation he'd had with Barefoot, and the question he had asked. *"What does God want from me?"* Barefoot had seemed the right person to ask. It seemed logical to assume that any man who knew the answer would be a happy man, and Barefoot was the happiest man Will knew. Yet Barefoot couldn't answer his question.

Coming back, the uphill walk out of the creek valley winded him a little, so he sat down to rest on a pine log at the edge of the Kilgore farm, not far from where, years ago, he had talked to Tobe for the last time. It was here that a new thought came to him.

Why not just ask God?

Will hadn't really tried to talk to God since he was excommunicated by the Amish. He and God had pretty much left each other alone after that. For over thirty years now he'd gone through the motions with Helen and the kids. It hadn't been that hard—walk the aisle, get baptized, memorize the songs, learn a few churchy words, wear a tie. It was all just stuff. Work. Pretending wasn't hard at all, and it made Helen happy. It wasn't that Will didn't believe in God. He had always believed in God; he just didn't think God believed in him. Now, having glimpsed his own mortality, he felt he had nothing left to lose. For a man already condemned it seemed a reasonable gamble, flinging a half angry challenge at God.

"So talk," he said, out loud, sitting on his pine log with his palms on his knees. "If you're there, talk to me. I'm listening. Tell me what you want from me."

But the noonday sun didn't flash any messages, the cotton-ball clouds didn't reshape themselves into words of wisdom, and the only sound from the weed-choked field in front of him was the drone of midsummer insects. He watched and listened patiently for any kind of sign, but nothing came.

Alone in the quiet, his thoughts strayed once again to Barefoot. It didn't make sense. Something deep inside him, some innate sense of rightness, told him that if anybody knew the secret to life and happiness, if anybody held the keys, if anybody knew how to get along with God himself, it had to be Barefoot.

A bobwhite called and brought Will back to himself, a little angry and a little frustrated because he had set himself down with the soundest intention of hearing what God had to tell him, and then drifted promptly away. His stomach said it was time for lunch. He got up, dusted himself off and headed back, growing more irritated by the minute because even as he walked back to the house with his hands in his pockets he couldn't shake the image of Barefoot sitting there by the pond pouring tea back and forth between two glasses, one sweet and one not.

He hung his cap on a peg just inside the kitchen door. Helen was stirring something on the stove, and it smelled good.

"Where you been?" she asked.

"Up by Kilgore's. Looks like they're finally going to cut that big stand of pine. There's machines parked up in the woods."

"You feel all right?" She looked him over, smiled.

"Better every day," he said. "I'm thinking I'll dig potatoes this afternoon." He was asking permission.

She nodded, ladling soup into bowls. "I guess by now you know your limits," she said.

He watched her for a minute. She was just dipping soup, but lately he had learned to see a delicate beauty in such moments. Moved, as he often was these days, by a loyalty he had finally come to see for the miracle it was, he went and stood behind her and put his hands on her shoulders until she laid down the ladle and turned to put her arms around him.

"Why are you still here?" he whispered in her ear. "After all I put you through."

She thought for a second and said, "I had the great misfortune to fall in love with you."

"A lot of people say that. Most of the time it won't weather a storm."

"Well then it's not love. Love forgives. That's how you can tell."

He finished his soup and sat for a minute, staring out the window at his garden. Rain had been plentiful. The garden had done just fine without him for a while, and harvest time was turning out to be exactly the therapy he needed at this point in his recovery. The garden called to him now, and he would go out as soon as he finished his tea.

The round kitchen table where they took their meals had for years accommodated the four of them—Will, Helen, Welch, and Riley—but now that the boys were gone it seemed half of the table had turned into a desk space that collected papers and pens, books, letters, junk mail, checkbook, and bills. Since the heart attack there had been a flood of doctor and hospital bills. Helen's Bible lay open on the table where she'd been reading that morning, and lying on top of it was a letter she'd gotten yesterday from Genevieve announcing that she and Riley were expecting another baby. Will had to listen to a lot of grandmother talk over his split-pea soup. Helen liked being a grandmother. It suited her.

She cleared the table and ran water in the sink while prattling happily about maybe going to California. Will was sort of half listening to her. The idle busyness of Helen's lunchtime talk had driven out the morning so that he completely forgot the question he'd flung out like a prayer earlier. Sitting there with his chin in his palm, he only wondered how big his potatoes would be. He reached over absently while he half listened to her, the way a man might doodle on a piece of paper while his mind drifts, and tugged Helen's Bible out from under Riley's letter to see what she'd been reading. There was a pen in the crease, and she had underlined something. He pinched his reading glasses from his shirt pocket, flicked his wrist, slid them onto his face, and read.

*"He hath shewed thee, O man, what is good; and what doth the Lord require of thee, but to do justly, and to love mercy, and to walk humbly with thy God?"*

He got up and left so quietly that Helen was still talking to him from the kitchen sink as he eased the screen door shut. He had no idea what she was saying.

Stopping by the barn, he laid a good stiff pitchfork on top of the wheelbarrow and trundled it out to the garden where he could think. He was shaken by what had happened. He had asked a question of God— *What do you want from me?*—and found the answer, in plain language, waiting for him in the Bible. It was not the answer itself that had shaken him, but the granting of it. It had come to him in such a small way that he knew beyond doubt that God had done it. God had heard his question, and answered it.

The dialog was open. *That* was what shook him.

322 | W. DALE CRAMER

Driving the pitchfork under the little ridge of potato plants with his boot, he pried against it, breaking the ground. His partnership with the earth was simple, and in it he found a kind of clarity, a stillness. He began to wonder what else he had missed. If God was speaking to him now, maybe He always had been. Maybe God had written other answers for him, not only in the Bible but in the earth, and in his own life—answers he had missed because he didn't know how to look.

He pulled up a cluster of potatoes bound together by root and soil, shook the dirt from them, and began to see that his idle reminiscences of Barefoot were not idle at all, but an answer, a clear and pointed message. Looking back across the years he saw himself surrounded by Jubal Barefoot, and Helen, and Tobe—people whose very lives spoke of kindness and justice and humility—and he understood, finally, that God *had* spoken to him.

Helen's voice came to him then, from a memory less than an hour old. He stopped and looked up into the sun, pulled the cap from his head, wiped his brow with it, and laughed. It was so simple, and it had been there all along. He just hadn't been able to hear it.

*"Love forgives,"* Helen said. *"That's how you can tell."*

It had stuck in his mind when she said it, though at the time he didn't know why. It was an echo. Now the words of the priest came back to him as clearly as if the little gray-haired man had been standing next to him in his garden, and not thirty years away in the middle of an ocean.

*"Somehow you must come to understand that God is love, that love is the proof of God, and forgiveness is the proof of love."*

Will understood it all at once, and for the first time in his life he knew—*knew*—that God loved him. Levi Mullet had simply been mistaken. Levi was not God, and his word was not the last word. No man could keep the Law; his only hope lay in the grace of God. The wrong Will had done and all the roots that had grown from it, all the lies he had told and all the harm that had come to those he loved because of it, *all of it* was covered by the grace of God.

He stood in his garden relieved, for the first time, of the weight of his own past—emptied, and then filled with light.

Leaning on his pitchfork, laughing to himself, he recalled vaguely that the priest had said something about planting a seed.

*Well,* he thought. *It has sprouted.*

## CHAPTER 37

*August 1978*

Will and Helen didn't make it to Ohio the year Will got his heart rebuilt, but the following summer they resumed their normal pattern and went up for a week. Things had changed. The first thing Will noticed, the thing that made him look for other signs, was the hat.

As soon as he could, Will nudged Helen and muttered, "Did you see the hat?" They were following Mose's wife down to look at something in the kitchen garden.

Helen looked around in confusion. They all wore hats.

"What hat?"

Mose was wearing a straw summer hat with a brim noticeably narrower than the Schwartzentruber hat all the men in the family had worn all their lives, and his hair was a bit shorter. Will could see his earlobes. Two of Mose's buggies now had rubber on the wheels, and the cornfield showed signs of having been harvested by a motorized corn picker. Things had definitely changed since Levi left. All of it was beneath Helen's notice, and yet it fairly shouted to Will.

"Oh, ja, we joined a new church," Mose said when Will finally asked him. He said it with a casual flip of the hand as if it were nothing, but Will knew better. It was not a small matter to leave the Old Order church, especially for Mose, who was almost sixty years old now. The differences between Old and New Order might have seemed slight to an outsider. Not so to an Amishman. Will didn't press the issue, but as the rest of the family came around to visit, or he went to visit them, he discovered that it was a mass exodus. Nearly all of his brothers and sisters had switched to a more liberal church. Daniel and Clara were the only holdouts as far as he could tell. Nevertheless, it wasn't something Will openly discussed, even with Mose, because he still thought of himself as an outsider.

Then, at mealtime, Will noticed the card table was missing from the corner, and as they gathered around the table Mose looked at Will and motioned casually to the chair next to his own. Will and Helen sat down at Mose's table and were treated as family. Nobody made a big deal of it, or even mentioned it, for the Amish studiously avoid prideful ceremony. But after everyone had pulled up to the table Mose turned to Will and said, "I wonder if you would like mebbe to ask out loud a blessing for this meal."

It was not the Amish custom to pray aloud at the table. Will had never heard of such a thing. Their mealtime prayer had always been silent, a bowing of heads for a moment. This was clearly a grand gesture of absolution. He prayed, thanking God for the meal and humbly requesting his continued blessings. It was an Amish kind of prayer, short and to the point, and he meant every word of it.

Mostly through hints and clues, some subtle and some not so subtle, Will figured out that by simply changing their allegiance to a New Order church that didn't hold the ban against him, his siblings had been able to quietly forget about it. Sitting at this table with this family for the first time in thirty-five years he saw it for the act of grace that it was, and he was moved to a deep and genuine gratitude. God does not change, but sometimes people change the way they see Him.

After lunch Will decided to drive up and visit his father at the Kauffman place in Geauga County. Mose offered to go along because he wanted to see Levi too, and because Will wasn't sure he could find the place. It was the first time Mose had ever ridden in a car with him.

Levi looked old. He seemed to have shrunk, and what was left of his hair had grown too thin to hide his ears, though it remained cut in the traditional bowl. His beard had turned yellow in the middle. His face, while hawkish and keen as ever, had developed new folds and liver spots. Will and Mose stayed only for a few hours, during which Levi never left his rocking chair on the front porch, calling out to Naomi whenever he wanted something. He ordered popcorn for the three of them and after a while she brought it, along with cups of water. Despite the warm afternoon, Levi kept a blanket draped over his knees the whole time. He was eighty years old. Though Will knew change was inevitable, he had never expected to one day find the incorruptible Levi Mullet wrapped in the husk of an old man.

They talked about crops and horses and weather and life on the Kauffman farm, yet despite the absolution granted him by the rest of the family, Will sensed no change in his father's attitude. Naomi was careful to give Will a separate bowl of popcorn. Once or twice the conversation veered dangerously close to the family's abdication of the Old Order church. When it did, Levi changed the subject. He was Schwartzentruber. The Kauffmans were Schwartzentruber. Levi would never be convinced that there was any other way to get to heaven. If God did not change, then neither would Levi Mullet.

In the end Will knew, and he knew that he had always known, that no matter what his brothers did, it was his father's pardon that mattered most. He couldn't explain it, might not ever even understand it, but he knew he had to have his father's blessing.

After a couple of hours Levi fell silent and still. When he hitched a little snore and they saw that he had fallen asleep in his chair, Will and Mose rose quietly and stepped inside to say goodbye to Naomi. On impulse, as he was leaving, Will stopped to pull the blanket up around his father, tucking it gently under his arms. He felt a great lost tenderness toward Levi in that moment, asleep in his rocker with bits of popcorn stuck in his yellowing beard, and would probably have kissed him gently on the forehead as he slept if he had not been Amish. Instead, he reached out very softly and brushed the backs of his fingers against his father's cheek.

"I *am* sorry," he whispered.

On the long drive back down to Apple Creek Mose fell silent for a while and then said, without preamble, "How much longer we'll have him with us, we don't know. We should bring everyone together so, before he dies, how God has blessed his life he can see."

Of all the words Mose had put together it was the "we" that moved Will. While there had been other reunions over the years, Will had never been invited. Once or twice when he was visiting, one of the women would start to talk about something that happened at a recent reunion— an ailing aunt had a seizure, or that roughneck Beachy boy broke little

Harvey's wrist playing baseball—but then they would invariably glance at Will or Helen and hastily change the subject. Will, being banned, was not part of the family, and was therefore not invited to reunions. Mose's "we," for Will, was a small word with profound implications.

## CHAPTER 38

*June 1979*

Mose made the reunion happen in June of the following year at his farm, the old homeplace in Apple Creek. Or perhaps it would be more correct to say that Mose *instigated* the reunion. Most of the preparation fell to the women while the men worked in the fields.

Welch and Sandy and their two kids came along, wheelchair strapped to the roof, and Helen tried hard to get Riley to bring his family from California, but it was not to be. In fact, she never even talked to Riley. Genevieve said it sounded nice and she'd like to do it if it was up to her, although frankly she didn't see it happening.

The news hit Helen hard, partly because news out of California had been scarce for a long time, and partly because the few letters Genevieve did write hinted at serious problems. Helen rarely called, and when she did Riley was never there. He was always either working or "off with some friends." He had done well, according to Genevieve—he'd made a lot of money. An "awful" lot of money, she said. But there was always a suppressed bitterness in her, and she made no secret of the fact that she was tired of Riley's drinking. And worse. Once she even slipped and said something about too much of his money going up his nose. Helen steamed and fretted and prayed, but she was too far away to do anything. When she tried to talk to Will about it he just shook his head.

"He's a grown man," Will said. "He made his choices and now he can live with them. He's not my problem anymore."

The day of the reunion dawned spectacularly clear. Mose's practiced hand had brought his farm to the peak of perfection so that everywhere Will looked he saw a postcard. A hawk drifted motionless, soaring high against a crystal sky, watching. A thick field of hay rippled like fine fur in a light breeze while a small herd of Haflingers galloped and romped across a strikingly green pasture, tossing their blond manes and racing each other down toward the pond. A pair of white herons stalked the edge of the water in the shade of an overhanging willow until a larger blue heron coasted in on top of them and chased them out. Strawberry plants and succulent young cornstalks boasted their health in a lush blue-green. Red and white and yellow flowers of all kinds ringed the house and garden, and a wood thrush sang from the sugar maple at the corner of the stable. The air smelled of cut hay.

Buggies lined up shoulder to shoulder by the barn and along the drive leading out the back way, their tongues resting on the ground. Some of the horses had been turned into the pasture for the day, but most of them had been put up in comfort either in the stables or in barn stalls. A line of large nondescript vans had parked down past the buggies—hired transportation for those who had come from out of state.

By the time Will and Helen arrived, the teenagers had all migrated down to the large front lawn for a volleyball game. Welch and Sandy couldn't help chuckling at the sight of boys in long pants and suspenders and girls in full dresses and white pilgrim coverings playing volleyball.

Married men stood around the barn, buggy shed, and stables in small groups talking about horse auctions and corn and hay and tobacco while their wives loaded the tables in the buggy shed with a potluck feast heavy on noodle casseroles, vegetables and "chello." The smaller children had gathered in a large cluster, sitting on the ground in the shade of an oak tree.

The buggy shed was basically a big deep three-bay garage taking up roughly half of a long building that housed stables in the other half. The flock of buggies, hacks, and wagons that normally resided here was moved around back to make room, and all the bay doors and windows opened to let the air flow through. The concrete floor had been scoured the day before, and the church benches brought in to serve as both tables and seats. Designed and built with Amish craftsmanship and thrift, the sturdy benches could be folded flat to fit tightly in the church wagon, or linked and stacked to make tables, or used in the conventional way as pews or benches.

Will stopped the car in front of the buggy shed to unload the wheelchair, and folks gathered around Welch right away. They waited turns to shake his hand and say hello, for they had not seen him since he was little and had never met his wife and children. Altogether nearly three hundred people milled around the old homeplace, dozens of whom were Welch's first cousins. He didn't recognize any of them.

Will took Welch around to meet everybody while the women whisked away Helen and Sandy and the kids. Even now, at such an informal and celebratory reunion, the women collected on the end of the buggy shed nearest where they were preparing the food, and the men wandered loosely elsewhere. Will was struck by the colors. So many of the family had switched to New Order that now there was a noticeable variety of color in their clothes, if not style. He saw shirts and dresses in shades of blue and green, and even a smattering of pink. Years ago, everything was black and white.

Though Welch rarely recognized a face, Simon sparked his memory by ogling him and his wheelchair with the same odd invasiveness Welch recalled from when he was a kid.

Daniel came by and offered a stiff, one-pump Amish handshake when Will introduced him, nodding and saying not a word. After he walked away Welch asked, "What happened to his forehead?"

"Donkey," Will said. "Ask me later."

Ben and Samuel introduced themselves, laughing, as always, like a couple of happy dwarves. They looked a little different to Will, now with the shortened hat brims and visible ears. Beards that had always hung down a hand's length were cropped short. Will made a little stroking motion against his chin with his fingers, smiling.

"Oh, ja!" Ben said. "We got clipped! I feel a liddle bit naked, these days. Don't you, Sammy?"

Samuel grabbed his earlobes and feigned a wide-eyed surprise, as if he'd just noticed his own haircut.

When he got the chance Will took Welch over to where the women had congregated so he could meet his aunts. Alma stood out because she wore the shorter dress of a Mennonite, the only print dress in attendance, apart from Helen and Sandy. The covering on the back of her head was smaller as well—about the size of a yarmulke. In the context of the Amish women, whose uncut hair was always hidden under the stiff white coverings as a sign of submission to their husbands, the postage stamp of cloth pinned to the back of Alma's head seemed to say that submission was more of a suggestion really. She was so liberal she'd flown in from Montana on a commercial airliner.

Welch said he remembered Clara, but barely. They found her sitting with a group of older women, the matriarchs of the clan. She spoke to them politely enough, but she maintained a kind of stiff formality. She and Will's brother Daniel had remained Old Order, and Will figured she was likely a little nervous about allowing him to eat from the table at the family reunion. Will hadn't eaten at Clara's house in twenty years—Helen refused to go there at mealtime—but he was pretty sure she would still keep the ban, even now. Like their father.

Cassie, at thirty-six, still had the gleam of mischief in her eyes when she smiled. Will was talking to Cassie when he became aware of someone waiting at his shoulder and turned around to find Katie.

"Katie! There you are!" he said, a little too enthusiastically, as he touched her elbow. "I've been looking for you."

She smiled a little, and Will could have sworn he saw the angel's kiss flash ever so lightly. "We just got here," she said. "Reuben is putting away the buggy yet."

"You remember Welch, don't you? Welch, this is your . . . cousin, Katie."

It was only a little pause, the tiniest little hesitation, but it threw Will's thoughts completely out of the moment, for he saw that it was precisely then—right there, in the middle of that little hesitation—that Katie's eyes dropped away from him.

Welch smiled, stuck out a hand, said something. Will had no idea what he said to her. Absorbed in his own thoughts, he wasn't listening. He had started to say "your sister." He really had. It was a fact, and it was something that everyone present knew for a fact, including Welch. Helen had told her sons the truth about Katie years ago when they were teen-agers, but neither of them had actually seen her since then. It came to Will that the only reason he had hesitated, and changed course, was that Clara was sitting nearby and glaring at him. If he wanted to make an excuse for himself he could say that he had done it out of respect for Clara. Or he could just give up and call it fear. Like Levi, Clara was righteous. She was the Law.

" . . . such a long time since I've seen you," Katie was saying. "I was so sorry to hear that you were wounded. Such a tragedy."

Will waited while Katie and Welch talked about their kids, but after a while he made an excuse and eased away, feeling a little wounded him-self. He felt a lot better when he spotted Sylvia and Toby.

He hadn't seen them in several years, during which time Toby, who was named after the father who died before he was born, had changed from a gawky teenager into the spitting image of Tobe. It was uncanny. It could have been a twenty-two-year-old Tobe standing here. Even the grin was the same.

Sylvia, true to her word, had stayed Amish, and would remain so for the rest of her life. Her father had died years before, but she stayed any-way because a promise is a promise. Will had talked to her about it once, and she admitted that it always felt a little like abandonment to her, as if she had betrayed Tobe in some small way by returning to what they, together, had left. She had raised her children Amish, even though her heart wasn't in it, and as all children do sooner or later, they saw through her. Each of them in turn, when they came of age, left the Amish. They didn't make a fuss about it, nor did the elders come to them and try to talk them out of it. It seemed to be understood as inevitable, as if the one thing bequeathed them by their too-brief father was a pair of wings.

"So, Toby," Will said, "how's the cabinet business?" He meant it as a joke. Toby inherited his father's genius with wood, and had started working at a local cabinet shop when he was fourteen years old. For years he'd been telling Will he was going to open his own shop—just like his father—but he was still just a kid in Will's eyes.

"Not too bad," Toby said. "I've already got an exclusive with two contractors. I'm doing all right." It turned out that he already *had* opened his own cabinet shop, and business was good.

Sylvia's eyes shined, looking at her son. It was easy to see where her heart lay. She leaned close and whispered to Will.

"Toby's getting married soon," she said. "He bought a house already, and there's a nice little mobile home that goes with it."

Will saw the outline of her plan instantly, and smiled. She'd lived all these years in a house without electricity and modern conveniences because she had given her word. But now that she was aging—and she had the makings of a first-rate grandmother, Will thought—she wouldn't mind having a few comforts. As an Amish woman she could not own such a place, but if her son, who was no longer Amish, wanted to put her up in a nice little mobile home with electricity and a nice bathroom, well, that would be all right.

While Will was talking to Sylvia and Toby, the crowd in the buggy shed seemed to thicken and he noticed that the throng of teenagers had abandoned their volleyball game and come up for lunch. Mose appeared carrying a bent-wood hickory rocker over his head, and he elbowed his way through the crowd to put it down in an open space near the food tables. Naomi escorted Levi up from the main house, and as the elder statesman of the Mullet clan, he took the seat of honor.

There was a distinctly Amish orderliness to the way people just sort of flowed to their seats at the tables, without any fuss or discussion or shouted directions. They just came in and sat down, women on one end, men on the other. Mose remained standing near his father.

"I was thinking we would mebbe go ahead and introduce ourselves first, and then we can eat," Mose said, rubbing his hands together and peering at the long food-laden tables down at the end. "Of course, we'll start with Dad." Then he sat down with his sons and let his father have the floor.

Levi leaned forward, pushing on the arms of his rocking chair. It took two tries but he finally got to his feet and stood rather uncertainly, clutching the back of the chair for support. Everything about him was bent—his knees, his back, even his head tilted a little to one side.

"My name is Levi," he rasped. "I am Eli-Jake Uri's Levi Mullet. I was born in 1898 in Holmes County, Ohio, and I cannot tell you the other date because I am not dead yet."

This brought a surprised burst of laughter from the crowd. Levi Mullet was not known for his sense of humor. The remark drew a hearty laugh of approval and would be repeated in his honor for years to come.

He continued. "The names of the children given to me by my first wife, Emma, are Mose and Clara and Tobe. The names of the children given to me by my second wife, Elizabeth, are Daniel, Ben, Samuel, Alma, Ada Mae, and Amanda." They each stood, briefly, as their names were called.

And that was it. He motioned with his free hand to Mose, yielding the floor, and then eased himself back down onto his chair. It was with unmistakable purpose that he refused to even glance in Will's direction, whereas a hundred others did. The absence of Will's name echoed from the rafters even after Levi had sat down.

Helen reached over and laid her hand softly on Will's arm. He didn't react. Staring at his shoes, smiling slightly, he slowly became aware that he had conquered his anger over his father's rejection. That particular freedom had come to him as part of the gift of absolution he'd found in his own garden two years before while digging potatoes, and it had gone unnoticed because, until now, it had gone untested. God would forgive him, but Levi wouldn't. Levi was human. But having seen his father as a fallible human being it had finally gotten through to Will that what he needed, almost as much as his father's forgiveness, was to forgive his father. What he wanted now, whether or not Levi ever changed his mind, was to try and find a way to heal some of the damage he had done. The truth about a man is in what he does, not what he says. Levi was right about that.

Mose took the floor and announced himself.

"My name is Mose Mullet," he said, standing beside his father's chair, "Eldest son of Levi Mullet." Mose had never liked the spotlight, but now he seemed even more reticent, as if he couldn't think what to say next. As if his thoughts troubled him.

Just as Levi had done, Mose went on to name his children in order of age. He pointed to each son and daughter, named them, and then, sometimes haltingly, named their children. Mose had eight children and twenty-seven grandchildren, so far. He named every one of them. There was an order to these proceedings, as with the Amish there is an order to all proceedings. When Mose finished naming his children he pointed to Clara and said, "My sister Clara has asked me to speak for her."

This was customary. If she wished to, a woman was allowed to stand and speak in a gathering like a reunion so long as the purpose of the gathering was purely nonreligious. Yet most Amish women did not wish to.

Mose named Clara's children in order of age, but he didn't bother to distinguish between her children, Simon's children, and the children they had in common.

And he still wasn't finished.

"My brother Tobe, who died while rabbit hunting years ago, left back a wife and three children. His widow, Sylvia, has asked me to speak for her too," Mose went on. He nodded to Sylvia, who sat with the women, near Clara. "Her children are Hannah, Rachel, and Toby."

Hannah and Rachel had not come. Toby stood watching the proceedings from the open bay door at the corner of the building, as though he were not quite fully there. Apart from the McGruders, he was the only one dressed in English clothes.

While he was listing Clara's and Sylvia's children Mose reached up without thinking and gripped his beard in his fist as he talked, and by the time he was finished he was squeezing so hard that his knuckles had turned white. It was an odd gesture, and he didn't appear to realize he was doing it.

In the awkward silence that fell then, Mose's fist came slowly down against his chest and pulled his face with it to stare for a moment at nothing, at the floor. His other hand rested on his hip. Suddenly Will knew, and he could tell from the stiff and nervous silence that all the Amish knew precisely what it was that troubled Mose so. Will had forgotten the order of things. If he had remembered, he very well might not have come. Now it was too late.

By listing Tobe and Sylvia's family after Clara's, technically Mose had already skipped Will. After all, the patriarch of the clan had not given

Will's name among his living children, and there was no mistaking Levi's intent. The proper thing for Mose to do now was to introduce Daniel and let him speak. Everyone in the room knew that would have been the proper thing.

Will waited to see what his older brother would decide. Whatever Mose did, Will would honor his decision.

Mose twisted at the waist and looked down at Levi. Still gripping his beard in his fist, it looked almost like Mose pulled his face around to make himself see his father. He muttered something very softly to him, in Dutch, and then straightened up.

"My brother Will," he announced. He said the name very clearly, gesturing with his hand, then promptly sat down among his sons and yielded the floor.

Will rose to his feet and took a couple of steps into the clear space by his father's chair. Levi said nothing, refusing to look at him. His beard ticked side to side slightly.

Will took a moment to scan the scores of eyes across the buggy shed, all fastened on him. He cleared his throat.

"My name is Will McGruder," he began. "I was born Will Mullet, the second son of Levi Mullet. Everybody here knows my story, and it seems kind of silly, now, to pretend like it's a secret. When I was young I fathered a child out of wedlock and then ran away and changed my name so nobody would find me. I sinned against the child, against her mother, and against God. I'm saying this now, not to make any claim to fatherhood—I gave away that privilege a long time ago—but to try and right a wrong, and to own a sin that if I had been any kind of a man I would have owned thirty-six years ago."

He shook his head. "There's no excuse. Nothing I can do now will take away any of the grief and pain I have caused. Even now, after all these years, there is still pain—*here, today*—because of what I did, and all I can say is I'm sorry. Words. Just words."

A terrifying stillness lay over the room. He held his fingertips tented against each other, and his face had drifted downward to stare at them as he spoke. When he looked up again he was astonished at what he saw in a sea of Amish faces. He expected judgment of some kind, or hardness. What he saw was compassion.

He found Katie with his eyes, and again saw compassion. Her hand covered her mouth.

"But the one thing I can *do* today is let the truth out, finally, so we don't have to whisper anymore. My oldest child is Katie Kurtz. She was raised as the daughter of Simon Schlabach, and the stepdaughter of my sister Clara. She is the wife of Reuben Kurtz. I am deeply thankful to Simon and Clara for raising my daughter into a finer woman than I ever could have done."

Will went on to name Helen and Welch and Riley and his grandchildren, then introduced Daniel and sat down. He tried very hard not to draw any further attention to himself, but he couldn't help noticing a change in the climate of the room. There was a small stirring of gladness among his Amish relatives after that, a kind of quiet relief, the beginning of a new acceptance of him. After all the family had been announced and all the outlying branches of cousin and aunt and uncle introduced, they quite consciously allowed Will to serve himself from the same buffet table as everyone else. Mose even made a point of ushering him to the front of the line. Welch followed Will, and made the mistake of starting down the opposite side of the buffet table, whereupon Mose actually grabbed the handles of his chair and steered him around it.

Mose seemed mildly embarrassed. "We don't do it that way in a big crowd," he said. "We thought it's more fair to the women this way, to let them go ahead and eat instead of waiting after all the men."

Welch did as he was told, but Will would have to explain it to him later. In the old days the men had always served their plates before the women, and the women before the children. It was just the order of things, probably instituted because the men came in hungry from doing heavy work. Now they let the women come at the same time as the men, only they had to serve themselves from the opposite side of the table. Welch had unknowingly started to help himself from the women's side.

Will didn't see his father for the rest of the afternoon. Levi must have been around someplace, though Will suspected that when everyone else lined up at the food table his father had slipped back to the main house for lunch rather than eat from the same table as his errant son. But on this day it didn't seem to matter. Will's attentions, on this day, had turned from his father to his daughter. Much of the afternoon would remain a blur in his memory, but he would always remember Katie's face, blushing, her angel's kiss clearly visible as she gripped his hands in front of her and whispered the words "Thank you."

## CHAPTER 39

*January 1985*

The Kauffman house in which Levi lived out his last years stands at the end of a long driveway that winds past a frozen pond where boys in sock hats play hockey while two teenage girls skate around the perimeter. The girls, in long coats and scarves, move slowly, taking baby steps because they are holding the hands of a skittering toddler between them, teaching her to ice-skate. It's a big pond. The far end where the deep water lies near the dam still has a large oval of gray slush in the middle of it, and whoever cleared the pond stopped short, leaving a bank of snow as a barrier to keep small children from wandering off onto the thin ice. Will's brothers have told him that until the last few days it has been unseasonably warm this winter, and some of the larger ponds still have soft spots.

A sleigh passes them going the other way as they pull up the long driveway. The sleek standard-bred mare arches her neck and trots proudly, glad to be working, and three kids in the sleigh throw mittened hands up in greeting. A broad field slopes down to the woods on the right, dotted with a grid of odd bumps where the snow has buried rows and rows of corn shocks.

The dawdi haus at the Kauffman farm consists of two rooms added to the back of the main house. Aaron Kauffman, Naomi's first husband, built the rooms because the addition was cheaper than a separate structure and because he worried constantly about Naomi's heart. He wanted her within shouting distance of the family. It seemed a miracle that this frail little woman outlived the robust Aaron, and beyond comprehension that she had married Levi a year later and then outlived him as well. The doctors weren't sure, but they estimated she'd had four heart attacks.

It's an Old Order house, Spartan, spotless, and big—two stories and spreading the way a family spreads, with additions in three directions. It's warm inside, and full of the semisweet smell of kerosene from the lanterns and woodsmoke from the stoves. Naomi is ready. Her bag is packed and waiting by the back door. Jonas, her son, helps her out to the car. He thanks Will profusely for coming to get her, apologizes for the inconvenience and says they'll all be down for the funeral in the morning. Riley takes the back seat so she can sit up front and talk to Will on the way.

Naomi sits hunchbacked in her heavy black cape and stares out the front window of the car, the curvature of her spine keeping her head well clear of the seat. In profile, her prominent nose and the white bun give her head an oblong, beaked appearance, adding to the impression of a bird. She speaks in a tiny, birdlike voice. All this traveling disturbs her, as she would much prefer to stay at home with her grandchildren and her kitchen. Of course it is no longer her kitchen, but she is honored in it.

"Have you ever in an airplane ridden?" she asks.

"Yes, I have," Will says, and then describes it for her—the cumulus clouds like little teapots, the high icy cirrus lying in rows like fish bones, and the way the sun glints off of the ocean like a pond.

"You've never flown at all?" Riley asks from the back seat.

"Oh, no!" she says. "We could never do that. It is not allowed. We would not even go in a boat if we cannot see land."

Riley thinks about it for a minute and says, "Then how did the Amish get here?"

"I believe the old ones came in wagons," she chirps, not entirely understanding the question. Fortunately, Riley lets it drop.

She doesn't seem terribly upset about Levi, but Levi was even older than she. At eighty-four she understands that every day is a gift. Levi was eighty-seven when he died—God gave him a good long life, and Naomi will not complain of its ending. Theirs had been a marriage for companionship, mostly, although Levi, being thoroughly Amish, would always need a wife to cook and clean for him. An Amishman will not do women's work. Naomi had married him because she liked him, which sometimes makes a better marriage than love.

From the corner of his eye Will sees her head turning toward him, like a weather vane twisting. Slowly, she reaches out a thin, shaking hand and just touches the back of his wrist with a fingertip.

"Your father," she says with a birdlike smile, "he liked that chicken."

It takes a minute for him to figure out what she means. Naomi's mind warps time in odd ways so that five years ago becomes yesterday, and then she speaks of it as if it *were* yesterday.

CHAPTER | 40

*October 1980*

The year after the reunion, Will and Helen went back to Ohio in the fall. Though the trees back home had not yet turned, in northern Ohio the frost had already come and painted the woods in a harvest palette of proud yellows and reds and browns.

Mose rode with them up to Geauga County. On the outskirts of Cleveland he noticed the time and said, "It looks like we'll be getting there chust before lunch. With three more mouths to feed, I'm thinking mebbe there won't be enough to go around."

He had a point. There was no way to let Naomi know she was about to have company.

"We could stop and eat before we get there," Will offered.

"If we do that you won't have much time to visit with your dad," Helen said. "We've got to be back for dinner at Ben's tonight."

"Right, I forgot. Well then, I'll just stop and pick up a bucket of chicken."

He couldn't hide all of his feelings. The shadow of an old weariness fell across his face and Helen saw it. She squeezed his arm.

"Listen, if they stick you in the kitchen, I'm eating with you," she said. "I'd rather have fried chicken anyway."

So would he, but he wasn't about to say it. Helen tended to forget about arterial plaque when they were on the road, and he knew better than to bring it up himself. Fried chicken would do nicely.

Levi Mullet seemed to shrink a little more every time Will saw him. When he got up from his chair by the stove in the living room he looked even shorter and thinner and more bent than last year. There was something else different about him too, though Will couldn't put his finger on it at first. Levi shook his hand the same as always, the same as he would have done for any outsider, but he looked Will in the eye now. He even smiled a little—not much, but a little. There was something different in his eyes.

Helen disappeared into the kitchen with Naomi and the other women to help prepare lunch while Will sat by the stove with the men. Mose and Jonas and Levi fell to comparing weather and crops, as always. It had been a good year for corn.

Then Levi kneaded his elbow and said how the coming of winter was aggravating his arthritis more than usual this year. The shift in conversation happened so subtly that Will didn't notice it at first. Next, Levi said something about his failing eyesight and looked over his shoulder to see where Naomi was before making a dry remark about what else was failing these days.

Awareness came to Will between the laughter, gathering upon him gradually, the way falling leaves cover the ground. He slowly realized that his father had allowed him into his company, that the ancient barrier between them had come down, at least partly. He wanted this peace to last, wished he could stretch the moment just the tiniest bit since he had waited such a long time for it. From the other room he could hear the clinking of plates and forks, the thumping of bowls and platters onto the table and the hushed voices of women. Soon they would call, lunch would be served, and Levi's barrier would go back up.

When Naomi's bird voice chirped out "Lunchtime," boys and girls and men and women flocked from all directions to the long table in the dining room. Jonas Kauffman stood at the head, for it was his farm now.

Will saw no separate table so he hung back, expecting to be sent to the kitchen. Helen came and stood at his side. Levi had already seated himself in the chair nearest Jonas, as the rest of the family took their places around the table until only two empty chairs remained—the two next to Levi. Jonas said nothing, though as he pulled out his own chair and seated himself he glanced at Will and Helen and pointed with his eyes to the two empty chairs.

Will could read no expression at all on Levi's face. He sat with his hands beside his plate, waiting.

Mose watched from the other end of the table, and when Will saw the little gleam in his brother's eye, he knew. It came to him then, with Levi not protesting as he and Helen took their places next to him, that it was over. It caught Will by surprise because he had been away too long and had become too English in his thinking, but he finally saw it. There would be no speech and ceremony because the Amish did not make speeches, nor stand on ceremony. Things would just be different now, that was all. A turning had been made, without fanfare. Will would now be Levi's son again.

Jonas bowed his head, and they all did likewise. Complete silence held for a minute until the rustling of cloth and the clinking of forks announced the end of prayer. In that moment Will said his own prayer of thanks, and by the squeeze that Helen gave his knee under the table he knew that she had done the same.

Levi never gave the slightest hint, as he was dipping from the same bowls of potatoes and gravy Will dipped from, that it was something he had not done in a very long time. An outsider watching them take a simple meal at the family table would have found absolutely nothing unusual in it. An outsider would have had no idea that something powerful and significant had happened when Will offered a red and white paper bucket of chicken to a shrunken, liver-spotted, bearded old man, who simply took a drumstick and handed the bucket on without a word. An outsider would have had no way of knowing that thirty-seven years of forgiveness flew as true as an arrow across the silence when Levi chose not to ask a simple question.

He did not ask who bought the chicken.

It was Levi's way, and it was enough. Will understood the message. His father had never quite trusted words. The truth about a man was in what he did.

## CHAPTER 41

*January 1985*

By the time he delivers Naomi to Mose's house, Will is exhausted from all the driving. Already it has been a long day. He spends an hour or so in the dawdi haus talking to some of the folks who have come to pay their respects to Levi, but Riley makes him nervous. Refusing to come in, Riley stays outside the whole time walking around in knee-deep snow in his tennis shoes just so he can smoke his cigarettes and be alone. After a while Will gives up and heads back to Sylvia's. They have to be at Toby's in a couple of hours anyway.

Riley takes the wheel and drives back to the mobile home, complaining of a headache the whole way. Will has never been sure if Riley's headaches are real, but it doesn't matter. The cure is always sleep, whatever the disease. Will doesn't quite understand depression, at least not long-term clinical depression like Riley's. He remembers some dark days and choppy seas, but he can't recall a time when he resigned himself to the sunless latitudes of the mind like Riley has, and stayed there.

Riley crashes when they get back to Sylvia's. He just flops down on the short bed in his little room at the far end of the trailer, pulls a pillow over his head and retreats into slumber.

Will lets himself down into an armchair and flips through a magazine for a minute, going through the motions, unable to make himself see the images or absorb the words. He tosses it aside. Sylvia's grandfather clock ticks ponderously and he becomes aware of the deep quiet. There's no television here, no radio, no stereo, no record player or cassette deck, and all at once he is certain that of all the subtle robberies committed by the late twentieth century, silence is the most grievous loss.

Riley never could tolerate the absence of noise, which, now that Will thinks about it, may be one of the things driving him under the pillow. In Riley's room at home a clock radio sits on the nightstand by the bed. It's just a little plastic thing, made in Japan, with one tinny-sounding speaker, but Riley keeps it on all the time, day and night. He brought it home with him last year, in his one suitcase. That was all he had left.

CHAPTER | 42

December 1983

It was Genevieve who finally called. Divorce papers were in the works, which seemed ironic to Will and Helen since they'd never heard anything about an actual marriage.

The divorce itself was no surprise. Riley had been drifting for a long time. The reason Genevieve called was to let them know he'd been arrested. She had already been through all this with Riley right before he ignored her last ultimatum and she threw him out. She had children to think about, and a job of her own. He could trash his career if he wanted, but she wasn't about to miss work and drag her kids through court hearings for him. Not now. He was on his own.

"I'll take care of *my* kids," she told Helen, "and you take care of yours."

Will and Helen went out to see what they could do. When they got to California they were shocked to find Riley still broadcasting arrogance, even though he was living out of a suitcase and paying a weekly rate for a dingy room in a cinder-block motel with a half-lit neon palm tree in the courtyard. His room smelled like an ashtray.

"Come on, Pops, it was a couple hits of coke, a few grams. It's not like I was trafficking or anything."

"Uh huh. Then there's the drunk driving charge—not the first, from what I hear."

"Bogus. I was *not* impaired. The cops needed to boost their revenues, that's all."

"When are you going to start taking this seriously, Riley? If the possession charge holds up you're going to have a *felony* on your record. Your wife and kids are gone. Your job is gone. What's it going to take?"

Riley was a lot more reserved in court. At least he kept his mouth shut while his lawyer and his father talked the judge into two years' probation. There was, as the lawyer put it, a "big bag of special conditions." Through something called an interstate compact, Riley would be confined to his father's house in Georgia, where for two years he would maintain a strict seven-to-seven curfew, do sixteen hours a week community service, and participate in drug and alcohol treatment as directed by a probation officer. His lawyer was happy. His lawyer said he got off light, given his record.

Riley carried a kind of self-righteous belligerence with him even after being confined to his parents' house. In the beginning he raged against a system that he insisted had singled him out and victimized him, but as the weeks wore on, as his probation officer made random curfew checks and personally took him in for random drug tests, Riley's fists came down and he sank into depression.

## CHAPTER 43

*January 1985*

Will raps on Riley's door, cracks it open.

"Riley. Six-thirty. We've got to go up the hill. Dinner at Toby's, remember?"

A moan from under the pillow. "Do I have to?"

Will shrugs. "Call Belliard and ask him. They're his rules." Dom Belliard is Riley's parole officer. He never gives an inch.

Riley flings the covers away, though they were not covering him, and manages to convey open hostility through the simple act of jerking a pair of shoes onto his feet.

Toby's house sits on the hill directly above them. His is a modest home by modern standards, an aging white clapboard split-level with two small bedrooms and only one bath, heated by a coal furnace in a partial basement whose door overlooks his mother's place. But Toby is an ambitious young man with a clear plan, and like the best of such men he has focused his energies on the means rather than the end. His cabinetmaking business thrives.

Through unbroken snow Will picks his way up the hill and around to the front of the house. Riley follows, stepping in his father's tracks where the footing is better. While they are still stomping snow off their shoes on the front porch Toby appears and ushers them in. He introduces Riley to his wife, Lauren, who smiles a lot and says little, pulling flaxen hair back from her face while clutching a yearling daughter on her hip. The baby is a wide-eyed, silent, bashful child, still in diapers. Toby treats Riley with a formality that seems odd to Will until he remembers that the last time Riley was here, Toby was five years old—a barefoot Amish kid who hadn't learned English yet.

Nothing in Toby's appearance gives away his Old Order upbringing. He wears carpenter jeans and a plaid flannel shirt, sleeves rolled up to the elbows, and he carries himself with the loose, shambling confidence of an athlete. Only his speech gives him away, for it is marked by the slow rolling lilt of a man born and raised Amish.

"So, Riley. It's good of you to help your dad drive up like you did." Something in his quick glance at Will says he knows enough about Riley not to ask how things are going. There might not be any good answer.

"I had nothing better to do," Riley says, and the slight edge in his voice warns Toby away. They all steer clear of Riley during dinner.

Toby has built a fire in the fireplace, so after dinner they retire to the den, to the comfortable chairs. Headlights sweep across the ceiling as a car pulls into the drive. Lauren gets up and goes to the front door. A minute later there's a stamping of feet on the stairs and a tangle of voices as Ben comes into the den, followed by Samuel, then Katie, and lastly by a man Will doesn't recognize. The stranger wears a fringe of beard, though his clothes are not Amish. Ben introduces him as Micah Weaver, a friend.

Katie is carrying a baby boy who looks to be the same age as Toby's little girl. She shifts the baby to a hip and greets Will and Riley with the customary handshake. Pulling the sock hat from the ruddy-cheeked child she looks on him with unabashed pride.

"This is your grandpa," she says to the child, and then, turning to Will, "I wrote to you about William, but I knew you'd want to meet him. Anyhow, he's not weaned yet, so I couldn't leave him back."

"Aw, he's a fine-looking young man," Will says. He reaches out to take the baby, but William clings to his mother and buries his face in her neck.

Katie smiles. "It's all right. He'll get used to you. He's chust a little shy."

"Is that your first grandchild?" Riley asks. He's sitting on one end of the couch. Lauren is at the other end, watching her baby crawl around on the carpet looking for something to put in her mouth. This is the first time Riley has perked up and shown an interest in anything.

"Oh, no! He's not a grandchild. This is *my* baby," Katie says.

Riley's eyebrows arch. His mouth hangs open for a second before he speaks. He knows Katie's story, knows she's several years older than he is—and he's thirty-five.

"What are you, forty?" he asks.

"Forty-one," she says genially, as she sits down beside him in the middle of the couch. It surprises even Will, who should have done the math. The years fly by too quickly. Only now does he notice the gray in the hair that peeks out from under her covering, and the crow's feet at the corners of her eyes. Will still sees a child when he looks at her.

"How many kids have you got?" Riley asks.

"This one makes nine," she says.

His mouth won't quite close. "So, was this like an accident, or what?" he asks, pointing loosely to the baby.

Katie smiles patiently, peeling a heavy coat from William's arms.

"God gives us what He gives us, and we are thankful," she says, and lets it go at that. The child, not a year old yet, wears Amish clothes on top of his diaper—heavy pants and blue shirt, with suspenders. What hair he has is already cut in a bowl shape.

Uncomfortable with the direction Riley is taking, Will searches for a way to change the subject. Ben is warming his hands at the fire when Will claps him on the shoulder and asks, "Was that a company car you drove up in, or have you gone Mennonite on us?" Everybody teases Ben because he teases them.

"Oh, ja, we woulda come in the buggy if it's chust the two of us." Meaning himself and Samuel, who lives next door to Ben. "But now Katie said she wanted to come, and that's too far in this weather. So we waited till after dark and come in the company car."

"I don't get it," Riley says. "Are Amish driving cars now?"

Ben turns to face him, putting his back to the fire. "Oh, no, we couldn't drive the car. We wouldn't have a license."

"But you own the company," Riley says.

Toby comes back with kitchen chairs and Will takes a seat. He hears the satire in Riley's voice and tries to head him off. "Well, Ben's company builds stables," he says, "and they used to be one of the biggest contractors around. They had to travel quite a bit."

Samuel is sitting on the hearth cracking nuts with his palms. "The shop is chust about a mile from the house," he explains, "so we take the buggy to work in the morning, and then if we go out to a job, Micah drives us."

"Let me get this straight," Riley says. "You can't own a car, but you can own a *company* that owns a car."

"That's right," Ben says. "So long as it's for business."

Riley spreads his hands, palms up. "But this isn't business."

"Well," Samuel says with a shrug, tossing a handful of nutshells into the fire, "that's why we waited till after dark."

Riley flops against the back of the couch shaking his head, a bemused grin on his face.

"So, Riley, what kind of work do you do?" Samuel asks. His face is brightly innocent and open. He knows nothing of Riley's recent past, or has forgotten.

"Oh, I was a problem solver with a little R and D skunk works out of . . . uh, I helped debug hardware for next-level game plat—" The lost look on their faces stops him in the middle of the word and the air goes out of him as if he's been punctured. He smirks, looks off to the side for a second, then says, "I work on computers."

Ben nods as if he understands. "That must be really interesting. We had a girl in our office that could work a computer, once. She's gone now. The stable business is not a very stable business," he says, grinning at his own pun.

Riley reads between the lines. "So I gather. You used to be big and now you're not. What happened?"

"Oh, well, some of the people we did work for mebbe weren't so honorable as they coulda been."

Riley instinctively looks to Will for an explanation.

"Some of the people he built stables for found out they didn't have to pay him. Because he's Amish."

Riley looks back and forth from Will to Ben, his puzzlement deepening.

"Amish won't sue," Will says. "They won't take a man to court to make him pay what he owes. Word gets around, and pretty soon customers just stop paying." He shrugs. "These days, money is money. Some people will do whatever they can get away with."

Riley's mouth hangs open for a second. "You're kidding, right? I mean seriously, you do good work but you're letting people walk off with the store because you don't believe in lawyers? You people are too much."

Ben starts to answer him, but Samuel reaches over and grabs a fistful of his pant leg. Ben has been standing with his back to the fire a little too long and his loose pant leg has heated up nicely. When Samuel jerks the pant leg hard against the back of his knee Ben shouts once and dances away, high-stepping to break his brother's grip. Samuel claps his hands and almost falls off the hearth laughing.

Riley just shakes his head. He starts to say something, but little William has crawled halfway onto him and now reaches up to his face. Riley pushes the baby's hand away and glances at Katie.

"He's curious," she says. "His papa's face has a beard. Yours is different."

Riley ducks his face away from the baby and tries again. "But, Ben, why couldn't you just hire a col—"

The baby grabs his chin, and he jerks away a little harder, glaring at Katie.

She smiles. "He *likes* you." She lifts the boy off of Riley, but as soon as she puts him down in her lap, he squirms and heads for Riley again.

"Look, you just can't run a business today without—"

The baby sticks his hand in Riley's mouth.

Riley sputters and recoils. He jerks the baby up and plunks him uncer-emoniously in his mother's lap, then springs to his feet.

"This is crazy!" he says, mostly to Will. "Look, Pops, something's wrong with the family tree somewhere. Seriously, somebody must have swapped babies in the hospital because I don't see how I could have come from this. You people are . . ." His face contorts with frustration, searching for the right word. He waves a hand at Ben and Samuel. "Hobbits! You're a bunch of *hobbits*, with your juvenile humor and backward ways. You live in your little holes in your little corner of the world, and you don't seem to care what you're missing."

He turns, suddenly, on Katie.

"Katie! Darlin'! Have you never heard of birth control?"

"Heard of it," she says, clutching her baby close. Will can see the outline of her angel's kiss as she darkens with embarrassment.

"Girl, if you can't control your husband, get your tubes tied! And Ben! Get a lawyer, dude!"

He takes a few steps toward the stair that leads to the front door, stops again and, waving his arms, says, "Get a *life*! Get a *clue*! Hobbits are nice in stories, but in real life they get stepped on by *big* people!"

Nobody moves or says anything. Riley rolls his eyes and stomps up the steps, grumbling. They hear him snatch his coat from the hall tree and slam the door on his way out.

"You think he's all right?" Toby asks, rising, peering up toward the door.

"Don't worry about it," Will says. "He'll just go down and sack out, sleep it off. That's what he always does. Look, I'm really sorry about this. Maybe he's right—maybe somebody swapped kids with me in the hospital." He shakes his head in profound embarrassment. "He sure doesn't feel like one of mine."

"He's been through a lot," Katie says softly, and there's genuine compassion in her eyes.

"Well," Ben says, patting his belly, "The Book tells us the Lord takes care of the flowers and the birds. I don't have much sense, I guess, but I got plenty food on my table and a good roof over my head yet."

Samuel is still sitting on the hearth, forearms across knees, staring pensively at the carpet.

"What's a hobbit?" he asks.

"I'm not sure," Will says. "I think it's from a book. Riley reads a lot."

Toby shakes his head. He doesn't know either.

They all sit silent for a time, and Will can't tell if they are moved to silence by shame or confusion. Or the shame *of* confusion. Tobe's voice comes to haunt him now, from the edge of a distant, weed-choked field. *"For better or worse, it's where you come from. It's who you are."* It was one of the last things his brother ever said to him.

"Remember when we were kids and we used to go snagging stone rollers in the creek?" Samuel asks.

Will is picking at his fingernails and his focus is there, in his lap. He is very nearly absent.

"That was a lot of fun," Ben says. "Sucker-mouth fish. They won't bite anything, but we could see 'em rootin' in the bottom and snag 'em."

"They weren't too good to eat either," Samuel says. "That creek—remember how we used to slip off from the plow sometimes and go skinny-dipping down there? Will, were you there the time I nearly drowned in the swimming hole? No, I think that was after you left."

Ben laughs. "Sammy never could swim a bit. We put syrup buckets in a sack and slung it under his arms to make him float."

"I swam good," Samuel says, offended.

Ben chuckles. "Sammy, *to this day* you still can't swim."

The evening goes the way it wants, and they are content to ride along with it. They talk of Tobe and his rabbit gun, Mose's keen eye and unnatural accuracy with a rock, and Will's prowess at wrestling in the haymow. They dust off memories Will has not opened in years.

"Remember the time we set fire to old man Bentwhistle's tree?" Samuel says.

Ben nods. "That was right before you left, Will. Tobe took a strapping for us that day."

"You were just little guys then," Will says. "Dad was crazy mad."

"What happened?" Toby asks. All of this happened before he was born, and he wants as many pieces of his father as he can find.

"Oh, it wasn't nothing," Ben says. "Me and Sammy and that old dog we had—"

"Boots, we called him," Samuel says.

"That's right. Boots chased a rabbit up in a old hollow oak on the rise up back of old man Bentwhistle's place and we couldn't get him out. Then Tobe comes along with some matches, so we kicked leaves up in that hole and set fire to 'em. Gonna smoke him out, you see."

Samuel waves his fingers in the air, looking up at imaginary smoke. "Fire went up through the middle of that old tree and comes right out the top, like a chimney. Boy, we took off," he laughs.

"Old man Bentwhistle—what was his real name, anyway?"

"I forget," Samuel says. "We never called him nothing else but Bentwhistle."

"Anyway, after old Bentwhistle put the fire out, he came straight to

Dad, and Dad strapped Tobe right in front of him. Pretty bad too. Oh, he was mad! Tobe never told him me and Sammy had a part in it. Not a word."

"Why did Granddad get so mad?" Toby asks.

Will answers for them. "He didn't like getting embarrassed, Toby. Especially in front of an Englisher. It wasn't so much what they did as how it made your grandfather look."

Katie yawns. Little William is curled asleep in her lap. An hour has passed since Lauren scooped up her baby and disappeared. Will glances at his watch, then stands up and stretches. "I didn't realize it was so late," he says. "I guess I should go down and check on my son."

He hears what he's saying, and the slightly sarcastic way he says it. His son. His embarrassing son.

*January 1985*

The moon has risen and the snow is lit. Will picks his way back down the hill in the same tracks he made coming up.

The little mobile home is warm and snug and silent, and he figures Riley must be dead asleep. He's about to hang his overcoat up when he sees that Riley's door is not closed. Riley never leaves the door open.

He tiptoes down and peeks inside. The bed is empty. He checks the bathroom—nothing. Sylvia's trailer is a small place, and Riley is definitely not in it. Nor could he have gone back up to Toby's without Will knowing it.

The car. Will remembers now that Riley drove home, and he kept the keys. Coming home from Toby's he had to have passed within feet of the car, but he can't recall now whether or not it was there. He simply hadn't noticed. With growing apprehension he steps out onto the front porch and looks. The car is still there, but it's not right. He remembers clearly that when they came home he made Riley back the car up the driveway so it would be facing downslope in the morning. Now it is turned the other way.

Riley has gone somewhere and come back.

Given Riley's mood, Will can guess where he went, and why. He has seen all this before and he mentally kicks himself for missing the signs— the headache, the increasing irritability, the irrational outburst. He should have seen it coming. The therapist said when Riley's under stress his first instinct is to escape, to get out from under the pressure of reality any way he can.

Will stands on the front porch searching his memory for a clue, some- thing Riley might have said or done to hint at where he would go on foot, at night, in the freezing cold a thousand miles from home. There is noth- ing, but it occurs to him finally that any idiot ought to be able to follow a man on foot through the snow. His eye scans the front yard sloping down to the road. The moon shines so brightly that a leafless tree at the corner of the trailer casts a clear shadow, a spider web of naked limbs on the snow. Will can see well enough to know after a single sweeping glance that there are no tracks across the front yard. The snow is unbroken, though it occurs to him that Riley could have followed the tire treads down the driveway. But then what? He knows no one here, and there is no bar or restaurant. It's a farm valley.

Buttoning his overcoat back up, Will walks gingerly down the drive- way to the road. He looks both ways. There are no cars. The road is as silent as the valley, yet it seems to Will that the cast-off banks of plowed snow crowd in tight against the lane so that a man on foot meeting a car would have little choice but to tumble headlong over the bank. No rational man would walk this road right now, but then Riley is not entirely rational.

On a hunch he goes across the road, stopping at the bank on the opposite side. And there it is—a clear line of footprints starting directly across from the driveway and heading straight down the middle of the valley.

His eyes are growing more accustomed to the semidarkness and now the valley shows itself to him, dressed in blue moonlight. Eventually he makes out every tree and shrub. He can see their shadows. Nearly a half mile away he sees a dark shape—a blotch, no more—under a tree at the edge of the flat expanse he knows is a pond. He can't tell if it's Riley, or even if it's a man, but it looks out of place and the tracks point right to it.

He steps across the bank of snow and follows the tracks. It's a long, hard walk through deep snow, and he tires long before he approaches the pond. His legs ache and the frosty air pains his throat from breathing too deeply. The thought that the dark shape ahead could be a man lying prone in the snow worries him until he realizes that it's much too large. A man's body would virtually bury itself in the snow and become invisible from any distance. Puffing from the exertion, he closes to within yards of the shape before it moves. A cigarette glows, and now he is close enough to see a plume of smoke blown straight up.

Riley is lying on his back on top of what appears to be an overturned flat-bottom boat painted in some dark color—probably green. Will stops at his feet. A pile of broken snow lies down both sides of the boat where Riley swept it clear before lying down on it. His hands are folded on his chest, and he doesn't move when Will comes and stops at his feet, but he finally speaks.

"Nice night," he says, and takes a drag from the cigarette without so much as raising his head. In the momentary glow Will can see a bottle of some kind nestled in the crook of Riley's arm. He can't tell exactly what it is, but he knows it's a fifth of something.

"Bit nippy." Will shrugs deeper into his overcoat. The long trudge through the snow has dampened the small of his back with sweat, and now that he has stopped walking it chills quickly.

"What's the matter?" he finally asks.

Riley raises his head for the first time and stares at him. Just his head.

"You mean, what's the matter with *me*?" The sneer is back in Riley's voice, fortified perhaps with alcohol.

"If you mean what's wrong with me in this one moment in time, I'd have to say practically nothing. For a change. I'm feeling fine, and getting finer by the minute." He sits up and spreads his arms in an unmistakable gesture of drunken bliss, the bottle sloshing in his hand. He swings his legs over and stands up.

"But if you mean, 'What's the matter with my life as a whole?' I'd say the answer to that may take another thirty thousand dollars' worth of psychoanalysis. And if you mean, 'What's wrong with the world as we know it?' I'd say nothing that can't be fixed with an all-out global thermonuclear war."

He's waving his arms around for emphasis, and leaning just a bit, but he can still talk just fine.

Will waits to make sure he's finished.

"I meant, why are you drinking?" Will says, very calmly.

Riley throws his head back, spreads his arms. "Because it's hard for a stranger from the Southfarthing to score cocaine in Hobbiton, is why I'm drinking. I would much prefer to snort a couple of lines, to tell you the truth. However, I did happen to spot a discreet little package store out by the interstate today." He raises the half empty bottle and shakes it for proof.

"Why were you so hard on them?" Will asks. "They're decent people, and they haven't done anything to you."

Riley's shoulders sag, and his arms drop. The overturned boat rumbles when he sits back down heavily. After a long pull on the bottle he jams it into the snow and drops his face into his hands.

"I tell you what, Pops," he mutters, "if you think these people haven't done anything to me, then you're the one who needs to see a shrink."

Will wishes he'd put on a hat before he left the trailer. His ears are cold. He turns up the collar of his overcoat and buttons the top button as he's sitting down next to Riley.

"Why do you say that?"

"Because I remember that little table in the corner. How could you let them do that to you? How could you let *anybody* do that to you?" Riley shakes his head slowly without taking his face out of his hands.

"You remember that?"

"I was twelve, the last time. I remember more than you think."

"And it bothered you?"

"Yes! After all these years, it *still* bothers me. I can't believe you'd let somebody do that to you."

"You didn't know my father," Will says. "In his world you had to pay for things, so I paid. Things are different now, but back then I thought it was what I had to do—a kind of penance, I guess. You just don't know. You can't know. There's no way you can understand what it was like growing up under that man. Never a kind word, never a bit of encouragement. I don't remember, even once, my father ever telling me he loved me—it just wasn't done. And you couldn't please him, he was—"

"Such a perfectionist," Riley interrupts in a hard voice, looking up, meeting his father's eyes for the first time. "He was just this brooding presence in the house, something to be avoided whenever possible."

"Yeah," Will says softly, studying his son's face in the half-light. "Yeah.

That's exactly what it was like. How did you...? Have I said all this before?"

"No," Riley says. "I wasn't talking about *your* dad. I was talking about mine."

He reaches for the bottle, turns it up, wipes his sleeve across his mouth and slides the bottle back into its neat hole in the snow. He stands up and walks away a few steps, then just stands there, mute, with his back to Will. His goose-down jacket is quilted in little hand-sized squares and it draws in tight to his waist. Riley says it makes him look like a hand grenade. The analogy, in light of what he just said, seems singularly appropriate.

"Okay," Will says quietly. "All right. It's hard for me to judge myself—I don't see myself the same way you do, I'm sure, but maybe you're right."

"I *know* I'm right. When you can't get your old man's approval no matter how hard you try, it makes you mad. It makes you want to strike back. It makes you want out. It makes you want to find approval somewhere else. My therapist will tell you all that."

He turns halfway, a moonlit silhouette looking over his shoulder at his father.

"What he hasn't told me is how you get past it. So tell me, Pops, how do you do it? I see how things are now, with you and your family. So how'd you do it? Give me your own personal twelve-step program."

Riley's voice is cold and cynical, but Will knows him a little better now. He thinks for a moment, and decides to just tell the truth.

"You're a wreck, Riley," he says. "And you're right, you're a wreck because your father was a wreck before you, and his father before him. We're human. We just can't get it right, and it takes some of us a lifetime to figure that out. You want *my* answer, I'll tell you, but you're not going to like it."

"Try me."

"It's God," Will says.

"Oh, please." His back is to Will, but even his voice rolls its eyes.

Will ignores him. "You asked me. Nothing changed for me until I finally figured out that people—human beings, every one as messed up as the next one—*can't* get past it. But God can. When I realized there really is a God and He cares about me in spite of everything, that He forgives me for all of it, *that* was the beginning of my twelve-step program. That's the truth."

Riley is still. He acknowledges nothing but neither does he argue with it.

"It was then that I started to understand my father," Will continues. "He's just like me, perfectly capable of getting it wrong because *his* father was the same way. The day I stopped trying to earn my father's forgiveness and gave him mine—*that* was the day things started to change."

Riley comes slowly to where Will is sitting, but then he leans down and plucks the bottle out of the snow. He takes a healthy slug, shoves it back into its hole in the snow and lights a cigarette, cupping his fingers around the lighter, his face lit by the flame.

"Church talk," he says, walking away again, shoving his hands in his coat. "Religion is a fabric of rules and regulations used by weak men to control other weak men. Our Amish cousins are fine examples of it with their picky little differences and fine-print loopholes."

He blows a cloud of smoke, spits, and says, "Your God is a myth, and your Law is an authoritarian tool."

"The Law," Will says, "was meant to put some distance between you and the things that will do you harm, that's all." As he is saying this he reaches down and pulls Riley's bottle out of the snow. Riley turns around as he's rising to his feet, and sees the bottle in his hand.

"What are you doing?" Riley says, as Will draws back his arm.

The arm whips, and the bottle sails high and far out over the frozen pond.

"Being a father," Will says. "It's my job."

Riley gazes at the pond. "*Now* you decide to be a father," he says. He shakes his head, and with a heavy sigh starts out onto the ice.

"Where are you going?" Will asks.

He stops a few steps out and looks back. "To get that bottle. I'm a drunk. It's my job."

"I wouldn't go out there if I were you. The ice won't hold you."

"Nice try," Riley says, turning away.

"I'm serious," Will calls out. "There are kids around here. Didn't you notice the snow hasn't been cleared from the pond? They'd be skating on it if it was safe."

Riley ignores him. He's maybe ten paces out onto the ice when from under his feet comes a sound like a piano string breaking. He stops, looks back.

Another piano string pops, louder than the first, and another right behind it. Riley turns around and takes a step back. The snow around his feet is turning to slush.

"Dad?" he says, and tries to run, but his feet slip and he goes belly down in the slush. Suddenly his feet are kicking water and he's trying to claw his way up a sloping piece of broken ice.

Will runs onto the edge of the pond, but he doesn't get three steps before he hears a long, grinding crack and feels the ice sag underneath his feet. He sidesteps and backs up to the bank.

"Dad?" Riley says again. He's swimming now, yet not going anyplace. Water-laden goose-down sleeves slap at the slanting ice. There's panic in his voice.

Will looks around, his mind racing. Riley is so close, but still out of reach. There has to be a way. His eyes fasten on the boat where he'd been sitting. He turns and slogs through the snow.

At the side of the overturned boat he plants his feet, then digs his fingers beneath the edge. Lifting with his legs, he throws his head back and heaves with all his might. Nothing moves—the boat is frozen to the ground. In the distance he can hear Riley's faint cry for help. His right foot finds something solid under the snow and his hand digs frantically. An oar. He pulls it free and slams it down hard, once, against the hull. Jamming the flat end under the edge he pries, and the extra leverage pays off. There's a ripping sound as the boat breaks loose.

Once free, the boat flips easily. He turns it toward the pond, toward Riley, and gets behind it, pushing, running. The cracked ice complains and shifts as he shoves the little boat onto it, and his street shoes slip, but he keeps going until his makeshift sleigh is almost there. At the last second, as he loses traction on the wet ice, Will throws himself into the back of the boat and scrambles over the middle seat. The bow has stopped right beside Riley, canting toward him a bit because the outer edge is still riding on ice. Riley ceases flailing now, and fumbles with numbing hands to grab the edge. Will keeps his weight back as far as he can to keep the boat from tipping while he latches on to Riley's coat and heaves. Riley helps all he can, shoving with his feet against the slab of broken ice under him, and between the two of them they manage to hoist him over the gunwale. He crumples in the bow of the boat, exhausted and shivering.

Will flops back in the boat gasping, trying to catch his breath. Riley cranes his neck and stares across the pond.

"Oh well," he says, coughing, "I've lost the buzz anyway."

They have to work together to get back to the bank, each hanging a leg over the side and pushing, but they get it done. Though Riley is completely soaked and shaking so hard he can barely talk, Will insists on putting the boat back where he found it before they head back to the mobile home.

Forty-five minutes later Riley is huddled on the edge of the couch clutching two quilts around him, gripping a second cup of coffee in his palms.

"You feeling better?" Will asks.

He nods. There's a steadiness in his eyes now.

"You were really babbling by the time we got here."

"Yeah, that would be hypothermia."

"How many fingers am I holding up?"

Riley looks, chuckles. "None."

"It was a trick question." Will rubs a hand over his nearly bald head. He sighs. "You know I . . . uh, that really scared me. Out there. I wasn't sure I could get you out."

Riley doesn't look up. He's holding his face in the steam from the coffee cup. "I wasn't sure you wanted to," he says.

He tosses the words off casually but there's a shadow of belief behind them. Will hears it, and it shakes him. Until now he really hadn't known how far he had thrown his son.

"Riley, look at me. Right here, look at me. There was never any thought about that. No decision. I never had a choice. Two of us would have come back here, or two of us would have drowned. It's that simple. You're my son."

Riley turns to his coffee as if he's looking for a distraction. Something here is too strong for him. He starts laughing.

"I gotta tell you, you looked pretty silly pushing that boat across the snow, Pops. You've got some seriously unorthodox rescue methods."

Will smiles. Unorthodox. The word conjures the face of a saint.

"A wise man once told me you can never have too much unorthodox," he says.

## CHAPTER 45

*January 1985*

On the morning of the funeral the big house is bathed in silence. People nod to each other outside and speak briefly in hushed tones, then lapse into complete silence when they step through the kitchen door into the house. The men reverently doff their hats as they enter so that, by the time Will and Riley come through, the kitchen counters are covered with piles of identical wide-brimmed black hats. The furniture has all been moved to the barn or the sheds, and the first-floor rooms have all been filled with rows of wooden benches—the same benches used for church services. They were brought in and set up the day before, after the house had been emptied and scrubbed clean.

The coffin sits closed atop two wooden sawhorses on one side of the big living room, far enough out from the wall for people to pass around it. An aisle has been left across the center of the room, and Levi's family sits on benches facing each other, the women on one side and the men on the other. Naomi is there, Levi's last wife, along with all nine living children. Most of his seventy-three grandchildren are in the room, and many of his nineteen great-grandchildren. Even in the large room where the family is seated a hierarchy is maintained among the men, the eldest sitting on the bench facing the aisle. The women are arranged differently, with the single girls taking the aisle seats. Behind them on the second row Naomi sits next to Levi's surviving sister, along with the elder women of the clan. The mothers with small children take the back row, nearest the door.

Levi's two remaining brothers take the first seats on the center aisle, facing the women. The sons of Levi Mullet fill the rest of the front row, and Will takes his place next to Mose.

All his life Will has known he was the second son of his generation, but now his position becomes a graphic reality, a charcoal drawing of his mortality. He sits fourth in line. Fourth, after two decrepit uncles and Mose, from the end of the bench. From the coffin.

Riley remains at Will's side because he doesn't know this is not proper. He should be on the next row back, with the sons of the sons, but no one points out his error and Will says nothing because it is not his place. They will let it pass. They understand that Riley does not know their ways.

Will keeps a nervous eye on his son. As the rest of the crowd fills the benches in the other rooms Riley seems fixated on the coffin. It's a simple six-sided box, made of pine, very plain and unadorned, yet the craftsmanship is evident. Built by a local Amish carpenter, every joint is tight and straight, and the hand-rubbed finish is flawless. The top is not flat, but peaked, the two halves of the lid sloping gently toward the edges. There are hinges across the middle of the lid so that the top sections can be folded back onto the bottom half when it is time to open it. There are no handles, no markings, no decorations of any kind on the outside. The room, like the coffin, is plain but neat and utterly clean. There are no funeral flowers, no pictures on the walls, no organ music. The royal blue curtains on the windows have all been tied back to let the sunshine in.

Riley looks about nervously once or twice, and Will knows what he is seeing. There must be two hundred people crammed into the house, but the two of them are the only ones dressed in suits and ties, the only men without beards.

After a while, when everyone is settled and the rustling has ceased, a grizzled old man rises and stands by the foot of the coffin with his hands behind his back. A life of manual labor has left him bent so that he cannot hold his head up straight and he always seems to be leaning forward. He calls for prayer. In unison, they all turn from their seats, get down on their knees, clasp their hands on the hard backless bench and lower their heads.

Riley kneels too. Will is relieved, but then he questions his own relief. Does he want his son, out of respect, to pretend a belief he does not own? In the end he decides it doesn't really matter. Sometimes there is value in ritual alone.

After the prayer there is a moment of awkwardness in the densely packed room as old men and women struggle to their feet, bumping each other as they turn around and take their seats again, shoulder to shoulder, hands folded in laps. The old man speaks for thirty or forty minutes, in Dutch. He uses no notes, no book—in fact, he keeps his hands clasped behind him most of the time—but his gravelly voice quotes from the Bible at great length with considerable fluency and conviction. Will understands most of it, though some of his Dutch has fallen away from him over the years. He wonders if Riley can tell from the singsong cadence that the minister is reciting long passages from the Psalms.

Everyone is still while the old man speaks. No one stirs.

When he is finished he simply stops talking and sits down. There is a mild rustling as people shift their feet and adjust themselves in the quiet space between speakers, and then a younger man rises and takes up the same position at the foot of the coffin. This one is maybe thirty years old, his hair still streaked with blond, his beard shorter and a little skimpy, his body still straight and strong. His blue eyes are full of kindness and a seasoned calm. He clears his throat and fumbles for words at first.

"I want to explain what I am doing," he says apologetically, enunciating every syllable. "I haven't ever done this before in English, but I seen there are some people here who don't speak Dutch. Please forgive me. I am too much of a Dutchman to talk good English, but I hope it's all right if I try. With God's help, I will do the best I can."

And so he does. Will watches furtively for a sign of objection among the older heads, but nothing happens. They may have something to say later. For now, they will not interrupt the service. The young pastor stammers often, faltering and straining to find the right word, for the Bible he has read all his life was written in German and he is forced to paraphrase whole long passages into English on the fly. But he does it.

He speaks at length about the traditions of the plain folk, and how faith without works is dead. He says that faith and works are like the oars on a boat, and that he believes a straight life cannot be lived without both. He says that it is good to avoid the traps of the world, and it is good to live a plain life and wear plain clothes that say to other men, "There is a better way, a higher path, a truer way to live."

"But we must watch out, always," he says. "We must be careful of pride. Pride is a wolf that will come dressed up like a sheep. Pride will make a man think he will go to heaven because he wears plain clothes, but that's not so. Your horse and buggy won't get you into heaven, but only the forgiveness bought by Jesus Christ, the Son of God." He pauses, wrinkles his face in concentration, then mutters a phrase in Dutch as he scratches his head. "*Welche der geist Gottes treibt, die sein Gottes kinder.*" He spreads his hands uncertainly, clearly afraid he might not adequately translate the words, and says to the crowd, "Them who are led by the Spirit of God—*they* are the sons of God."

Will is stunned. Growing up, he never heard such words from a minister. "*Your horse and buggy won't get you into heaven.*" No Amish preacher he had ever encountered would have uttered such words in public. Will's eyes roam the room. Some of the younger heads nod ever so slightly at the minister's words, eyes in agreement, and he realizes suddenly that this is not something new to them. They have heard it before. *The times,* he thought, *they are a-changin'.*

After the second preacher stops talking and sits down, a third rises to take his place. This one, too, speaks at great length without the aid of notes or books. He is tall and stern and weathered about the face by many seasons out of doors. Quoting long passages from the book of John he speaks in Dutch with a deep and resonant voice about the love and grace of God. Referring occasionally to Levi Mullet, a man he had known all his life, the minister claims no promises and makes no guarantees about where Levi's soul has gone. He speaks only of hope and faith and diligence, for that is the Amish way.

By the time the third preacher is finished, two hours have passed and still there is very little movement among the hundreds of people in the house. Even the children in the back rows remain calm and attentive.

A man with a dark beard and thick glasses gets up as soon as the last preacher sits down and, without a word, lays back the upper lids to the coffin, then stands aside with his hands folded in front of him. It is only this action that identifies him as the funeral director, since his clothes and his demeanor are precisely the same as every other Amishman present.

No words are spoken by anyone and no signal is given, but everyone rises to their feet and waits while a line forms and the crowd files silently past the open coffin. They come in a precise order, distant relatives and friends first, reserving the last goodbyes for the immediate family. Many of them pause for a moment, gazing one last time on a face they will not see again in this world. Some of the women are crying, dabbing at their eyes with handkerchiefs, but they do it quietly.

Some of the men have brought small sons with them and the fathers urge the sons to touch the body, usually on the face. The boys comply, hesitantly. After a reassuring glance at Dad, their small fingers reach out and brush against Levi's cheek. It's a little thing, but a clear and poignant reminder to Will of an Amish father's dutiful and patient educating of his sons. They would not have their sons growing up without seeing that this life is temporary, and that death is a part of it. They want their sons to participate in death, to touch it and understand not only that each of us must face it, but that we must help each other through it. The sight leaves Will with a deep pang of regret that, for once, has nothing to do with his father.

When most of the people have filed by and gone outside, the sons and daughters of Levi Mullet linger. Levi's face is relaxed and serene in a way that it never was in life, and as Will stands looking down on his father, he is moved simultaneously with a deep grief for the years irretrievably lost between them and a quiet joy arising from the certain knowledge that they did, in the end, make their peace.

Riley stands beside Will, his expression blank. He never really knew his grandfather, only saw him a few times in his childhood and barely remembers him. Will doesn't know where the sudden impulse comes from, nor does he question it. Gently, he takes his son's hand and guides it to the face of his father so that the tips of Riley's fingers graze the pallid cheek. Riley does not resist.

After Levi's sons and daughters have said their final silent goodbyes, the director quietly folds the hinged lids over, closing the coffin. He pulls a flat-head screwdriver from his pants pocket, places a handful of screws in predrilled holes and runs them down tight while Levi's children look on. His every movement is unhurried and precise, workmanlike. The last turns of the screws pry little squeaks of protest from the wood, a sound that will remain intact in Will's ears for the rest of his life, conjuring memories of this day whenever he hears a sound like it. The brothers contain themselves, all of them cast in a bronze Amish stoicism, but Clara breaks down and weeps openly. It is the only time anyone can actually be heard weeping during the entire ceremony.

Six men surround the coffin and lift it while the director whisks away the sawhorses from underneath, and then with ponderous effort they maneuver the box around lengthwise so that it can go out the door feet first.

Leaving the dim house and emerging into the midday brightness of sunlit snow, Riley reaches into his shirt pocket for his cigarettes, then takes a sweeping glance at the people around him and withdraws the hand, empty. Touching Will's shoulder he leans close and asks, "Are you okay?"

Will nods, looks up. "I'm fine," he says. "It's warming up a little."

Where the snow has been shoveled away from the paths and lanes around the house the sun has begun to do its work. Water drips off the ends of a row of icicles hanging from the eves. The ice has melted in the thin places where the snow has been cleared from the path, leaving slush between clumps of soggy grass. A heavy, matronly woman hikes her dress a few inches and totters uncertainly on the high spots, making her way to her buggy. The men go to fetch horses and hitch up for the ride to the graveyard a mile away. A long hack, specially covered for duty as a hearse, waits beside the house, its horse tossing his head and stamping impatiently in the traces, its driver sitting solemnly, holding the reins loosely on his knees, waiting for the line to form up behind him.

Will stops to pay his respects to Naomi and speaks briefly to his aunt and uncles before he heads gingerly up the lane to where the car is parked, doing his best to keep the slush out of his shoes.

The car creeps along the road at a walking pace behind the long line of buggies making up the funeral procession. Riley stares out the window at the snow-covered hills for a while, then reaches under the seat and pulls out his paperback copy of *Atlantis Requiem*. He doesn't open it; he just holds it in his lap and looks at the cover.

"They've set their God very high," he says quietly.

Will waits. He has no idea what Riley is talking about.

Riley sees the puzzled look and explains. "Adrian Ott," he says, turning the cover of the book toward Will. "Main character."

His tone lacks its usual air of superiority—he sounds utterly sincere for a change, almost subdued—but Will still doesn't know anything about an Adrian Ott.

"I don't read much," he says.

"It was after a funeral. I guess that's what made me think of it." Riley flips through the book, stopping at a passage on a dog-eared page. "He's talking about a carpet merchant from Venice named Oscar Solarte, a real social climber. Trophy wife, the right clubs, all the right connections—sort of a modern-day Ivan Ilyich. He dies of liver cancer, and then listen to what Ott says about him: 'He raged against the ending of his days, for he found too late he had set his gods too low. With great clarity of purpose he had sacrificed himself, and poured his life out on a place that came, in the end, to be no place at all.'" Riley sighs, closes the book. "Maybe Adrian Ott was onto something."

Will has listened closely and he is moved. He hears something in the tone of Riley's voice and he understands that behind the words lies a tacit admission. Somehow Riley sees his own pale reflection in this Oscar Solarte.

A few buggies have already reached the graveyard and parked in a row beside it. Riley's eyes survey the distant clutch of Amish in their pilgrim clothes. They are beginning to filter out of the row of parked buggies and walk somberly up the hill toward the gate in the low picket fence surrounding the graveyard.

"There's an uncommon grace in these people. They seem so small at first," Riley says quietly. "But they're not. They only seem so because they believe in a very high God. He's real—to them."

"He's real to me," Will answers, without taking his eyes from the road. "I've seen the proof."

He feels Riley staring at him for a long moment but he says nothing else. A hundred yards short of where the little dirt road turns up beside the graveyard Will pulls onto the shoulder and parks behind a large van. He sets the brake, switches off the ignition, and when neither of them makes a move to get out, Will senses an opening, a chance to lengthen the bridge toward his son.

"What is it?" Will asks. In the quiet capsule of the car it's almost a whisper. "What are you thinking? Talk to me."

Riley shakes his head, looks away for a second.

"That preacher," he finally says. "The one who did his thing in English."

"Ah." Will nods. "Yeah. He said some good things. I'm glad you—"

"It wasn't what he said. I've heard all that before—all of it. You made me go to church the whole time I was growing up, remember? Three times a week. There's not a sermon I haven't heard, or a pitch I can't see through. It's not that."

"What then?"

Riley is still holding the paperback in his hands, fluttering the pages absently with his thumb to give his eyes something to focus on besides his father.

"It was unusual, wasn't it? What he did."

"What?"

"English. He said he'd never preached in English before, and it was obviously the truth. I was looking at Katie when he said he was going to speak English. She was surprised. I could see it in her eyes, and she wasn't the only one. If I understand these people and their reverence for tradition, that guy was sticking his neck out. It was tough on him, and he didn't have to do it. He did it, like he said, just because there were people there who didn't speak Dutch."

Riley stops thumbing the book and looks straight at his father.

"In your whole life, how many times have you ever heard an Amish preacher do his thing in English?"

Will considers briefly and shakes his head. "Never. It was a first, that's for sure."

"Now think. You knew just about everybody there. Even the drivers from the vans had beards and looked sort of half Amish. Think hard. How many actual non-Dutch speaking people did you see in that house?"

Will rubs his face and stares at the steering wheel, going over the scene in his mind very carefully because he has begun to see the importance of it. Every face he has seen, every voice he has heard since getting out of the car at his father's house flashes through his mind. He doesn't answer until he is sure.

"One," he says.

"Yeah." Riley nods, and his gaze drifts up toward the graveyard. "Yeah. That's what I thought."

The little picket fence is fragile and low, only about thigh high, for it is not here to keep anyone in or out but merely to mark the boundaries of a place ruled by reverence and memory. All the headstones are the same size, the same simple design, except for two rows of smaller ones pushed up against the near fence. These are closer together, because children don't need as much space. A great round oak tree stands guard over the highest corner of the graveyard, its bare snow-frosted limbs creaking in a brittle wind.

The cemetery slopes gently downward. Will and Riley are among the last to arrive, and rather than elbow through to where the family stands at the head of the grave, they move quietly toward the edge of the crowd at the side. Someone has cleared the snow from the middle of the graveyard and shoveled a wide path up to the gate, but there are no mounds or ridges of cast-off snow. Whoever did it took pains to haul away the snow rather than pile it on top of someone else's grave. The uncovered ground is soggy, thawed by a bright sun and stirred into mud by the passing of many feet. The Amish pay no attention to the mud on their boots. It will wash off.

The widow Naomi sits in a lawn chair at the foot of the grave where she can see everything clearly, with Levi's children gathered around her, standing. All of the men are bareheaded. Some are holding their hats in front of them; others have left them in their buggies.

The minister who preached last at the house, the tall one with the stern face, stands near Naomi and begins reading from a book. His voice is clear and strong. The wind plays with his thinning white hair and ruffles the pages of his book so that he has to hold a hand flat on top of it to keep his place, but he pays it no mind. He is reading the first verse of the ancient funeral song, a long and passionate poem of farewell from the deceased to those who are left.

"'Good night, my beloved . . . my heart's friend,'" he reads, in Dutch. "'Good night, you who grieve and weep for love of me. . . .'"

The coffin sits across two planks at the edge of the grave, a hand-dug hole six feet deep with corners neatly squared. In the bottom waits a rough-sawn oak frame nailed to stakes—the sides of a wooden vault. As the minister reads the first lines of the ancient hymn, four stout young men come forward to pass ropes underneath the coffin, then they stand on opposite sides of the hole and lift it, gently, with the ropes. When it is centered over the hole, the ropes inch through four strong sets of hands in perfectly smooth accord until the coffin rests inside the oaken vault, and the ropes are pulled out and taken away. One of the men lets himself down into the hole, his feet landing gingerly on the sides of the vault. A stack of thick two-foot long oak planks rests near the end of the grave. Now a young man begins handing the short planks down to the man in the hole, who lays them across the frame one at a time until the coffin is covered. He then reaches up, a strong hand grips his wrist and he is hoisted lightly out of the hole.

Four young men stand shoulder to shoulder on the far side with small, worn hymnbooks in their hands, waiting. Once the minister stops reading the four begin to sing, a cappella, the next verse. Their voices are clear and strong, man voices, uninhibited by the fact that they are not beautiful, not professional.

A little sob escapes Naomi as she sees the vault completed and her husband's body taken one step farther from her sight, yet she recovers quickly. She never averts her eyes, never breaks down. She knows, in the end, everyone goes back to the earth. It is written. When she is asked about it she will say, "'The Lord gives, and the Lord takes away. Blessed be the name of the Lord.'"

There are two ridges of dirt flanking the grave, and now four men with shovels take up positions atop the piles and begin unceremoniously shoveling dirt into the hole. They work briskly, like Amishmen, and dirt lands on the oak planks of the vault with a resounding *whump-whump . . . whump-whump*, which can be heard between the words of the ancient song of the quartet.

The sound softens as the boards get covered. After a few minutes the four are relieved by a fresh team, and eight strong arms keep up the pace.

The minister reads again, the men sing again, and they go back and forth in this way while the grave is filled in.

Riley takes all of it in, standing ramrod straight and looking distinguished in his long black wool overcoat. He couldn't possibly understand what's being said, but it's clear from his rapt expression that his eyes are seeing something profound.

The four singers' faces are lifted slightly with their eyes closed as they sing, no doubt partly because of the wind that keeps blowing their long hair into their eyes. They pay no attention to their hair. They are not singing for themselves.

A baby cries out. Peering through the crowd, Will sees that it's Katie's son, William. Katie is holding him. She smiles at the baby and tries to shush him, but he only cries louder. She is standing near Naomi, and Will sees a brief embarrassed glance. Then Katie turns and begins threading her way out of the throng. She moves toward the gate but stops once she's clear of the crowd. She bounces the baby in her arms and coos at him until he quiets and then, rather than disturb the family by elbowing her way back to where she had been standing, she comes slowly down, still bouncing William, to stand beside Will and Riley on the sparse perimeter of the crowd.

The baby sees Riley and reaches for his face again, but Katie pulls his arm down, frowns at him, says no. He wails louder than ever, and no amount of jostling will deter him. Katie frowns, touches her nose to the baby's face, but he bends his little body away from her and wails. Her angel's kiss is beginning to show.

Will turns to her and starts to ask if there is anything he can do, even though he knows there is not. Yet before he can speak, Riley holds his hands out toward Katie. His eyes ask permission. She hesitates at first, but then, smiling shyly, she gently hands the baby over. "This is your uncle Riley," she whispers.

Riley holds the infant up near his face. Instantly, William stops wailing. The beginning of a smile opens his toothless mouth and he seizes Riley's chin in a chubby fist. Riley winces when the baby hooks a thumb in his nose and yanks with surprising strength, but he is chuckling. The baby laughs too, the guileless silver laugh of a brand-new soul.

The job is almost finished. The mounding dirt is visible above the rim of the hole now. The piles are nearly gone. It strikes Will that there are no brass and copper trimmings here, no canvas canopy to protect a ten-thousand-dollar casket from the elements, no Astroturf to keep expensive footwear from being soiled by contact with the earth—only dirt and sky and snow and the tender care of those who will not avert their eyes, even from death. There is no intermission to let the mourners turn their backs while paid professionals make death disappear smoothly, as if by magic, leaving in its place a mountain of fresh-cut flowers.

Mose stands behind Naomi, staunchly supporting a stepmother he barely knows. His face is focused and serene. The four singers pour out their rugged best rendition of an ancient hymn, and the sound of it blends with the sounds of a buffeting wind and the rhythm of the dirt whumping softly on a father's grave.

In the distance, across the road, a wide field slopes down to a line of leafless gray hardwood trees along the creek. The field lies under a deep comforter of new snow, and the high sun beats against it. The air is crisp and achingly clear. The earth shines.

Will has not noticed it until now, but in the middle of the broad snow-covered field across the road lies a dark patch roughly a hundred feet square that is crosshatched with manure and straw, where an Amish farmer has just this morning cleaned out his barn and spread the fertilizer on top of the snow. Will is there with him. He feels the sting of the predawn cold and the promise of first light on his face, hears the rumble of the heavy door as it slides open, smells the warm earthy scent of the barn spilling from the darkness. He feels the slick haunch of the horse and the leather of the traces, hears the snuffle of anticipation as he hitches up the wagon. He feels the soreness of the shovel in his hands and shoulders and back—not the bone-joint ache that he's become accustomed to these days but the glad soreness he knew in his youth, the song of triumphant strength. He sees through the farmer's eyes as he looks out over his field and gauges precisely where to spread the load. He knows his land like he knows his own body, and despite the deep snow his eye tells him unerringly where he left off last time. He stands in the back of the wagon leaning on his shovel when the job is done, gazing out over his land with the pride of a lesser partner in a grand and time-honored enterprise. Though the land is asleep and there is little to see, he grants himself a good long look, the way a mother will stand and look at a sleeping child, and for the same reason. The farmer knows it is a kind of prayer.

Will knows it too, now, and it fills him with peace and light. The God of the farmer is a very high God. Come spring the snow will melt, and that which is old and broken and dead will be made new again.

Come spring.

ACKNOWLEDGMENTS

First, last, and always, I thank God for showing me the keys.
I also owe a debt of gratitude to:

My parents, Howard and Ann Cramer. Although the characters in this story are entirely of my own creation, the major turning points of the novel are loosely based on actual events in my parents' lives. They are survivors in the finest sense of the word.

My wife, Pam, who named this book.

My sister Fannie and her husband, George, as well as my cousin Miriam Scholl, for advice and insight.

My cousin Linda Miller, whose home provided much of the setting, and my late uncle Jake, whose funeral provided even more.

The early draft readers—Eddie Starrett, Cindy Schade, Patty Ivers, Bobbie Winkelman, Pam Baker, Marita Paulhamus, Jim Martin, and my sister Susan Holloway—who have saved me from many a blunder.

My family at MCC, whose prayers give me wings.

Bobby Johnston, for kitchen dialogs full of graceful thought and thoughtful grace.

Joy Cobb, for her parole and extradition expertise.

Luke Hinrichs, for his unflagging support and attention to detail.

Janet Kobobel Grant, the best agent in the business.

Lori Patrick, for her invaluable input on the cover copy, and Rachel Patrick, for words of wisdom.

The surviving members of The Purple Plastic Psychedelic Cigarette Machine, for the use of the name, and I probably should apologize for smudging their artistic reputation.

ABOUT THE AUTHOR

W. DALE CRAMER, author of critically acclaimed novels *Sutter's Cross* and *Bad Ground,* lives in Georgia with his wife, Pam, and their two sons.

For more information visit www.dalecramer.com, or readers may write to Dale at P.O. Box 25, Hampton, GA 30228.